HILDA

Rebecca was born in Chester, En[...] the three-day week, the world [...] and McDonalds opening their [...] mother educated her on a diet of T Rex, Adam and the Ants, Bob Dylan and Leonard Cohen and she grew up thinking that Frank Zappa was her dad (sadly untrue). She studied at Exeter University during the heyday of Blur, Oasis, The Offspring and The Spice Girls, when life was sweet and everything cost £1 and has had a variety of jobs that have taken her to some very interesting places, including four years teaching in a Category C male prison.

Rebecca has been attempting to parent since the start of the millennium and currently lives in South-West England with her husband and three children. When not working her day job or frantically writing, she can often be found either engaged in the fruitless pursuit of trying to find a bra that genuinely does its job or the less frustrating pastime of drinking prosecco.

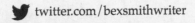 twitter.com/bexsmithwriter

Also by Rebecca Smith

More Than Just Mum

FAKING IT

REBECCA SMITH

One More Chapter
a division of HarperCollins*Publishers* Ltd
The News Building
1 London Bridge Street
London SE1 9GF
www.harpercollins.co.uk

This paperback edition 2020
First published in Great Britain in ebook format
by HarperCollins*Publishers* 2020

A catalogue record of this book
is available from the British Library

ISBN: 978-0-00-837019-0

Printed and bound in Great Britain by
CPI Group (UK) Ltd, Croydon CR0 4YY

This book is dedicated to everyone who is brave enough to confess that they don't have a clue about what they are doing – and carries on regardless...

'Would it be possible for you to move a little to the left?' I enquire politely.

I don't wish to be rude but I've been stuck in this position for a good five minutes now and my right leg is going to sleep. I didn't say anything initially because I wasn't sure how long we'd be here but the evidence would suggest that I could be in for the long-haul and I'm starting to lose sensation in my toes. All hopes of this being a quickie are totally out of the window.

Nick shifts slightly to the side and continues banging away. I try to stay focused because I am very aware that this is a two-person task and I don't want to be accused of lying flat on my back and expecting Nick to put in all the effort. It's happened before. But, as often happens when I'm in this position, my mind can't help wandering and before I know it, I'm compiling a mental shopping list for tomorrow's trip to the supermarket and wondering whether I locked the back door because there's been a spate of burglaries in this area and you can't be too careful.

Nick grunts loudly and I wince.

'Be quiet,' I hiss. 'You'll wake up the bloody kids.'

I don't know why I'm bothering. His relentless hammering can probably be heard halfway down the street.

Nick looks down at me. 'Well, if you were more involved then it might be a bit less effort and I might be a little quieter and I'd almost definitely be finished a whole lot quicker.'

'I *am* involved,' I snap back. 'I'm here, aren't I?'

I'm not really. I'm bored and I'm chilly and I just want to go to sleep but apparently this *has* to happen now, despite the fact that we already did it a few hours ago.

I can remember a time before all of this. A time when evenings were our sanctuary: a place where we could play and explore and voice our wildest thoughts with abandon, not stifle every sound for fear of disturbing our offspring. That was before we had kids though, when the world was big and exciting and filled with potential. Not exhausting and predictable and filled with necessary marital duties.

'Yes!' Nick punches the air in triumph and I roll my eyes. It's like he thinks he's the first man to ever do this and, as I have often assured him, he really isn't. Nor will he be the last. But it doesn't seem to matter what I say – his pleasure and self-satisfaction knows no bounds, and if I'm honest, his enthusiasm is quite sweet.

'Well done,' I tell him, scooting out from underneath him. 'It's still dripping though. Is that normal?'

Nick bends down and takes a closer look. 'I think it'll stop in a minute,' he says. 'It should be fine.'

I grit my teeth and try not to sigh. 'You said that last time,' I remind him. 'And yet we had a full-blown flood two hours later. I'm tired, Nick. I'm too old to spend my nights doing stuff like this.'

He shrugs. 'I don't love it either, Hannah, but it has to be done.'

I pull myself to my feet and put down the torch. We both stare at the newly fixed bathroom pipe and the tap that is attached to it. Its random leaking makes me think that it could somehow be a metaphor for our lives but I'm too exhausted to figure out exactly how.

'How tired are you?' asks Nick, reaching out for my hand. 'Only, the kids don't seem to have woken up and the night is still young!'

I glance at my watch. The night is as young as I am, which is not very. Then again, this is the first evening in ages that our teenagers have been asleep before we are which does afford us a rare opportunity. And I've already spent some time on my back tonight.

I'm not completely averse to doing it again.

Chapter One

The shoes are utterly ridiculous. Seriously. I can't think of a single occasion when I might actually wear them and I definitely don't own any items of clothing that will go with them. They are impractical and unnecessary and I could pay for two driving lessons for Scarlet for the same cost.

I really, really want them.

'Are you sure that they fit?' enquires Nick as I attempt to stuff my foot inside the first shoe. 'You look like you're struggling a bit there, Hannah.'

'I always wear size six,' I complain, scowling at my unhelpful feet. 'I just don't understand it.'

'Well, why don't you ask for the next size up?' Nick glances at his phone. 'Surely that's the logical solution?'

'I already did,' I mutter. 'They don't have them. But it's not a problem because these are fine.'

I take a deep breath and push my feet inside.

'There! They fit perfectly!' I stand and smile

5

triumphantly at Nick. 'Let's buy them and then we can pop to the pub on the way home and have a cheeky drink to celebrate being out on a school day.'

This shopping trip is the first proper time we've had together in ages and I want to milk every last moment before we have to return to normality.

Nick frowns at me. 'I don't think—'

'I love them!' I interrupt, thrusting one foot out in front of me. 'Look how long they make my legs look. They're everything a person could possibly ask for in a shoe and I'll be happy for the rest of eternity when I own them.'

'Everything a person could ask for other than them actually fitting you,' retorts Nick. 'Which I would have thought was a pre-requisite in any item of footwear.'

'They fit me just fine,' I snap back. 'I am a grown-ass woman and I am clever enough to know whether a pair of shoes fit me or not.'

Nick raises his eyebrows. 'Come on, Hannah, why can't you just admit it? The shoes don't fit but that's not a problem – there are plenty of others to choose from.'

But the others are not like these beautiful creatures, I wail in my head. *I don't want other, less exotic, more* comfortable *shoes. I want these shoes. I deserve these shoes. I have waited an eternity for shoes covered in sequins with a glitter heel and I am not leaving this shop without them. They are going to make my life better, I just know it.*

I gaze at my husband, bestowing him with my most gracious and beatific smile, which feels surprisingly natural now that I've got these shoes on. I actually feel a bit like a princess. I really think that purchasing them will revolutionise my life; there's nothing that I won't be able to do when I'm wearing footwear as striking as this.

'They're perfect,' I tell him. 'They're exactly what I need.'

I sit back down and slip them off (ignoring the slight sense of relief that they are no longer viciously pinching at my toes) before handing them to the sales assistant.

Nick shakes his head at me as she starts boxing them up, but I can see a smile tugging at the edge of his mouth.

'You're sure they fit?' he asks. 'We're supposed to be buying you a pair of celebratory book-publishing shoes, not a piece of medieval torture equipment.'

I finish lacing up my trainers and reach out to take his hand.

'I love them,' I tell him, keeping my voice quiet so that nobody will overhear us, while also cleverly evading his question. 'And every time I look at them I'm going to remember what they represent, which is me being an authentic, genuine author.'

'They *are* very nice,' Nick agrees kindly. 'And you're going to look stunning in them.'

The sales assistant hands me a boutiquey-looking paper bag and Nick hands over his credit card. And then we leave the shop, the bag swinging back and forth in my hand. This is who I am now. I am a woman who wears impracticable high heels and who shops in dinky little bespoke stores and goes into town with her husband after work just because *she feels like it*. I am confident and secure and, for the first time in ages, at peace with who I am. I am a wife, a mother, a teacher and a (secretly) published author of an erotic novel.

Life is sweet.

'Oh my bloody god!' Scarlet's shriek slaps me in the face the second that we walk through the front door. 'I honestly can't believe you, Mother!'

It turns out that my sweet life and newfound peace lasted for exactly eighty-three minutes. I don't know why I'm surprised. I'm lucky I even had that long.

I drop my lovely paper bag and its even lovelier contents on the floor and freeze. This is it. The moment I've been waiting for. The charade is up and my identity has been revealed. Life as I know it is over. In some ways it's a relief – I've been living in such fear of being found out in the weeks since *More Than Sex* was published and at least now, with the cat well and truly out of the bag, I can relax. No more hiding in the shadows. No more denying who I really am. Maybe this will be a good thing?

I am a complete and utter fantasist.

'You've done some whack stuff in the past,' my daughter yells, her face scrunched up in anger. 'But *this*? Congratulations, Mum – you've totally outdone yourself this time.'

'What are you screeching about now?' asks Dylan, opening the living room door.

'Yeah,' joins in Benji, peering under his older brother's arm. 'Why are you being so rude to Mum? Again.'

Dogger nudges her way in between his legs and joins in

the staring, her big, brown eyes darting between us as she too tries to make sense of this terrible situation.

Nick pushes past me and gives Scarlet a stern look. 'I don't know what has upset you but whatever it is, I am not prepared to listen to another word while you're shouting.'

'I think she *knows*.' I put a slightly shaky hand on his arm. 'She's obviously going to be feeling a bit upset, Nick. We've always understood that.'

Nick turns to look at me, his face draining of blood.

'We agreed to keep it a secret, Hannah,' he mutters. 'How have they found out?'

'Not *they*,' I hiss back. 'Scarlet. And I have no idea. But they're *all* going to know now, aren't they?'

I gaze over his shoulder at my children. Scarlet and Dylan are seventeen and eighteen now, almost adults themselves. I have no idea what this discovery is going to do to them at such a crucial and formative stage of life or how I'm ever going to look them in the eye again, now that they know what I've been getting up to. Particularly Scarlet. There's no way that she's ever going to accept my new career. Not without an almighty teen-fuelled meltdown, anyway. And I can live without that.

And then there's Benji. My sweet, loving, innocent ten-year-old boy who has no comprehension of a world where a mother's actions can bring lasting shame and humiliation upon her unwitting offspring. He'll be shunned from every party and the days of sleepovers and playdates are long gone. I'm pretty sure that none of the other mothers will let the child of an erotic writer associate with their offspring. Nobody is going to care that I only did it because my hours had been cut at work and I needed to find a way to fund the ever-increasing needs of our children. Well, that and to prove that I could be more than just a mum.

This is *not* a relief. I am *not* relaxed. I will happily live a farce, a pantomime, a fake life that is a total sham if it means my children, and everyone else on the planet, never find out about what I have done.

What I am *doing*.

I close my eyes for a second and pull on every last bit of strength that I can find. And then I open them and address my teenage daughter.

'How did you find out?' I ask, trying to keep my voice steady. 'Who else knows?'

Maybe there's a way of carrying out some degree of damage limitation. The kids discovering the truth is bad enough but what if this information came via school? I won't be able to walk into work on Monday morning if everyone in the staffroom *knows*. But perhaps she found out online on some dodgy website.

Maybe there's still some hope.

'The whole school is talking about it,' she snarls at me. 'I doubt there's a single person who *doesn't* know.'

Oh fucking fuck. This is bad.

'We can explain,' starts Nick but Scarlet rounds on him, her cheeks flaming red.

'This hasn't got anything to do with you,' she says. 'It's not *you* who wrote it.'

Nick nods his head. 'That's true. But I fully support your mother in everything that she does and this is no exception. In fact...'

He pauses for a second and I see him gulp slightly as he prepares to incriminate himself alongside me. God, I love this man. He won't let me walk to the gallows on my own.

'In fact, it was me who encouraged her to send it once it was written. And I stand by that decision.'

Scarlet's mouth drops open in horror and I step forward to stand beside my husband. We are united in solidarity. If we fall, we fall together.

'I don't actually believe this,' she murmurs. The shock has clearly got to her and I peer closely at her lips, trying to see if they're turning blue and wondering if I should make her a cup of sweet tea.

'What has Mum written?' Dylan leans against the doorframe and looks at us all with interest. 'What've I missed?'

'It's important that you understand the context that this was written in,' I begin. I might as well own the announcement now. 'First and foremost, what I want you all to remember is that there are many different types of writing and erot—'

'A *detention slip*!' bellows Scarlet, drowning out my words. She's obviously recovered from the shock, which I am thankful for on a number of levels. 'For Ashley.'

'What?' asks Nick, confusion etched across his face. 'You've written what now, Hannah?'

I start to laugh as I let go of his hand and slump down against the wall, relief making my legs weak.

'And now you're going to laugh about it?' Scarlet's voice is raised in pitch by several octaves. 'Well, that's bloody marvelous, Mother.'

'I'm not laughing about *that*,' I gasp, struggling to take a breath. 'I'm laughing because, well—'

'Yes?' asks Dylan. 'What's so funny?'

I look up and see all four members of my family gazing down at me. Benji is smiling encouragingly, as if I'm about to tell them a joke. Dylan has the look on his face that he gets when he suspects that we're up to something and I know he won't rest until he finds out what – he's learnt from the best – Scarlet is glowering with what looks like serious murderous intent while tapping her foot on the ground impatiently, waiting to hear my excuse, and Nick is staring at me with what can only be described as fear, his eyes pleading with me not to cock this up.

I nod my head and gather my thoughts and then I throw myself onto the sacrificial altar.

'You're right,' I lie. 'I'm laughing because I wrote Ashley Dunsford a detention note.'

Dogger pads across the hallway and stares at me balefully.

'You are a terrible parent,' my daughter lovingly hisses. 'There are literally hundreds of people at our school and yet you decided to single *him* out. Why couldn't you have chosen another kid to punish?'

I push myself off the ground and look her in the eye, my relieved laughing fit over. I don't need her to tell me that I'm not going to be winning *Mother of the Year* anytime soon. I'm pretty sure that the award criterion doesn't include spending your days trying to figure out the sexiest way to describe a penis.

12

Although for what it's worth, in my esteemed opinion there is no sexy way to describe a penis.

'Because it wasn't "another kid" who was vandalising school property with a can of spray paint, was it?' I give her a firm look. 'It was Ashley Dunsford and quite frankly, he should consider himself extremely fortunate that I only gave him a detention and not community service or a prison sentence.'

'I don't think that's your jurisdiction, is it?' enquires Nick, relief plastered across his face. 'I'll make us some tea.'

'Can we get back to the game?' Benji asks Dylan. 'I think Scarlet's stopped yelling at Mum now.'

Dylan nods but I see him giving me another curious glance before he disappears back into the living room and I know that he's suspicious. I'm going to have to cover my tracks even more carefully if he's going to start sniffing around my business.

'*Have* you stopped yelling?' I ask Scarlet, once the door is closed.

She nods, her face flushing pink.

'And do you have anything else that you'd like to say to me?' I enquire. The terror that my secret was out is abating and I'm ready to address the appalling manners of my daughter.

'I'm sorry,' she mumbles and I resist the urge to ask her to enunciate her apology more clearly. 'I shouldn't have shouted at you. I was just really embarrassed that you'd given Ashley a detention. It makes me look bad.'

'It doesn't have anything to do with you,' I tell her. 'He

did something stupid and now he has to deal with the consequences. That's the end of it.'

'I just thought that he might, you know...' Scarlet shuffles from one foot to the other. 'He might blame me for you giving him a detention and then he might go off me.'

'Oh darling, that's not going to happen!' I say.

More's the pity.

'Not that I really like him anymore,' she rushes on. 'So don't go thinking that I care or anything, because I don't. I've got bigger stuff going on like running for Head Girl, which is way more important than boys.'

She pauses and flicks her hair over one shoulder. 'And he doesn't even think about me like that now we're in the Sixth Form. Obviously.'

'Obviously,' I agree, as she starts to head up the stairs. 'But perhaps you could inform him that if I catch him graffitiing the words *"Scarlett Thompson Is Blazing"* on the wall of the gym ever again, I will not be held accountable for my actions.'

Her head whips round.

'Is that what he wrote?' she asks. 'Oh my god! He's such a dick. I'm never going to live this down at school. I'm *mortified*!'

The huge grin plastered across her face suggests otherwise.

'You can also tell him that *Scarlet* is spelled with just one "t". If he likes you enough to get a detention for you he should take the time to learn how to correctly spell your name.'

But my words are lost in a draught of floral body spray

as Scarlet dashes upstairs, her phone out and her thumbs darting across the screen as she rushes to update her friends on this new and scintillating detail.

'Here you go, Hannah.' Nick hands me a mug as I step inside the kitchen. 'That was a bit of a close call, wasn't it?'

I shudder and wrap my hands around the warm tea.

'I really thought they'd found out about the book,' I tell him. 'I think I've aged about ten years in the last ten minutes.'

Nick nods and sinks down onto a chair. 'I know what you mean. But I suppose we should think about what we're going to say when they do find out. Because they *will* find out, Hannah – you know they will.'

I sit down next to him, resisting the urge to ditch the tea and pour a glass of wine instead.

'We can't let that happen,' I tell him. 'They are in no way mature enough to understand what I'm doing – they'd totally get the wrong end of the stick and it'd all get completely out of hand.'

He nods again thoughtfully and stares out of the window. 'We're just going to have to be more careful. You can't panic like that again – you almost told them everything.'

I make a huffing sound. 'It's a shame you didn't think about that when you sent off my manuscript to an agent then, isn't it? None of this would even be a thing if you and Cassie hadn't stuck your big noses into my business.'

He turns to look at me, the corner of his mouth twitching. 'Right. So you wish we hadn't helped to launch your porn writing career, then? You hate everything about it and you're never going to write another word?'

For the love of all that is holy. If I've told him once, I've told him fifty gazillion times; I do not write *porn*. I write tasteful, informative and highly accurate erotica.

And I don't hate it.

I actually love it.

It's the first time in forever that I've had something that is purely just for me and, on the days when I'm stressed about my teaching job or the kids are driving me insane or everything just seems like hard work, my writing is a warm little secret. It makes me feel special and daring and unique.

I take a sip of tea and think about what just happened. Nick does have a point. The kids don't know about the book but I almost blew the whole thing. I'm going to have to be much cooler if I want to maintain my anonymity, which I absolutely must do at all costs. There's no way that I can allow anyone to find out about my side-hustle. Other than Nick, my best friend Cassie, and my mother, nobody knows that Twinky Malone, the author of *More Than Sex*, is really me – and they never can.

I've shared every aspect of myself since becoming a wife and a mother but I'm not sharing this. Even if sometimes I want to shout about my triumphs from the rooftops, I know that I have to keep quiet. Not that I don't imagine myself being interviewed on daytime television sometimes (mostly when I'm in the bath after having drunk a couple of glasses on Wine Wednesday). The presenter will ask me how I came to write erotic fiction and I will smile at her coyly before telling her what I told myself on the day that I stumbled onto this particular side-hustle.

I wanted a job that I loved and I wanted my teenagers to see me as more than just 'Mum'. I also needed to make some money so I had a good, long think about what sells and the answer was right there because, as everybody knows, there is one thing in the world that has always *sold.*

Sex. Sex sells. So I decided to have a go at writing erotica because I thought it would be easy, but I can tell you right now. It's hard. Very, very hard.

And that is usually where my fantasy ends because by then, one of my delightful children is usually hammering on the bathroom door and demanding that I vacate my bubble bath because they need a wee and they need it now…

Chapter Two

I t's Friday night and I've invited my mother to join us for a nice, relaxing family meal. One day I'm sure that I'll figure out that those four words don't belong in the same sentence, but that day is clearly not today.

I serve up plates of my specialty dish and sink into my seat, reaching gratefully for my glass before remembering that I am absolutely determined to complete Dry September and, as I have somehow managed to make it to the fifth day of the month without a single drop of alcohol, a glass of wine is out of the question. Which is a shame because, in retrospect, September was not the wisest of months to choose for this particular challenge. I'd probably be finding it a bit easier if I'd chosen a nice relaxing month like July, rather than the horror that is Back-To-School, especially when we've got Off-To-University to contend with too, not to mention the fact that I'm supposed to be writing the sequel to my first book.

I spent a large part of today at The Daily Grind, our local

coffee shop, trying to get started and I'm actually pretty tired. Unless you've ever tried to write a book it's impossible to understand how challenging and exhausting it is just to even think of an appropriate title. I tried for several hours before deciding that it was probably acceptable to refer to it as Book Two (untitled) and that maybe my time would be better spent trying to think of a plot.

'Cheers!' I say, to the table at large, raising my glass of water. 'Bon appetit.'

'This looks lovely, darling,' says my mum. 'What do you call it?'

'Pesto pasta,' I tell her. 'With sausages.'

'I was thinking about going out tomorrow.' Scarlet's voice is suspiciously nonchalant. 'Is that okay with you guys? And can I borrow your scarf?'

I mentally review the calendar. We don't have any plans for this weekend and quite honestly, with the way that Scarlet and Dylan are always winding each other up these days, it might be a bit of a relief to have her out of the house for a few hours.

'That's fine,' I say, scooping up a forkful of pasta. 'And if you mean the scarf that Dad gave me for my birthday then yes, you can borrow it as long as you don't lose it. So where are you going?'

Scarlet makes a mumbling sound and when I glance up at her she is smiling at me so sweetly that it instantly makes my blood run cold. I know this look and it only heralds the start of bad things.

'I didn't quite catch that, sweetheart,' I tell her, returning my laden fork to the plate. '*Where* are you going? And who are you going with?'

Scarlet takes a long swig from her glass. I know this tactic. She's stalling for time while she tries to decide how much of the truth to tell me. I need to be alert and on top of my game. This is not a time for taking my eye off the ball and I may well require backup. Surreptitiously, I reach out my foot and try to kick Nick on the ankle.

'Ow,' howls my mother. 'That was my leg!'

'Oh god, Mum – I'm so sorry!' I wince sympathetically and reach across to put my hand on her arm. 'I was aiming for Nick, not you.'

We both glance at my husband who is deep in conversation with Dylan and Benji about an article he read in his latest *Land Rover* magazine.

'I think you're going to need more than a kick to get his attention,' murmurs Mum. 'He hasn't stopped banging on about that ridiculous vehicle since I got here.'

I turn back to Scarlet and wait patiently until she has drained every last drop of water in her glass. She blinks twice (which I happen to know is another one of her tells and suggests that she's keen to introduce some kind of conflict to our relaxing evening meal) and then sits back in her chair, attempting a look of extreme relaxation.

'I'm just going to hang out at a friend's house,' she informs me, her voice impressively casual. 'Nothing exciting.'

I lean back in my own chair. We are like two cowboys facing off in a Spaghetti Western, the kitchen our OK Corral.

'I don't think so,' I say, my voice dripping with insouciance. 'Not unless this *friend* has a name.'

Scarlet scowls. 'What difference does it make whether they have a name or not? Why do you need to know?'

I scowl back. 'I need to know their name so that I know where they live. If you think I'm letting you go off without us knowing where you are, then you're daft.'

'She is incredibly daft,' Dylan informs me, joining in the entertainment. 'So she probably did think that.'

'I'll have my mobile though, won't I?' Scarlet rolls her eyes and I grit my teeth. I'm determined to enjoy a pleasant family mealtime even if it kills me and I'm not going to let her goad me into shouting at her. 'You can ring me whenever you want to.'

I smile at her, hoping that I'm hiding my insincerity. 'No name and address – no hanging out. It's that simple. Now can you pass the water jug please, Dylan?'

'There's no need to be snarky about it,' she sniffs. 'God – it's like living in a prison. I'm applying to be the Head Girl at school, you know? You'd think my own mother would treat me with a bit of respect.'

I do know that she's applying to be the Head Girl. Possibly because she has mentioned it approximately seventy-five times a day since nominating herself.

'You're very lucky, Hannah,' my mother tells me. I raise one eyebrow, wondering what it is about this particular exchange that labels me as blessed. 'When *you* were a teenager I had no way of knowing what you were up to. If you went out for the evening I just had to hope you eventually came back – I couldn't stalk you, the way you do with *your* kids. There was none of this Track My Phone business back then, oh no.'

She. Did. Not. Just. Say. That.

This calls for some instant damage limitation.

'Oooooh, *snap!*' crows Dylan, tipping back in his chair. 'This should be interesting.'

'Yes, well – what we're actually talking about here is—'

'Track my *what*, now?' Scarlet's voice is so chilly that my arms erupt with goose bumps. 'What is Granny talking about, Mum?'

I laugh merrily. 'Oh, nothing darling! She's just a bit confused. Technology can be rather baffling to the older generation, you know? So, as I was saying—'

'I am neither *confused* nor *baffled*,' barks my mother, slamming her fork onto the table. 'And quite honestly, Hannah, I resent the implication that just because I'm no longer in my youth then I don't have a clue. I'm surprised at you, I really am. You need to be a bit less judgemental about others.'

'*Burn!*' snorts my oldest and most disloyal child, while Scarlet holds her hands in the air.

'Preach it, Granny.'

I shoot them both a quick glare and then turn back to my mum.

'I didn't mean to offend you,' I tell her, soothingly. 'It's just that all this silly talk about stalking makes it sound more devious than it really is and I don't want Scarlet getting the wrong idea.'

I don't want Scarlet getting any idea about it at all, full stop.

So thank you very much, Mother. You've just completely destroyed my cover.

'Have you been tracking me?' asks Scarlet and my goose bumps disappear under the heat of her fierce gaze. 'Tell me the truth.'

'It's called maternal protection,' I snap back. 'And you should be thanking me for keeping you safe.'

'It's called *stalking*!' howls my daughter. 'And it's a complete invasion of my privacy! I can't believe you sometimes, Mum.'

'I told you it'd end in tears, Hannah,' my mother helpfully adds. 'No good can ever come from meddling in your child's business.'

The irony of this sentence is clearly completely lost on her.

'For the record, I've known about this for ages,' says Dylan, smirking smugly at his sister. 'It's not really a problem unless you're going somewhere that you shouldn't be.'

'Don't lie,' snaps Scarlet. 'You've just disabled the app on your phone.'

'Is that what you've—' I start, turning to Dylan but Scarlet interrupts me.

'Well, you don't need me to give you my friend's name then, do you?' she says, narrowing her eyes at me. 'Not when you can follow my every move from the comfort of the sofa. God. It's so pathetic.'

'I don't track you from the comfort of the sofa,' I hiss. 'I'd be so lucky. No – I'm too busy running around picking up all the half-empty cups of tea that you leave strewn around the place as if it's a hotel.'

'What are you on about?' Scarlet's face is screwed up in fury. 'What's that got to do with anything?'

My weak attempt at regaining the moral high ground is obviously failing.

Nick finally stops his fascinating monologue about Betty the Land Rover's rust problem and looks across at us. 'What's going on?'

'Our daughter wants to hang out with a friend,' I inform him, retreating to a safer foothold. 'A friend who has *no name.*'

'That's sad,' says Benji, through a mouthful of pasta. 'Imagine having no name.'

Scarlet groans under her breath.

'Why are you so stupid?' she asks him. 'Like, actually? It's a genuine question. How have you even survived this long with so few brain cells?'

Benji wrinkles up his face, the way he always does when he gets upset and I leap in before Scarlet's attempt to distract us from the real conversation is a success.

'I'm assuming that your reluctance to share information means that it's a boy?' I enquire. 'Does he go to school with you? Have I taught him?'

My daughter shakes her head. 'I didn't say that it was a boy, did I?'

'Yeah, Mum,' adds Dylan. 'Did you just assume her sexuality?'

'It wouldn't surprise me,' Scarlet retorts. 'She makes out

like she knows everything but she doesn't actually have a clue about what it's like to be Gen Z.'

'Who are we talking about?' asks Nick, looking confused. 'And why?'

'I just want to hang out with some friends, Dad,' Scarlet tells him, throwing him a huge smile. 'Tomorrow evening. I was just checking that you guys didn't have any plans.'

Nick smiles back at her. 'It's fine with me,' he says. 'I'm intending on spending most of the weekend underneath Betty, sorting out her under-carriage.'

For fuck's sake. It's like I am the only adult in the room with a pair of functioning ears.

'Can we just back this conversation up a bit?' I sit up straight and stare at Scarlet. 'Number one, is it "friends" plural or "friend" singular that we're talking about here?'

'Friends plural,' she mutters.

'Good. And where exactly are you meeting them?'

Scarlet pauses but my mother leans forwards and gives her a smile.

'You may as well tell her, darling,' she advises. 'She can locate your exact whereabouts on her phone in five seconds flat if she wants to. I've seen her do it. It's very impressive – I think she might have had a good career in the Secret Service in another life.'

Yes, another life where I'm not constantly needed to solve my family's problems and keep them out of trouble. Another life where I roam the streets of Paris wearing nothing but high heels and a trench coat instead of roaming the supermarket aisles wearing an old waterproof jacket and scuffed-up shoes.

'We're getting together at Petra's house,' she says, the

words pushing themselves reluctantly out of her mouth. 'A couple of us from school and some of her new friends from college.'

I sit back in my chair. 'That wasn't so hard, was it?' I tell her. 'And if you'd only said that in the first place, then we could have avoided this whole conversation. Of course you can go to Petra's house – I'm sure you've got lots to catch up on.'

'And are you going to keep on stalking me?' she asks. 'Even though you know that it's an invasion of my human rights? You really do need to get a life, you know, Mum.'

'Have you been tracking her phone again?' asks Nick, frowning. 'I thought we agreed that we'd only use that function if there was an emergency.'

Sometime it feels like the entire universe is out to get me, it really does.

I sigh. 'If you feel that strongly about it, then no – I won't track your location. But don't come crying to me if you get kidnapped and nobody notices.'

'Hannah!' exclaims my mother. 'What a thing to say! Nobody is going to kidnap Scarlet!'

'Nobody in their right mind, anyway,' huffs Benji, finally getting his own back. 'And even if they did, they'd soon give her back when they realised how annoying she is.'

In the ensuing carnage all attention is diverted from me and the fingers that I am frantically crossing under the kitchen table, which is good, because I have absolutely no intention of stopping utilising new technological advances to keep a maternal and watchful eye on my children. It's the only reason I pay for their bloody phone contracts in the first place.

The meal finally ends and the kids do some token cleaning up before disappearing to their rooms. Nick mutters something about fixing a Land Rover part and heads out of the back door in the direction of the shed and I know that I won't see him again for hours.

My mother looks at the clock.

'I'd better be off,' she says. 'I'm meeting an old friend for drinks tonight and I can't be late for Barbara. I think she's heard about my new calling in life and is hoping for a bit of free advice.'

While it was somewhat unexpected when my sixty-four-year-old mother announced that she was taking up a new career, it wasn't a complete shock. She was a mother who my school-friends described as *cool* and their parents probably called *unconventional*. Or maybe *bohemian*, if they were being kind. Whatever word they used, I knew what it meant. My mother was the exciting, interesting member of our family, constantly throwing herself into new experiences and learning new things and I was the steady, sensible one. It bothered me less when I was growing up than it does now, which I think could possibly tell me something about my insecurities, if I was inclined to think about it.

Which I absolutely am not.

There are very few topics of conversation that my mother thinks are out of bounds and she prides herself on being able to talk about anything to anybody, regardless of how keen they may or may not be to discuss their most private thoughts with her. Over the years she has subjected me to her earnest and heartfelt opinions on every aspect of my life, from my career to my parenting to the provenance of my groceries. And I know that she does all this because she's constantly absorbing new information and she wants to share it and I'm probably the only person in the universe who will actually listen to her – but good god, it's completely infuriating and she drives me utterly insane.

Anyway, her new direction is entirely my own fault. When I had the idea of buying her credits for an online course, I was imagining her dabbling in genealogy or perhaps art history. Not *'Let's Talk About Sex, Baby! Foundation One, Access to Counselling.'*

'But you're not even qualified yet,' I point out, resisting the urge to sigh. 'Don't you think you should be careful about offering advice when you don't really know what you're talking about?'

My mother laughs and stands up. 'When you get to my age, you *know* what you're talking about. Speaking of which – how are the sales of your book doing?'

I glance at the kitchen door but the kids are long gone.

'Okay, I think. It's kind of hard to know for sure just yet.'

Mum fixes me with a familiar look and I brace myself.

'Well, you know my thoughts on the matter, Hannah.'

I do, because you insist on telling me every single time I speak to you.

'Uh-huh,' I mutter, non-committally.

'I'd be very happy to spread the word about your literary debut,' she continues, shrugging her shoulders into her coat. 'All this silly secrecy is costing you in book sales, you know.'

I do, because you also inform me of this on a regular basis.

'I've been trying to figure out the second book but it's a bit trickier than I thought it'd be,' I find myself saying. 'I'm not entirely sure that I can do it.'

Mum turns to look at me. 'Of course you can do it,' she says. 'You've already written one book, Hannah. Just do it again.'

'It's not that simple though.' I lean back in my chair and shake my head. 'There wasn't any pressure last time. I was just writing for me and I didn't even know what I was doing half the time.'

'Well, I rather think that was the beauty of it,' Mum tells me. 'It came from the heart. You just need to chill out and relax. I mean, you're writing porn. How hard can it be?'

I stare at her suspiciously.

'This isn't a laughing matter, Mother. And I'm not writing *porn*, as you very well know. It's erotica and it's absolutely mainstream and there's nothing remotely pornographic about it.'

Mum's forehead creases into wrinkles. 'I'm not entirely sure that I understand the difference between erotica and porn,' she says.

So, that online course isn't exactly making you an expert, then? Funny, that.

'But if you ever want my informed critique on the sex scenes then you only have to ask, darling.' She beams at me. 'I'm learning so much on my course and I'd be very happy to share my knowledge with you. In fact, I'm doing a fascinating module at the moment called *Marital Sex: Use it or Lose it,* which may be of particular interest to you.'

Which seems as good a place as any to shut this conversation down and show her the door.

I give her a hug and watch as she gets into her car, waving until I'm sure that she's actually gone. And then I go back into the kitchen, put the kettle on and slump onto the battered old sofa that Dogger has claimed as her own. My mother might be right about my desire for anonymity impacting on my sales but it's a price I'm willing to pay.

Writing about sex is terrifying and difficult and my guiltiest pleasure and I just don't think it'll feel the same if everyone knows that I'm doing it. And as for any discussion about the state of my marriage, well – that's just ridiculous. Nick and I are fine. Everything is lovely. And nice. We're lucky that we've been together for all these years and we're still attracted to each other. Lots of people aren't as fortunate. And there's nothing wrong with lovely and nice. Who wouldn't want that?

I sink into the cushions and groan. Damn my mother and her stupid online course. *Use it or Lose it*? What's that supposed to mean? How often are we supposed to be using it before we're at risk of it vanishing forever? And we probably aren't as adventurous as we once were but just because I'm always a bit knackered and Nick seems more in love with his Land Rover than me, it doesn't mean we have issues. We've been married forever and it's a marathon, not a sprint.

Although the one hundred metre dash is probably a better description of our sexual liaisons, rather than a twenty-six-mile endurance event. And part of me has been wondering whether an author of erotic fiction should be being a little more daring in her own exploits. Just to stay on-brand, you know?

Fuck it. I mentally add rejuvenating my marriage to my to-do list and turn on the television. I may not have any chill and but I do have Netflix.

Chapter Three

'I can't believe we've only been back at school for one week. It feels like the summer never happened.' Cassie slumps down next to me and closes her eyes. 'I just had to explain to my new Year Seven class that Chemistry is not, in fact, going to be, and I quote, "all about making potions" and that Westhill Academy is not even a tiny bit *"like Hogwarts"*. I swear these kids are getting younger every year.'

I wince, imagining Benji walking through our hallowed halls this time next year and renew my vow to enroll him in some self-defence classes over the next twelve months.

'At least you managed to get a break this summer,' I remind her. 'I feel like I need a holiday from my holiday.'

I have tried not to envy my best friend and her three weeks in Crete at an all-inclusive resort without any kids to worry about. I have also failed in that task.

Cassie opens her eyes and gives me a frown. 'But you

had two weeks in France,' she says. 'What happened? Did you overdo it on the vin rouge?'

I sigh. 'There isn't enough cheap plonk in the whole of France to ease the pain of attempting a nice, family holiday. You have no idea how stressful it is going away with my lot.'

Cassie looks unmoved. 'You should have done what I did then,' she says. 'Taken some time to find yourself.'

I open my mouth to reply and then close it again. There's no point in even trying to explain. She doesn't understand that I would sell my soul for some time. Time to do anything. In fact, *finding myself* would probably be quite low down on my list of priorities after curling up and reading more than one page of a book or having a bath without interruption. Or maybe even having an intimate date night with my husband, if I could entice him out of the shed.

The bell rings and a collective groan goes up from those teachers scattered around the room who are teaching next period, which appears to be everyone except for Cassie and me.

'I don't want to go back to lessons,' whines Peter, who has been having a quick nap in the chair opposite us. 'I'm getting too old for this crap. Teaching English to teenagers is a young man's game. All I want is a nice little nest-egg so that I can retire somewhere where there aren't any people – is that so much to ask?'

'You need to set yourself free from that kind of limiting attitude,' Adele, the drama teacher, tells him as she breezes past with Danny hot on her heels. 'I'd have hoped that last week's Inset Day would have given you some strategies for dealing with self-negativity and extraneous brain noise.'

'I'm not being negative about *me*,' Peter mutters as she wafts out of the room, heading to the drama department where some hapless class will be forced to listen to her waffling. 'And *you're* extraneous brain noise.'

'I thought it was an excellent activity,' gushes Danny, only he times his comment too late and Adele has left the room. 'It's like Adele said last week – it's in the darkest times that we can really find our strengths.'

Peter scowls so hard that his glasses start to slip down his nose. 'Well, the darkest time I've had recently was at that bloody awful drama session and it in no way equipped me with the necessary strength required to teach my Year Eight class, none of whom have the slightest desire to string more than two words together in a coherent manner.'

I shudder. I'm still trying to recover from the horrors of last week's Inset Day but some things can't ever be forgotten: Adele making us all participate in expressive mime as we learnt to *connect with our inner child* being only one of them.

'That's my point,' says Danny. 'You need to be more positive, mate.'

Peter drags himself out of his chair and towers over Danny.

'It was bloody weird, *mate*,' he snarls. 'And if I don't win on the lottery next weekend then it might be wise for everyone to stay out of my way.'

'There's only seven more weeks to go until half-term' I

call, as Peter wearily picks up his bag. 'I've started a countdown on the calendar at home.'

It's true. I know I shouldn't be wishing the days away (as Scarlet keeps reminding me, I'm not getting any younger) but ever since Miriam took over as Headteacher, school has been even more unbearable. She's appointed herself a personal assistant – a little old lady called Miss Pritchard – and has taken to prowling the corridors during lesson times, peering in through classroom doors and barking notes for Miss Pritchard to scrawl down in the notebook that never seems to leave her hands. It's like being on the set of an incredibly dull horror film where nothing ever happens but there's still a constant feeling that terror might be just around the corner.

Peter gives me a tired smile and plods out into the corridor, followed by our other reluctant colleagues and a still-enthusiastic Danny, whose newly qualified perkiness has been in no way dampened by Peter's not-very-veiled threats. Cassie waits until the room is empty and then turns to look at me, her eyes sparkling.

'Right then,' she says, rubbing her hands together. 'There's nobody here now so we can stop talking about boring crap and have the conversation that I've been dying to have all week. How's it all going with the book? We haven't even spoken properly since it came out. Tell me everything, Hannah!'

I glance around to check that we really are alone. *More Than Sex* has been out for a few weeks now and I'm desperate to talk to someone other than Nick about it.

It's fair to say that being a published author has both

pros and cons. The first con is that, contrary to what people may believe, the publishing industry doesn't exactly throw money about. Not that I thought writing a book would make me loaded.

Definitely not.

Not for one. Single. Second.

Sure, it's possible that on the night I received the call from my new agent, telling me that she wanted to represent me, Nick and I may have got slightly ahead of ourselves. And by 'getting ahead', I absolutely do not mean sending an email to Miriam Wallace, telling her where she could stick her stupid job offer of teaching English.

She was quite gracious about that, actually. Once my agent had explained to me that the kind of money we were talking about would be just enough to pay for driving lessons and the occasional bottle of Prosecco, I was forced to write a painfully cringe-worthy email to Miriam, begging for my old part-time job back. She said that as she'd already advertised the position, I'd have to interview along with all the other applicants but it turns out, quite unsurprisingly, that people are not queuing up to deal with fourteen-year-olds murdering Shakespeare so I was the only one in the running. My interview consisted of Miriam piling yet more work onto my already exploding timetable and me pathetically agreeing to all of her demands. I did tentatively enquire about whether there may be enough money in the school budget to reinstate me in a full-time teaching position, but once she'd stopped her mirthless laughter she told me that three days was all that was on offer and I could take it or leave it.

The next slightly challenging aspect is that I had to agree to write another book and, while I don't want to seem ungrateful, this wasn't really what I was aiming for when I wrote *More Than Sex*. Sure, I was hoping to earn a bit of extra money but it wasn't only about that. I wanted to be someone different to the Hannah Thompson that I saw every time I looked in the mirror. I'm just not entirely convinced that the *someone different* I wanted to become was a writer of erotic fiction and certainly not comedy-erotica. I'm not sure that's who I really am.

The school staffroom isn't the *ideal* location for this discussion but, other than Nick and my mother, I've had nobody to share this with and I can't wait any longer. Because honestly, despite the slight negatives, having a book published is genuinely the best feeling ever.

'It's been incredible,' I tell her, keeping my voice low. 'Honestly, Cassie – I can't begin to tell you.'

Cassie squeals. 'I *knew* that Nick and I sending your manuscript off was the right thing, even if you were in a mood with us for weeks! This is brilliant!'

I grin at her. 'Well, I'd definitely never have had the confidence to share it, so yeah – it was the right thing! My agent is lovely and my publisher is some kind of genius and has worked wonders with the edits – and now it's out there and people are reading it and some of them actually seem to like it!'

'So they should.' Cassie reaches into her bag and pulls something out, brandishing it in front of my face. 'Will you sign my copy? Write something meaningful about how you'd never have done it without me and that you owe all your success to my amazing friendship. Or words to that effect.'

I swear that my heart actually stops beating for a couple of seconds. Grabbing the book out of her hand, I clutch it to my chest while my eyes dart feverishly around the room.

'Cassie! What are you doing? You can't bring that in here – what if someone saw it?'

Cassie rolls her eyes dramatically and gestures at the empty chairs. 'There's nobody else here, Mrs Paranoia. And even if anyone did see it, they wouldn't know that you wrote it, would they? You need to relax.'

I do relax slightly and look down at the book in my hands. I've spent a lot of time staring at the cover over the last month but I don't think I'll ever get tired of seeing it. The sugared-almond-pink background, which contrasts with the sensible and sturdy pair of black knickers on the front and the title: *More Than Sex*. I approved of the cover the instant that I saw it – the knickers in particular are completely perfect, because the image conveys practicality and comfort which is obviously important considering that the main character, Bella Rose, spends the majority of her time engaged in manual labour on a ranch. It's not exactly logical to imagine anyone mucking out horses while wearing scanty, lace underwear and, more than anything else, I want my book to be honest and real.

Cassie is right. I do need to relax. There's nothing to link me with being the author of this novel. Nobody will find out that I have penned a deliciously raunchy story of sensual desire that apparently is *one of a kind*. It turns out that Nick was wrong – it *is* possible to be both erotic and sexy while remaining informational and factually correct. According to my publisher, it's a highly amusing mash-up of genres.

I think I might be what is popularly known as *zeitgeist*. I'm not sure if this knowledge makes me want to whoop with joy or hide under my duvet.

But none of this means that I want anybody to know about it.

'So how are you keeping the whole thing a secret from your kids?' asks Cassie, interrupting my thoughts. 'What do they think you're up to when you're off being a famous author?'

'I'm hardly famous,' I say, shaking my head.

Not that I haven't thought about what it would be like to be a celebrity. As well as my private bathroom interviews, every time I go shopping I imagine being mobbed by hordes of excited fans. Not that it will ever happen, because one of the things I have insisted on is absolutely no photograph of me in any publicity. Scarlet's ability to access information on the Internet rivals that of Wikileaks and I know she'd sniff me out in a matter of seconds if I allowed my publisher to include a picture on my author page. It's been a bit of a source of conflict between us, actually. Binky, my lovely but slightly scary editor, has sent me several emails explaining the importance of readers being able to put a face to the name and making a connection with the author, but for now I'm standing firm. I'm scared of Binky but I'm terrified of Scarlet.

'Anyway,' I continue. 'I haven't had to go anywhere or do anything yet so there hasn't been anything *to* explain.'

'But surely you're going to have to start promoting the book soon?' Cassie looks confused. 'They're going to want you to help publicise it, to increase sales.'

'I don't think it works like that when you're at my level,' I tell her, glancing at the clock. 'I don't think they're expecting me to hit the bestseller lists anytime soon! Which is a bit of a problem because I only got a tiny advance and most of it went on the car breaking down on our way home from our holiday. I'm more broke than I've ever been and I'm pretty sure that my writing isn't going to help pay for Dylan's university costs. Nick's applying for a new forestry contract at the moment and if he gets it then that'll help boost his existing income quite a lot – but there's no guarantee. The tree surgeon world is fierce.'

'That's the whole point of you doing some publicity though,' Cassie says tells me. 'I think you need to dream big, Hannah. See where this new journey might take you.'

I stand and look at the cover of the book again.

My book.

It would be wonderful to be able to focus on *developing my craft* (I read that phrase in a book that Nick bought me over the summer called *How to Write a Bestselling Novel*) but that kind of thing doesn't happen to just anyone. Cassie really doesn't understand how it works.

'Why do you think I'm back here, facing yet another term of teaching English to the delightful Year Nine, Class C?' I ask her. 'I wouldn't be doing that if I was about to hit the big time.'

'They're Year *Ten*, Class C, now,' Cassie helpfully

reminds me. 'Not that they're going to be any more mature just because they've gone up a year group.'

'Well, I've got three days a week of dealing with them, which right now feels like an eternity.' I hand her back her copy of *More Than Sex*. 'Put this away and for god's sake don't bring it into school again. Can you imagine if Brandon Hopkins got his sweaty little hands on it?'

'I'm still going to get a signature from you,' Cassie promises, shoving it into her bag. 'Then I'm going to keep it in a completely pristine condition so that I can flog it on eBay as a first edition when you're rich and famous.'

She pulls herself to her feet and we walk together towards the staffroom door.

'So, did you meet any eligible bachelors over the summer?' I ask as I reach for the handle.

There's a pause and when I turn back to look at my best friend, her face is uncharacteristically flushed.

'Maybe,' she murmurs.

'Cassie!' I push the door closed again with my foot. 'I can't believe that you haven't told me this already! I *knew* there must be a good reason for why you couldn't meet up with me last week. Who is he? Do I know him? Is it serious?'

I know I'm being nosy but the glow on her cheeks is reliably informing me that my best friend has been finding more than just *herself* this summer and if I have to live vicariously through her sexual exploits, then so be it.

'It's too early to talk about it,' she says, looking everywhere but at me. 'We're still figuring things out.'

'Oh my god.' I take a step forward and peer at her face.

'You like him. As in, you actually *like him* like him. It's a goddamned Christmas miracle!'

'It's September, Hannah.' Cassie pushes past me and pulls open the door. 'Not even you can start talking about Christmas yet.'

'Don't change the subject,' I follow her out into the corridor, ignoring the sight of three Year Eleven girls giggling loudly and disappearing into the toilets. 'I can't wait to meet him!'

'Well, I wouldn't hold your breath,' Cassie says, heading off towards the Science department. 'You might pass out.'

I watch her go, trying to decide if she's walking with an extra jaunty spring in her step, and then I turn and make my way to the stairs and up to my classroom, where in twenty minutes I will have the deepest joy of explaining to Year Ten, Class C that GCSEs are about to dominate their every waking moment for the next two years and that they are going to be required to do a tiny bit of work.

Chapter Four

The building is absolutely massive. And shiny. It is not what I was expecting in the slightest and my legs start to tremble slightly as I look up at the fifty-gazillion windows that stare out across the River Thames. I'm not ready for this and I don't know what I was thinking. People like me don't belong in places like this. This is for the sparkly, beautiful people who have the world at their feet – not the middle-aged mothers who had to get up at an ungodly hour so that they could attempt to put some make-up on and sort out their uncooperative hair and organise the packed lunches and do last night's washing up and *then* change their outfit four times, the first three because of a crisis of confidence and the last time because of fear-sweat.

But if I want even the slightest chance of continuing with my writing career then I need to pull myself together and get a grip because my editor wants to see me to discuss my second book and I can't just run away. Tottering slightly on my fabulous but impractical author shoes, I push open the huge door and walk inside. I am woman and I will not allow my fears about 'belonging' to stop me from pursuing my own dreams and desires.

Besides, I'm here now so I might as well go in, fraudster or not.

The reception area is even more intimidating than the exterior. Security guards lurk menacingly, eyeing everyone with suspicion, and I immediately feel guilty and want to avoid eye contact with them. But that makes a person look even more suspicious, so I do what I always do when I feel guilty by suggestion and overcompensate.

'Good morning!' I trill, making firm eye contact with one of the guards. 'Isn't it a beautiful day? A little chilly, perhaps – but then it is autumn, after all! And winter will be upon us before we know it!'

He narrows his eyes until I can barely see his pupils. 'Move along to the desk, please, Madam.'

This is the problem with London. Nobody wants to have a conversation. It was the same on the train. The man sitting opposite me actually moved seats after I tried to engage him in some casual chitchat.

It's me.

I know it is.

I talk when I'm nervous. I've always been that way.

An incredibly well-groomed woman is typing efficiently on her keyboard as I approach the desk. She doesn't look up and so I stand quietly for a full one point three seconds and then launch into my friendliest banter.

'Gosh! You're fast at typing, aren't you? I wish I were that quick. It takes me forever to write one page which isn't very good when you consider that I'm trying to make a living out of it!'

She mutters something into her headset and I stop talking. Eventually, after what feels like forever but my watch assures me is less than thirty seconds, she looks up and gives me a tight smile.

'Name?'

'Hannah Thompson,' I say, beaming widely. 'My name is Hannah Thompson.'

'Here to see?'

'Binky,' I tell her. 'She's expecting me.'

The receptionist peers over her glasses. 'And does Binky have a surname?'

I laugh nervously. 'I'm sure she does but I can't remember it right now.'

She looks me dead in the eye and I swear, for a brief moment, my heart stops beating.

'That's going to be a problem, Madam. We have over three thousand people working in this building and I'm going to need a little more to go on.'

I laugh. 'But surely you must know whom I mean? You can't possibly have more than one person called Binky working here?'

She tuts. 'I know of at least three Binkys on the fourth floor alone.'

This is ridiculous. I have not come all this way and psyched myself up for nothing. I lean casually onto the desk and give my brightest teacher-smile.

'Well, can you just look for *my* name then? Maybe that will shed some light on which of the Binkys I'm supposed to be meeting.'

'Your name isn't in the system,' she intones. 'I've got a Twinky Malone meeting Binky Sanderson at eleven-thirty but nothing for a Hannah Thompson.'

'That's me!' I shout. '*I'm* Twinky Malone. And I've remembered now – it *is* Binky Sanderson who I'm meeting!'

'How convenient,' mutters the receptionist.

'Not really,' I tell her. 'It would have been much more convenient if I'd remembered her full name when you first asked me, then we could have avoided all this hassle.'

She stretches her hand out across the desk and my tension fades. Maybe I was wrong about London. Maybe people do want to communicate and engage with others. Perhaps they're all just waiting for someone like me to jolt them out of their hard shells, through the power of friendliness and chitter-chatter. Maybe I should start a business, travelling around the capital city dispensing *joi de vivre* wherever I go.

I reach out and grasp her hand.

'It's lovely to meet you,' I gush.

'Identification,' she barks, yanking her hand out of mine. 'I was asking for your ID. To prove that you're Twinky Malone.'

Oh. My bad.

'I don't have any,' I confess, my heart sinking. 'It's my pseudonym and so I don't have any official paperwork with it on. Is that a problem? What do other authors do? Should I find someone to issue me with some fake ID? Do you know anyone who can help?'

The receptionist sighs deeply and taps something onto the screen.

'I've sent an alert to Binky Sanderson and she's on her way down. I can't give you a visitor pass until she vouches for you and you can't get through the security gate without a pass.' She points behind me to a row of occupied chairs. 'Take a seat and she'll be here shortly.'

I nod gratefully and head across the polished floor to a free seat where I sink down gratefully, glad to have a moment to prepare myself. This place is insane, from the over-the-top flower displays to the works of art on the walls. I can't quite believe that I'm here. I gaze around, soaking it all in, desperate not to miss a single thing.

There's a sudden surge of activity, with people entering the building and rushing up the stairs on the other side of the security gate. I crane past them to admire the view of the autumn sun sparkling off the river.

'Did you see her!' hisses the young woman sitting next to me and I whip my head round to look at her. 'Oh. My. God.'

'Who?' I ask. 'Who was it?'

'I can't believe you didn't see her!' she howl-whispers, her eyes staring wildly at the people who are just moving out of sight at the top of the stairs. 'She was standing right in front of you. You couldn't miss her!'

'Who was it?' I repeat, feeling cross with myself. Scarlet is very interested in anything celebrity-related and I could have won myself some real brownie points if I'd gone home with some kind of a story to tell. Although the reality is that it doesn't matter who I might see today because I'm not actually here. The kids think I'm out on a course for school and while I don't enjoy lying to them, it's far better than the alternative option of telling them the truth.

'Your one off the telly!' the young woman huffs, rolling her eyes at me. 'You know? The blonde one? Does a load of stuff with the brunette one. She's funny.'

I shake my head sadly. 'Sorry. I don't know who you mean.'

'Well, you should pay more attention in a place like this,' she says. 'Who are *you*, anyway? What are you doing here?'

She tilts her head to one side and appraises me, trying to decide if I'm a person of interest.

'Oh, I'm not anybody,' I rush to assure her. 'My name is Ha—'

And then I stop.

Because I am sitting here in a swanky publishing house and I am here for a reason. And there is a very tiny part of me screaming incredibly loudly that it might be quite nice to own my success instead of constantly being focused on hiding it away like it's something shameful.

There is also a very large part of me whispering quietly that I shouldn't do something I might later regret.

I tell that part of me that it can do one and turn to face the celebrity-spotting woman.

'I'm an author,' I announce, sitting up straighter. 'You might have heard of me. My name is Twinky Malone.'

'What do you write?' she asks, sounding bored. My proclamation has clearly not excited her. 'Is it like, cookery books or something?'

'There you are!'

I turn and see Binky coming towards me. I know her from her online profile picture and she must recognise me from the photo that I sent with the strictest instructions that it was not to be used for any publicity. I stand and fix a professional yet pleasant look to my face. First impressions count and I want my editor to think that I'm utterly in control of everything.

'It's so great to finally meet you,' she says, shaking my hand with a warmth that was definitely lacking in the receptionist. 'We're all so excited that you're coming into the office today! Let's get your pass sorted and then we can head upstairs and introduce you to everyone.'

She turns towards the desk and I start to follow her before pausing and spinning back to the young woman.

'It's not cookery books that I write,' I call. 'It's erotic fiction. The very incredibly sexy kind.'

Her jaw drops open and I give her a grin before heading to the desk where the receptionist reluctantly hands me a visitor pass and grants me access to the halls beyond the security gate.

In the lift, Binky talks enthusiastically about *More Than Sex* and by the time we arrive at the sixth floor I feel as if I've known her forever.

'Readers are loving the mash-up of erotica and comedy,' she tells me as we leave the lift and walk into the office space. 'I really think you can build on that with Book Two.'

'Absolutely,' I agree, trying not to gasp at the sight of London spread out beneath me. 'I can absolutely do that. Funny fornication is my bread and butter.'

I've been struggling just the tiniest bit with the fact that everyone seems to think my first book is amusing as well as sexy. That wasn't my intention in the slightest when I wrote it – as far as I was concerned I had written something that was highly risqué and also packed with informative facts. I'm trying to come to terms with my new role as comedic sex-woman but it isn't easy. It's as if now that I know I'm supposed to be funny, I can't think of a single joke. I have no idea how stand-up comics perform to order, night after night.

Binky laughs. 'You're hilarious,' she tells me. 'Now, can I get you a drink?'

I accept a cup of tea and follow her into a small meeting room. I wasn't trying to be humorous (obviously) but as I'm rapidly discovering, sometimes it's better just to go with the flow.

Once I'm settled on a sofa, another woman enters the room and gives me a welcoming smile.

'This is Alice!' enthuses Binky. 'She's our publicity manager and she's another big fan of your book!'

'Twinky! It's great to meet you at last,' says Alice, walking over and shaking my hand. 'I've been telling Binky for ages that we need to get you in and start working on a publicity campaign but I gather that you've had some reservations?'

I nod and take a sip of my tea.

'It's just that, being a mum as well as a writer, I have to consider the wellbeing of my children, you know?'

They both nod understandingly.

'I'm sure you're run off your feet,' says Alice, sitting down next to me. 'Three kids and writing, not to mention your day job! But you're here now and we've got some great plans.'

'Oh, it's not so much the time issue,' I tell her. 'Although obviously, a few extra hours in the day would be wonderful!'

They laugh dutifully. I join in, even though I'm lying. A few extra hours in the day sounds like a terrible idea. You can guarantee that if the government suddenly decided that the day had to last twenty-seven hours (and I wouldn't put it past this lot) then I would not be spending that extra time relaxing or sleeping or doing anything remotely enjoyable. I, along with a large percentage of the population, would just end up with even more jobs to do. A few extra hours in the day would just extend the misery before I actually get to sink into a wine-fuelled bliss.

'No – it's more the genre in which I am writing,' I continue, trying to sound intelligent. 'I don't want to risk being outed as an erotic author. It doesn't seem like the most appropriate thing for a mother to be doing.'

Alice stares at me for a second, her face perplexed.

'Are you saying that you think it's embarrassing that you've written erotic fiction?' she asks slowly. 'Is that the problem?'

'No, no!' I laugh. 'Not embarrassing, per se…'

'What then?' She leans forward and peers at me, her kind face open and honest. She isn't judging me. She's genuinely interested.

'Okay, it is a *bit* embarrassing,' I whisper. 'I'm writing about sex, for goodness' sake. I don't want my kids to know about that. Or anyone else who knows me, for that matter.'

'Okay.' Alice sits back and shoots a quick look at Binky. 'So what you're saying is that it's the *sex* aspect that you're worried about?'

'Yes!' I take another sip of tea. 'I don't want anyone to look at me and judge me. I don't want them thinking differently about me because they've read my book and seen what my fevered imagination is capable of concocting.'

'I really don't think that you need to worry,' Alice says, her voice shaking slightly. 'I've read a lot of erotic fiction and your first book isn't exactly what I'd describe as *hardcore*.'

'It's actually very mild,' agrees Binky. 'In fact, we had a huge discussion about whether we could class it as erotica in the first place.'

'Due to the minimal amount of actual copulation,' adds Alice.

'You should enjoy the fact that you've written a book that readers are raving about,' says Binky. 'And now that you've hooked them in and made them fall in love with Bella Rose and Daxx, we need to keep them reading – which means that Book Two needs to be *more*.'

'More?' I put down my teacup. 'More of what?'

'More sex,' states Alice firmly. 'And more humour.'

Binky nods. 'Definitely more sex.'

'Oh.' I gulp slightly. 'I see. More sex. Excellent.'

Binky leans across and pats my hand kindly. 'You've got a very original voice, Hannah,' she tells me. 'We'd really like to see you let yourself have fun with this book. Let loose a little and see where you can take Daxx and Bella

Rose on their sexual journey of enlightenment. How far are you prepared to go?'

Buggering hell. I do not like the sound of a sexual journey of enlightenment one bit.

I turn and look out of the window at the majestic skyline. I'm going to have to tell them that while it's been a wonderfully exciting adventure and I'm very grateful for the experience, this is where I have to get off the bus. I wasn't even supposed to be on this bus in the first place. I thought that writing erotica would be easy but it isn't. And it's even harder when the reason you're a success is because your definition of raunchiness is other people's definition of outrageously funny.

More Than Sex was only published because the sex is so bad that everyone thought it was a joke. They're laughing *at* me, not with me, even if they don't realise it – because it wasn't a joke to me. It was the sexiest, most X-rated, taboo thing that I could possibly think of, regardless of whether everyone who reads it thinks it's the lamest sex imaginable. There's no way I can write something that's *more* than that.

I can't do it.

Can I?

I take a deep breath and let myself think about upping the ante and pushing myself to write something even riskier than my first book. I cannot deny that the thought is giving me a slight thrill of excitement. And I don't know how far I'm prepared to go – but maybe it could be fun figuring it out. Plus I still have my dire financial situation to consider. I can't just throw away an amazing opportunity because I feel a bit uncomfortable.

'You really shouldn't be embarrassed about it,' Alice assures me. 'You're writing under a pseudonym and nobody has to know it's you if you really don't want them to. But surely it'd be empowering for your family and friends to know that you've followed your dreams and achieved something brilliant?'

I sit back and think about what they're saying. Maybe I've been overreacting about remaining anonymous? Maybe the world won't judge me too harshly if word gets out that I'm a published author of erotica? Maybe we've evolved to a level where women are entitled to be sexual without being slut-shamed?

'Anyway...' Alice's voice is wheedling. 'Why *shouldn't* you write erotica? It's not like mothers aren't allowed to do it.'

Oh my god. Absolutely this.

'I think they had to do *it* to become mothers in the first place,' quips Binky.

Alice nods her head. 'E. L. James has got two kids and I bet she stood in the playground with her head held high once *Fifty Shades of Grey* came out. And I bet none of the kids cared about it.'

'Women have sex.' Binky gives me a firm look. 'It's not just for the men, is it? That's what we love about your book – it's honest and funny and messy and awkward and it's for women.'

It is this that sways me.

Why the hell shouldn't I have sex? And why the hell shouldn't I write about sex? And, now that I've written about it, why the hell shouldn't I do everything that I can to get better and write about even more sex?

I am a teacher and a wife and a mother and a daughter and I've spent my entire life pretending that I know how to do stuff that I know literally nothing about. This is no different to when a newborn Dylan was placed into my arms and I was told that I could take him home from the hospital. I didn't have the first clue about what I was supposed to be doing and he's turned out okay, hasn't he? I've brought up three kids and I've winged it all the way. I sure as shit can fake my way through writing Book Two (untitled) and it's going to be the most informative, most factually correct and most goddamned provocative, titillating and libidinous work to ever grace the comedy-erotic fiction shelves.

'Let's do it,' I say, looking at Binky and Alice and beaming widely. 'Let's get our freak on.'

I sing this last bit in my best hip-hop voice but, from the looks on their faces, I think it is safe to assume there are no Missy Elliot fans in the house.

I can do this.

My freak is ready to rumble.

Chapter Five

It's Friday and quite honestly, it isn't really being the day that I was hoping for. I felt so inspired and up-for-it after meeting with Binky and Alice yesterday and their enthusiasm and confidence was quite contagious.

However, it turns out that writing the sequel is proving to be every bit as hard as I suspected it might be. I sat at my usual table in The Daily Grind this morning (the fact that I have a usual table makes me feel like a totally legitimate author) and tried to imagine how Bella Rose would feel when she saw Daxx walking shirtless into the kitchen but I kept getting completely distracted by the new barista, whose ability to whip up a whipped caramel latte is truly second to none. Plus his muscles kept rippling every time he pulled down the lever on the coffee machine and it made the tiger tattoo on his arm move in a very enthralling manner. So I didn't actually get very much done at all and ended up coming home, in the hopes that I'd be more productive here.

And while the whole writing thing is all very exciting and I know that I'm very lucky, it does feel slightly different this time. When I was writing before, I wasn't sure that I'd ever let anyone read it. Now, every word that I choose feels like it has to be perfect. All I can think about when I sit down to write is a faceless, unknown reader, selecting *my* book over one of the millions of others that are out there – and then finding it lacking. I've been calling her *Valerie* in my head, in an attempt to make her seem less intimidating but I think I've just compounded the problem because she's started to take on a personality all of her own. And Valerie is a very demanding mistress when it comes to her choice of erotic fiction.

It's all mildly terrifying and I'm pretty sure that I've got writer's block because so far, the only thing that I've got is the first six words of the first chapter. And Valerie thinks that they are all quite rubbish.

There is one very excellent thing about being a writer though and, glancing up at the clock, I can see that it's finally time for me to stop labouring over my manuscript and indulge in some author-reader connectivity or, as others might call it, some Googling of myself. I put the kettle on and then take my laptop across to the sofa by the back door, making myself comfortable beside Dogger. I've had to develop some rules for working from home because otherwise it's all a bit too easy for the day to disappear. So I'm being strict with myself now. Writing happens at the kitchen table with a glass of water – and relaxation time happens on the sofa with a cup of tea. I'm actually getting quite good at being disciplined. As soon as my break is over

I'll return to the table, delete the six words that are on the screen and start again.

I've been eagerly anticipating this moment for the last hour. This is fast becoming my favourite thing to do and one of the best bits about being a writer. I hadn't given it much thought to begin with because everything happened so quickly – but a few days after *More Than Sex* was released, the reviews started to come in and that was it. I was hooked. If I'm truly honest, another reason for the lack of progress with Book Two (untitled) is possibly due to the amount of time that I have spent searching for reviews online. Not that there's anything wrong with that. It's just Continued Professional Development – I'm keen to read what people say about the book, good or bad, and then use that to further my writing skills. I appreciate and take on board each and every comment. It's like I tell the kids at school – a person is never too old to learn and it's important to keep your mind open to the opinions of others.

I've had to limit my looking though, after Nick asked me yesterday how my writing was going and I complained that I didn't have enough time to get anything done and that he was going to have to cook supper because I'd been so busy working on my book. Well, I told *him* that I was working. The reality was that I spent several hours searching for reviews online and twenty-eight minutes writing my opening paragraph. And twenty-one of those minutes consisted of me staring vacantly at the screen, wondering what Valerie would make of a first chapter that started with the words:

Bella Rose's skin started to prickle with unbridled passion and also as a result of the temperature in Tulsa, Oklahoma being ninety-six degrees Fahrenheit (which in real money is thirty-five point five degrees Celsius). The high propensity of buildings meant that the trapped heat made it feel much hotter, which Bella Rose knew was part of the phenomenon known as Urban Heat Island and made living in this new city a very different experience to the ranch back in Wyoming. Not that the meteorological conditions were a problem. Bella Rose liked her climate the way she liked her men. And also her coffee. Hot and steamy and ~~tattooed~~. Hot and steamy was good. Hot and steamy was what Bella Rose liked best. Long, sultry nights filled with sizzling, torrid passion as she and Daxx made wanton, steamy love into the early hours.

It took a lot of reading and re-reading for me to come to conclusion that Valerie would think it in no way realistic or even particularly sexy despite the fact that it includes the words *sizzling* and *wanton*. So I deleted everything except the first six words and I haven't been able to come up with anything else since, which is why I'm trialing this new way of working. My new plan is to write for one hour and then check for any new reviews instead of refreshing my screen on a two-minute basis, which will hopefully mean that I'll get some actual writing done and stop getting too distracted.

It hasn't worked so far today but then again, maybe I'm just the kind of writer who needs feedback from her audience in order to thrive. That sounds reasonable. I cannot write in a vacuum. I need to bounce off the opinions of others and hone my craft, acknowledging that without the reader, there *is* no writer.

My new career might be fraught with risk and challenge but I can't lie – it's also incredibly exciting. Every time I think about the fact that I have written an actual, genuine book that actual, genuine people are reading I feel a thrill of utter euphoria and reading their comments makes me feel like I'm someone a bit special. Opening the first tab, I can see immediately that there are four new reviews since I last looked. My heart starts to beat a little faster and I lean closer to the screen, ready to soak in lots of lovely, critical appraisal.

The words from the first review leap off the screen and punch me in the face.

What the actual fuck? I don't know who Heather0933 is, but I sure as shit know that she does not have a clue what she is talking about. If she's such a bloody expert on what entails good erotic fiction then where is her book, hey?

I struggled with this book and the beginning nearly had me giving up.

Well, I wish you had *given up, if you were just going to be unkind about it.*

I scan down to the next review.

The humour felt forced and unnatural and there's very little plot.

It wasn't supposed to be funny when I wrote it. Although she possibly has a point about the lack of plot –

but does it really matter? Do readers really pick up erotica for the plot?

However, what she says next about some of my information being wrong is just plain ignorant. I fact-checked everything that went in. There's no way I would include something that I hadn't ensured was accurate. I spent hours researching, making sure that I had up-to-date knowledge about the setting in Wyoming and Nick and I re-enacted all the explicit scenes to guarantee that they were physically do-able. Any suggestion otherwise is just libelous. I could probably sue.

I'm quite fortunate that Nick didn't try to sue me himself, if I'm honest. My surprise purchase of a sex manual entitled *Kama Sutra: Three hundred and sixty-five positions* resulted in an evening that neither of us is ever likely to forget. I still have the occasional night where I will wake drenched in sweat and clutching the duvet in horror as I re-enact the moment that Dylan and Scarlet walked in on us attempting to recreate the Coiled Cobra position. The fact that we were fully clothed did little to dispel the awkwardness.

I ended up donating the totally useless manual to the school charity sale, hidden under a pile of Enid Blyton books. That's another thing that wakes me up now and again – the knowledge that I almost definitely inscribed my name inside the front cover, as is my habit on purchasing a new book. Nobody has confronted me about it though, so I'm either safe or it was bought by someone who hasn't learnt to read yet.

Blinking hard, I scroll down to look at the next review.

Kevin from Hull has given me three stars and the comment reads:

Very nice. Just what I've been looking for. My mother-in-law is delighted.

I wonder if Kevin from Hull has possibly confused my erotic novel with his new kettle purchase.

I fervently hope so.

Thankfully, I get lucky with the fourth reviewer who says that she's never read anything so funny in her life and that she hadn't known that sex could be so entertaining.

Neither did I, until I unwittingly struck comedy-sex gold. Now all I've got to do is tap that again.

Heaving a big sigh, I give Dogger's fur a quick ruffle and then return to the table. This book isn't going to write itself and Valerie is waiting. I can't let her down. I need to find a way to write in a sexy manner while injecting a jocular note into every sensual act that Bella Rose and the brooding, yet slightly stupid, Daxx perform.

I stare at the screen and try to remember what I did last time. After I'd read all the *Fifty Shades of Grey* books and been inspired to do a better job, I read a few other erotic works and tried to find a pattern. But what really worked was writing about what made *me* feel excited. And that was making sure that Bella Rose was a kick-ass, take-no-nonsense woman who knew what she wanted. It was all about writing a character that secretly, I would quite like to be.

So all I've got to do now is figure out what Bella Rose

wants next and send her on a new journey. Her journey of sexual awakening or enlightenment or whatever, which presumably means that she's going to be having quite a lot of it. Sex, that is.

I flex my fingers and position them over my keyboard. There are worse things that a woman could have to do with her time than fantasise about wanton, impassioned coitus.

I type the raunchiest word that I know onto the screen to get me started.

And then the phone rings and when I glance at the screen I see that it's my mother. Of course it is. She's always had the ability to interrupt any moments of illicit pleasure that I may be attempting to enjoy.

I could ignore her. I should ignore her.

I am incapable of ignoring her.

'Hi, Mum,' I say, lowering the lid of my laptop which I know is ridiculous but I just don't feel comfortable talking to her with *that word* leaping off the screen. 'Is everything okay?'

'Everything is fine, darling!' she trills merrily. 'I've just finished this week's online learning session and it made me think about you. We need to have a quick chat.'

For fuck's sake. This is literally the last thing that I need right now. Whatever she's about to say is guaranteed to ruin my mood and dampen my vibe for the rest of the day.

'I'm actually a bit busy, Mum,' I start but I'm wasting my breath. Short of hanging up on her, there is nothing I can do to stop her when she wants to *have a quick chat*. Which is code for a lengthy monologue.

'It's about you and Nick,' she says, plowing straight

ahead. 'I'm worried that you're spending too much time on your phones and computers and devices and not enough time investing in your relationship as lovers.'

I close my eyes and start trying to count to ten. I don't make it past two.

'The Internet is killing sex,' she states. 'And you need to do something about it.'

Incredible. I'll add it to the list of things that demand my attention.

'The first thing you need to do is remove your mobile phones from the bedroom,' she continues. 'Hannah? Are you listening to me?'

'I'm not having a conversation about this with you, Mother,' I say firmly. 'It's just like last week, when you rang me up and tried to tell me that I need to do something about harmonising the domestic and sensual halves of myself, right when I was in the middle of trying to unblock the dishwasher filter. I am not your sex-counselling guinea pig, okay? Find someone else to trial this stuff on.'

There is silence at the other end of the line and I instantly feel bad.

'But you're probably right,' I concede, grudgingly. 'I'm sure it would be better for our health if we didn't charge our phones next to the bed every night.'

'Definitely better for your sexual health,' agrees my mother, bouncing back. 'That's sorted then. Excellent!'

'Marvellous,' I mutter. 'Thanks for calling.'

'My pleasure,' she chirrups. 'Just shout if you want any more advice, Hannah. I'm always here to help. Now, sorry to cut you short, darling, but I must go. I was just heading out to the shops when you called.'

'But Mum, you rang—' I start, but the dialing tone buzzes back at me. I shake my head and hang up before lifting my laptop lid, but even *the sexiest word* isn't enough to get me back in the zone so I delete it and try again. Binky said that I should push my characters further and take more chances. Her insinuation was that I need to loosen up which was a bit rude because I've always liked to think of myself as a very chilled out, laid-back yet also passionate kind of woman and any suggestion otherwise is a teeny bit insulting.

I'll show her just how loose I can be. I shake my arms and shrug the tension out of my shoulders and then I start typing, really letting myself go. I dig as deep as I possibly can and type without thinking, which is another thing I read about in *How to Write a Bestselling Novel*. It's called 'Free Writing' and the whole point is to write without fear of being judged or worrying about normal conventions. And the end result may be a little raw and in need of a polish but it will be real and honest and from the heart and that's exactly what I'm after.

I write an entire paragraph and then pause, nervously reading what I've written back to myself. This is the moment of truth.

Bella Rose's skin started to prickle. She had always been susceptible to blocked sweat glands, particularly under her breasts and on her upper thighs and most of the time a simple application of an antiperspirant usually did the trick. The best solution of all, of course, was to avoid any activity that would result in her perspiring but right here, with Daxx standing in front of her with such unbridled passion and lust in his eyes that it made her knees tremble, Bella Rose was prepared to throw all caution aside. This was a man she would gladly perspire for. Heck, just the sight of him unbuttoning his shirt made her damp.

The end result is…a little shit.

It's not even sexy by my (apparently) low standards, despite the mention of both thighs and breasts. No wonder my own mother seems to think that I need marriage guidance. If I can't even write about this stuff then what chance do I have of spicing up my own love life?

I need help.

Chapter Six

I am sitting in the empty staffroom, attempting to find the energy and inclination to mark Year Ten, Class C's English homework when Cassie finds me.

'You've got a face like a slapped kipper,' she says, flopping down into the seat opposite me. 'Why so glum? Is it because Scarlet has got the entire Sixth Form petitioning to go on strike if the canteen doesn't start serving bacon and brie panini? Because I have to tell you, Hannah, a lot of the teaching staff are very onboard with the whole thing.'

I drop my pen and rest my chin on my hands.

'It's not that,' I tell her. 'I knew nothing about that but I'm ecstatic that my daughter is putting her Head Girl powers to good use since her appointment to the position, all of two days ago.'

'So what is it then?'

'Nothing is right.' I exhale loudly. 'I feel like I spend my entire time working as hard as I can and getting absolutely nowhere.'

Cassie nods sympathetically. 'I get it. This job is getting more thankless by the day. Do you know, Miriam told me last week that she's taken away the budget for the Chemistry department but that is in no way an excuse for anyone to make less progress? Seriously! How am I supposed to teach about chemical reactions without any buggering chemicals?'

I gaze out of the window. 'It's not just this place. It's everything.'

'Like what?'

I sigh. 'Oh, I don't know. Life.'

Cassie snorts. 'You're going to have to be a bit more specific than that, Hannah. Honestly – what's pissing you off?'

I turn back to look at her, shrugging my shoulders.

'I can't be more specific because I don't *know*. Everything just feels wrong.' I shake my head in despair. 'I feel like I spend every day trying to run up the down escalator and it's knackering and pointless and I've had enough.'

Cassie raises an exquisitely shaped eyebrow and I feel something snap inside.

'And that's another thing. Surely by now, after forty-four years on this planet, I should be able to find some time and money for myself? I should be able to get my eyebrows waxed or have a relaxing massage if I want to, shouldn't I?'

'You should,' she agrees, kindly ignoring my random complaint.

'It shouldn't be this hard.' I bang my fist on the table. 'And I'm bloody sick and tired of pretending that I know what I'm doing all the time. Would it be so awful just to admit that I don't actually possess all the answers in the universe?'

Cassie leans forward and gives me a firm look. 'Yes. Yes it would. We are women, Hannah and our one superpower is knowing everything about everything. If we let them suspect, for even one second, that we aren't fully in control then we'll be left with nothing. Do you understand me?'

I nod my head wearily but I don't actually think I do understand. I just know that it all feels wrong right now.

'What's this actually about, Hannah?' Cassie softens her grimace and gives me a concerned look. 'Is it Nick? Or the kids?'

'Yes.' I slump back into my chair. 'No. Oh god, I don't know. I just know that I'm tired all the time and it feels like I've been breaking bits off myself to give to everyone else for so long that I didn't even realise there was nothing left for me. Never mind time to focus on my actual marriage.'

Cassie smiles. 'What you need is a date night,' she tells me. 'Go somewhere nice with Nick. Just the two of you.'

I suppress a howl. I've barely seen Nick properly in the last few weeks. He's constantly busy either at work or fixing his bloody Land Rover and even when we are together, we're both either utterly exhausted or end up talking about money and how the hell we're going to pay for everything that needs paying for.

Plus it feels like our family is in some kind of strange limbo, waiting for Dylan to go to university. None of us quite know how we're supposed to be feeling and there's nothing that I can do to 'fix' it because it's supposed to be this way. We were never going to stay being the five of us forever, I know that. It's making me feel like everything is layered with a thin sprinkling of sadness and I just don't know if Nick feels the same way that I do. I'd ask him but I'm scared that I won't like the answer.

'I don't think that's going to help,' I say. 'A meal out is not going to solve my problems.'

A concerned look passes over Cassie's face.

'Are you guys having trouble?' she asks quietly, glancing around to make sure that nobody can overhear. 'You can talk to me about it if you are, Hannah. God knows if anyone will understand man trouble then it's me. And men can get very challenging in their middle years, believe me.'

I shake my head. 'It's not really man trouble though. It's woman trouble. It's me.'

Cassie frowns and I elaborate.

'I'm just feeling a bit – well, a bit boring.'

I pause, unsure how much to tell her but then decide that if I can't talk to Cassie then the only other option is my mother and that is never happening, no matter how happy it would make her.

'And it's not just my life and who I am that's a bit dull,' I whisper, even though the staffroom is still empty. 'It's more than that. I think I'm maybe a bit boring in the bedroom. You know. When it comes to being sexy?'

Cassie starts to laugh but then sees my face and quickly stops.

'What do you mean? Why would you think that? Has Nick said something to you?'

'No!' I shudder. 'Of course he hasn't. He'd never be so insensitive. No – I just think that I'm not very imaginative. I've been desperately trying to write some erotic scenes for Bella Rose and Daxx but I can't get it right.'

'I think you're super sexy,' says Cassie loyally, but I can see her mouth twitching. I shouldn't have expected her to understand. The woman gets a facial twice a month and has a gym membership that she actually uses, plus a very active Tinder account. Her life is way more exciting than mine can ever hope to be. 'You're just having a bad day.'

'It's not just that though,' I tell her. 'Scarlet keeps banging on about me being middle-aged and I'm usually able to ignore her but lately it's been getting harder and harder.'

Cassie shrugs her shoulders. 'What's the definition of middle-age?' she asks me. 'Is it a number or a state of mind? And as much as I love her, Scarlet can be a bit much sometimes, Hannah. Don't let her get to you.'

'That's easy for you to say,' I retort, sniffing loudly. 'You don't have to deal with her every day. And anyway, I'm starting to think that she might be right. I've looked online and I'm definitely displaying some of the symptoms of aging.'

'We're all aging, Hannah.' Cassie sounds amused. 'But go on – I'll bite. Which ones?'

'Well, I forgot all about Benji needing to take cakes in for the school cake sale the other day,' I tell her. 'Which was mortifying because the PTA specifically tasked me with providing *sugar-free flapjacks* for those children whose parents actually care about their teeth. And so now, if any of the little cherubs require *any* kind of dental work in the next six months, then I am going to be held solely responsible.'

Cassie tuts. 'You're always forgetting stuff for Benji's school,' she says, clearly unmoved. 'That's down to your organizational skills, Hannah – not getting old and past it.'

'Fine!' I lean towards her. 'I didn't want to have to share this with you because I don't want to gross you out, but you obviously aren't taking me seriously. It's not just *aging* that I'm showing signs of. It's the peri-menopause too.' I lower my voice further. 'I'm fairly sure that I have a reduced libido.'

I sit back, smug. There's no way she can minimise *that* little nugget of information.

'And you are basing this on what, exactly?' Cassie does not look grossed out. She looks highly entertained.

I hold my hand up and start counting off on my fingers.

'One: If we watch a film then I'm always asleep before it's even halfway through. Two: Sometimes, if I had to choose, I'd rather have a hot bath and read my book than engage in any other nocturnal activity. Three: If we do actually have *you-know-what* then it's not unheard of for my mind to start roaming onto other things and I'm not talking about sexy things – I'm talking about what food there is in the fridge and when the car is due for its next service and whether Dogger needs a top-up of worming pills. And four: As previously mentioned, I am struggling to write about anything that could be classed as even a bit sexually adventurous which is a problem when I'm supposed to be a writer of erotica and I'm currently attempting to write Book Two, which so far doesn't even have a bloody title.'

I take a deep breath and blink hard. 'I just don't think I'm a very sexual person and that makes me want to cry. Quite a lot.'

Cassie jumps out of her seat and comes around the table, enveloping me in a big hug.

'Hannah. My lovely but ever-so-slightly ridiculous friend. There is nothing wrong with you, okay?'

I pull away. 'Did you not just hear the list of woe that I am dealing with? I'm only two steps away from needing to book into a retirement home.'

Cassie laughs. 'I didn't hear anything that any woman hasn't felt at some time. I happen to do some of my best problem-solving during sex – it's the only time that I'm not distracted.'

Relatable.

'So you don't think I'm menopausal?' I ask, as Cassie heads back to her side of the table. 'Or getting old?'

She shrugs again. 'Who knows? I'm not a doctor. You might be menopausal but so what? Gone are the days when that meant a woman was all dried up and written off. We've got to own that shit now.'

I suppress a groan. I do not want to *own* the menopause. I only mentioned it in the first place because I wanted her to tell me that I'm being ridiculous and that there's no way I can possibly be at that stage of life.

'I mean, you're getting old*er* but you're definitely not getting *old*,' muses my so-called best friend. 'What I do know is that you're tired and over-worked and that's making you a tiny bit stressed out right now.'

I nod in agreement. 'I am all of those things.'

'You need to take a chill pill, Hannah.' Cassie flops back onto her chair. 'Stop taking everything so seriously. Chill out. Do something just for you. And lighten up.'

Chapter Seven

M y phone beeps just as I'm debating what to cook for supper.

'I suppose I'm going to have to collect him,' I say to Nick, eyeing the can of beer in his hand as I tip some fish fingers onto a baking tray. 'Seeing as you've already started the weekend.'

'You snooze, you lose,' he tells me, stretching his legs out in front of him and sighing in pleasure. 'I offered you a glass of wine, remember?'

I narrow my eyes at him. 'Not today, Satan. *Some* of us have self-control and willpower.'

I pick up my phone and swipe the screen, suddenly keen to jump in the car and spend some quality time with my oldest child before he flies the nest and does whatever baby birds do when they're ready to spread their wings and leave their mummies, which hopefully won't involve too many failed attempts at flying or any lurking cats. But instead of the text that I am expecting from Dylan, requesting a lift home from his girlfriend's house, the green WhatsApp icon shows a notification and a very tiny part of me dies inside.

I didn't even want to be on WhatsApp in the first place. If the kids need me and I'm not within screeching distance then they text like every other normal person. But the Parent Teacher Association at Benji's school decided that every class should have a private messaging group and Allegra, our terrifyingly efficient class representative and Chair of the PTA, made me join. I suppose that in some ways it's quite useful – if I'd been part of the group chat last year then I'd at least have had a heads-up about bastarding World Book Day.

However, the positives are quite hard to remember when the negatives far outweigh them.

And the missive that has just slid into my DMs is about as negative as they get.

'You've got to be kidding me.' I read the words and then lower my phone to gape at Nick. 'This is a new all-time low, even for Allegra.'

'What's wrong now?' he asks half-heartedly. 'Did she catch you trying to pass off shop-bought cake as your own again?'

'It's worse than that,' I mutter, shaking my head. And then I read her message aloud, keeping my voice low so that I can't be overheard.

'Hannah. I would very much appreciate it if you would address Benji's use of language. Auberon came home from school today and told me that Benji called him a *penis*. Yes. A *penis*. He says that Benji shouted it at him in front of the whole of Chestnut Class when they were in the playground at lunchtime, which means that we may very well have a large penis epidemic on our hands. I'm sure that you understand just how serious this is. Unfortunately, Ophelia's ballet class had been cancelled so she heard everything and you know how impressionable six-year-olds can be. She's now running around the house and shouting "*You're a penis*" at the dog, which is upsetting for all of us. Please help – I'm at my wit's end here.'

'Bloody hell,' murmurs Nick, when I'm finished. 'That sounds like a right cock-up. What does a penis epidemic look like?'

'She's clearly unhinged,' I say, putting down my phone. 'But I can't just ignore the situation, not if he's going round saying rude things at school. God – what if he's overheard us talking about the plot of *More Than Sex*? What if my writing is somehow corrupting him?' I grimace and turn to face the kitchen door. 'Benji! Can you come in here please?'

'Is it really necessary to drag him into this?' asks Nick. 'It's not a big deal, Hannah. All kids say stuff like this – and he doesn't know anything about your book. Just calm down.'

I narrow my eyes at my husband. 'You might not think it's a big deal, *Nick* – but if we let him get away with inappropriate language now then where's it going to end up, hey? *Penis* might only be the start of it.'

'I hardly think this is a gateway to—' starts Nick and then our youngest son appears in the doorway and the interrogation can begin.

'Is supper ready?' he asks, sniffing the air apprehensively. 'I can't smell burning.'

'Give it time,' says Nick.

I ignore them both and gesture Benji to sit down.

'How was your day?' I start. I don't want to leap right into the gritty stuff straight away.

'It was okay,' Benji tells me. 'Mrs Cowl got cross with me because Logan was talking and so I wasn't allowed to use an iPad but I didn't mind because I got to read a book instead.'

'Reading a book isn't a punishment!' I exclaim.

'Why did you get told off if Logan was the one talking?' Nick asks at the same time.

Benji shrugs at both our responses and I move on.

'Did anything happen in the playground at lunchtime?' I prompt. 'Maybe with Auberon? Perhaps some kind of argument that got a bit silly?'

Benji wrinkles up his forehead. 'No. We played football for a bit until Logan kicked it over the fence.'

'It's just that Auberon's mum seems to think that you said a rude word to Auberon,' I say, pulling my sad face. 'A not-very-nice word that has made Auberon's mum feel quite upset.'

Benji stares at me blankly. 'I didn't say anything.'

I pause. I've never known Benji to lie to me but that doesn't mean that he doesn't. He might just be exceptionally good at it.

'Well, Auberon's mum is quite sure that you said an offensive word.' I pull out a chair and sit down opposite Benji. 'It's better to admit it now and then we can move on.'

Benji's upper lip starts to tremble. 'I didn't say anything bad!' he insists. 'Honestly, Mum.'

I maintain eye contact and try to channel a calm but firm manner. 'So you didn't say the word *penis* at school, then?'

Benji bursts out laughing, which is not the reaction that I was expecting.

'Oh that! Yeah, I said *that*! I thought you said that it was a *not-very-nice* word?'

I glance at Nick for support but he seems to be thoroughly enjoying the entertainment being laid on before him and just waves his hand nonchalantly at me, which is no help whatsoever.

'Well, it's not a word that should be shouted at other people,' I tell him. 'You know better than that.'

Benji nods. 'I do know better than that. Which is why, when Auberon was shouting "*You're a willy*" to the people who were walking their dog on the other side of the fence, I told him that you shouldn't be embarrassed about using the proper word for things and that he should really be shouting "*You're a penis*".' He pauses and stares at me. 'Was that wrong? Because you've always told us that there's nothing embarrassing about using the right word for body stuff.'

'You *have* always told them that,' agrees Nick, nodding seriously. I resist the urge to knock his can of beer off the table.

'It's clearly just a misunderstanding,' I say. 'I'll let Auberon's mum know what happened and then we can forget all about it.'

'Why did you say that *penis* is a rude and offensive word?' Benji is obviously not prepared to forget all about it.

'I've got one and so does Dad and Dylan. Does that mean that *we're* rude and offensive too?'

The grin on Nick's face is large enough to house one man and his dog which is handy, because if he keeps this up then he's certainly not sleeping under this roof tonight.

'Only sometimes,' I mutter. 'But it's not necessarily linked to your genitalia. More of a personality thing, I'd say.'

'So can I go then?' Benji pushes his chair back and stands up. 'Only I'm in the middle of a game with Logan and if I'm gone for too long then he's going to destroy my house and I'll have to start building it again.'

I nod. 'You've got twenty more minutes of screen-time and then you'll have to come off, okay?'

Benji groans. 'Can't I stay on a bit longer? Logan's Mum lets him stay on for *hours*.'

'Well, I'm not Logan's Mum,' I retort, looking meaningfully at the kitchen clock. 'Time is ticking, Benji – you've only got nineteen minutes left now.'

The kitchen door slams closed behind him as he sprints off to claim his precious allocated time on the computer. I pick up my phone and then pause.

'What am I going to tell Allegra?' I ask Nick.

He shrugs. 'The truth. It's not that complicated, Hannah.'

The laugh that pushes itself through my tightly pursed lips is as humourless as I feel.

'*Not that complicated*? Are you insane?' I lean back in my chair and stare at my husband. 'I can hardly send *Mrs*

Perfect Mother a WhatsApp message telling her that her perfect son was shouting abuse at complete strangers.'

'Why not?' Nick looks puzzled. 'That's what happened. Benji shouldn't be branded as the problem here – her kid was the one doing something stupid, not him.'

'But it doesn't work like that,' I tell him. 'If I tell Allegra that Auberon was behaving in a less-than-fabulous manner then she's going to make my life a living hell. You know the phrase "don't shoot the messenger"? Well, Allegra won't do anything as humane as to shoot me. That would be far too easy. She'll spin this out and exact her own brand of torture for the rest of the school year until I'm begging her to just put me out of misery.'

Nick laughs. 'You're being a total drama-queen! Just tell her that Auberon was being a bit daft. What on earth can she possibly do to you?'

I lean across the table and fix him with a firm look.

'She can do anything she likes,' I intone. 'Because she is in charge of the goddamned world, *Nick*.'

'Really?' Nick rolls his eyes at me. 'The goddamned world?'

I nod. 'If I get on the wrong side of her then the rest of the school year is going to be a complete misery. She'll act all nice to my face and bitch about me behind my back and I'll end up being given all the crappy jobs at every school event.'

Nick stands up and stretches his arms and I find myself hoping that he's not about to disappear off to start working on his bloody Land Rover again. Annoying as this conversation is, it's quite nice being here in the kitchen together.

'I still think you're overreacting. Tell her what happened in the playground with Auberon and Benji and then let it go. And if she tries to get you to do anything that you don't want to do then just refuse.'

Sometimes, the extent of Nick's naivety is hard to fathom.

'One does not simply "say no" to Allegra,' I snap, shaking my head. 'It's not a word that she understands.'

'Come off it, Hannah.' Nick sighs loudly. 'Just send her a message and let's try to enjoy the evening. I've had a knackering week and I've spent the last five days stuck halfway up a tree with a chainsaw in my hand. Right now, all I want to do is chill out for a bit.'

'Is there any more news on that forestry contract you were going after?' I ask. 'It's been ages.'

'Are you sending that message or not?' replies Nick, and then my phone beeps again with another missive from Allegra, this time in the form of the *praying hands* emoji. She's clearly getting desperate.

'Fine.' I swipe my screen and start to type. 'As long as you're aware that it won't only be me who suffers. She's currently on the search for a willing dad to dress up as Father Christmas for this year's Festive Fete and I've heard a rumour that you're in the running. This probably isn't the time to raise your head above the parapet unless you're prepared to spend five hours sweating in a cheap Santa suit while small children try to pull your beard off.'

'Not a chance.' Nick wrinkles up his nose. 'You don't seriously think that she'd ask me to do it?'

'I do,' I tell him. 'I definitely heard her talking to one of the other mothers about how *"that sexy tree surgeon"* would be the perfect choice and as far as I know you're the only parent who fits that description. Well, the tree surgeon part anyway.'

Nick scowls at me and I suppress a grin. 'So I'll send this message telling her that Auberon was yelling about his willy because as you said, it's only the truth and it's not that complicated.'

'No!' Nick darts across the kitchen and snatches the phone from my hands. 'Are you insane? I'm not dressing up as sodding Father Christmas.'

I smile sweetly up at him. 'So we're on the same page then? We're in this together?'

Nick grits his teeth and nods. And then we throw Benji under the metaphorical bus and write a penitent message to Allegra, apologising profusely for our son's use of the word *penis* and assuring her that he will never use the correct terminology for that particular appendage ever again. And did we say how sorry we were?

'I feel like a traitor,' Nick says when we've finally pressed *send*.

'That's because we are,' I tell him. 'Treacherous, cowardly, disloyal parents who care more about what other people think about us than the moral high ground.'

'It's for the best though, isn't it?' He pulls another can of beer from the fridge and pops the top open. 'It would be more damaging for Benji to see me prancing around as

Father Christmas than it is to be considered a bit rude, surely?'

'Absolutely,' I agree. 'Although I might have quite enjoyed the performance.'

Nick grins. 'Maybe we can have our own Festive Fete. You could dress up as a sexy fairy with glittery wings and a fairy wand.'

My phone beeps again, saving me from telling him exactly where he can stick his fairy wand – this time with a message from someone I'm actually happy to hear from.

'Dylan wants collecting,' I say, standing up. 'Can you finish cooking the fish fingers?'

'If by *finish*, you actually mean can I *start* cooking the fish fingers, then yes, I can.' He takes a swig of beer and gestures at the still-cold oven.

'That's the spirit,' I tell him. 'I'll be back in a minute. And maybe you can get Scarlet to run her Head Girl speech for the new pupils past you while I'm gone? I heard it the other day and it needs a bit of toning down.'

Our daughter has obviously confused our school with a totalitarian dictatorship, if her welcome address is anything to go by. Not that Miriam would necessarily disagree with her. I'm torn between being impressed and alarmed by her tenacity.

Outside, the air smells like autumn. The leaves are still on the trees but it won't be long until they're gone and Dylan will be gone with them. There's two weeks to go before he heads off to university and it's impossible to figure out how I'm supposed to be feeling. Part of me wants the next fourteen days to last forever but part of me wishes that we could just be at that point already because the anticipation and waiting for him to leave is half-killing me.

I pull up outside his girlfriend's house and think about how unprepared I am for him not to be living at home. I'm excited for him, of course I am, but I'm scared too. Scared that he'll be lonely and unhappy. Scared that he won't make friends or that he'll hate his course. Scared that he's committing to more debt than I can bring myself to calculate. And selfishly, scared that we won't survive him going. We've been a family of five (well, six, with Dogger) forever and I can't imagine it ever feeling okay with only four of us in the house.

The car door opens and my boy throws himself down onto the passenger seat.

'Thanks for picking me up, Mum,' he says, leaning across and giving me a quick kiss on the cheek. 'How was your day?'

He always asks me about my day. How am I supposed to let him go when he's so bloody lovely?

'It was fine,' I say, checking the mirrors and pulling away from the kerb. 'How about you? Was it alright saying goodbye to Zoe?'

He leans forward and retrieves his phone from his back pocket. 'Yeah, I guess? I mean, it's a bit weird and awkward and everything but it was okay.'

His phone pings and he starts to type. I focus on the road and try to think about something else but it's impossible – nothing feels as big as Dylan's impending departure.

'Is Zoe nervous about leaving so early?' I ask, after a few minutes of silence. 'And how are her parents doing?

I am obsessed with how other parents are handling this major life event. I've spent hours online looking for forums where people (mostly women) talk about how they coped with their children leaving home, looking for tactics and strategies that might help my brain to calm down, just for a bit.

'She's a bit anxious about meeting her flatmates,' Dylan tells me. 'They haven't got a group chat like my flat has so she isn't sure what they're going to be like. But her parents are chill with it all, you know?'

'Oh, they're chill?' I indicate and pull left onto our street. 'Of course they are. Because why wouldn't they be? It's a chill thing, isn't it? I am also chill. And cool. Totally cool. Because it's all going to be absolutely fine and brilliant and amazing.'

Dylan gives me a look as I turn off the engine.

'Are you doing okay, Mum?'

It's so important that I don't project my fears and emotions onto him. This isn't about me. It's about my darling, sweet, first-born child and I have got to be strong enough for both of us.

'Me?' I laugh in a light-hearted manner. 'I'm absolutely fine! Why wouldn't I be? I won't have to wash your stinky socks or spend hours collecting dirty plates and mugs from your room or chauffer you around the place because you decided that driving lessons weren't that interesting!' I plaster on my chirpiest smile. 'I should have sent you packing years ago!'

Dylan puts his hand on my arm. 'It's going to be okay,' he says quietly. 'I'm ready for the next adventure, Mum.'

'Of course you are.' I turn away to open the door so that he can't see my face because I'm getting this all the wrong way round and he's not the one who is supposed to be comforting me. 'You're absolutely ready.'

It's me who isn't ready. And I don't think I ever will be.

Chapter Eight

The instant that we step inside the doors of Ikea, I start to regret my life choices. The place is heaving and, judging from the strained expressions on the faces of the adults in front of me, lots of them are here on the same mission as us.

'So,' I say, in the cheeriest tone that I can muster. 'Here we are! I've got a list and if we stick to it then I think we can get this done pretty quickly.'

Scarlet snorts sarcastically. 'I think we're going to be lucky to get out of here before closing time.' She nods in the direction of Dylan, who has already wandered off and is now staring at a mocked-up display of a bedroom with wide eyes.

I shake my head and start to weave my way through the assembled throng, pulling Scarlet behind me. I've been dreading this trip all summer. Nick half-heartedly offered to join us and I initially thought that maybe the whole thing would be more bearable if we turned it into a family day out – but then I came to my senses and remembered the last time that Nick stepped foot inside this shop. My usually mild-mannered husband morphed into a raving sociopath and there was very nearly a nasty incident when he insisted on walking the wrong way around the shop floor, despite the fact that there are clearly marked arrows. He ranted that if they wanted his money then he wasn't going to be herded around like cattle and that if he felt like turning left instead of right then he damn well would. It was highly embarrassing and I vowed never to cross the threshold of this particular store in his presence again.

Plus, by the time we got to the checkout, the trolley was filled with a ton of useless crap that he insisted were necessary purchases and that are all, despite his protestations, still crammed into the back of the kitchen cupboard. He hasn't cut a cucumber into a fancy spiral shape even once.

Anyway, Nick is at home with Benji and I am here, attempting to make light of the fact that today is all about helping my son to leave home. I was slightly surprised that Scarlet wanted to join us but I'm glad that she's here. She reminds me that I'm still going to be a mum; that there are still people who need me.

'Look at this,' says Dylan as we battle our way towards him. 'I definitely need one of these.'

I look at where he is pointing. 'Absolutely,' I agree, pulling out my list. 'I've got *duvet cover* written down here. But these are just the show rooms. I think we're better off waiting until we get down to the next floor – then you can see all the choices and we can find something that's practical and cheap. You don't want anything that's going to be too high-maintenance to wash.'

'No, not that. *This*.' Dylan moves forward and picks up a cactus plant. 'This will look brilliant in my new room!'

'That's actually adorable,' says Scarlet, joining him. 'They've got them in three different coloured pots – you should get one of each. But Mum's right – this floor is boring. Let's get down to the good stuff on the next floor.'

'I don't think—' I start, but my words are lost in the air because it's as if someone has just announced the start of a race. Dylan and Scarlet are off, bounding across the room, pointing things out to each other as they go but never breaking their stride.

I dash after them, pushing my way through the other shoppers. This is not what I had envisaged in the slightest. I thought we would wander through the room displays and I could show Dylan my vision for how his room at university should look. And then maybe we'd get a coffee and perhaps a plate of meatballs before making informed, sensible choices about our purchases. I did not think that I'd be spending the morning hurtling after my children while they witter on about cacti. We are here on serious business and I can feel myself starting to get prickly.

I catch up with them at the moving walkway. Dylan flashes me a big grin and beside him, Scarlet is beaming with happiness.

'There's so much to get,' he tells me. 'My room's going to look dope.'

'Totally,' agrees Scarlet. 'Plus, I've seen one or two things that I really need too.'

So *that's* why she's here. I must really be losing my game for not seeing that coming.

'We're here to kit Dylan out for uni,' I remind her.

'Oh yeah, of course.' She nods earnestly and then puts her hand on my arm. 'They're only tiny things and I can always pay for them myself. Or just wait until it's my turn to leave home.'

I know what she's doing. Of course I do, I'm not a compete imbecile. It still doesn't stop my heart from crumpling in my chest at the thought of her being gone, along with Dylan.

'Well, perhaps I can get you something,' I tell her. 'As long as it's cheap.'

We step off the walkway and Dylan rushes across to where the trollies are parked.

'We're going to do this sensibly and logically,' I tell them both as we move towards the first set of shelves. 'My list is organised into sections and there will be no deviating from the list, understood?'

'Sir, yes sir!' Dylan whips his hand up to his head and clicks his heels together in the same way that's he's been responding to my commands since he was fourteen and that has consistently driven me crazy for the past four years. Nobody is going to salute me once he's gone and the knowledge of this makes me suddenly want to cry.

But there's no time scheduled for tears today. He's going to be off before we know it and this is our chance to make sure that he has everything that he could possibly need. We've spent eighteen years equipping him with life skills –

and now the time has come to provide him with the appropriate tools necessary for his survival.

It turns out that we have ever so slightly differing opinions on the definition of *survival tools*. We haven't even made it past the first set of kitchen implements before the conflict begins.

'You need some basic crockery,' I say, picking up a cheap but perfectly functional set of two white dinner plates with matching side plates and bowls.

'*Basic* is right,' sniffs Scarlet. 'They look like they're made out of paper.'

'I like these,' says Dylan, gesturing to a dramatic (and tacky) dinner set. 'The purple splatter effect really stands out against the black background.'

'You're going to be eating beans on toast,' I point out. 'I hardly think that the décor of the plate is going to enhance the culinary experience.'

He huffs a bit but I stand my ground and the basic plate set is placed into the trolley.

Round One to me.

'Okay, now we need to find you a mug.' I consult my list. 'Actually, we'll get you two mugs just in case you have a friend over and want to make them a cup of tea.'

I ignore Scarlet's snort of derision and march across to the mug aisle.

'How about this one?' I ask, reaching up. 'I think the dark blue will work well with the white plates.'

But when I turn around, Dylan and Scarlet have disappeared. Sighing, I replace the mug and then push the trolley towards the sound of my children who, for some reason, appear to be howling with laughter.

I find them in the next aisle. 'Hey! I'm not doing this if you're not going to take it seriously. You can't just bugger off and leave me to do all the work. I wanted to know what mug you'd like to get but it would appear that *I'm* the mug for doing everything while you two just mess about.'

'Sorry, Mum.' Dylan looks contrite. 'I saw this display stand and it reminded me that there's some other stuff on the list that I need.'

I gaze at the contents in his hand and then glance back down at my list.

'Nope. I told you before, there will be no deviating from the list and I can assure you that those items are absolutely not written down here.'

Dylan grins at me. 'They might not be on your list but they *are* on my list. Look!'

He pulls a piece of paper out of his pocket and brandishes it in front of me.

He's made a list.

His very own list.

My heart swells with so much pride that for a second I think it might actually burst, right here in the kitchen department. Finally, after all those years of hard work and effort, he is starting to take responsibility for himself.

My son, the list-maker.

He's actually going to be okay.

My parenting work here is done and I can't lie, it's a bittersweet success.

'Have you read his list, Mum?' asks Scarlet, ruining the moment and yanking me back to reality. 'It's *really* sensible.'

I pull the piece of paper out of Dylan's hands and scan my moist eyes across the scrawled handwriting.

It is *not* sensible. It would *only* be sensible if it were, in fact, the list of a stressed-out parent planning a particularly boisterous child's birthday party.

'I don't see why you could possibly need jelly moulds,' I tell him, a small frown furrowing onto my forehead. 'Or fairy lights. Or inflatable toys. Or ping pong balls. Or a fancy-dress outfit.'

Dylan throws an arm around my shoulder and ushers me back towards the mug section, but not before I see him pass the jelly moulds to Scarlet who places them into the trolley.

Round Two to Dylan.

'You want me to make friends, don't you?' he asks. 'And nothing says *friendship* like a vodka jelly on our first night in the flat.'

'But you don't drink alcohol,' I say, pulling away and staring up at him. 'Why can't you just make a regular jelly, if the aim is to get to know your flatmates? Or I could ask Granny to make you some of her yummy brownies.'

'I don't drink *now*,' Dylan agrees. 'But I'm going to uni, Mum. You're the one who told me that it was all about starting a new adventure and that I should embrace every opportunity that comes my way.'

'I'm pretty sure I didn't say that,' I mutter. I'm lying. I did say that, one warm evening in France when I'd had some wine to drink and the kids were lying on the grass pointing out shooting stars and the world seemed wonderful and filled with potential. I felt brave that night, as if everything was happening exactly the way that it should.

But right now, in this harshly lit shop with hundreds of people pushing past me, I feel less brave and definitely less filled with awe and wonder.

'Well, what about the other stuff?' I say, moving on. The moulds are already in the trolley and in all honesty, I can't see Dylan having the patience to faff around with vodka jelly. I speak from experience when I say that the concept is a whole lot more fun than the reality. Getting the vodka to set in the first place is challenging enough – and then cleaning jelly-coloured vomit out of carpets in rented student accommodation is the cherry on the cake. I'm tempted to tell him to just eat a packet of raw jelly and then drink a few vodka shots to save himself the hassle – but I won't because a) that would be irresponsible parenting and b) some life lessons have to be experienced first-hand to really make an impact.

'I need a fancy-dress costume for Fresher's Week,' he says, waving his hand dismissively. 'And the toy is for one of the nightclubs – apparently you get in for free if you bring an inflatable with you.'

I stand still and try to process this ridiculous information.

'You should try and buy yourself an inflatable woman,' Scarlet informs him. 'That's the best chance *you've* got of getting a girlfriend when you're at uni.'

'He's got a girlfriend,' I say, leaping to his defence. 'And that's not a very nice thing to say to your brother. Apologise.'

I turn, just in time to see Dylan flicking Scarlet the finger.

'Dylan!' I hiss. 'That's not an appropriate gesture to make in public. Or anywhere else, come to that. Say sorry.'

They both roll their eyes and turn back to the shelves of crockery.

'I need the fairy lights to make my room look appealing and cosy and to create a chilled ambience,' he continues, picking up the exact same mug that I had selected, scowling at it and then putting it back on the shelf. 'The ping pong balls are for impromptu games of beer pong.'

'Not very impromptu if you're planning for it now,' I quip, ignoring the second reference to alcohol in the last twenty seconds. 'And I suppose fairy lights could be quite nice. I'm just a bit surprised, that's all. You've never shown the slightest interest in interior decorating and *ambience* before.'

'But I've never had my own room before,' he says. 'Can I get these mugs with the chunky handles?'

I nod, distracted by what he's just said. He's always had his own room but I know what he means, even though it pains me to admit it. Going away to uni is purely his and nothing to do with Nick or me. And I know that's part of the reason for going – he'll get a whole load of life experiences and skills alongside his degree and I'm beyond happy that he's feeling confident and ready.

I am *so very freaking happy*. These are definitely happy

tears that are threatening to leak from my eyes. The breaking of my heart is a *happy* breaking, it really is.

'So can I get the lights?' he asks. 'You know, for the ambience?'

I am a lost cause.

Eventually, after what feels like many, many hours, we make our way to the checkout. Scarlet is now the proud owner of a number of photo frames, a new bedspread and several thousand cushions and will apparently *love me forever*. I have never been the kind of woman who feels as if she needs to buy her children's affection but right now, I'll take whatever I can get.

It's possible that I am a teeny bit needy at the moment.

The trolley is laden with pots and pans and other student paraphernalia. We have had a prolonged discussion about the merits of two different potato mashers, with me insisting that the cheap, plastic one will do just as adequate a job as the Gucci version in stainless steel that he had his eye on and I have enjoyed eavesdropping on another family who were engaged in a lively and fun debate about the necessity of owning not one, but two pizza cutters *'in case of emergencies'*.

'I don't think that went too badly,' I say, putting the plastic potato masher on the conveyor belt. 'We've got everything on my list and none of it was too expensive.'

Then the cashier quotes me a price that makes my eyes

well up yet again, only this time I am not having a nostalgic Mummy-moment.

'How much?' I screech. Scarlet whips her head round, her cheeks flushing with humiliation as she checks to see if anyone has witnessed my outburst. She needn't worry – every checkout is filled with parents and their lanky, teenage offspring and my words are lost in the cacophony of disbelief and horror as credit cards are fumbled and faces pale as they acknowledge that their child may well be off to university with everything they could possibly require, but their own food and drink budget is about to be wildly slashed to compensate for the massive bill that they have just been presented with.

'At least you won't have to feed me when I'm away,' Dylan says, once I've paid.

I release the breath that I've been holding and uncross my fingers and toes. The credit card went through and for that I am truly thankful, seeing as my side-hustle isn't exactly proving to be especially lucrative yet.

'That's true,' I tell him. 'In fact, at this rate you're going to be the one sending food parcels home to *us*. We're going to be living on baked potatoes for months.'

'Oh god,' huffs Scarlet, her shoulders drooping. 'I hate bloody baked potatoes. In fact, I hate potatoes full stop. I mean, what's the point of them? They're ridiculous – if you want to grow a potato then you have to plant a potato. It's like, how is that even a thing?'

'What came first, the potato or the potato?' adds Dylan. 'It's worse than the whole chicken and egg conundrum.'

'Well, you're going to have plenty of time to contemplate

it,' I say, attempting to get the trolley towards the lift. 'While you're eating all those lovely potatoes for every meal.'

'But I hate potatoes,' Scarlet repeats, with a whine in her voice.

I am absolutely not in the mood for this.

'But you love your gorgeous new bedspread and photo frames and cushions, don't you?' I snap. 'Or shall we go back and ask for a refund?'

Scarlet leaps next to me and puts her hand on the trolley.

'I'll help you with this,' she says, smiling enthusiastically. 'And I've just remembered that I love potatoes and I'm very grateful for anything you feed us.'

Then she turns her head so that she's looking at her brother.

'As long as they're in chip form,' she murmurs and I decide to go along with the pretence that if she can't *see* me, then I obviously can't *hear* her. Sometimes Scarlet behaves more like a seven-year-old than a seventeen-year-old.

Dylan moves up on my other side and helps wrangle the trolley inside the opening lift doors.

'Thanks Mum,' he says quietly. 'I know it's a lot but having you help me kit out my room is going to really help when I'm there on my own. It's going to make it feel like I've got a bit of home with me.'

And I am slayed for the third time today.

But in a good way, I think.

Chapter Nine

There are two things waiting for me when I get home from work on Monday. The first assaults my senses when I step out of the car and I shudder. I love living in this house very, very much, but the fact remains that it is needier than all of our children put together and something is always breaking or going wrong or demanding attention. And right now, a person does not need superhero senses to identify that the septic tank is due its regular emptying. It is at times like this that I entertain the idea of moving somewhere with new and swanky commodities such as mains drainage.

'Urgh – that's disgusting!' mumbles Scarlet, slamming the passenger door and clamping her hand against her face. 'I can't believe I have to live like this. I hope the rest of the street are all out. It's mortifying.'

'It's your poo too,' Benji helpfully points out. 'You shouldn't be embarrassed about something that comes from your own body.'

She growls something unintelligible and makes a dash for the front door. I glance around, keeping my fingers crossed that our closest neighbours aren't home. Benji can make as many self-affirming, body-empowering statements as he likes. The stench really is foul and it really is humiliating.

'Afternoon, Mrs Thompson.' Rob, our friendly septic tank engineer/emptier, walks across the front lawn with Dylan at his side. Rob informed me the first time we met that he has no sense of smell. Never has a person been so well suited for a job. Sadly for Dylan, he would appear to possess a fully working nasal system and his face has gone a bit pale. 'I'm afraid we've got a bit of a problem.'

I press my lips together and give Rob a tight smile, steeling my inner resolve. Whatever it is, we can handle it. And it's probably not even that big a deal. This is poo we're talking about. How much of a problem can poo possibly be?

'Hit me with it,' I say, trying to sound chirpy while not inhaling too deeply. It might be my imagination but the stink seems to be getting worse.

'Your tank has imploded,' he says, his voice monotone. 'The lads emptied it out as usual and the whole thing just collapsed. The contents were the only thing keeping it together.'

'Oh shit,' says Dylan.

Somebody had to.

'What does that actually mean?' I enquire, trying to stay calm. 'Is it something that can be easily fixed?'

Rob laughs, the same way he laughed when I asked him if it was true that throwing a dead badger into the septic tank would mean that it didn't need emptying, as the previous house owner had assured us.

'It means that you've got two choices. The first is that you can spend an extortionate amount of money on replacing the tank.'

I shake my head. That doesn't sound good.

'The second is that you can spend an extortionate amount of money and finally get connected to a mains drainage.'

'Is there a third option?' I ask weakly. 'One that doesn't involve extortion?'

He grins at me. 'You could do what my old mum used to do and use a bucket.'

'She'll pay,' Dylan tells him and I nod.

He's right. One way or another, I'll definitely end up paying.

I always do.

Once Rob has explained that we can continue to use the bathroom and the kitchen but that we should expect some degree of aroma and seepage until he can return in two weeks to sort out the mains connection, I stumble inside the house and head straight to the shower where I spend at least fifteen minutes scrubbing the smell from my hair.

Then I head downstairs to the kitchen where I find the second surprise of the day waiting for me in my inbox.

I read it once and then I sit down and read it again. And then I stand and make my way to the fridge, pulling out a full bottle of very cold and very alcoholic white wine, which I pour into a glass and take outside into the garden after giving Dylan strict instructions to cook some pasta for everyone. The front garden still has essence of shite in the air so I make my way to the very end of the back garden, as far away as possible from both the house and the smell.

I'm still out there when Nick gets home sometime later, his face lined with exhaustion after another long day. He sits down next to me and raises his eyebrows when he sees the almost empty wine bottle next to my open laptop.

'What happened to Dry September? I thought you were determined to see it through this time – you've made a proper song and dance about how virtuous you're being and you've only got two days to go.'

I drain the last few drops and wave the glass at him.

'Twinky Malone would never do anything so ridiculous as to attempt not to drink in September. And as I'm going to have to *be* her, then the least I can do is respect her wishes. *Hannah* can deal with the consequences another time.'

Nick eyes me suspiciously. 'What're you on about? And why are you referring to yourself in the third person. Are you having some kind of crisis?'

'If you want answers then you're going to need your own glass of wine,' I tell him. 'And bring that packet of kettle chips from the back of the cupboard.'

I lean back in my chair and look up at the sky while he goes indoors. It's still light but dusk is creeping in around the edges of the garden and everything has a soft, sepia-like tint as if it's an old photograph that's aged over time. That or the wine has gone straight to my head.

'Here you go.' Nick is back and I'm pleased to see that he's brought another bottle. 'Now tell me what's going on.'

The world snaps back into view and I sit up, reaching for my glass.

'It's been a bit of a day,' I start. 'There's some not-so-good news.'

Nick reaches across the table and puts his hand on mine. 'Is it to do with your book?'

I shake my head. 'The septic tank is dead,' I inform him. 'As in deceased, no more, cannot be revived. We're going to have to pay up and go on mains drainage.'

I quote him the number that Rob told me and his face falls.

'Bloody hell, Hannah. We can't afford that.' He lets go of my hand and rubs his face.

'Let's cross all our fingers and toes that your forestry contract comes through soon because I'm not quite sure what we're going to be living on otherwise.' I take a slurp of wine. 'In the meantime, I've had an email from my editor.'

Nick reaches for his own wine, nodding at me to continue.

'Apparently, the sales of the book for the first few weeks have been okay. Not top of the book charts but not awful either. And now one of the big supermarkets wants to sell it. They've put in a massive order and it's going to be sold as a paperback in most of their stores. Binky said that it's the kind of book that women will pick up along with their weekly grocery shopping.'

'Seriously?' His shoulders relax a little and finally I see something that almost resembles a smile on his face. 'That's incredible! We should drink a toast to all the mummies who want to buy some porn along with their Parmesan!'

'It's not bloody porn,' I mumble. 'I've told you about a gazillion times already.'

Nick raises his glass and toasts me mid-air.

'Po-tay-to, po-ta-to,' he says. 'I don't know why you get in such a strop about it. Erotica, porn – same difference.'

'As it currently stands, the sales of the books are not going to be enough to pay for the septic tank,' I plough on, choosing to ignore his stupid comment. I've got enough to worry about without adding the education of my husband on the classification of sexual fiction. 'The supermarket buys them at a huge discount and they'd need to sell loads of them for me to make any decent money. But Binky did mention something else that might help with that.'

Something about the serious tone of my voice finally gets his attention and he lowers his glass to look at me properly.

'What is it, babe?' he asks. 'You actually look quite pale. Are you alright?'

I shake my head violently. 'No. I am not alright. Or maybe I am alright and it'll all be fine. Perhaps I'm making a big deal out of nothing, you know?'

Nick swallows loudly. 'Whatever it is, we'll get through it together,' he says. 'Like we've always done. Just spit it out, Hannah. Tell me what's going on – and then I need to tell you something too.'

'The supermarket taking on the book is great,' I tell him, trying to get a grip on my rising hysteria. 'But we still need readers to actually buy a copy when they go to the shop.' I pause and take another sip of wine. 'Binky says that this is my chance to actually make some real money but the only way to do that is to help promote the book and commit to some publicity. And by *some publicity*, she means *this*.'

I wake up my screen and spin my laptop to face him. Nick peers closer and starts to read the email that Binky sent me earlier.

Dear Hannah,

I hope all is well with you and yours. It is with great pleasure that I am writing to inform you that More Than Sex *is going to be stocked in—*

'Not that bit,' I tell him. 'Read the bit at the end. The thing that she forwarded to me.'

Nick's eyes scan down the screen and then widen.

'*Calling all Sex Goddesses*,' he reads aloud. '*We are delighted that you will be joining us as part of the panel at this year's Sex Con. Our aim is to bring you all together for a frank and open discussion as part of our "Real Sex Talk" event and we know that our delegates will all benefit hugely from the expertise that you will bring. Further details to follow in due course.*'

I stare across the table at my husband. 'I'm going to have to be *seen*, Nick. People are going to know that I write erotica and our kids are going to find out *and* the other teachers at school, and that's before I even start thinking about what will happen if Year Ten, Class C ever discover it. And what if Allegra hears something? My life is going to be over.'

Nick grins at me, which is not exactly the reaction that I am expecting.

'They're calling you a *Sex Goddess*, Hannah. I think I quite like being married to someone with that title!'

I stare at him in disbelief. 'Did you not hear me? Binky is demanding that I reveal myself in public. There is nothing okay about this situation, not least the fact that I am clearly *not* a Sex Goddess and if I turn up at Sex Con then I'm going to make an almighty fool of myself.'

My loving husband shrugs and helps himself to some more wine.

'Well, I think you're super sexy. What is Sex Con anyway? Is it like Comic Con without the superheroes?'

I shake my head. 'I have no idea. Probably because I am totally out of my depth here and this invitation has clearly been sent by mistake.'

'No, it hasn't.' He points at the screen. 'Binky says that they nominated you for a place on the *Real Sex Talk* panel and that it's a huge honour that you've been accepted.' He looks over at me. 'You have to do it, Hannah.'

'I. Am. Not. A. Sex. Goddess,' I hiss, through gritted teeth. 'And I can't risk anyone recognising me – you know that. It's one thing writing this stuff in secret but it's something else entirely going out there and *talking* about it, for god's sake!'

Nick rolls his eyes at me. 'But you've already got the solution. You told me yourself that you're just going to have to be Twinky Malone. She writes porn for a living – I'm pretty sure that qualifies her for the position of Sex Goddess. Go as her.'

'But I'm still going to be *me*, aren't I?' My wail carries through the garden and I see Scarlet peering suspiciously out of the kitchen window. 'People will still know who I am.'

Nick takes another sip of wine. 'You're making this all way harder than it needs to be, babe. Just put something on your head and they'll be none the wiser.'

I am married to a blithering buffoon.

'I hardly think that a *hat* is going to provide me with a foolproof disguise,' I hiss, conscious that our teenagers have bat-like levels of hearing. 'I'm going to have to do a bit more than that, *Nick*.'

There's a crash from inside the house and then the unmistakable sound of Benji howling. Nick stands up and puts his hands on the table, leaning down until he can see right into my eyes.

'So do more,' he tells me. 'Do whatever it takes and then get out there and enjoy yourself. You've been saying that you want to be more than just Mum for years now – so do it. Find your Sex Goddess and let her out.'

'Like it's that easy,' I scoff. 'Anyway – what did you want to talk about?'

He shakes his head. 'It can wait, babe.' Then he drops a quick kiss on top of my head and goes inside to deal with whatever chaos our youngest child has managed to create, leaving me alone in the garden with the wine bottles and my thoughts.

Nick might be a bit insensitive to my needs at times but he's completely right on this. I *do* want to be more than just Mum. And maybe I can kill three birds with one stone. I'll embrace the idea of myself as a confident, sassy writer of comedy-erotica while transforming myself into a Sex Goddess for the Sex Con event *and* breathe some new life into my marriage at the same time.

But if I'm going to do it properly then I'm going to have to consider the whole package. It won't be enough to just *look* different. I'm going to need to find my inner diva and embrace every inch of her. Her personality. Her charisma. Her hopes and dreams.

I'm going to need to go full Twinky Malone.

I spend my next day off outlining the plot of my second book in detail. This was another suggestion in the *How to Write a Bestselling Novel* book and I've been meaning to do it for a while. I'm actually quite pleased with myself – it turns out that teaching English for the last year has actually given me a few skills in this department and when I step back and look at the large piece of paper that I've covered in sticky notes, I feel a huge sense of pride. I have a beginning, middle and an end, all presented as a huge mind map. All I've got to do now is actually write it.

I'm just about to start tidying up when the front door crashes open and seconds later, Scarlet flies into the kitchen.

'It stinks in this house,' she snarls. 'When's that gross septic tank getting sorted?'

'Soon,' I snap back, hurriedly rolling up my mind map.

I am aware of the aroma. It's not even that strong but it seems to permeate everything and leave a tinge of decay and horror in the air. It's not the ideal environment for a person who may be attempting to get their sexy on, that's for sure.

Scarlet doesn't even glance in my direction. Instead she stomps across to the fridge and pulls out a carton of orange juice before emptying the majority of the contents into a pint glass and rather impressively downing it in one. I blink, trying to chase away the image of my baby girl out-drinking everyone at the bar and remember that I have some parenting to do.

'Why are you home?' I ask.

It's a reasonable question.

'God!' she groans. 'Why does everyone have to know everything about me and what I'm doing, all of the time?'

I raise an eyebrow and gesture to the seat opposite me. She hesitates for a second and I think that the situation might be about to escalate but then her shoulders slump and she throws herself onto the chair.

'School doesn't finish for another hour,' I say, in as non-confrontational a tone as I can muster. I've been here before and I know that I need to act as if I'm calming a savage beast if I want to get anything out of her. If I give her the slightest chance to feel persecuted or 'got at' then she'll flounce off feeling aggrieved and I'll have to bide my time until she's ready to share what's upsetting her.

And today I just don't have the time to wait.

'I walked out,' she says, resting her head on the table. 'And I'm not going back.'

'No way,' I say, losing the calm voice. 'You are not quitting school, young lady. You've only just started Sixth

Form and there's bound to be a few teething problems but you have to stick it out it for the good of your education.'

She raises her head and looks at me wearily.

'I'm not going back *this afternoon*,' she tells me. 'So chill out, okay?'

I heave a sigh of relief and lean back in my chair.

'So what's the problem?'

Her head flops back down onto the table and I have to strain to hear her muffled voice. It's impossible to catch every word but I think I hear the words '*Ashley Dunsford*' and '*Twat-bucket*' and I definitely hear the phrase '*never going to even look at a boy again*', so I get the gist of the issue.

'Shall I make us a nice cup of tea and we can have a good chat?' I say, once she's stopped muttering. 'I think I've got some emergency chocolate hidden in the cupboard that the boys haven't found yet.'

Scarlet sighs and then stands up.

'I phoned Granny on the way home and she said that I can go over to her house and have a chat. I think she'll probably be really helpful, you know?'

No. I don't know. I am your mother and it's my job to be there for you in your hour of need. We should be cuddling up on the sofa and talking about boys and maybe painting our nails, before watching a sad yet ultimately uplifting film. And you will snuggle up next to me and I will feel your pain but also be warmed by our bond because I am your mum and you should need me.

'I'm sure she'll be great,' I say, forcing myself to smile at my daughter. 'She was always very understanding whenever I needed someone to talk to.'

My lucky, lucky mother to be blessed with a daughter like me, who actually shared my worries with her. And now Scarlet is doing the same thing and choosing her as a confidant and I know that a good mother would rejoice that their child has someone she can trust with matters of the heart.

I am clearly not a good mother.

I wait until the front door has slammed shut and then pick up my laptop and ram it into my bag. I may be a bad parent and a terrible teacher and quite honestly, a bit of a wreck right now but that doesn't mean that I have to fail at everything. I am one hundred percent determined that Book Two (untitled) will be the raunchiest, sexiest, most orgiastic work of our time and there is only one place to go for the divine inspiration that writing of this calibre requires and that is The Daily Grind.

For the hot and steamy coffee, obviously.

Chapter Ten

My alarm beeps at 6 a.m. but it doesn't need to bother. I've barely slept. The night lasted forever as I lay awake, trying not to think about the day ahead but unable to think about anything else. Occasionally I would doze for a few minutes, but my dreams were filled with nightmares about me leaving a very small child on a plane and having to watch helplessly as it toddled off to the cockpit and started taxiing down the runway.

There's a slim possibility that I am not really handling Dylan heading off to university very well.

'Wake up,' I whisper at my sleeping husband, resisting the urge to hit him on the head with my pillow. 'You promised that you'd cook a proper breakfast before we have to leave.'

Nick grunts and rolls over. I wait for three seconds and then prod him in the ribs. 'Nick! Wake up and cook the sausages.'

Blearily, he opens his eyes and squints at the clock on his bedside table.

'Hannah. It's six o'clock in the morning. We don't have to leave until ten o'clock. Sausages do not take four hours to cook. Go back to sleep.'

I attempt a chuckle but it comes out more like a strangulated yelp.

'Go back to *sleep*? Go *back* to sleep? I'd need to have slept in order to do that, Nick – and I can assure you that I have not been doing much sleeping. Because one of us needs to be sure that Dylan has got everything he needs and actually, it's a very good job that I wasn't asleep because I remembered at two-fifteen this morning that he didn't have any drawing pins for his noticeboard and what on earth is the point of a noticeboard without any pins, hey? Tell me that! So I went and had a rummage around in the kitchen drawers and found a whole packet of pins and I've put them in his rucksack but you need to remind me to tell him where they are because he won't know otherwise and then he'll be in real trouble if he needs to put something up on the board.'

I pause to breathe and Nick pulls me into his arms.

'He's going to be fine, babe,' he tells me. 'You don't need to worry, okay? Now will you please try to get some rest?'

I relax my shoulders and close my eyes but then another thought makes me sit bolt upright.

'Should we have had him vaccinated before he went?' I ask, frowning as I try to remember all the advice that I have trawled through online.

Nick sighs and sits up. 'He's going two and a half hours

down the road, Hannah – not to another continent. I don't think vaccinations are required. Last I heard, rabies and yellow fever weren't prevalent in the south of England.'

I do not appreciate his tone.

'But it's a known fact that people get ill when they move somewhere new,' I snap back. 'It's to do with new germs and viruses and stuff. And Fresher's Flu – that's definitely a thing.' I leap up and stare down at Nick. 'Oh god. What if he gets sick and I'm not there?'

'You *won't* be there, will you?' points out my loving and understanding husband. 'And if he does get sick then he'll deal with it, just like every other eighteen-year-old who leaves home.'

I shake my head. 'We need to do everything that we can to keep him healthy and safe. I can't handle the thought of him being unwell when he's away from us, I just can't. And I read an article about students all getting scurvy because they don't have enough Vitamin C but I haven't bought him any!'

Nick throws back the duvet and walks round the bed to stand in front of me. He puts his hands on my arms and looks me right in the eye.

'My darling wife,' he says quietly. 'You are being ever so slightly insane right now, okay?'

I open my mouth to protest but he keeps talking.

'I'm going to go downstairs and make you some coffee. In the meantime, I want you to take a nice, long shower. Then we'll cook some sausages and wake the kids up and have a leisurely and relaxed last breakfast before we go.'

The last breakfast. It all sounds so final and, for the

millionth time this week, I feel tears springing up behind my eyes. But I have to get a grip. I'm not going to make this any easier for Dylan by behaving like a middle-aged drama-queen. I force my shoulders back and attempt a smile. Nick bends down and gives me a kiss, which nearly makes me cry *again* because if it weren't for us getting together all those years ago then we wouldn't even have a child to take to uni.

I take my time in the shower and by the time I get out there's a hot cup of coffee next to the bed and the smell of sausages wafting up the stairs. I put on the clothes that I have chosen for today's outing and that absolutely didn't demand two hours of my time yesterday afternoon, standing in front of the mirror and swearing at my reflection as I tried to find items that suggested *cool-and-funky-mother* while also projecting a *do-not-mess-with-my-offspring* vibe, which is a harder call than one might have initially anticipated. Then I take a deep breath and head out to face the day.

The car journey is strangely stilted and completely unlike every other trip that we've made this summer, where the kids could only communicate at two hundred decibels while Nick and I attempted to hold deep and meaningful conversations in between navigating disasters. This time the backseat is quiet and I find myself reverting to the kind of mothering that went out of fashion around the time of Benji's fifth birthday. My attempts at encouraging a quick round of 'I-Spy' fail miserably and nobody is even remotely interested when I propose a family game of 'Yellow Car' which is alarming because they normally leap at any opportunity to give each other a smack and this game practically legalises sibling abuse. When I enthusiastically point out a tractor on the other side of the road, Nick leans across and quietly suggests that we just listen to the radio and I grudgingly acquiesce.

When we reach the campus, smiling students in purple T-shirts direct us to a car park. Nick turns off the engine and I twist in my seat, not knowing what words to say to my slightly nervous-looking son.

'So—' I begin and then a tapping at the window distracts me.

A grinning student is gesturing to us to get out of the car.

'Welcome to campus!' he trills as we open the doors. 'You're Dylan Thompson, right? My name's Liam and I am going to be your student mentor during Fresher's Week. We're on a bit of a tight schedule so if we can get you moving then that'd be great!'

'How does he know who you are?' I hiss at my son.

Dylan grins. 'My reputation precedes me.'

Scarlet groans. 'Plus his name is on that massive sign that you had to put on the windscreen when we got here.'

Nick walks round to the boot and opens it up. It's crammed with Dylan's belongings, all stuffed into every bag that we own and when we ran out of those, plastic bin bags.

'Do you want to take his kitchen bag first?' he asks me

but before I can reply I am gently but firmly maneuvered out of the way by a group of students who have materialised from nowhere and who now begin to very efficiently empty the contents of our car boot onto luggage trollies.

'If you come with me I'll get you signed in and sorted with your key,' one of them says to a stunned Dylan, and then she whisks him off before I can even say goodbye.

'I'll just get his clothes bag,' says Nick, stepping forward, but he's stopped before he can get within touching distance of the car.

'We've got it covered,' Liam assures him. 'We know what we're doing so it's probably best if you guys just stand back and let us get on with it, yeah?'

I wince. Nick is ridiculously territorial about packing and unpacking the car and I'm sure that he's about to assert his authority and demand that anyone under the age of twenty step away from the vehicle. But instead, he gives Liam a quick nod and moves back to stand with the rest of us.

'I think we've been demoted,' I whisper to him. 'I feel like an old person.'

'Are we going to get to say goodbye to Dylan?' asks Benji, looking worried. 'Because I've made him a card and I haven't given it to him yet.'

I give my youngest child a calming smile. 'Of course we will! We won't leave without seeing him first.'

Hell no, we won't. Not if I have to stalk every last inch of this campus to find him.

In front of us, the car is rapidly emptied and Dylan's

bags taken off to god-knows-where by beaming students who appear to be livening up their day by undertaking their own version of Wacky Races with the luggage trollies. I think about the chocolate brownies that my mother lovingly baked for him to share with the rest of his flat and wince again, hoping that they make it to their final destination in one piece.

'If you come with me, I'll show you where Dylan's room is,' says Liam, giving us another fifty-watt grin. 'I need to check in with him and make sure he knows what's what.' Then he sets off at a brisk pace and we have to dash to keep up with him.

'Why are they all smiling so much?' I hiss to Nick as we charge through the main entrance.

'They're probably on drugs,' he whispers back.

I screech to a halt. 'If you think I'm leaving our son here with—'

Nick bursts out laughing. 'I'm *joking*, Hannah. *Obviously.*' He gestures to the laughing, cheery young people milling around us. 'They're smiling because they're happy and they're happy because they think this is a good and safe university, okay? Now hurry up because Liam is on a schedule and he isn't waiting for us. And neither are Scarlet and Benji so unless you want to leave them all here, we need to catch up.'

I scowl at my husband and scurry after him. There is a time and a place for humour and merriment and this is *not* it. Not that Scarlet seems to understand the gravitas of the situation any better than Nick does. I can see her up ahead, deep in conversation with Liam. This would not necessarily be a problem on its own but I can tell from here that she's gone to full Scarlet mode. If Liam is chirpy then Scarlet is the equivalent of an entire flock of pigeons.

She's obviously re-thought her boy ban.

The poor lad doesn't stand a chance.

Liam makes a comment and Scarlet's peals of delighted laughter ring out around the campus. He turns to look at her and she throws back her hair like she's starring in her own shampoo advert and it's only now that I notice her wearing my very lovely, very expensive birthday scarf, which she definitely did not ask permission to borrow. I narrow my eyes, reminding myself to take it back just as soon as we've got Dylan settled.

Once we're inside the hall of residence, I calm down a bit. The place is filled with anxious-looking parents all doing their best to keep it together and it's absolutely true that misery loves company. I walk along the corridors, eagerly observing the scenes around me and taking comfort that I do not, in fact, appear to have a monopoly on crazed-mother status.

'I've put twenty-six stamped, addressed envelopes in your bag,' says one nervy mother to her daughter as we walk past. 'So you can write to me twice a week and it won't cost you a penny. I've even written most of the letters for you – all you have to do is fill in the blank spaces to let me know how you're feeling and what you're doing.'

I wonder briefly if I should have done this for Dylan and then give myself a reality check. I'll be lucky to get a text message, never mind an actual letter written on actual paper. That mother is even more deluded than me and I love her for it.

Inside Dylan's flat, it is organised chaos. There are bags and people everywhere and the noise is deafening. Liam leads us down the corridor and then stops at an open door.

'You all settled in then, mate?' he asks as Dylan appears in front of us. 'Unpacking done?'

'Yeah, all sorted. Thanks.'

'Excellent! In that case, you'll probably be up for the first socialiser event at four o'clock, yeah? I'll swing by the flat and pick you all up and then we can head down to the Student Union.'

Dylan nods enthusiastically. 'Is that the toga tea party?'

Liam smirks. 'Yeah, mate. You got a toga sorted out yet? Don't worry if you haven't – just use one of your sheets. You won't be sleeping in your bed tonight anyway so it's not like you're going to need it!'

My head is turning between the two of them so quickly that I'm at risk of getting whiplash and my brain is on overdrive with questions. How can Dylan have unpacked so quickly? Why won't he be sleeping in his bed tonight? What on earth is a toga tea party?

The last question is half-answered almost immediately by a retreating Liam.

'One bit of advice,' he calls as he walks down the corridor.

Thank god. Finally he's going to do some student mentoring.

'Have something to eat before we go out. Drinking

tequila out of teacups can be a bit brutal unless you're used to it. See you later!'

I gawp at him as he gives Scarlet a slightly scared look before scurrying out of the door and then I turn to gawp at Nick.

'Who is *used* to drinking tequila out of a teacup?' I ask, my voice incredulous. '*Who*, Nick? And what do togas have to do with tequila?'

My husband shakes his head silently, clearly as confused as I am.

'Let's see your room, then,' says Scarlet. Other than her brief attempt to seduce cheery Liam she has been uncharacteristically quiet so far and I'm sure she's taking everything in, storing information just in case it can be used to her advantage at a later date. She muscles past me and steps inside and I follow her, eager to see my son's new abode.

He is not *all settled* and his room is not *sorted*. Instead, bags are strewn across the floor, the contents spilling out onto the carpet as if some kind of burglary has taken place.

'Nice.' Scarlet doesn't appear to notice the mess. 'You've got your own en-suite bathroom too – you're so lucky. I've been asking Mum and Dad for an en-suite for years.'

'And when you're earning enough money to pay for the house extension that would be required for you to have private bathroom facilities then you can get back to me,' Nick tells her.

I clap my hands. 'Right then! If we all pitch in then I think we can probably get this place unpacked and ordered in the next few hours. Nick – why don't you put his lamp together? Benji and Scarlet, you can start putting his toiletries in the bathroom and Dylan, you can help me make up the bed because, regardless of what helpful Liam may think, you *are* actually going to need somewhere to sleep tonight.'

I lean down to find the bag containing his bedding but a hand on my arm stops me.

'Actually, Mum – I think I'm good to do this myself.' His voice is quiet and when I glance up at him, he looks worried. 'I need something to do when you all leave, otherwise I'm just going to be sitting here feeling weird.'

I stand and Nick puts his arm around me, pulling me close.

'I think it's probably time we headed off,' he murmurs in my ear. 'Give him a chance to meet his new flatmates and sort himself out.'

No. Absolutely not. Not happening. He's not ready for us to go.

'Look at him,' whispers Nick. 'He's ready.'

I'm not ready.

'I suppose we should let you get on with it,' I say, taking a very deep breath. 'But promise me that you'll make your bed before you go out.'

Dylan laughs. 'I promise.'

I can do this. I can find the strength from somewhere very deep within me to smile at my boy and give him a final hug and then walk away without making a scene. This is not a time for sobbing. This is a positive, life-affirming moment and we are incredibly lucky to be experiencing it.

This is where Dylan is supposed to be. It's a good thing. The important thing now is not to cry.

'I don't want you to go to university!' The howl bursts out of Benji like a coiled spring and when I spin round, his face is red and streaked with tears. I move towards him but Dylan beats me to it.

'Hey, little bro. No cry-face, okay? I'll be home soon and you can text me whenever you want.'

Scarlet joins her brothers and the three of them stand in the middle of the room, their arms wrapped round each other.

'Be safe,' she murmurs to Dylan. 'Don't do anything that I wouldn't do.'

'God, Scarlet.' Dylan pulls out of the hug and stares at her. 'That gives me a lot of options. I thought you said that I should stay safe?'

Scarlet punches him on the arm. 'Whatever, loser.'

Dylan grins. 'You're going to miss me really, you know you are.'

Scarlet opens her mouth to utter a retort and then she stops, her eyes glistening suspiciously. I swallow hard and press my lips together. Scarlet never cries and if she starts now then I'm totally done for.

'I got you these,' she says instead, reaching into her bag and pulling out a family-size pack of chocolate bars. 'So that you won't starve to death. And also these, so that you don't get any minging diseases or, god forbid, spawn any gross offspring.'

She tosses both the chocolate and a packet of condoms

onto the bed and then marches past us to the door. 'Are we going then?'

I wonder briefly if I should remove the condoms before deciding that, awkward as it is to see them lying there in front of us, deliberately taking contraception aids away from one's teenager is probably not deemed to be good parenting practice.

Nick nods. 'The traffic's going to be awful. We should probably head on if we want to be home before teatime.'

Dylan gives Benji another squeeze and then looks at me.

'It's easiest if you just go,' he says. The nervousness in his voice brings me to attention and I snap into mother-mode.

'Absolutely,' I agree, pulling him in for a hug. And in my head, I am speeding through a camera-reel of images, revisiting all the times that I have held this boy in my arms. Remembering the crying baby and the naughty toddler. The worried little boy and the determined, life-loving young man. And it's so bloody hard but I remind myself that I am not losing him.

I can't rid myself of the feeling that I am losing part of myself, though.

'Have a wonderful time,' I say, finally releasing him so that Nick can have a last hug. 'And text me now and again, okay? Just so that I know you're doing alright.'

'I'll text you loads,' Dylan promises, blinking hard.

'The occasional proof of life would be great,' Nick tells him. 'Just so we don't worry.'

The walk down the corridor from his room to the exit simultaneously lasts no time and also forever.

'Make your bed as soon as you're back in your room,' I remind him. 'And hang your towel up in the bathroom.'

'Yes, Mum,' Dylan says. 'You don't have to panic.'

'I'm not panicking.' I dismiss his comment with a casual flick of my hand. 'But also, I packed you some milk and it'll need to go straight into the fridge. And you should probably have a proper lunch if you're going out later so maybe you could cook some pasta.'

'I could,' agrees Dylan mildly. 'I'll see what everyone else is doing first though.'

We reach the door.

'I made you a card,' sniffs Benji, putting his hand in his pocket and pulling out a crumpled piece of paper. 'So that you don't forget about me.'

Dylan takes it from him. 'I love it,' he says, his voice catching. 'And I love you. I'm not going to forget about you, Benji – I promise.'

'See you later,' says Scarlet and then she grabs Benji's hand and holds it tightly.

'Have adventures,' I tell him, not wanting my parting words to be sad. 'Although, maybe not too many all at once. And only safe adventures, okay?'

'Bye guys.' He waves his hand as we step outside. 'I'll see you soon.'

And then we're doing it. We are putting one foot in front of the other and walking away, leaving our first-born child to the tender mercies of a group of strangers. Nick holds my hand and together we take one, two, three, four, five steps towards our new normal life.

Until Nick wrenches his hand out of mine and sprints

back to where Dylan is standing in the open doorway. I watch as he puts his hand in his jacket pocket and pulls out an orange, which he thrusts at our bemused son.

'Eat it!' he shouts, as he jogs back to me. 'And I've left you a packet of Vitamin C in your rucksack so you don't get scurvy.'

I reach out and grab his hand and we watch as Dylan gives us a salute and then closes the door.

'Are you okay?' I ask, my voice wobbling with the effort of not bursting into tears.

Nick makes a gulping noise and rubs his eyes with the back of his other hand. 'I'm fine. No, I'm not fine. This is crap and I hate it and I don't know how we're supposed to do this.'

'Neither do I,' I tell him. 'But other people do it so I guess it must be possible. Shall we go home and drink all the wine?'

He nods and we turn around and make ourselves walk towards Scarlet and Benji who, from the look on their faces, have been having their own emotional moment.

The journey home is even quieter than the previous trip.

'At least you don't have to share the backseat with Dylan,' I quip after half an hour, in a pathetic attempt to lighten the atmosphere.

There's a pause and then Benji speaks up.

'I was thinking that only being two of us in the back would be good,' he tells us. 'But it isn't as great as I thought it'd be.'

There's not really a lot that I can say to that.

Chapter Eleven

O ur new normal life is not feeling normal in the slightest. Despite our very best efforts to keep moving forward in a calm and positive manner, our offspring seem utterly determined to make everything as difficult as possible. Dylan started the dramatics by texting us three hours after we'd arrived home from dropping him off, casually informing us that he'd *chopped the top of his thumb off* when he was slicing an onion and was currently en route to A&E by bus. At least that was where he *hoped* the bus was going.

It was only the fact that Nick and I had wholeheartedly thrown ourselves into our vow to drink all the wine that stopped me leaping into the car and driving straight back down to rescue him. Instead I had to make do with some frantic Googling of bus timetables so that I could assure both him and us that medical attention was in his near future. And *then* the hospital was dealing with some kind of environmental crisis that meant he was told there would be an eight-hour wait to be seen. So he went back to his flat and FaceTimed Nick, who with the aid of a bottle of ketchup, a supply of bandages and my thumb as a prop, proceeded to talk him through patching himself up.

The only positive thing about the entire, stressful experience is that he was chopping an onion in the first place, therefore slightly reducing my fear of him surviving on boil-in-the-bag rice and cereal alone.

Then Scarlet decided that the stench coming from the collapsed septic tank was making her feel nauseous and that the remedy included me giving her twenty quid to go to the cinema with Petra. And then Benji had an argument with Logan and it took several hours of emotional and in-depth analysis (which naturally, he waited to have until I was tucking him into bed) for him to realise that a disagreement about the strengths and weaknesses of various Pokémon was not a reason to lose a best friend. By which point Nick was asleep on the sofa and my white wine had lost all of its chill.

A bit like me.

It's been over a week since I received the email about Sex Con and resolved to throw myself into my reinvention as a Sex Goddess, while also injecting huge amounts of carnal pleasure and hilarity into Book Two (still untitled), yet my progress has been painfully slow. It's not that I haven't been trying – it's just that Dylan going to university has really changed the dynamic in the house and I feel bereft and slightly pointless. I'd talk to Nick about it but I feel like he's avoiding me, and it isn't exactly aiding my efforts to become more sexy when he won't even look at me.

However, by Thursday afternoon, after I've spent *quite* a long time on research because it's obviously important to ensure that my work is factually correct, I think I'm finally ready to get down to some proper writing. I've made the executive decision to stop worrying about the humourous aspect of my writing for the time being and concentrate on one thing at a time. Which for now is making sure that my writing is erotic. Which means getting in a sensual state of mind.

It's not easy though, being here in my own kitchen, which is not a location where I'm particularly inclined to feel raunchy.

I put the kettle on and pace, trying to conjure up a racy vibe.

'Ooh, sex,' I murmur to myself, walking past the huge pile of laundry that's waiting to be put in the washing machine. 'I am so, so sexy right now – oh shit!'

I've reached the end of the room where the big family calendar is attached to the wall and I've just seen that I was supposed to be at a PTA meeting ten minutes ago. I spin towards the door but then stop. I *could* dash over there now with my profuse apologies but then I won't ever get the chance to solve my sex problem. This is one of those times where I'm going to have to come first and the consequences can be damned. Swallowing hard and steeling my inner resolve, I start to pace the room again, forcing my head back into the game.

'Sexy, sexy, sexy,' I say, marching past the sink where last night's washing-up is still stacked up in a basin of cold and now-greasy water. Not only have I still not managed to book an appointment with the dishwasher repair company, I have also spectacularly failed at creating a washing-up rota, meaning that unless I want to serve tonight's supper on paper plates then I'm going to have to deal with the situation at some point very soon.

I keep walking and trying to convince myself that I'm feeling seductive and alluring but it's no good. I know other writers of erotica manage to just *switch it on* like a vacuum cleaner but I don't even know how to start. Grabbing a mug, I pour hot water onto a teabag and stare out of the window. It's exactly as I feared. I'm a forty-four-year-old woman who has spent so long dealing with kids and work and house stuff and the general mundanity of life that I've lost it and I didn't even notice it was going.

I've lost my sensuality and I have no idea how to get it back because, unlike Benji's homework, it is unlikely to be down the back of the bloody sofa.

Sighing deeply, I finish making my cup of tea and sit back down at my laptop. It's hopeless even trying to write so I let my fingers roam across the keyboard and allow myself to sink into the world of social media for a few minutes. I scroll down the screen, reading the various status updates on Facebook and scowling at the picture-perfect lives that are presented like works of art for the rest of us to admire. I don't know why I even bother to come on here because it only ever makes me cross. It's all fakery and pretence and designed to make everyone feel insecure about their existence.

I exit the screen and read my emails, hoping for some distraction there. I have two unread messages. One is from Binky, reminding me that she'd like to read the first few chapters of Book Two 'in the very near future', just to ensure that I'm on the 'right path' and please can I get back to her as soon as possible? I groan and take a sip of tea. I am not on the right path. I'm not even going in the right direction.

The other message is a reminder from Rob, asking me to pay the invoice for our connection to mains drainage. I've been delaying slightly, hoping that Nick's new contract will get confirmed but time is clearly up. The already-groaning credit card is just going to have to take a deep breath and suck up yet more debt.

Admitting defeat and giving up isn't even an option anymore. I can't tell Binky that I can't write another book and I don't want to have to tell myself that the reason for my failure is that I can't do sexy. Because there's a lot riding on this, not just writing Book Two. I need to stop feeling so damn sorry for myself. There are people in the world with real problems and I am not one of them. I need to figure out how to fake it until I make it and I know exactly how to do that.

Sitting up straight, I shove my shoulders back and flex my fingers.

Hannah Thompson is bringing sexy back the only way she knows how.

Through the power of Google.

Working quickly, my fingers fly across the keys. There are many ultimate questions in life, including *Who Am I?*

and *Why Am I Here?* But none are as ultimate as the words that I am typing into my laptop: *how can I get into a sexy state of mind?* I press enter and sit back as Google presents me with 94,700,000 answers in 0.69 seconds and then I smile because really, with odds like that, how can I possibly go wrong? I read the first article, my brain whirring as if I'm studying for an exam and then I stand, pushing any doubts to one side. I need to do this and I can't do it sitting at my kitchen table.

Heading into the hall, I check that the front door is locked. The last thing I need right now is Scarlet coming home early from school and finding me in a compromising position. It would scar her for life and I don't need the grief. Then I walk upstairs and into my bedroom, running through the suggestions that the World Wide Web had to offer.

The first one sounded easy enough so I head over to the wooden chest on my side of the room and open up my underwear drawer. Well, I call it the underwear drawer. In theory, that is what it's supposed to be. In reality, it's the drawer where I shove everything that I haven't got another home for. But now isn't the time to be worrying about my clothing organization so I push aside the ugly one-piece swimming costume that I bought after Benji was born and the sparkly bikini that I haven't worn in the last nineteen years but that I can't quite bring myself to believe will never fit me again. I rummage amongst the winter tights and the pop socks and the strapless bra that has only been worn once because it turns out that straps are what actually make a bra work and without them you might as well be slapping a lettuce leaf on your breasts and asking it to do the impossible.

I forage in between odd socks and belts and a suspender belt that is circa 1996 and was a bad idea even then. I toss aside many, many pairs of what Scarlet unkindly refers to as *fug knickers* and I call my *big girl pants* and will only throw away when the one remaining strand of elastic finally breathes its last breath because there are certain times in the month when only big girl pants will do. And finally, after a strenuous archeological dig, I find what I am looking for.

My one and only thong.

Yanking off my jeans and current fuggish underwear, I pick it up and step inside, pulling the delicate fabric up my legs. Nick bought me this several years ago on our wedding anniversary and while I appreciated the gesture (and while obviously recognising that this was a gift for him, not me), in all honesty I'd have preferred a multipack of cotton briefs. I'd have definitely got more wear out of them, that's for sure.

But Google has assured me that if I want to feel sexy then I need to dress the part. There was a whole article on embracing womanhood and treating your body like the precious thing that it is and apparently, wearing knickers that droop at the back is not particularly sensual.

I pull my jeans back on and wriggle a bit, trying to get the thong part into a slightly more comfortable position. My brain conjures up an image of a cheese-wire and I shake it away. I need to push through the discomfort and the sensation that my butt cheeks are being dissected and release the inner Sex Goddess that lies within.

Even if the article did neglect to mention that I would be releasing her through my arse.

Wincing slightly, I walk over to the mirror on the wall and try to remember what I'm supposed to do for step two. I know that the article suggested that I *make friends with the mirror* by starting every single day voicing aloud one thing that I love about myself, so I strike a pose and stare at my reflection.

'Hello, you,' I say, feeling a tiny bit self-conscious. 'You're looking super-hot today.'

It's a lie. I am not looking super-hot. My hair needs a wash and I just flung on the first clothes that I could find this morning, which happens to be an old cardigan and my reliable mum-jeans. But I'm wearing provocative underwear and I can't lie – the sensation of my bare skin rubbing against the denim is not unpleasant. In fact, I'd go as far as to say that it's making me feel kind of racy.

'So.' I give myself a shy smile. 'I just wanted to say that one thing I really, really love about you is your—'

The doorbell rings and I jolt backwards, feeling exposed.

It rings a second time and there's a hammering sound.

'Coming!' I yell, running down the stairs. 'Just hang on a minute!'

I unlock the front door and wrench it open, hyper-aware that my sexy thong doesn't leave a lot to the imagination and that underneath my jeans, I am practically naked.

'Morning, love,' says the postman. 'I've got a parcel that needs signing for.'

'Ooh, how exciting,' I say, reaching over and scrawling

my finger across the device that he is holding out. 'I hope it's for me!'

'The parcel isn't for you,' purrs the postman and when I look up he is gazing at me through lowered eyelashes. 'But I've got something else here that you might like.'

'Is it a special delivery?' I ask, slightly breathlessly. 'I haven't had one of those in a while.'

He puts his post satchel on the ground and beckons me to step closer.

'I'll let you be the judge of that,' he says, putting his hands on my waist. 'But I haven't had any complaints about the standard of service yet.'

I close my eyes and wait for his lips to land on mine. As a woman of the world I have had many experiences but being ravished on my doorstep has not been one of them.

He leans closer and my thighs clench in anticipation as the smell of his aftershave wafts towards me.

'This is why I love the Royal Male,' I whisper, just as he—

'It's not for you,' the postman says, lifting the parcel off the ground. 'It's for your husband. And from the size of it he's been ordering more parts for that beaten up old Land Rover of his.'

What in the name of fuck was that? I blink rapidly, feeling like I've just emerged from some kind of sex bubble. Please, for the love of god, tell me that those sighs of pleasure stayed in my head and that I did not inadvertently sex-groan in the poor postman's face? I glance over at him but he remains impassive, which tells me nothing. Maybe he's accustomed to middle-aged women having sexual fantasies about him on their doorsteps? Maybe this happens to him all the time and it's no big deal?

He passes me a box and I stagger under the weight.

'Thanks very much,' I say brightly, kicking the door closed behind me and dumping the box on the hall floor where hopefully Nick will trip over it and break his stupid neck when he arrives home. If I have just accidently caused a sex scandal then it's all Nick's fault for bringing the postman to the door in the first place. And I know that we've had a conversation about not buying anything else this month unless it is a complete necessity and, as he drove off to work in Betty this morning, whatever is inside this box can't be that vital. Not vital enough to risk me getting a conviction for sexual harassment, that's for sure.

I walk back into the kitchen and sit down at the table before my legs give out beneath me. Bloody hell fire. I know that I was trying to become Twinky Malone but I didn't think she'd emerge that quickly. And now that my heart rate has calmed down I'm starting to feel quite proud of myself. If that is what happens when all I've done is put on a thong then the possibilities are endless. I feel like a woman who has just discovered that she has witchy powers. I decide here and now that I will do whatever it takes to learn how to harness my gifts and I will only ever utilise them for the forces of good.

And for becoming as sexy as I damn well can. Obviously.

I lean back and take another look at my laptop screen. I've sorted the underwear situation and made a start on my friendship with the mirror. Now I need to surround myself with delicious scents and wrap myself in luxury fabrics. How tricky can that be? If I'd had any idea about how easy it was going to be to unleash my inner Sex Goddess then I'd have done this *ages* ago.

Glancing at the clock, I see that I need to get a move on if I'm going to get any writing done before it's time to collect Scarlet and Benji but that's okay because I've got the next two aspects on my 'sexy state of mind' list covered. The delicious scent is dealt with by locating the highly expensive candle that Cassie gave me for my last birthday and there's a very soft blanket hanging over the back of the kitchen sofa. It might *technically* belong to Dogger but beggars can't be choosers and I can already feel my sensual side surging forth.

Well, I will just as soon as I get this torturous thong off because I have come to the evidence-based conclusion that, while it may have helped me channel some of my inner depths, it is also delving into one abyss that I wish to remain unexplored.

I deal with the underwear situation. Then, pausing only to slap on a bit of hand cream and therefore achieving both step five (*indulge in some pampering*) and also helping to ease the pain of my poor, chapped hands which are suffering after days of having to actually do the arsing washing-up, I sit down at my laptop, take a deep breath and channel my inner Sex Goddess.

Bella Rose stared out of the penthouse window, at the impressive Tulsa skyline. She couldn't see all 186.8 square miles of it, obviously but what she could see, she approved of.

'That's business taken care of for today.'

At the sound of his deep, masculine voice reverberating around the room, Bella Rose span round and took in the sight before her. Like the Tulsa skyline, it was impressive. The front of his trousers struggled to hide the package that lay beneath and Bella Rose knew that if she were to take a closer look then it would absolutely have her name emblazoned along the side (author's note: check this. It is meant to be a subtle reference to both the address on a parcel and also a tattoo but I am not actually sure that it is possible to tattoo that particular part of the male anatomy. It certainly doesn't seem like a sensible idea).

'Was everything okay?' asked Bella Rose, taking a sip from her glass of wine. 'Has your great-uncle left everything in good order?'

Daxx shrugged, the movement highlighting his delectable muscle tone. Bella Rose gulped as she observed the tiger tattoo on his arm quivering slightly, as if it were about to launch itself into the air and pin her to the ground.

'It's oil,' he told her, his eyes hooded with desire. 'And I'm now an oil billionaire. There are people who can deal with the day-to-day stuff. All we need to do is each other.'

Bella Rose watched as he pulled off his trousers, smiling when he remembered to fold them neatly and then take them into the bedroom to put them away. Billionaire or not, she was unprepared to clean up after him. And anyway, he might not be retaining his billionaire status once she'd arranged the meeting with the accountant. There would be no tax-dodging or shady shenanigans while Daxx was with Bella Rose, she'd make sure of that.

Joining the Billionaire Club was not going to turn him into a twat, not if she could help it.

Daxx came back into the room, giving Bella Rose one of his legendary, trademark grins. The work clothes were all gone now and he was clearly feeling warm because there wasn't a stitch on him. He stared intently at her, as if he could read her mind – which Bella Rose knew was extremely unlikely because she'd been trying to direct him towards her G-spot for months now using only telepathy so as to spare his feelings, but the message still wasn't getting through. She was seriously considering taking things to the next level and writing him some instructions, although as Daxx was more of a visual learner it would probably be prudent to include a labeled diagram too.

'I've missed you,' he growled, prowling across the carpet. 'I think we should have sex.'

At the mention of the word sex, Daxx's brain sent nerve signals to his muscles, telling them to relax. This allowed his blood to fill the tissue around his ~~Johnson pecker~~ *penis – which had the fortuitous byproduct of causing it to stiffen (author's note: research other ways to describe an erection. There must be a way to make it sound sensual and not merely functional and utilitarian although god only knows how).*

Bella Rose raised one eyebrow and turned back to the darkening skyline.

It was true what they said. Everything was bigger in Tulsa. And by everything what she really meant was Daxx's huge, pulsating ~~tool member~~ *phallus.*

She thought she might quite like it.

I read my work back, feeling my cheeks flush slightly at

the pure brazenness of the whole thing. It's a good start, I think – but I'm not quite there yet. I still need to build the tension and come to the climax.

Of the plot, obviously.

On the one hand, this is some of my best writing to date. Binky wanted me to add more sex and I've literally written the actual word. I'm not even alluding to what's about to happen – it's utterly explicit, right there on the page and nobody can say that this isn't provocative. It's the perfect storm for sex – the dramatic cityscape, the naked skin, the smell of wealth coupled with a responsible, community-minded approach to taxes. That last one is important because I hate anything that jolts me out of the narrative and nothing would distract me more than thinking that Daxx was about to evade paying his taxes by having an off-shore tax haven in the Channel Islands.

It's got almost everything that the reader of erotic fiction requires.

But something is still missing. If Valerie was reading this then I think she'd say that it could be even sexier. Despite my increased sexual vocabulary, I am not *entirely* convinced that it would get her hot under the collar. And even though just the thought of Daxx ravishing Bella Rose with only his brooding eyes makes me feel like I'm having a hot flush, I am easily cooled off again by the description of his stiffy. I take my hat off to erotica writers who manage to make this sound appealing, I really do.

I'm going to need to do more. But in the meantime, I might send Nick a text and see if there's any chance of him knocking off at a decent time today and then maybe we can get rid of the kids and have an early night. Not all my research has to be done on my own, after all. And I think it might be time to use my new sexy-talk skills in the bedroom.

I'm ready to let Twinky Malone show me exactly what she's capable of. Nick would be wise to hold onto his own hat.

Chapter Twelve

He fell asleep. After all the effort I went to, bribing Scarlet with money to go ten-pin bowling and then watching a hideously boring film about skateboarding with Benji so that I could get away with sending him to bed a bit earlier than normal, Nick bloody well fell asleep. I thought we could start with our regular, vanilla sex and then take it up a notch and things were looking promising at first. But as soon as our usual performance had ended he was out for the count without a glimmer of interest in an encore. I didn't even manage to get my sensual candle lit or change into my sexy thong or start talking about anything even remotely throbbing before he was snoring. I was tempted to wake him up and yell at him but on reflection, decided that it wasn't worth the bother. It wasn't like it would enhance the erotic mood of the bedroom. And truthfully, it might not have been the best plan. I'd fondly imagined that Twinky Malone would be up for taking several curtain calls a night but it turns out that her stamina isn't any better than Nick's.

Still, it would have been nice to have entertained the possibility.

So screw him. Or not. Whatever. Twinky Malone wouldn't mope about, bemoaning her husband's lack of interest in exploring new sexual dimensions. Hell no. She'd take matters into her own hands and that's exactly what I intend to do, just as soon as I've written the next chapter of my book and figured out what exactly it will take to get Nick to realise that we are rapidly at risk of becoming old.

The Daily Grind is fairly empty at this time of day. I order my drink and take a seat at my usual table, settling down to enjoy the view.

'Caramel latte?'

My first thought is that his voice is exactly how I imagined Daxx's voice would be, if Daxx had been born in the East End of London and not, in fact, America. My second is that he smells like sex in a bottle. Not actual sex, obviously – that would be a bit disgusting – but more the *concept* of sex.

He places my coffee on the table and throws me a casual smile. My eyes alight on his name badge. Apparently he's called Levi and he's *here to help*. All I have to do is ask.

But I don't want to ask. Not with words anyway. Sometimes these things can be discussed without anyone uttering a single word. Slowly, without breaking eye contact, I stand and then I lower the zip on my waterproof jacket and shrug it seductively from my shoulders. It lands in a heap at my feet but I don't bother to pick it up. Instead, I reach out and pick up the coffee cup, cradling it in my hands and peeping at him over the rim, my eyes wide with lust.

'Is this roasted?' I whisper, my voice dripping with desire.

'No.' He shakes his head. 'But that can be arranged, Madam.'

I smile – and it's the kind of smile that a female spider might give her mate after she's done with him and is about to enjoy him for dessert because a) she's fucking ravenous and b) why not?

'The roasting can wait,' I croon, crooking my index finger and beckoning him to come closer. 'I have other needs that you can help me with right now.'

My hand twitches and I knock my cup, sending a bit of frothy milk onto the table.

'I've seen you in here before,' he says, whipping out a dishcloth and mopping up the spilt liquid. 'You always look so focused on your work.'

I swallow loudly and give a quick nod, checking that my jacket is still zipped up to my neck. It's hard to figure out if Twinky Malone is content with staying in my head or if she's about to emerge, like in the film *Alien*, only instead of a baby Xenomorph it will be a fully-fledged Sex Goddess that bursts out of my chest.

'Yep. I'm very focused. Totally focused.'

'So what is it you're doing then?' he asks. 'When you're sitting here for hours?'

'Nothing!' I laugh nervously. 'Just being focused, that's all. On my work.'

'Okay, then.' He gives me a slightly quizzical look and backs away from the table as if I'm a dangerous animal.

Levi obviously has a good instinct for survival and I obviously have a teeny bit of a sex bubble problem. But everyone knows what you have to do with bubbles. Blow them.

And that's exactly what I intend to do. But this time I won't wait for Twinky Malone to emerge in time for dessert. This time she's going to be there for the main course. Nick is not going to know what's hit him.

Binky emails later on Friday afternoon with the details of the *Real Sex Talk* panel for Sex Con, which is still one month away but apparently *'will be here before you know it'*. It is probably not meant to sound as threatening as it does.

My attempts at Twinky-fying myself are off to an okay start (if I ignore my husband's lack of interest and the potentially embarrassing sex bubble incidents), but I'm very aware that I've been mostly focusing on my attitude and state of mind and still have the pressing issue of my appearance to address. This in itself raises two major problems. The first is that there's still been no mention of Nick's new forestry contract and after the incident with the septic tank, the credit card is stretched out further than a bungee cord and so I haven't got any money to waste; and the second is that I hate going clothes shopping. The lights are too bright and the mirrors too reflective and I always end up feeling hideous and filled with self-loathing. And right now, when I'm struggling with Dylan leaving home and Nick barely being here and a million different worries going through my head about the kids and money and my stupid job and writing Book Two (untitled), the last thing I need is more pressure.

I will deal with the situation another time, when I'm

feeling slightly more confident and sure of exactly who it is that I want to be. What I need now is a calm, relaxing weekend so that I can reflect on my progress and figure out my next steps.

They say that when man makes plans, God laughs. What they are missing is that when woman makes plans, her teenagers howl with merriment. After Dylan's sliced thumb and Benji's argument with Logan, which demanded numerous back-and-forths between me and Logan's mother and has resulted in a much-anticipated sleepover at Logan's house tonight, I am obviously ready for the next ambush, because only a fool wouldn't anticipate that Scarlet was not yet done with the Thompson family drama-thon. At least I *thought* I was ready. Turns out that there are many different types of fool and none so foolish as the mother of a teenage girl who thinks she might have a handle on what to expect.

She waits until early on Friday evening when I have just poured myself a cheeky glass of wine and slumped down onto the sofa with the pure intent of losing myself in two hours of mindless Netflix viewing. Nick is down in his shed (quelle surprise) and I have the remote control all to myself.

'So, how was your day, Mum?'

I am instantly on the alert and poised for battle. She never asks me this. I think she genuinely believes that I cease to exist when she doesn't have a requirement for me.

'What do you want?' I ask, putting my glass down carefully and trying not to sigh. It has not been the easiest of weeks and I've earned this drink. I don't want it being hijacked by my daughter. 'I thought you were going out with Petra tonight?'

'I want eighty quid.' She flicks her hair over her shoulder and gets straight to the point. 'Please. There's a festival in the summer and we're all going but I need to get my ticket now before they sell out.'

I shake my head. 'Not happening, I'm afraid. Every penny we've got is paying for the septic tank disaster.'

'God.' Scarlet groans and rolls her eyes. 'I hope I'm not this boring when I'm an adult. You guys have got way more cash than I have but you spend it on stuff that's totally crap.'

'Language,' I tell her, although in this case she's accurate. Never did I imagine that I would be dragging my sorry arse to work and slogging it out in the classroom three days a week just to pay to have the family's poo deposits conveniently disposed of.

'So can I have the money then?' she asks, her voice filled with the blind optimism that only teenagers possess.

I could go easy on her but her comment about us having more cash than she does is rankling.

'How much money do you have in your room right now?' I ask casually. 'Just as a matter of interest.'

She pauses, looking up at the ceiling and muttering under her breath while she figures it out, which is revealing in itself.

'Dunno,' she says eventually, shrugging. 'I've got some birthday money left and the money I got from helping out at those weddings as a waitress – oh, and Granny gave me twenty quid last week. So maybe about two hundred pounds?'

I raise one eyebrow at her enquiringly and she smiles sweetly back.

'I've got plans for that money,' she informs me, giving a small laugh. 'I can't possibly spend it on festival tickets.'

'Do you know how much I've got?' I enquire, not leaving a gap for her to reply. 'Let me enlighten you. My wallet currently has about four pounds in loose change which is all that was left after I had to buy food for Dogger *and* we ran out of washing powder and that isn't cheap and *then* Miss Pritchard cornered me and forced me to pay my tea and coffee dues for the staffroom.'

Scarlet grimaces. 'That's what I'm talking about. I swear I'm not going to be this dull when I'm middle-aged. You need to get a life.'

I pick up my wine and slug back half the glass. The time for savouring the moment is well and truly out of the window. As is any desire to help my daughter out. It's every woman for herself and I have just about had enough.

'You can pay for your festival ticket yourself,' I tell her.

Scarlet opens her mouth as if she's about to protest but then wisely clamps it shut again and turns to leave the room.

I can't resist one final last word.

'Although whether we'll actually let you go is another thing altogether.'

She spins round, her face registering her shock. 'You wouldn't do that,' she states. 'But while I'm here, how would you feel if I went out with someone who owns a motorbike?'

It's a feeble attempt to regain the upper hand. She's clearly off her game this evening.

'I'd feel sorry for his mother,' I tell her.

'Mum!' Her indignant shriek makes my ears ring. 'That's a horrible thing to say.'

'Not because he was going out with you,' I clarify. 'I'd be sorry for her because she'd be constantly stressed out at the thought of her child on one of those death machines. Also, where's my scarf after you borrowed it *without asking*?'

'So you haven't changed your mind about me going on a motorbike then?'

I raise an eyebrow at my daughter. 'My scarf?'

Scarlet exhales loudly (actually she sighs, but I'm trying to reframe her more challenging behavior in a positive light in a pathetic attempt to retain my sanity) and stomps out of the room. Everyone has their limits and I have just been pushed beyond mine. I am no longer prepared to be written off as a boring middle-aged mother. I will fight against a world (and a daughter) that expects me conform to its outdated expectations and I will spend some of my hard-earned cash on myself for a change. If my attitude isn't enough to signal my new persona then I'm going to have to get more explicit.

It's time to go sexy shopping – but I don't want to do it on my own.

This calls for the kind of loyalty that only a best friend can provide and so I text Cassie that I've got a crisis and arrange to meet her tomorrow evening at the new wine bar in town. I'm fairly sure that Twinky Malone would not be seen dead in the tatty, stinky pub that we usually frequent and if I'm going to get into character then I need to do this properly.

Not that I necessarily have to wait until tomorrow to get more explicit. The house is empty. Now is the perfect time to carry out some research for my next scene with Daxx and Bella Rose while also showing Nick that we can rock the changes. Pouring myself another teeny glass of wine I pull my laptop towards me and open the lid. I may have been a little hasty giving away *Kama Sutra: Three hundred and sixty-five positions* but it doesn't matter. There is a wealth of information on the Internet. A person just has to know where to look and fortunately, I am the mistress of Google.

I type my key words into the search engine and then click on images.

Fuck me. My eyes widen as the screen fills with pictures of people engaged in what can only be described as shagging. For some reason I wasn't expecting them to be so realistic and I look frantically for the ClipArt versions in the hope that they might feel less pornographic, before clicking back to the information screen. I didn't really think that through. I am clearly more of a text-based learner than a pervy-photo kind of learner.

Taking a breath, I try again, scanning down the list of suggestions in front of me. One in particular leaps out and after a quick scan of the instructions, I'm good to go. I just need Nick because I might be a burgeoning Sex Goddess now, but even I can't pull this off on my own.

It takes me a few minutes to prepare myself but by the time I hear the back door open I am ready and in position. Nick's footsteps heading up the stairs match the thumping of my heart and by the time he opens the bedroom door I am almost breathless with anticipation.

'Hey,' he says, his eyes lighting up as he sees what I'm wearing. 'You should have told me that you were ready to go to bed. I could have come sooner.'

I give him my sexiest smile. 'That's the last thing that I want you to do,' I purr. 'Tonight is all about sensual exploration. It's about pushing our limits and facing our fears. How far are you prepared to go, Nicholas?'

His face drops and he looks hurriedly around the room. 'What do you mean? Facing what fears?' He takes a step back. 'Is this another one of your weird attempts to get me over my phobia, Hannah? Because I don't care how sexy you look – I am not holding a spider.'

'No!' I gesture to my almost entirely naked body, showing him that I do not have a stash of arachnids hidden about my person. 'There are no spiders. What do you take me for?'

His head is still darting around the room suspiciously. 'So what fears am I supposed to be facing then? You're acting very strangely and that usually means that you're plotting something.'

'I shouldn't have said anything about facing any fears,' I placate, trying not to sigh. 'It was a figure of speech. Now can we get on with our evening of sensuality, please?' I pat the bed next to me. 'You're over-dressed.'

It's a good job that I didn't choose position five from my Google list. He'd have been put off sex for life if I'd suggested that we attempt to reenact The Spider.

Once Nick is assured that he is not about to ambushed

by a cluster of tarantulas, he relaxes slightly. It takes him seconds to disrobe and then he walks across the room towards me.

'The kids are all out, yeah?' he confirms, giving me his sexiest smile. 'It's just you and me tonight?'

I nod and push myself off the bed, stopping him before he can sink down next to me.

'It's just you and me,' I confirm. 'And we have all night if we need it. Which we may very well do because what I have in mind is possibly going to take a few goes.'

Nick's face drops. 'Oh god, no. Tell me that this isn't going to be another Kama Sutra fiasco because honestly, Hannah – my knee has only just recovered from last time.'

I laugh seductively and shake my head. 'This isn't anything to do with the Kama Sutra. And your knees are going to be fine. Now, if you lie down on the carpet I can get myself into position and we can take it from there. You'll love it.'

'You're looking gorgeous,' Nick tells me, taking hold of my hand. 'I'd really like it if we could just—'

'You'll like this,' I say, gazing up at him with pleading eyes. 'I promise. It's going to be great.'

I need him to see that we can do new things. I need to know that there's more to us than the same old Hannah and Nick who always do the same old things. I need to know that I can do sexy.

He pauses for a moment and I hold my breath.

'Is this research for your book?' he asks eventually.

I nod eagerly. 'Totally. I'm just trying to figure out how Daxx and Bella Rose can take it to the next level.'

And us, Nick! I'm trying to figure out how we can take it to the next level because despite my sensual candle and my up-the-bum thong and my daily self-affirming conversations with myself in the mirror, we are still doing what we've always done. And I'm terrified that we're going to wake up one morning and suddenly realise that we are old. And if Googling 'sexual positions that may surprise your husband' doesn't add some spice to our life then I'm all out of ideas.

Nick stares at me and for a second his eyes are filled with something that looks a bit like disappointment.

'It's called The Butter Churner,' I tell him brightly, trying to lighten the mood. 'That doesn't sound too tricky, does it?'

He raises his eyebrows and gives my hand a squeeze. 'Just try not to kill me, okay?'

I can't promise anything. According to the website that I found this particular position on, it is ranked twenty-eighth on a list entitled 'Positions He's Secretly Dying For You To Try In Bed'.

I grin back at him. 'There are worse ways to go. At least you'd die a happy man.'

Chapter Thirteen

Cassie is already seated when I arrive, perched up at the bar and deep in conversation with the outrageously attractive bartender. I fling myself onto the stool next to her and try to get my breathing under control.

'Tell me again why I thought having kids was a good idea?' I ask.

Cassie frowns back at me. 'I have no idea,' she tells me. 'They seem to take you for everything you have and give very little back in return. In terms of investment, they're pretty rubbish to be honest.'

This is both fair and accurate.

'Scarlet spent most of today at my mother's house,' I complain. 'She tried telling me it was because of the stink at our house and when I pointed out that the septic tank has been dealt with and we are now the proud owners of stench-free mains drainage she had the audacity to tell me that the smell she was referring to was the stench of my hypocrisy and she'd still be spending the day with Granny.'

'What were you being hypocritical about?' Cassie asks.

I shrug. 'I have no idea. I rather suspect that she was talking out of her arse and just looking for an excuse to escape my company.'

'I'd let her go,' Cassie states. 'Sounds like it'd be a much easier day if she wasn't at home.'

'Well, yes – but that's not really the point.'

I am her mother. She's supposed to want to spend time with me. It's not about easy.

'Anyway.' Cassie sits back on her stool and gives me a long look. 'We're not here to talk about your kids. You said that you were having a crisis, so spit it out, Hannah. What's going on? Is Nick having an affair? Are you?'

'No!' I stare at her, my mouth gaping open. 'Why would you say that?'

I did have a rather interesting dream last night, though. Not that dreaming about someone you aren't married to counts as having an affair, although I'm not entirely sure how I'd feel if Nick was having dreams about sexy baristas. Especially when our romantic evening didn't end entirely the way that I had planned. It was a shame about The Butter Churner actually. I think we could have had a shot at it if I hadn't misinterpreted the diagram and reversed our positions. It turns out that it would be a physical impossibility to do what I was proposing. Not without risking hospitalisation and six weeks in a neck brace, anyway.

So that was a bit of a flop.

'So if your crisis isn't to do with your relationship then what is it?' pushes Cassie, gesturing to the gorgeous man behind the bar to bring more wine. 'Have you finally got to the bottom of Scarlet's crime ring? Has Dylan got a crack habit? Did Benji finally snap and take out that little shit, Auberon?'

'What has got into you tonight?' I ask her, watching as she takes the bottle from the slightly alarmed-looking bartender and fills her glass to the brim. 'You're in a proper hot mood.'

Cassie grimaces. 'Sorry. I've had a bad day and I don't mean to take it out on you.'

I reach across and put my hand on her arm. 'What is it? Is it something to do with that guy you've been seeing?'

She closes her eyes briefly and when she opens them they are sparkling with a ferocity that makes me gulp.

'*Been* seeing is right. Turns out that while we were making plans for a long weekend break in Brighton, his wife was making plans to give birth to their fourth child.'

I wince. 'Oh Cassie. And you didn't know?'

She glares at me. 'Of course I didn't arsing know. I wouldn't have even spoken to him if I'd known. Twat.'

'Twat,' I agree, clinking my wine glass against hers. 'Do you want to talk about it?'

She shakes her head. 'I do not. Talking about it makes me angry and when I'm angry I make rash decisions, you know?'

I do know. This is not the first time that Cassie has had a bad experience with a partner and I have been there on several occasions to prevent her from doing something that they may well have come to regret.

'You'd think that I'd have found someone decent by

now,' she complains, pulling apart a beer mat. 'Is it so much to ask for? I just want to meet a nice, kind, funny, intelligent, honest man with a good work ethic who doesn't have shit taste in clothes, food or music and who doesn't have an entire family sitting at home waiting for them to return. Am I being too picky, Hannah? Am I?'

I sip some more wine and wonder how to let her down gently.

'You're definitely not being too picky on the whole *already-having-a-family* thing,' I say, nodding encouragingly. 'But I do wonder if your absolute hatred of anyone who doesn't agree that Jon Bon Jovi is the best singer of all time is limiting your options just a *tiny* bit. Also, your refusal to acknowledge anything vegan as actual food is slightly offensive to people who choose not to eat meat or dairy products.'

Cassie scowls at me. 'I'd rather be single for life than compromise on either of those issues.'

I nod, keeping my thoughts that this may well be the case to myself.

'What I need now is a distraction.' Cassie pushes the decimated beer mat to one side and turns to face me. 'Tell me all about your crisis, Hannah. And it'd better be good.'

'Well, it might not exactly be a *crisis*,' I admit. But you know my book?' I lower my voice, just in case someone might overhear. Now that *More Than Sex* is out in the world I can never be sure who could be listening.

Cassie nods.

'And you know how it's written by Twinky Malone and nobody knows that she is me?'

Cassie sips her wine and nods again.

'I have to become her.' I blurt the words out in a rush. 'Well, actually – I'm sort of already becoming her. But I'm still not quite at full *Twinky* and I need your help. I need you to help me look like a Sex Goddess.'

Cassie stares at me. 'I have no idea what you're wittering on about, Hannah. Why do you need to look like a Sex Goddess? Is this you worrying about being old and boring again because I already told you, that menopause crap is obsolete.'

'It's not that.' I lower my glass. 'And I don't think I'm boring anymore. Not in my head, anyway.'

She stares at me, interest lighting up her eyes, but I move on. I'm not prepared to talk about my sex bubbles with her. Not right now, anyway.

'I need to turn myself into a Sex Goddess because everything that you said would happen, *is* happening,' I tell her. 'I have to publicise *More Than Sex* and as part of that I'm going to be on a talk panel at Sex Con. So, will you help me?'

Cassie sits up straight.

'*You're* going to be talking at Sex Con?' she asks. 'Holy fuck, Hannah! That's massive! And insane!'

I nod. 'I thought about just saying no, but Binky, my editor, has made it clear that this is something she wants me to do and it's the only way to make any money out of this whole thing. And it's not enough for me to take on a new persona. I need to look the part too.'

Cassie casts her eyes down my body, taking in my scruffy hair that has been wrangled into a ponytail, my baggy top and my mum-jeans. And I don't mean *mum-jeans* as in the trendy, high-waist fashion item. I mean jeans that I have actually been wearing since I became a mum.

'You're right,' she says thoughtfully, chewing her bottom lip. 'This is definitely not a look that's going to sell sex.'

'Thank you for that.' I slump further onto my stool, feeling slightly dejected. 'I wouldn't have asked you to help if I thought you were just going to mock me.'

'But we can do something about your outdated style!' Cassie sits up straight and gives me the first smile of the evening. 'I need a challenge and god only knows, turning you from *mumsy* into a Sex Goddess is going to be the challenge of a lifetime. Not impossible, but it's going to take time, effort and money. And you'll have to do exactly as I say and be one hundred percent committed to your transformation. Are you committed, Hannah?'

I nod slowly, trying not to be too offended at her harsh appraisal. I need her help and now is not the time to hash over the fact that my best friend thinks I look *mumsy*.

No. Three o'clock in the morning is the time that I'll be doing that, thank you so much.

'This calls for more wine!' bellows Cassie, sloshing the last of the bottle into my glass. I have no idea where the rest of it went so quickly. 'Here's to the reinvention of Hannah Thompson!'

Oh, honey, you are so late to the party. My reinvention started ages ago. I just need you to help me put the cherry on the cake.

We clink our glasses and agree to meet in the High Street at two o'clock tomorrow, which by the time I fall into bed many hours later is the one detail that I can remember from the entire evening.

I am slightly less sure of my newfound determination to revamp my look when I wake up the next morning but there's no way that I'm backing out. Partly because I'm owed this and it's the natural next step in my evolution but also because Cassie threatened to start reading extracts from my book aloud in the staffroom if I stood her up. And I don't want to piss her off because I need some help if I'm going to sexify my image and Cassie is absolutely the woman for the job. This knowledge doesn't stop my stomach from churning with mild terror at the prospect though. I've been friends with Cassie for years and one thing I know for sure is that she's ruthless. Once she sets her mind on something then nothing can get in her way. She's a bit like Scarlet in that respect and I wonder briefly what it says about me that I am surrounded by females who scare me rigid.

'What are you shopping for, anyway?' asks Nick as I drag my sorry ass out of bed and start searching for clothes that will achieve the dual mission of making me feel safe and comfortable while also generating a look that is trendy and as un-mumsy as possible.

'Oh, we're just browsing really,' I say casually, taking off my pajamas and pulling on my most reassuring underwear. 'I might buy a new cardigan if I see something that I like.'

Nick smiles. 'Treat yourself, babe. You deserve it.'

I squint up at him suspiciously. I know his game.

'What have you bought?' I ask. 'Go on. Just tell me.'

He wrinkles his nose and then waves his hand in the air. He's aiming for dismissive but I've been married to this man for long enough to know his traits. The more laid-back he appears, the more he's spent and I know exactly what he's spent it on. Or who he's spent it on, anyway.

'What did Betty need this time?' I enquire, yanking on a long sleeve T-shirt. 'Because quite honestly, I wouldn't have thought there was any part of her left to replace. If she was a woman, she'd be a cosmetic surgeon's wet dream.'

Nick looks offended. 'There's nothing cosmetic about replacing Land Rover parts, I can assure you of that, Hannah. And as I keep telling you, it's—'

'—an investment,' I finish for him.

This is not the first time we've had this fascinating conversation.

'So how much did you spend?' I ask, moving on from what he's actually purchased because honestly, I have zero interest in prop shafts and fuel filters and head gasket seals.

Nick mumbles an exorbitant figure and I spin round to face him, my indignation only slightly diminished by the fact that I'm trying to force one leg into my tights and the rapid movement puts me at extreme risk of falling over onto the bedroom floor.

'You spent *how much*?' I screech. 'What were you thinking? You are aware that we've just been slapped with a fucking astronomical bill for the twatting septic tank fiasco?'

'I was *thinking* that if I didn't replace the part then it was going to end up costing us a lot more, further down the line,' he tells me. 'It can be my birthday present, okay?'

And your Christmas present and your anniversary present and next year's birthday present and don't even think about expecting an Easter egg, I think, ready to open my mouth and let rip. But then I remember what Cassie said about the reinvention of Hannah Thompson requiring time, effort and money and I clamp my lips together. Perhaps having a go at my husband for spending so much wouldn't be the most prudent move right now.

'Look, Hannah – we both work hard,' Nick says, pulling me in for a hug. 'I just think we need to remember to live a little. Virtually every penny we earn goes on the kids – or this house. It doesn't hurt to send some of it our way, every now and again. Otherwise, what's the bloody point of it all?'

He's right. I can't remember the last time Nick had any new clothes and we haven't been out together for ages. Buying parts for Betty really is his one indulgence.

'Fine.' I give him a squeeze and then return to the task of getting both legs into my tights. 'Maybe I'll go wild and buy *two* cardigans.'

I do feel a tiny bit bad for not telling him what Cassie and I are doing but I just don't know how to put it into words. It's not every day that a woman attempts to transform herself into a Sex Goddess and it's making me feel slightly vulnerable, like the more I talk about it the less chance I have of actually achieving my goal.

I'm a bit like an athlete, gearing up for a big event. I

think that I need to get in the *zone* and prepare myself mentally for the challenge that lies ahead and I can't do that if everyone is invading my mental space.

I'm just relying on Cassie to know what getting in the zone actually entails because I truly do not have a clue.

Chapter Fourteen

'Sorry I'm late,' I tell Cassie, pulling an apologetic face when I meet her in the High Street a little while later. 'I was determined to be on time but Scarlet decided to wait until I had one foot out of the door before telling me that her new objective is to be the most powerful and notorious Head Girl that the school has ever seen, which obviously meant that I had to talk to her for the next twenty minutes about responsibilities and commitment and also disillusion her of the belief that becoming Head Girl entitles her to, quote: "*rule the school and do whatever I want*".'

Cassie grins. 'At least she's got ambition,' she tells me. 'Most parents would applaud that in a teenager, Hannah.'

I sigh quietly and shake my head. It's not a lack of ambition that worries me about my daughter – it's more her fierce and immovable belief that she can achieve anything if she wants it badly enough. Part of me is proud of her confidence but another part of me quivers in fear. In an ideal world her attitude would be fine but we do not live in an ideal world and her inability to perceive her own weakness makes her vulnerable. And it's incredibly tricky trying to protect a girl who thinks that she is utterly invincible.

'But it isn't her ambition that we're here to address,' Cassie reminds me. 'Now, let's get started. If we're going to turn you into a sex kitten then you're going to have to loosen up a bit. I've got a battle plan all mapped out.'

'Can I ask that you refrain from using the phrase *sex kitten*? There's nothing sexy about kittens. Also, I'm slightly concerned that you are referring to this shopping trip as a battle.'

'But it is.' Cassie raises one eyebrow at me. 'The challenge that lies ahead is not going to be fun. It is not going to be easy. But if you choose to accept this mission it will revolutionise your life and there'll be no looking back.'

'You make it sound so serious,' I laugh. 'We're just shopping for a few new clothes. I thought we could start at M&S. I've bought some nice things from there in the past.'

Cassie winces.

'Oh, Hannah. This is why you need me. No Sex Goddess would never darken the doors of that place, not if it was the last shop on earth.'

I follow Cassie as she marches ahead, striding past all the shops that I would usually frequent. The pavements are slick with rain and I scurry along with my head down, trying to keep up with her.

Just as I'm starting to think that we aren't going shopping at all, Cassie stops.

'Here we are. This is the place for you, Hannah.'

I look at the shop in front of us and instinctively take a step backwards.

'Hell, no.'

Cassie grabs my hand before I can make my escape.

'Hell, yes,' she responds. 'This is exactly where we need to be shopping if we're going to turn you into a sex bomb.'

I glance at the window display and then look quickly away. I might want to reinvent myself but I have no intention of my transformation including anything that involves my nipples.

'Cassie.' I keep my voice quiet in case anyone walking past hears us and judges me accordingly. 'I am fairly sure that this establishment is what is known as a *sex shop*. I can't go in there.'

'Why not?' Cassie puts her hands on her hips and glares at me. 'There's a whole load of clothes in here that I think would look great on you.'

I jerk my head towards the window.

'Seriously? You think that what I need right now is S&M gear, do you? I'll get arrested if I try and leave the house looking like that.'

'You might – if you get lucky,' quips Cassie.

I close my eyes briefly, enjoying the sudden image of a sexy police officer telling me to *'spread 'em'* and that he's writing me a parking ticket because I've got *fine* written all over me.

'If being sexy was a crime then you'd be guilty as charged,' he says as I gaze at his extraordinarily large baton and swallow hard.

'Just take a look, will you?' Cassie whips me out of my

bubble before it can get interesting. 'Consider it an educational experience.'

I think for a second. I do have a passion for learning, it's true. And I'm not one to turn down an opportunity to better myself.

I stare at the shop again, wondering if I can really do this.

Cassie rolls her eyes. 'Hannah. Did you or did you not tell me that Binky has requested more sexiness in your next book?'

I shrug. 'She might have mentioned words to that effect. Possibly.'

'This shop is oozing sexiness,' Cassie tells me. 'Let's just go in and have a look. You never know, you might find some inspiration in here, even if you don't find any clothes! Becoming a Sex Goddess isn't just about the paraphernalia, Hannah. It's a way of life.'

She's absolutely right. This is excellent research for Book Two. I'm sure that Daxx is exactly the kind of guy who'd give Bella Rose something slightly freaky for her birthday and I can well imagine him shopping in an establishment such as this one.

I take a deep breath. I've got my big girl knickers on. I can do this and if I can't, then Twinky Malone can. It's not a big deal. It's a shop, just like all other shops. There's nothing to worry about.

I glance furtively around to check that nobody is watching and then I follow Cassie inside, blinking while my eyes adjust to the slightly red-tinted light.

Oh my sweet lord. Once again, I have been proven to be

spectacularly wrong. There *was* something to worry about. There are whole shelves of something to worry about. And this is not a shop like any I've ever frequented. I'm not sure who the target audience is but I'm fairly sure that it isn't me.

My eyes alight on a pair of handcuffs and a sexy police outfit and I quiver slightly.

Then again, maybe this is a sign.

It's like it was meant to be.

Perhaps the target audience isn't Hannah Thompson but that's okay. Because I've been *her* for the last forty-four years. I am way overdue for some excitement and if I can't find it in here then I don't know where I will.

'Can I help you?' asks an assistant, appearing beside me as if by magic.

'Err, no thank you very much,' I say, stumbling over my words. 'I'm just browsing.'

Bloody hell, why did I say that? Who goes into a sex shop to browse?

'Are you seeking anything in particular?' she enquires. 'Maybe something for a special occasion?'

I know that she's only doing her job and she seems very friendly and pleasant but I really, really wish that she'd just leave me alone so that I examine the merchandise in private. I'm willing to be open-minded but that doesn't mean that I want to have a lengthy discussion about it with a total stranger. Am I the only person in the world who understands that a person can enjoy writing about sex but not want to engage in conversation about it?

'Umm, no not really,' I tell her, jiggling from foot to foot.

'Just, you know—' I gesture wildly around the shop. 'Some *sex things*.'

She gives me a weird look and retreats to the counter. 'Okay, then. Feel free to give me a shout if you need further information on any of the products.'

'Hannah!' Cassie's voice floats through the air, rescuing me before I can say anything else ridiculous. 'Come and check out these clothes.'

I walk down the aisle, trying to not gawp at the items lining the shelves. The stock is piled high and everything is attractively packaged in pastel-coloured boxes. This place is like Toys"R"Us for adults. Cassie is standing by a rail at the far side of the shop, holding something that I'm fairly sure doesn't have enough material to cover a Barbie doll.

'That's not *clothes*,' I tell her, stopping a couple of feet away. 'It's a crime.'

The hunky policeman in my mind gives me a wink and I regretfully shake my head, sending him away for now. I need to stay focused.

Cassie grins. 'It's sexy.'

I contemplate the slip of fabric in her hands. 'I can just imagine Nick's reaction if I put that on and marched into the bedroom. I doubt there's enough material on that to cover both my arse cheeks. He'd probably have a heart attack. If he didn't die of laughter.'

'He would if you *marched* in,' Cassie retorts. 'Clothes like this are made for slinking, Hannah.' She gives me an appraising look. 'You do know how to *slink*, don't you?'

'Of course I do,' I scoff, making a mental note to Google *slinking* at the first available opportunity. 'But I need something to wear to Sex Con and there's no way that I've got the confidence to walk in wearing that.'

'Well, I think you're wrong about Nick's reaction. I think he'd bloody love it if you wore this one night. But it's your call.'

I watch as she replaces the skimpy, pretty, lacy item and feel a pang of regret. Maybe she's right. Maybe Nick would love it. But what if she's wrong and it doesn't make a difference? What if he thinks I'm being stupid and weird? It's probably better to be safe than sorry.

I am suddenly filled with inexplicable sorrow.

Cassie takes a few steps to the side and then pulls something else off the rack. 'What about this jumpsuit, then? It's perfect for Sex Con.'

It certainly has more material. If you can actually call it that.

'What is it made of?' I ask, stepping forward and prodding it suspiciously. 'Is that *rubber*?'

'I think it's latex,' says Cassie, peering at the label. 'Oh, my mistake. It's ninety-four percent polyester.'

'I didn't think polyester could look so aggressive,' I say weakly.

'It's supposed to make you fearsome,' Cassie says, holding it up in front of me. 'It's called "the dominatrix jumpsuit".'

'Yes, well it was definitely not designed with forty-four-year-old women who have had three babies in mind, I can tell you that.' I twist to the side and stare at it, still feeling hollow inside. 'Who the hell can actually wear this stuff?'

'Anyone can wear it,' Cassie tells me. 'And I'm

disappointed in you, Hannah. Are you saying that age and motherly status is a barrier to your sensuality, because that's not very empowered of you.'

'No!' I grab the jumpsuit from her and clutch it to my chest. 'I'm absolutely not saying that.'

Yes. That's exactly what I'm saying. It is very hard to channel your inner Sex Goddess when you spend every waking moment engaged in dealing with other people's shit and are coming to the terrifying realization that unless you do something radical, this boring, normal person is who you are now, forever and ever, and may the goddess have mercy on your soul.

But Twinky Malone doesn't have those problems. Twinky Malone writes erotic novels and buys impractical shoes and if she needs to rejuvenate her marriage and her life by rocking the changes then she buggering well will. Twinky Malone can absolutely rock a wet-look, figure-hugging, plunge-neckline jumpsuit because she's a goddamned rock star.

Tossing my ponytail over my shoulder, I strut into the changing room. It's time for the next step of my transformation and I'm not just doing this for me. I'm doing it for women everywhere, for anyone who has ever felt invisible or forgotten just because they're over the age of thirty-five or someone's mum. When I walk down the street wearing my dominatrix jumpsuit, people (and by *people* I mostly mean Nick) will see me as a living, breathing, sexual person and not just the woman cooking the tea and making sure the dog is up to date with her vaccinations and taking the kids to school.

And from henceforth, all my steps will be slinked…or slunk…or possibly slank? I'm not entirely sure.

Pulling off my clothes, I step into the jumpsuit and pull it up my legs. It's pretty tight and I realise immediately that my bra is going to have to come off, which is an alarming prospect. I have a complex love/hate relationship with my bra. On the one hand, it is uncomfortable and restrictive and my shoulders have deep ridges from where the straps have dug in, which can't be healthy. On the other hand, it stops my breasts from tripping me up.

It's tricky.

'How are you getting on in there?' calls Cassie from the other side of the curtain. 'Are you ready to show me your new look?'

'One minute,' I shout back, wrestling my arms into the sleeves. 'I've just got to do it up.'

I start pulling on the laces at the front, yanking as tightly as I can in an attempt to bring my breasts under control. My first attempt squishes them into a strange position under my armpits and so I try again, this time bending over as far as I can (which isn't that far in this thing) and asking gravity to give me a helping hand for once in my life.

By the time the laces are tied and my breasts are somewhere in the vague proximity of my chest, I am red-faced and slightly out of breath.

'You've got to hand it to these dominatrix types,' I call. 'They're prepared to work for it.'

'Just show me!' pleads Cassie and so I throw back the curtain and step out for my grand reveal.

'Crikey, Hannah.' Cassie puts her hand up to her mouth. 'Wow.'

'Is it that bad?' I ask, turning to peer in the mirror. 'Oh.'

'It's not *bad*,' Cassie says to my reflection. 'It's just – I don't know how to put it.'

'It's a lot,' I say, twisting round so that I can see myself from a different angle. Cassie nods enthusiastically.

'It's definitely a lot,' she agrees. 'You actually do look incredible. I had no idea you were hiding such sexy curves under all those cardigans!'

'Neither did I,' I tell her. 'Although there's no way on this planet that I'd be able to go out in public looking like this. Perhaps I could tone it down with a scarf? I've got one that Nick gave me for my last birthday which would work really well.'

Cassie gawps at me. 'What the hell are you wittering on about? You can't wear a scarf with a dominatrix jumpsuit!' She turns away and starts to walk back down the shop. 'You look amazing but I know that there's not a snowflake's chance in hell of you actually buying it. I've got a bit of my own purchasing to do – come and find me when you're ready.'

I go back into the changing cubicle and close the curtain. I have never, in my entire life, even contemplated wearing something as risqué as this. I have never had the courage.

'I don't look anything like me,' I whisper to myself, gazing into the mirror.

The woman staring back at me is one percent Hannah Thompson and ninety-nine percent Twinky Malone and I think I might be a bit in love with her.

I twist round so that I can read the price tag on the neck and then I start to undo the laces on the bodice, folding the jumpsuit up as carefully as if it were made of spun gold, which it might well be, considering what I'm about to pay for it.

You can't put a price on sexual confidence and I have never owned an item of clothing that has made me feel like this one does. This jumpsuit is going to be the answer to all my problems. My writing is going to ooze with sensuality and I'm going to strut my stuff at Sex Con and Nick is going to be seduced by my temptress ways.

I am going to bloody well slay those three birds with this one, possibly overpriced and slightly uncomfortable but massively sexy stone.

It's worth every penny.

Chapter Fifteen

It is with some trepidation that I open the door to my mother after work on Tuesday. Benji has gone for tea with Logan, and Scarlet left the house this morning muttering about seeing Petra after school. I have no idea if that's really what she's doing but I am working on my trust issues and have so far resisted tracking her phone. And while I'm busy having faith in my daughter, I have graciously decided to get over the hurt that she would rather speak to her grandmother than to me. As such, I have invited my mother over for coffee...so I can grill her for information about why Scarlet has been going to see her so much and then using that intel to do some actual parenting.

I wait until she's dumped her shopping bags on the floor and we're sitting in the kitchen with cups of coffee and slices of lemon cake and then I open my mouth to start talking.

She beats me to it.

'Now tell me, Hannah. How's that book coming along? Have you finished it yet?'

I nod firmly, determined not to be distracted from my mission.

'Absolutely,' I state. 'Pretty much done with it now, to be honest. Just one or two finer details to clear up and then I'll be sorted. But anyway, Mum – I wanted to ask you about—'

Mum laughs knowingly. 'So you're struggling, then.'

I glare back at her. 'I am *not* struggling, thank you very much. In fact, I'm almost halfway through and I think it's possibly going to be even better than the first book, *actually*.'

Mum raises an eyebrow. 'Well, I should hope so,' she tells me, her voice firm. 'There are rules for writing a sequel, you know. And the first and most important rule is that Book Two needs to be far superior to Book One.'

'What do you know about it?' I sniff, vaguely aware that I sound like Scarlet. 'You've never written a book.'

Mum pats my knee kindly. 'That's because I'm not a writer, darling. I'm a do-er.'

Excellent.

'Now why don't you tell me what the problem is and I'll see if I can bring any of my years of experience to help solve the issue?' She takes a sip of her coffee. 'I've just completed Module 2 of my Sex Therapy course and I'm sure I can be of some use to you.'

'I don't have a problem!' I wail.

I might have a *bit* of a problem. After a surge of writing when I got home from buying the dominatrix outfit I've hit a very small brick wall with Book Two (*why are titles so bloody hard?*) and if it was anyone else offering to have this conversation with me then I'd bite their arm off. It'd be great to have the opportunity to talk about writing and plot and how to make this second book both sexy and funny with someone whom I trust.

So, not with my mother.

Although she *is* one of the only people I know who will listen to my woes and then find a solution while only mildly judging my ineptitude or life choices. And she probably has a point. She's more qualified to talk about this stuff than I am.

'Fine.' I lean across the table and grab my notebook. 'I'm listening. But don't say anything that's going to gross me out, okay? You're my mother – you have standards to uphold.'

Mum clears her throat officiously and launches right in. 'I've been giving it some thought and I've found some porn-writing top tips that should help you with writing a sequel. I've been on the Internet and there's lots of advice out there. You really could have done it yourself, Hannah.'

I resist the urge to tell her that between teaching three days a week and trying to write a book, as well as the challenges presented by my youngest two offspring plus spending every waking moment wondering if Dylan is okay and trying to pretend that I don't miss him constantly while also trying to address the pressing need to reinvent myself, I have been *slightly* short of time. And also, for the fifty-millionth time, that I am *not* writing porn. But I bite my lip and I stay quiet.

I need her help.

I *need* her porn top tips.

'Okay, top tip number one,' she starts. 'Don't just pick up where the last story left off. Your readers want to think that time has passed and that this next book has something new to offer them.'

'Okay.' I scribble a note and then look up at her. 'That's good. I think I've got that one covered. At the end of *More Than Sex*, I left Bella Rose and Daxx in the barn at the Wyoming ranch. But the next book is based in Tulsa, Oklahoma.'

'Why Oklahoma?' asks Mum. 'What's the importance of that particular location to the plot?'

I shrug. 'Well, it could have been set anywhere, really. But I wanted to change the location and Oklahoma just leapt out at me when I looked at a map of the United States. So, what's top tip two then? What other words of wisdom do you have for me?'

Mum picks up her lemon cake. 'Give the reader something new,' she states. 'Book Two definitely needs to be more exciting than Book One.'

'Okay.' I think for a moment. 'I've got that too. This book isn't about life on a ranch – it's completely different. Daxx has come into a huge inheritance and is now a billionaire. Billionaires are very popular in erotic fiction, I know that from my extensive research.'

Mum takes a bite of cake. 'Top tip three is that you need to make the book the same,' she mumbles. 'Readers want more of what they've already read.'

I stare at her. 'Make your mind up. Which is it? The same old thing or something new? I can't write both.'

'That's a very defeatist approach, darling,' Mum tells me. 'If you don't mind me saying so.'

I do, actually. I mind quite a lot that I need some help and you're sitting here spouting utter rubbish. I can do that all on my own, thanks.

I shrug as nonchalantly as I am able. 'I don't see myself as defeatist,' I tell her. 'More pragmatist. Or realist. I am not a magician, Mother. I cannot write a book that is both the same and also not the same. It's impossible.'

Mum laughs. 'You need to write something that's the same but different. So keep the things about the first book that made it so special and then mix things up a bit. It's like taking a tried and tested recipe for sponge cake and then adding something extra, like chocolate or cinnamon or brandy. It's the same but with extra spice.'

I think about what she's saying.

'I guess it makes sense,' I say, slightly grudgingly. 'I think I can do that.'

'Of course you can!' trills my mother. 'Now, the next thing that you need to remember is that you have to kill your darlings.'

'No way.' The words tumble out of my mouth in an instant. 'I'm committed to Daxx and Bella Rose now. I'm not making one of them die.'

'Then maybe you could bring in a new love interest?' she suggests. 'Something to up the stakes and keep it kinky. But darling, all of this is just snippets of advice. The most important thing is that you write about what you know.'

Write about what I know? I thought she said she'd read

my book? Does she think that I've got first-hand experience of sex on the barn floors of Wyoming with sultry ranchers?

'Tell me the main themes of the sequel,' my mother says, putting her plate down on the arm of the sofa.

'Err, probably sex and humour,' I say. 'That's generally what I'm aiming for.'

Mum tuts at me. 'No, no, no. Tell me what's important for the characters. What do they want from life?'

I sit up a bit straighter. I can totally answer this question. 'Bella Rose wants to reinvent herself,' I murmur. 'She wants to show the world that she's more than meets the eye. She wants to feel loved and sexy and also capable. She wants to push herself out of her comfort zone and be rewarded in the process.'

My mother smiles smugly. 'Well, there you are then. *You* need to experience new things and acknowledge the benefits. It's all about cause and consequence, Hannah. Action and reward. You need to experience the things that you want your characters to feel and then write about it.'

She hasn't got a clue about how any of this works. I knew I was wasting my time engaging in any kind of conversation with her about this.

And yet – and yet, there is the nugget of an idea forming in the back of my mind. But before I can let it loose I need to address the reason I asked her to come over here in the first place.

'Why does Scarlet keep coming over to your house?' I ask, keeping my voice casual. 'She seems to be spending an awful lot of time with you. What does she talk about?'

Mum gives me a little smile and then shakes her head.

'I can't tell you that, Hannah! Surely you know about client-therapist confidentiality? Plus, it's crucial that I don't break the Circle of Trust that I have with Scarlet.' She pats my hand kindly. 'You understand, don't you?'

Oh yes – I understand all too bloody well. The *'Let's Talk About Sex, Baby!' Foundation One, Access to Counselling* online course has turned my mother into a hip and valuable font of knowledge, and me into a defunct, obsolete loser, as far as my daughter is concerned.

I just want my daughter to talk to me. Why is that so hard for anyone else to understand? I have spent years giving her my all and eagerly anticipating the day when my teenager would turn to me and see that I have so much to offer. And now she's turning to my bloody mother instead. I dealt with the dirty nappies and the sleepless nights and the stomach bugs. I should be the one she confides in. It's not arsing fair.

'Well, thanks so much for all your help,' I say, standing up. 'I feel full of inspiration and ready to get cracking right away. So, if you could see yourself out then I can make a start.'

'If you're sure.' She seems a bit miffed that I'm kicking her out so unceremoniously but thankfully she pulls herself to her feet and starts gathering her bags. 'Enjoy the rest of your day, Hannah.' She leans over and gives me a kiss on the cheek. 'I've got a good feeling about this book, you know. The last one was a hoot, darling. Just try to relax and channel that same energy.'

I watch her walk down the garden path and then I close the door and race back to the kitchen where a quick rummage in the drawers of the big cupboard provide me with the tools I need.

I've been struggling to write because I haven't really understood Bella Rose's motivation. I know that I want her to be brave and adventurous and above all, a Sex Goddess but that is not enough. I need to write about what I know, and what I *know* is that I don't want Bella Rose pinning all her chances of happiness and success on someone else – she needs to take responsibility for her own wellbeing and self-worth and not rely on the people around her to make her feel good about herself because they won't, not in one million years. Not even if they happen to be her very own flesh and blood.

Which means that I need to do those things too. I need to push myself. It's as my mother said – it's all about action and reward and I know exactly how to motivate myself to keep trying new things. It's what I used to do for the kids when they were struggling to take responsibility and needed a bit of a visual reminder.

I get to work, using a large piece of paper and a ruler and a selection of felt tip pens. And then I walk across to the fridge and pull down the kids' sticker chart that has been stuck on with fridge magnets for the last three years and forgotten for approximately two years and eleven months. In its place, I put my new creation with its rows of blank squares, hanging a sheet of gold star stickers next to it that were left over from one of my many attempts to encourage Benji to relinquish his nappy and use the potty.

But this chart doesn't have a checklist of duties like the old one. I am not going to be rewarding myself for washing up or cleaning out the hamster or mowing the lawn. Hell no. Mummy will be rewarding herself with stickers for activities far dirtier than emptying the kitchen bin and there's no way that I can write them down for all to see.

Not that this is a problem. I'll know what I've done, every single time I put a sticker on another square. This is the perfect way to channel my efforts into the three things that are giving me the most grief right now: writing the sexiest scenes that I can imagine, turning myself into a Sex Goddess and rejuvenating my slightly limp marriage.

It's going to be perfect.

Chapter Sixteen

The front door slams shut and seconds later Scarlet storms into the kitchen with a face like thunder.

This is becoming something of a habit.

'How come you're home so early?' I ask, glancing up at the clock. 'School doesn't finish for another hour.'

'I had a driving lesson and now I've got a free period.' She marches across the kitchen and opens the fridge door. 'I did tell you this morning but clearly you weren't listening.'

I sit back in my chair and give her a firm look.

'I'm sure that I *was* listening,' I tell her. 'However, I do have a few other things on my mind, you know. I don't spend all day only thinking about your timetable. I've got my own stuff to do.'

'I thought you had a day off?' Scarlet pulls out a yoghurt pot and joins me at the table. 'What are you doing, anyway?'

I slam the lid of my laptop closed, hiding my manuscript.

'I was researching something,' I say, thinking fast. 'For school.' I need to distract her from what I was *actually* doing, which was trying to figure out what Daxx's reaction would be if Bella Rose appeared in the bedroom in a dominatrix jumpsuit. I just can't decide whether he'd be horny or horrified – it's impossible to predict and I think I may need this to be a Gold Star Challenge, no matter how nervous that makes me feel.

I've been thinking a lot about my initial reactions to certain situations and have decided that I need to rethink my mantra. From now on my motto is that it is better to be sorry than safe and I am prepared to die on that hill. Although Scarlet discovering my identity of Twinky Malone is naturally exempt. I may be experimenting with new things but masochism is not one of them. It's possible that I might have a bit of a flair for sadism though.

'I thought that I could do a topic on how it is better to try something and fail than forever live your life wondering about the missed possibilities.' I beam at her. 'We live in a success-driven society and I'm not sure that it makes us particularly open to adventures.'

Scarlet rolls her eyes. She hates it when I try to voice anything that sounds like I might be being remotely trendy and constantly reminds me that I still think the 1980s were twenty years ago.

Which is fair, to be honest.

'Yeah, well, sometimes it's better not to bother trying in the first place.' She lowers her head onto the table. 'Like my stupid driving lessons. I'm seriously crap – my driving instructor actually made me stop halfway through today's lesson so that he could *"have a moment to recover and calm down".'*

'That's not really what I'm talking about—' I start and then I think about what she's just said. 'Scarlet? Are you having problems with your driving lessons? Why haven't you mentioned this before?'

Her groan reverberates around the room.

'I didn't mention it because I knew you'd make a massive fuss about it,' she mumbles, her head still firmly pressed to the kitchen table. 'And I didn't need the stress.'

She didn't need the stress? Am I actually hearing this correctly? She didn't tell me that she was struggling with driving because she thought I'd make a massive fuss and she didn't need the bloody stress? Scarlet is clearly following in Dylan's ambivalent footsteps, leaving Nick and I with yet another teenager who claims to want to learn to drive but who would rather take fifty times longer than everyone else while racking up a ludicrously insane bill.

Well, I've had enough. No more Mrs-Nice-Mother. Hannah Thompson might be happy to treated like a doormat by her ungrateful children, but Twinky Malone is not.

'We're cancelling your driving lessons,' I tell Scarlet, ignoring the shock that rolls in great waves across her face. 'I'll teach you myself.'

Scarlet folds her arms across her chest and scowls at me. 'No way. I've told you before – you'll do my head in. I'm not getting in a car with you.'

I look at her. As in, I *properly* look at her. This seventeen-year-old girl whom I would do anything for. I would battle demons and run into burning buildings and stop speeding bullets with one hand in order to save her from any harm. She is the light of my life, the meaning to my world – and also, a bit of a pain in my ass. And right now, she doesn't need me to lay my life on the line to keep her safe. She needs me to bloody well parent her.

'Okay.' I shrug my shoulders. 'That's your choice to make. I don't want to make a *massive fuss* about it, after all.'

She relaxes slightly and heaves out a deep breath. 'Thank god for that. There's no way that you'd be able to—'

'I'm still cancelling your driving lessons,' I interrupt. 'So you have three options, as far as I can see. You can come out with me or you can pay for your own lessons or you can forget about driving all together.'

Her mouth gapes open.

'How am I supposed to pay for my own driving lessons?' she snarls. 'They cost a fortune.'

Yes. Yes they bloody do.

'You can get a job.' My voice is calm and measured, like the cool-headed parent that I am but inside I am like a cobra, coiled and waiting, ready to parry her every strike with a better countermove.

'You paid for Dylan's lessons,' she retorts. 'It's not fair if you don't pay for mine. It's not *equality*.'

Teenagers are so predictable. She's not even making this a challenge.

'Equality isn't about you all getting the exact same thing,' I inform her, reaching into my bag and pulling out a nail file. 'It's about ensuring that you all get what you need. And what you need right now is to stop acting like a brat and cop on.' I buff my nails casually, as if this conversation is boring me. 'So you can either pay for your own lessons or you can gratefully accept my very generous offer to teach you to drive. What's it going to be?'

Scarlet sucks in air, like she's struggling to breathe. The room is silent apart from the sound of my nail file and I resist the urge to make eye contact. I am in control here. It doesn't matter to me either way what she decides. I couldn't care less whether she learns to drive or not. I'm not even going to—

'Will you teach me to drive?' Her voice is so quiet that it's almost a whisper. 'Please?'

Thank Christ for that. I wasn't entirely sure how I was going to explain to Nick that I'd just stopped our daughter from ever being able to drive and that we were probably going to be on chauffeur duty for the rest of our lives.

'I suppose I can do that,' I say, trying to sound reluctant while flinging my file to the table and leaping out of my chair. 'I've got an hour until I need to collect Benji – we'll go for a drive and then pick him up from school at the end.'

Scarlet starts to speak but I'm already up and heading for the hall.

'Come on!' I call over my shoulder. 'There's not time like the present.'

Honestly, I wish I'd tried to channel Twinky Malone years ago. Just imagine the parenting wins I'd have achieved if I'd been a bit more forthright and feisty instead of constantly worrying about stuff like their wellbeing and self-confidence and mental health.

I find my shoes and wait while Scarlet reluctantly plods to the front door.

'My instructor has dual-controls in his car,' she tells me, as we walk to the car. 'And I've never had a lesson where he hasn't had to use them at least three times.'

I put my arm around her shoulders and give her a quick hug. Just because I'm being a bit firmer doesn't mean that I have to remove all the love.

'And that is probably part of the problem,' I explain. 'You've got the safety net of him being able to brake or whatever and so you're not invested in your own progress. Honestly sweetheart, you just have to trust me.'

I open the car door and swing into the passenger seat. Scarlet goes around to the other side and I wait until she's safely strapped in before turning and giving her my most bolstering smile.

'You're going to be fine. Just do everything that you normally do in a driving lesson and I'll give you advice as you need it. Okay?'

Scarlet grips the steering wheel and nods.

'If you're absolutely sure?' she asks.

'I'm sure,' I trill, feeling quite excited. Maybe this will be the start of a whole new dynamic between us. I have a ton of parenting energy to spare now that Dylan has gone to uni and god knows, Scarlet has always required more than her fair share of my time and attention. This way I can show her that I am absolutely here for her when she needs me and maybe she'll stop stomping off to talk to my mother about her problems and will actually trust me with her feelings.

I will be an uber-parent, solving all of her issues while sharing my own life experiences in a fun, non-threatening, Twinky Malone kind of way.

Starting right now.

'You just need the freedom of driving without the fallback of knowing that someone can take over from you,' I say. 'You need to take responsibility for your actions and solve your own problems.'

I'm quite good at this. I wonder why I never considered becoming a driving instructor before – the amount of money I've spent on lessons is surely evidence that they must all be multi-millionaires?

Scarlet tentatively turns the key and the engine roars to life.

'It's like that bit in *Wind in The Willows*!' I tell her, chuckling lightly. 'You know, when Mr Toad gets a car and all he wants to do is travel on the open road? Poop, poop!'

Scarlet makes a strained noise and then releases the clutch.

And I am suddenly re-enacting a mash-up of *Wind in The Willows* meets *The Fast and the Furious* and I could happily give myself a good slapping for thinking that freedom was the answer to Scarlet's driving woes when it is quite clearly the very last thing that she needs.

'Perhaps slow down a little?' I croak, trying to make myself heard over the whining of the engine.

'Don't scream at me!' yells Scarlet. 'I need a calm environment or this is going to end very badly.'

I hold out my hands to placate her and then keep them up – I have a feeling that I might need to use them to brace myself in the very near future.

'I'm not screaming. I'm merely pointing out that there is a speed limit on our road and I suspect that you're exceeding it by some tiny margin.' I glance at the speedometer. 'Bloody hell, Scarlet – you need to slow down.'

Her eyes dart wildly to the dashboard. 'The dial is only on six!' she shrieks. 'I'm nowhere near the speed limit. Stop freaking me out!'

'You're looking at the rev counter,' I inform her in what I think is a very measured and controlled tone of voice. 'If you look at the dial next to it, you will see that you're actually going fifteen miles over the speed limit and if you're caught on camera then you could get points on your licence.'

I'm not actually sure that this is true. Can learner drivers even get points before they've passed their test? It'd be just my bloody luck if they gave them to me instead, as the so-called responsible driver.

'Alright, alright!' howls my daughter. 'Just stop stressing me out, okay? I can't drive under these kinds of conditions. You need to relax, Mum.'

I am starting to wonder if she can drive under *any* kind of condition but I wisely keep this thought to myself and Scarlet finally eases off the accelerator, bringing the car back to both a safe and legal speed.

'You're going to turn left at the end of the road,' I say, as we approach the junction. 'Remember to look in the rear-view mirror and then proceed when it is safe to do so.'

I can totally provide a chilled vibe. I will create a calm and nurturing in-car environment and Scarlet will pick up on the confidence that I have in her abilities and she will thrive on my trust and support.

I lean back into my seat, showing her that I have enough faith to relax while she is in control. It's so important to practise what you preach and my words alone will have limited impact. She needs to see that I am utterly composed and serene; that I know I am in safe hands and have no need to micro-manage her every—

'I said turn left!' I jolt upright as Scarlet pulls out of the junction. 'Left! No! The *other* left!'

The car lurches across the central white line and then back again as Scarlet wrenches the steering wheel from side to side.

'That's it,' I say encouragingly as she maneuvers us into the correct lane, waving my hand apologetically at the slightly stunned-looking driver on the other side of the road. 'And maybe try to listen to the directions that you're given next time.'

'I *was* listening,' Scarlet mutters. 'It's not my fault that I sometimes get my left and right muddled up, is it? Stop pressuring me.'

The car starts to gain speed and I'm struggling to hear myself think over the howling of the engine. And then the sky suddenly darkens and the very worst thing that I could possibly conceive of happens.

'Is that rain?' whimpers Scarlet. 'I haven't driven in rain yet. I don't have the skills.'

'It's fine,' I tell her, more breezily than I feel. 'Just flip the wipers on and keep doing what you're doing.'

Scarlet fumbles around and the indicator lights start to flash.

'Try the other one,' I suggest. 'And quickly, darling, before the rain gets much worse.'

'I can't find it!' wails Scarlet. 'And I can't see properly out of the windscreen! I'm just going to pull over.'

I lean across and activate the wipers. 'No need to panic! And you're not stopping now, for goodness' sake. If you're going to drive in this country then you need to be able to cope with a tiny bit of drizzle!'

The heavens respond by tipping three months' worth of precipitation onto our exact location.

'You need to put the headlights on so that we can be seen,' I instruct, as the cars in the oncoming lane start flicking on their beams. Scarlet moans under her breath but she successfully finds the light switch and we keep moving forward in a vague approximation of a straight line. I allow myself two seconds of self-congratulation and then resume instructor-mode. My work here is not done. I would appear to be making some progress with her though. I am a genuine, qualified teacher after all and once you've learnt the concepts of how good learning occurs, it's surely possibly to teach anything to anyone? It's a highly diverse skill.

'I'm wondering if it might be the right time to think about changing gear?' I enquire now, in such a mild voice that I think I convincingly make it sound like a serving suggestion. 'Second gear is mostly used at lower speeds, as a general rule of thumb and you've yet to move into third gear on this journey.'

'Give me a minute,' snarls Scarlet. 'God – you want me to do everything at once, don't you? Slow down, change gear, put the lights on, find the windscreen wipers—'

'Watch out for that cat!' I bellow. 'Stop!'

The car lurches forward as Scarlet slams her foot on the accelerator, I assume in panic and not in a dark desire to mow down an innocent kitty.

'Not *that* stop!' I scream. 'The *other* stop!'

We screech to a halt in the middle of the road, the car silent for a brief, wonderful moment until Scarlet recovers enough to start shouting.

'That's exactly what I'm talking about, Mum!' She grips the steering wheel. 'It's too much! You're asking me to use the clutch and change gears and steer the car and do all that other stuff and now you want me to look out for cats as well? I'm only human – I can't do everything! You're going to have to choose what you want me to focus on, okay? You're putting way too much pressure on me!'

Superb. Apparently I can add being a useless driving instructor to all my other maternal weaknesses.

A car sounds its horn and I swivel my head to watch as an irate old man indicates and pulls around us, gesturing rudely as he drives past.

She's right though. It *is* too much. All of it. And it's relentless – it never, ever stops. Learning to drive is only the start of it.

'We'll take it one step at a time.' I remove my hands from their brace position on the dashboard and give her knee a quick pat. 'And at least we now know that you can implement an effective emergency stop, which is excellent news!'

In retrospect, I don't think that we've been paying her driving instructor anywhere near enough money.

Chapter Seventeen

'I'm so excited about this, Hannah!' Caroline is beaming at me in the mirror as she fastens the robe around my neck. 'It isn't often that I get to do a colour change as dramatic as this one!'

I smile bravely at her. 'And you really think it's the right move?' I ask for the tenth time since I entered the hair salon. 'Because going silver feels like a really big deal. Like – am I going to look like a vixen or a granny? I don't think there's a middle ground here.' I look at my reflection and gulp. 'I could always just dye the roots again and maybe lose a few inches off the bottom.'

Caroline shakes her head. 'We've been doing that since I met you. You said you wanted something new and we've discussed this before. If not now, when?'

'It's just that being brunette is part of my identity,' I tell her. 'It's who I am, you know?'

'But it isn't, is it?' Caroline puts her hands on her hips and gives me a blunt look. 'I've been slopping hair dye onto your head for the last ten years. You know as well as I do that if we stopped doing that then you'd be grey in a month.'

I nod balefully. It's true. I spotted my first grey hair when I was sixteen and I've been doing whatever I can to hide them ever since. It wasn't so bad in my teens and while I was at university – I'd either experiment with henna, which was mostly unsuccessful, or cover them up with mascara, which was fine unless it rained. Once I started having kids though, the grey hairs developed a life of their own and I had to start dying them on a regular basis. And since I turned forty they've got a full-grown personality and social life and like Baby, they refuse to be put in the corner.

What would Twinky do? Well, she wouldn't waste hours of her life every four weeks, pathetically trying to hide the real her. She wouldn't stand in the front of the mirror and sob at the sight of white hair. She would take control of the situation and woman-the-fuck up. Anyway, I've already decided that tonight is the night when I take being Twinky to the next level and the new hair is a big part of my Gold Star Challenge. I can't back out now.

'You could always go the natural route,' Caroline suggests, seeing my worried face and taking pity on me. 'Plenty of people do it. If you go on Instagram and search for #silversisters or #greyhairdontcare, there's loads of pictures of women who are letting their grey grow out.'

I sit up straighter and fix her with a firm stare.

'Let's do this thing,' I tell her, my voice resolute.

Maybe I'm vain. Maybe I'm self-obsessed and conceited and narcissistic and all the things that mothers are definitely not supposed to be. But there is absolutely no way that I can just let my grey hair do its funky thing and grow out slowly. Go big or go home, that's what Twinky says. I'll invent my own hashtag if I have to.

#greyhairyesIfuckingcare

#fortyfournoteightyfour

Caroline returns with a large bowl of dye.

'You're absolutely sure?' she checks. 'You really want to do this?'

'If you can't beat them, join them,' I tell her, nodding. And then I sit back and watch as my hairdresser proceeds to remove every last bit of colour from my hair.

'It's all the rage now, you know,' she tells me while we're waiting for the bleach to take effect. 'Loads of celebrities have done it. Kim Kardashian and Ariana Grande and Rihanna – they've all gone silver.'

'Excellent,' I say, wondering if the burning sensation on top of my scalp is normal. 'I'm in vogue for the first time in my life.'

Caroline laughs. 'It's not just the women, either. Idris Elba has got silver hair in his beard, did you know that?'

I frown. 'Not quite the same, though, is it? I'm fairly sure that Idris Elba has not dyed his hair silver in an attempt to prevent society from making snap judgements about him due to the fact that some of his hairs have lost their pigmentation.'

My hairdresser sniffs. 'I'd have a word to say to anyone who thought they were in a position to judge Idris Elba, that's for sure. The man's a god.'

'Well, obviously,' I agree. 'But doesn't it strike you as a

teeny bit unfair that women with grey hair are seen as being old and past it, while men are seen as being sexy?'

'Are you saying that you don't think he's sexy?' demands Caroline, her eyes flashing in a way that is slightly alarming considering that she is holding the future of my hair literally in her hands.

'I am not saying that at all,' I assure her. 'I just wonder if I'd be so desperate to cover the fact that I'm going grey if we lived in a world where women aren't constantly judged on their age and appearance and where perpetual youth is celebrated.' I smile at her in the mirror. 'Which has always struck me as ridiculous, you know – because you only have to look at teenagers to know that the very idea of perpetual youth is actually a nightmare. And the thing is, that even though they might—'

'There's the timer!' interrupts Caroline, sounding relieved. 'Let's get you over to the basins and wash this off and then we can see what we're dealing with.'

That sounds a bit ominous.

'I thought we knew what we were dealing with,' I say as we walk across the salon. 'You said that the bleach would strip out all the colour and then we could put on a lovely toner and I would be walking out of here with beautiful, shiny, silver hair.'

'I didn't actually say that,' Caroline corrects, ushering me towards a chair. 'Do you want to sit down or lie back?'

'Lie back,' I say. 'And what do you mean?'

'Put this towel around your shoulders and lie down when you're ready,' she answers. 'And what I *actually* said was that we wouldn't know how much lift we had until we washed out the bleach. That's what we're doing now.'

'Lift?' I lie down and try to relax. This is usually my favourite part of a trip to the salon. The indulgence of someone washing my hair. The relaxing head massage that never lasts for as long as I want it to.

'I explained all of this to you, Hannah.' Caroline turns on the taps but I can still hear the frustration in her voice. 'All hair is different and some hair can be resistant to removing the colour. In which case, it can be a little difficult to achieve the required end result.'

A tiny bit of my brain is reminding me that I have possibly heard these words before, but it was when I'd just started to read a very fascinating article called 'Hen Nights Gone Bad' and there's a slim chance that I zoned out on Caroline's pep talk.

'Well, can't you just leave the bleach on until all the colour has gone?' I ask, wincing as the water runs cold for a second.

'Sure,' drawls Caroline and I swear I can hear her rolling her eyes. 'As long as you don't mind your hair all snapping off. Look Hannah, you have to trust me, yeah? I've left the bleach on for as long as I possibly can without causing irreparable damage to your hair. Let's wash it off and then we can take it from there.'

I force myself not to speak for the remainder of the hair washing and then, once Caroline is satisfied that every last drop of bleach has been removed we troop back to the mirror, ready for the moment of truth.

'Now, it's going to appear darker because it's wet,' she warns me. 'And we still need to add the silver toner, okay?'

I hold my breath as she removes the towel from my head.

'Oh.'

Caroline stares at my reflection and for a second our eyes lock with each other.

'Is that normal?' I ask, trying to keep calm. 'Is that what you were expecting to see?'

'It's fine,' Caroline assures me, hurriedly covering my hair back up with the towel.

'Are you sure?' I stare anxiously at her in the mirror. 'Because it looked a tiny bit orange to me.'

Caroline forces a chuckle. 'No! Absolutely not! I mean, it might have a slightly more *burnt hue* than we were aiming for but these things are a work in progress. They take time.'

I gawp at her. 'How much time?'

I don't have *time*. *Time* is the last bloody thing that I possess. This hair appointment *is* my fucking *time*.

'Are you going to be able to sort it out?' I ask, inhaling deeply and trying to remember some of the mindfulness techniques that Drama teacher Adele is always going on about. 'Or am I going to be walking out of here with an orange head?'

'I'm telling you – it's one hundred percent *not* orange. It's going to be fine, Hannah.'

'But is it going to be *silver*?' I push. 'Am I going to slink my way home looking like a sex vixen? *Am* I, Caroline?'

She stares at the back of my head, as if lost in thought.

'Caroline? Just tell me the truth. Am I going to look ridiculous?'

My words jolt her back to reality and she shakes her head.

'There's really no need to be so dramatic,' she scolds and then she turns and calls over her shoulder. 'Freddie? Can you come in here for a moment, please?'

Her attempt to sound casual makes my heart race even faster.

'What is it?' Freddie yells back. 'I'm kind of in the middle of something here.'

'It'll just take a minute.' Caroline averts her gaze from mine as she tells the blatant lie. We both know that the situation before us is going to demand much longer than sixty seconds to resolve.

If a resolution is even on the cards.

Freddie huffs his way into the room and stomps across to where I'm sitting.

'I'm in the middle of a perm, Caroline,' he moans. 'And you know how time-sensitive that can...' He pauses as Caroline removes the towel, his hand flying to his mouth in horror.

'I could do with a second opinion here,' Caroline tells him.

'It's definitely orange,' he states, lowering his hand to his hip. 'If that's what you're asking.'

I moan quietly.

'I think it's more amber,' Caroline interjects. 'Or possibly titian.'

Freddie tilts his head to one side. 'It could be salmon, or possibly coral,' he says reluctantly. 'At a push.'

'It's orange!' I wail. 'I'm not going to be *slinking* anywhere. I'm going to roll out of here like a giant fucking satsuma.'

This is an abject disaster. I have plans for this evening and I need to look perfect.

Caroline hurriedly throws the towel back over my head. I'm not sure whether this is an act of sensitivity or to protect her eyes from the blinding glare of my clementine locks.

'I'm not going to let that happen,' she promises. 'We have options.'

'Like shaving it all off,' mutters Freddie. 'Or possibly a wig.'

'You're not helping.' Caroline glares at him. 'Do you reckon I can go again with the peroxide?'

Freddie steps forward and tugs a piece of my hair out from under the towel, rubbing it between his fingers and staring at it critically. I hold my breath.

'Possibly,' he says, after several long seconds. 'If you proceed with caution and check every few minutes for breakage.' He drops my hair and gives me a firm look in the mirror. 'There's a chance that your hair could all snap off if we leave the bleach on for too long. Is that a risk you're willing to take? Because my advice is to leave it a few weeks to recover and then try again.'

Stay like this for a few weeks? The man doesn't have a clue.

'Absolutely,' I tell him. 'Just get rid of the orange.'

He shrugs. 'On your head be it.'

Obviously, *Freddie*. That's the entire problem. I'd be

enjoying this whole drama quite a lot more if it were someone else's head that had just turned into the main attraction from *James and the Giant Peach*.

'I'll just go and mix up some more bleach,' Caroline tells me. 'Can I get you anything? Tea? Coffee? Valium?'

'Maybe a hat, if this next lot of bleach doesn't do the trick?' I joke weakly. She smiles and heads off to the back room and I am left wondering if the offer of antidepressants was genuine and if so, whether they might possibly take the edge off.

Once the bleach is back on (and I'm sure that by now she's just pouring Domestos onto my scalp) I sit for another forty-five minutes, trying to distract myself in the world of footballers' wives and Instagram scandals and celebrity weddings – but nothing can prevent me from growing increasingly freaked out about what is occurring on top of my head. The minutes tick by, punctuated by Caroline frequently coming over to unwrap the tin foil that is covering my hair and checking that it hasn't all splintered into tiny fragments. I scrutinise her face each time, trying to gain information but her poker face is highly professional and she's giving nothing away.

Finally, after what feels like forever, I am led across to the basin for a second time and the bleach is washed out. There is no relaxing head massage or chitchat this time. Caroline is all business. Once my hair is clean, we repeat the walk of doom back to the chair and I clench my teeth as she removes the towel.

It's only hair, I tell myself. *Nobody died. Get a grip and stop being so bloody self-centred. Tonight's liaison can still go ahead. You'll just have to wear a sexy headpiece.*

'That's definitely not orange!' Caroline's voice is light with relief. 'And it hasn't all fallen out, either!'

'Thank Christ for that!' I exclaim, staring at my reflection.

It's not only hair, *actually*. It's my identity and I'm already feeling a bit weird about not being brunette anymore. If that makes me self-absorbed and vain then so be it.

Caroline starts talking about toner and how it might take a few more appointments for my hair to be properly silver but I'm not really listening. Instead, I'm gazing at the person in front of me. She looks like someone who makes choices instead of accepting her lot in life. She looks like someone who invests time and energy in herself instead of giving it all to everyone else. She looks like she could kick some ass.

She looks like Twinky Malone. My transformation is complete.

It's another hour before I can leave the salon. My hair has been toned and conditioned and trimmed and I have handed over an extortionate amount of cash to Caroline, alongside proclamations of gratitude for her perseverance and skill.

But when I step outside into the busy street, I do not merely walk. I do not button up my sensible waterproof and bow my head against the driving rain like I would normally do, nor do I sprint for the cover of the car. Instead, I remember the YouTube clip that I managed to watch thirty seconds of last night before Scarlet walked in and I had to quickly minimise the screen and pretend that I was watching *Bake-Off*.

And then I slink my way down the High Street, effortlessly weaving my way in between bin bags and puddles and one very irresponsibly left pile of dog shit, like the carefree, sensual being that I now am.

Chapter Eighteen

'What have you done to your hair?' Scarlet stares at me as I stumble into the kitchen. My carefree sensuality lasted for all of two minutes before I remembered that there was no food in the house and that unless I wanted the kids to starve to death while I was out tonight then I was going to have to visit the supermarket. I did attempt to maintain some element of sexy but it's surprisingly tricky to slink when pushing a shopping trolley with a wonky wheel. Plus, I spent at least five minutes lurking around the book section, waiting to see if anyone was going to pick up *More Than Sex* and slinking is not necessarily synonymous with discreet behavior.

'Do you like it?' I ask, dumping the bags on the kitchen counter and looking at her apprehensively. I am feeling surprisingly vulnerable and I'm not sure that I can handle teenage brutality right now.

Scarlet wrinkles up her nose and walks around me, scrutinising my new look from every angle. I hold my breath and tell myself that I do not need her approval to validate myself.

'I love it,' she declares once she's completed her circuit. 'It's actually very empowering that you've decided to embrace the grey, Mum. I reckon if I inherit your genetics then I'm not going to bother dying it. You're totally on-trend.'

'It's silver, not grey,' I correct, but in my head I am whooping with joy.

Oh. My. God. Not only am I a sex vixen, I'm also an inspiration to the younger generation. I'll probably get asked to contribute to one of those thought-provoking books where powerful women write letters to their daughters or their sixteen-year-old selves. My letter will touch on the importance of self-belief and refusal to conform to societal expectations and also a word of advice about not waiting until you are in the fifth decade of life to embrace your true identity.

I am lost in the depths of my own self-awareness when Benji barrels into the room and screeches to a halt in front of me.

'It *is* you!' he says triumphantly. 'I knew it!'

'You're a genius,' deadpans Scarlet, walking across to the fridge. 'I am truly blessed to have such an Einstein for a brother.

'I was looking out of my window, seeing if I could spot any *suspicious goings-on*,' Benji continues, ignoring Scarlet. He's been obsessed with *suspicious goings-on* ever since he saw an old episode of *Sherlock*. To begin with I encouraged him, mostly because I thought him doing anything that used his brain could only be a good thing but I've got to be honest, it's wearing pretty thin now. The last thing I need is yet another skeptical, questioning child in this house, not when I'm attempting to conceal an entire identity from my offspring. And I'm seriously regretting buying him that ridiculous deerstalker hat.

'*Anyway*,' Benji says loudly, 'then I saw a woman walking down our garden path. At first I thought that it was Granny because the woman had exactly the same hair as Granny but then I looked again.'

'Words are coming out of your mouth but you're literally not saying anything.' Scarlet pulls the carton of orange juice out and turns to glare at Benji. 'Why are you still talking?'

I would tell her to stop being so unkind if I weren't reeling from the deathblow that my youngest child has just delivered. *My hair looks like my mother's? Is he fucking serious?*

'And then I realised that when Granny walks she always looks a bit like she's dancing but this woman was staggering so it couldn't be her.'

The knife plunges a bit deeper.

I was staggering under the weight of three bags of shopping, you ungrateful little—

'And then I noticed that the woman was wearing your coat so I deduced that it must be you, wearing a wig. Is that a wig?' Benji beams, clearly proud of his detective skills.

'It's not a wig,' I say brightly, plastering a massive smile across my face in an attempt to hide my inner agony. 'It's my new hair and I'm very pleased with it.'

'Oh.' Benji grabs an apple from the fruit bowl. 'You don't look like you anymore though. Did you know that?'

'That was kind of the entire point,' I say, through gritted teeth. 'It's good to have a change every now and then.'

'I suppose so.' He takes a big bite and munches loudly. 'I don't know if I want you to change though.'

The knife twists in my heart. Of course he doesn't want me to change. I'm his mum and I'm not supposed to do anything new. I get that. The unspoken agreement is that our children grow and develop and learn and make mistakes and then go off and have adventures. We have to stay exactly where they left us, ready to be there when they next require our attention. That's the deal. I'm messing with the rules by trying to mix things up a bit.

It *is* only a change of hair colour, though. I'm not exactly staging a parenting revolution over here. Not tonight, anyway.

'It might take a bit of time to get used to it.' I step forward and pull him in for a hug. 'I kept giving myself a shock when I was driving home. I thought there was a strange woman sitting in the back of the car every time I looked in the rear-view mirror.'

'Well, this is fascinating and all,' drawls Scarlet. 'But I'm going to have to love you and leave you.'

I shake my head and block her exit from the kitchen.

'You're clearly forgetting our arrangement,' I tell her. 'You're babysitting tonight because I'm going out and Dad isn't going to be home until late.'

Oh yes, I'm going out. I'm going out to find me some sexy time and I won't be home until my mission is a success.

The voice in my head sometimes makes me cringe.

Scarlet scowls. 'What arrangement? Are you paying me?'

I nod firmly. 'Yes, of course and it's double-bubble this evening. Not only do you get all of your food and lodgings absolutely for free but I won't be charging you for the endless love and affection that I show you on a daily basis.'

I smile sweetly at her and she rolls her eyes.

'You're hilarious,' she says. 'Have you at least bought us anything to eat because the cupboards are as bare as Mother Hubbard's? Dogger is the only one in this house who's actually got any food.'

It gives me a warm swell of happiness to hear her make a literary reference and I make a mental note to discuss the possibility of her applying for an English degree at university next year.

'There's pizza,' I tell her, pointing at my abandoned shopping. 'Don't worry, you won't have to eat dog kibble tonight.'

'It's not that bad,' Benji tells us as we start to unpack the bags. 'It's like eating crunchy cereal that tastes like marmite.'

'You're an animal,' Scarlet tells him, in between some dramatic fake retching. 'You're actually disgusting.'

'You should try it.' Benji is unperturbed. 'It's better than that chicken toothpaste Mum bought the other week.'

'Benji!' I swivel round and stare at him. 'Tell me that you didn't use that. It's for Dogger!'

He shrugs and takes another bite of apple. 'You said that I couldn't go out on my bike until I'd cleaned my teeth,' he mumbles through masticated apple. 'And I couldn't find any toothpaste in the bathroom so I thought I'd use that instead.'

I put two tins of baked beans onto the shelf and then close the door, contemplating whether I should be asking Google whether canine toothpaste is harmful to small boys. But then I catch sight of the time and decide that the damage is already done.

'Very inventive,' I tell him, ignoring Scarlet's howl of protest. 'But don't do it again, okay? Now, I'm going to get ready and then I'll be heading out. Benji – Scarlet is in charge so make sure that you listen to her. However, if she says anything that you're even a bit unsure about then text me. We don't want a repeat of the kitten incident.'

'Are you going to keep going on about that for the rest of my life?' Scarlet protests. 'I was nine years old!'

I turn to look at my daughter. 'Yes. Yes, you were. You were entirely old enough to know that sending your two-year-old brother out into the street to rescue a stray kitten was a bad idea, but you still did it, didn't you?'

Scarlet scowls. 'I knew he was your favourite child so you wouldn't be as mad at him,' she mutters. 'And I really wanted a kitten.'

'Darling, that's just not true,' I tell her, shaking my head. 'None of you are my favourite child. Now, please look after your brother and don't be a dictator. You do not, I repeat, DO NOT, have the authority to instigate sanctions *as you see fit*. Your Head Girl privileges have no jurisdiction in this house. Have I made myself understood?'

She nods reluctantly. 'I'm not sure what's in this for me

then,' she mutters. 'If I can't even give him a warning card or a detention every time he talks with his mouth full.'

'I bought you a bar of chocolate,' I tell her. 'And you can both have some popcorn.'

She smiles and turns towards the cupboard. 'Have a great time,' she says. 'We'll be fine.'

Sometimes, teenagers are bewilderingly easy to please. I know that I should appreciate it but it just makes me uneasy.

'By the way, have you seen my scarf?' I ask, turning back to look at Scarlet as I reach the kitchen door. 'I still haven't seen it since you *stole* it on the day we took Dylan to uni.'

'Nope.' Scarlet busies herself with the popcorn. 'I haven't seen it anywhere.'

I could challenge her but now really isn't the time so, resolving to ask her again tomorrow, I head up the stairs. Sounds of music waft towards me when I reach the top, followed by laughter. Scarlet and Benji are obviously engaged in one of their rare moments of unity which is excellent news for me because I really, really don't want to be interrupted. It would be very bad news for all of us.

Heading into my bedroom, I close the door and then pause. I'm about to do something massive. Something that I've never done before and that, in all honesty, is making me feel extremely nervous. This is a big move and I need to be absolutely sure that I can do it. It's all very well and good telling myself that it's in the name of research but surely I have to consider the ethics too? If I were a crime author then I wouldn't just go out and kill someone so that I'd have the necessary knowledge to write about it. Maybe what I'm doing isn't so very different. I've had to lie to my husband and I'm abandoning my children to an evening alone just so that I can find my inner sexy.

I feel ruthless. Because tonight isn't just about helping me to write Book Two (*I am never going to think of a title*). Sure, I want to know what Daxx's reaction would be to Bella Rose surprising him wearing unexpected attire but it's more than that.

I want this.

I need this.

Pulling the dominatrix jumpsuit out from where it is hidden at the bottom of my wardrobe, I quickly undress before I can change my mind and then hoik it and yank it and tug it until it's on. When I look in the mirror, a small gasp escapes my lips. It seems more daring now than it did in the shop and my almost-silver hair makes the black wet-look fabric seem even more aggressive.

And Cassie was right. It doesn't need a scarf.

But there's no time to dally. I have a date and he's not going to hang around if I'm late. I thrust my feet into my celebratory author shoes, feeling a momentary pang of guilt. This is definitely not what Nick envisaged when we bought them. Then I totter over to my mirror and slap on some very red lipstick that's lurking at the bottom of my make-up bag and which I have no recollection of ever buying and ring my eyes with a black kohl pencil before glancing again at the time.

I'll have to do.

I lurch downstairs clinging on to the banister for dear life and then grab a coat from the hooks in the hall.

'See you later!' I call towards the kitchen and opening the front door. 'No need to come out!'

'Mum!' The kitchen door flies open and Benji races towards me. I frantically do up the coat and then turn around, praying that Scarlet hasn't followed him. Her eyes are like lasers and there's no way that I'll get this outfit past her.

'You were just going to leave,' he says accusingly. 'You can't go without saying goodnight.'

I am a bad, bad mother.

'Of course I wasn't,' I tell him, trying to bend over to kiss his head but giving up halfway. This jumpsuit is very unforgiving. 'I was just about to come and find you.' I pat his hair and push him gently back into the kitchen. 'And I'll tuck you into bed when I get home later.'

And then, feeling like the worst kind of double agent, I leave.

The Uber that I've ordered is waiting for me outside the house. It's not a particularly long walk into town but it might as well be Timbuktu in these heels. I like the idea of arriving in real style and for one mad minute yesterday was toying with whether I could justify the cost of a rented limousine because that does seem like the kind of transport that Twinky Malone would use. Then I got a grip and thought about how much Prosecco I could buy for the cost of one hour in a stretch car. It's a lot.

Checking the registration plate, I lean towards the car and smile at the driver.

'Hi,' I say. 'Can I check your name?'

I am nothing if not street savvy.

The man behind the wheel looks across at me. 'I'm Matthew,' he says, smiling. 'Are you Hannah?'

I shake my head and grin. 'Not tonight. Tonight Matthew, I'm going to be *Twinky Malone*!'

Matthew eyes me warily. 'Then I'm not your Uber,' he tells me. 'Sorry, love.'

He puts the car into gear, forcing me to grab hold of the handle and open the door.

'No! I'm sorry!' I say, flinging myself onto the back seat. 'I am Hannah really.'

He looks at me in the rear-view mirror and frowns. 'Which is it, then? Hannah, or that other name? Because if I take you and my genuine passenger gives me a crappy rating then I'm not going to be very happy.'

'I *am* your genuine passenger,' I assure him. 'I ordered an Uber to take me into town, to that new wine bar on Bridge Street. Is that the destination that you had?'

He nods reluctantly and pulls away from the pavement. The car fills with silence and I try to focus on what I'm about to do, calming my mind in readiness for what lies ahead. The problem is that it's exceptionally difficult to find any kind of tranquility when my jumpsuit is making it almost impossible to sit in any position other than bolt upright.

I wriggle backwards in an attempt to get more comfortable but the wet-look fabric squeaks on the leather seats, making an awkward noise that could easily be mistaken for flatulence. Some people would probably deal with this situation with laughter. I do what I always do in these situations and ignore it. Unfortunately for me, the jumpsuit fabric is not playing ball and instantly emits another vaporous-sounding squeal.

'You alright back there?' calls Matthew, sounding concerned. Probably for the upholstery of his vehicle.

'I'm fine!' I trill. 'And just so you know, I'm not – you know – *passing wind.* This jumpsuit is wipe-clean which I guess is a plus when it's being used in a dominatrix scenario but doesn't make it the most practical for travel purposes!'

I glance at Matthew just in time to see him gulp.

'Not that I'm a dominatrix,' I add hurriedly. 'God, no. I couldn't be doing with all those needy men begging me to do weird stuff to them.'

My mouth has a life if its own when I get nervous.

'Right you are,' says Matthew, fixing his eyes firmly on the road ahead.

I am pathetic. I am in no way equipped for the role that I am about to play. I can't even pretend to the Uber driver that I'm someone I'm not, so how the hell am I going to fool the man that I'm about to meet?

'My husband has no idea about what I'm up to tonight,' I say, as we pull up at the traffic lights. 'And I have to confess, that's making me feel nervous.'

I turn and look out of the window. 'But then again, if we just keep doing what we've always done then we're going to get what we've always got and that's not working for me anymore. What is life without a few risks, am I right, Matthew?'

Matthew makes a non-committal noise and turns on the radio and we spend the rest of the journey in silence.

The car arrives at the wine bar and Matthew pulls over.

'Have a nice evening,' he says as I clamber squeakily out of the car. 'Don't do anything that you might regret.'

I laugh nervously. 'I intend to have as many regrets from this evening as possible,' I tell him.

And then, trying not to fall over I stumble towards the wine bar entrance, hoping that I don't bump into anyone I know. I can do this. I can walk into a public place wearing what can only be described as bondage gear because something has got to change and I am prepared to go to extreme lengths to get myself out of this rut. I'm not just doing this for me. I'm doing it for my readers too. And my marriage. And with any luck I'll have arrived first and will have time for a glass of Dutch courage.

Or maybe two glasses.

I see him before he sees me. Taking a deep breath, I shrug off my coat and hand it to the doorman. Then I slink across the room and sidle up to the bar, gesturing to the bartender to bring me a drink as I clamber onto the stool next to his. He's engrossed in his phone and doesn't notice me sitting there which is funny for the first few seconds and then quickly becomes irritating.

'What's a nice man like you doing in a seedy joint like this?' I purr in my sexiest voice, which is also a bit American for some reason, but that's fine because everyone knows that America is sexier than England, which is obviously why I've chosen it as the setting for both my books. And then, very seductively, I stroke his arm.

He jerks away in shock, flinging his hand and mobile up into the air. 'Bloody hell, my phone!'

I wait while he bends down to retrieve it, fixing my most alluring smile to my face. I can do this. I can be any woman I want to be and when this man *sees* me, his mind is going to be blown.

I keep waiting while he examines the screen and mutters not very quietly about the cost of the damage.

I wait a little longer while he checks that he can still receive his emails and that Facebook still works.

And then I get bored of waiting for him to *see* me because he's clearly forgotten that I'm even here. So I do what Twinky would do, which is to speed things up a bit.

'Can I offer you a drink?' I murmur in my American accent. 'By way of recompense?'

He turns and his face registers so many kinds of bewilderment that I can't count them all.

And I am finally *seen*.

In retrospect, I shouldn't have tried to keep it a secret. The hair was a big enough surprise, I can kind of understand that now. Coupled with the dominatrix jumpsuit and my seductive accent, which was apparently utterly convincing (I may have a future in Hollywood after all), Nick was, in his own words, completely and utterly shell-shocked by my appearance.

Which is the excuse that he is using for turning my romantic evening into a complete and utter farce.

'Where is your sense of adventure?' I wail at him as we stagger out of the wine bar three hours later.

'I was just a bit surprised, that's all,' Nick tells me for the hundredth time, raising his arm to wave at our Uber. 'I've never seen you dressed like that before.'

'Exactly!' I snap. 'And is it any wonder, when I get a reaction like that one?'

I can still hear his voice in my head, asking me *what the fuckety-fuck I was wearing.* I expect I'll be able to hear it until my dying day.

At least I'll be able to write a credible scene for Book Two now. One where Bella Rose tries to do something exciting and Daxx pisses all over her parade like the knobhead that he is.

'You look incredible, Hannah,' Nick says, grabbing hold of my arm as I stumble on an uneven paving slab. 'I've told you that many, many times over the past few hours.'

'Not enough times to wipe out your initial shitty reaction though,' I snarl as we clamber into the car. 'And I clearly don't look incredible enough for you to have a one-night stand with me despite the fact that I have humiliated and degraded myself by leaving the house dressed like a dominatrix. Hello, Matthew.'

'I thought I told you not to do anything you'd regret,' Matthew says, shooting Nick a very dirty look in the mirror. 'Is this man taking advantage of you?'

'No!' I howl. 'I went to all this effort and he isn't even

prepared to have an affair with me which is incredibly selfish of him, not to mention completely unsupportive.'

'I don't understand what it is that you want!' Nick tells me, throwing his hands in the air. 'I've said that you look amazing and as soon as I'd got over the shock of seeing you I told you that we should head straight home for a night in. And I *love* your new grey hair.'

'It's silver!' I cry, trying and failing to plug in my seatbelt. 'There is a whole world of difference between those two colours. Silver is lustrous and metallic and glamorous and grey is – well, it's old. Are you saying that I look *old*, Nick? Are you?'

'I am not saying that,' he replies calmly, leaning over and fastening my seat belt. 'I think you look gorgeous.'

'So why won't you have a one-night stand with me then?' I whimper. 'It's not fair.'

'What do you mean?' Nick asks and I can hear the frustration in his voice. 'I don't know what it is that you want, Hannah! I've been asking you all evening if we can just go home and spend some time together.'

'I think she wants to have sex with you,' calls Matthew helpfully, pulling away from the kerb. 'But you should know, mate – she's married.'

'I know she's married,' says Nick.

'It's not about sex!' I shriek at the same time. 'God, why are men so dense? I know how to have *sex*. This was about injecting some fun into our relationship. It's called fantasy, Nick. It's about the *thrill*! I was trying to spice up our marriage but I have no idea why I'm even bothering.'

'I just don't see why you'd want me to pretend to be

someone else,' Nick says, shuddering. 'I hate all that kind of stuff, Hannah – you know that.'

It's true. He's always had a distinct loathing of anything that requires acting or role-play. In retrospect, it wasn't the wisest choice of activity to choose for this evening. Especially when Nick thought he was meeting up with one of his mates from work. And I suppose it is quite sweet that he didn't even want to look at me when he thought I was another woman.

'If you want us to do something that's a bit different but that's also a thrill then we could go on that off-road driving day that I told you about,' he continues. 'Loads of people go as a couple. I think you might really enjoy it.'

I slam my hand down on the seat and glare at my husband. 'That is *not* the kind of thrill that I'm talking about and the fact that you think a *Land Rover driving day* will provide what I need speaks volumes, Nick. *Volumes!*'

He shrugs. 'Okay. How about we go out in the kayaks then? Just the two of us. We could take a picnic and go down to the coast and paddle out to a remote spot.' His eyes light up. 'Like we used to do.'

That is actually quite a nice idea.

But nice ideas are not going to help me identify my inner Sex Goddess and they're not going to address the tiny issue of whether my husband is going off me, either.

'Look.' I twist in my seat, ignoring the squeaky noise. 'I want to remember what it's like to be excited. I can't write about the thrill of a liaison if I'm not experiencing it. That's what tonight was supposed to be about. The excitement of someone new. The way your heart races when they walk into the room. The intoxicating feeling of your eyes meeting and the knowledge that the adventure is only just beginning.'

I slump back into the seat.

'My heart still races when you walk into the room,' Nick tells me, reaching out for my hand. 'I don't need anyone new – and I love that we're in the middle of our adventure together and not at the start.'

I stare at him, struggling to process his words.

'I thought you might have gone off me,' I say quietly. 'You're always busy and I'm always tired and I just wanted us to reconnect.'

'I think we're *connected*,' Nick sounds confused. 'And I could never *go off* you. It's just that I thought that you might be...'

'What?' I squeeze his hand. 'You thought that I might be *what*?'

'It doesn't matter now.' He turns to stare out of the window. 'We can talk another time – when we're not both pissed.'

I don't know what that means but I do know that it doesn't sound good.

'We can talk now,' I whisper, feeling my heart starting to race. 'Nick? What is it?'

He shakes his head and then twists back round to look at me. 'It's nothing, babe. Forget I said anything. I just don't want to play stupid games and pretend that we're other people. I love *you*.'

'I love you, too,' I sniff.

'So you two are married then?' Matthew gawks at us in

the mirror. 'Crikey – I thought me and my missus had problems but you guys make us look like the Beckhams.' He pauses for a minute. 'They're still together, right?'

'Keep calling her your *missus* and you're going to have even more problems before too long,' I murmur.

We sit in silence as Matthew navigates the rainy streets. It's warm inside the car and I like sitting here with my hand tucked inside Nick's. It's as if real life is on pause for a few minutes and we can just *be*. The worries can all fade into the background.

'Here you go then,' says Matthew, pulling up outside our house. 'And good luck to the two of you. I think you're going to need it!'

Nick leaps out and I shuffle across the seat, keen to take as few steps as possible in these torturous shoes. And then he holds my arm and we walk up the garden path, lights blaring from every room in the house despite the fact that Scarlet and Benji will both be in bed by now.

Nick squeezes my hand as we reach the front door. 'We can give it another go,' he offers. 'Now that I know what you were aiming for. You can be Twinky Malone, Sex Goddess, and I can be whoever you want me to be.'

'I want you to be *you*,' I tell him, shaking my head and then stretching up to kiss him.

He kisses me back and then breathes a sigh of relief. 'Thank god for that,' he tells me, unlocking the door. 'Because I wasn't sure for a bit back there and I'm pretty shit at doing accents.'

We walk inside the silent house and I lurch across the

hallway to collapse down onto the stairs. 'God, my feet are killing me.'

I undo the straps and ease my shoes off, rubbing my sore heels with my hands. When I glance up, Nick is gazing at me with a look that makes my heart speed up.

'You've got no idea how beautiful you are, do you?' he murmurs.

'It's the dominatrix jumpsuit,' I tell him, pulling a daft face. 'What can I say? I'm gorgeous.'

He shakes his head. 'You're definitely gorgeous but not because of the outfit. It's you, Hannah.' He walks across to where I'm sitting and holds out his hand. 'It's always been you.'

He pulls me to my feet and we walk slowly up the stairs. And I know that Nick is right and that we need to talk properly. I know that the worries haven't gone for good and tomorrow they'll be waiting for me when I walk back down these very stairs, but right now, the answer to everything is that I give zero fucks.

Well, maybe not quite zero. Maybe I've got *one* left to give tonight.

Chapter Nineteen

'Can you both please hurry up?' I shout as I walk into the kitchen. 'We should have left for school ages ago.'

'I can't find my PE kit,' moans Benji. 'Have you seen it?'

I glare at him. 'Well, where did you leave it?'

He stares back at me. 'I don't know. If I knew where I'd left it then I'd be able to find it, wouldn't I?'

I narrow my eyes even further. I am not in the mood. Not this morning.

'Don't be so rude,' I tell him. 'And find your kit.'

His face wrinkles up in confusion. 'I wasn't trying to be rude. I was just telling the truth.'

'Yes, well – if you weren't being rude then you were being illogical and that's almost as bad,' I snap.

'He was actually being highly logical,' Scarlet informs me, getting up from the kitchen table. 'He *would* know where his kit was if he knew where he'd left it.'

'Don't start,' I warn her. 'And wash up your own cereal

bowl. I'm not your slave. And where did you put my scarf after you'd borrowed it? I haven't seen it anywhere.'

Scarlet shrugs. 'Maybe it's in the same place as Benji's PE kit?'

'I'll put the milk away,' says Benji enthusiastically, clearly keen to distract me. He bounds across the room to the fridge and then pulls up short. 'Hey! Why have you got your own sticker chart on here? Where's ours? That's not fair!'

I grab my bag and start to look inside, checking that I've got my wallet and diary. 'Yours has been gone for almost a week and neither of you have noticed so I think it's safe to say that it's entirely fair. Plus, I'm the only person around here who does any actual work, so why shouldn't I have my own reward chart?' I straighten up and sling my bag onto my shoulder. 'I'm leaving in two minutes, with or without you.'

'Excellent. I'll just go back to bed then,' mutters Scarlet, holding her hands up in self-defence when I shoot her a glare. 'Just joking. God – someone woke up on the wrong side of the bed this morning.'

She scurries out of the room and I exhale slowly. She's not wrong. I did wake up on the wrong side of the bed – Nick's side. I hadn't even realised that he'd left for work until my alarm went off and he was nowhere to be seen. He did text me, saying that he couldn't sleep so he'd decided to get an early start but it's done nothing to calm the swirling, aching sensation in my stomach and the growing suspicion that I am doing something wrong.

'Why have you got two gold stars on here?' asks Benji, staring at the chart. 'What did you do to get them?'

'Have you found that PE kit?' I ask, whirling to face him. 'No? Then you've now got one minute to find a solution and get yourself out to the car.' I clap my hands. 'There's no time to lose. Come on – chop, chop.'

He opens the fridge door and flings the milk inside and then dashes past me, his face a picture of panic.

'You could try looking on the upstairs landing,' I call helpfully after him. 'Where you dropped it yesterday.'

Sure, I could have told him that when he first asked. The old me would have told him, if she hadn't already picked up his kit and hung it up on his coat hook in the hall. But the new me isn't such a pushover. The new me would rather leave his bag exactly where he dropped it and if any of us had broken our necks by tripping over it and falling down the stairs, then he would have learnt a valuable life lesson about taking responsibility for his belongings.

I am a parenting guru. I should probably think about writing a book about this shit.

Two hours later I am sitting in the staffroom and my mood has not improved. I've sent Nick several texts and had perfectly pleasant if slightly brisk responses which is not where I hoped we'd be after my attempt at date night. Both of those gold stars on my reward chart were a result of our not-entirely disastrous night and I thought that we'd managed to even things out between us a little. But he's still super distracted all the time and I keep replaying the conversation we had on the way home from the wine bar.

'I thought that you might be—'

I know what he was going to say. It's totally obvious and I'm not stupid. He thinks I'm cheating on him. It makes perfect sense if you think about it. I'm spending all this time transforming myself into someone different and he's got to be wondering why. I thought I was being quite subtle about my attempts to stoke up the fires of our passion but if The Butter Churner night made him suspicious then my crack at role-play has possibly pushed him over the edge.

I hate the idea of Nick thinking that I'm having an affair and under normal circumstances I would have it out with him in a heartbeat. But it's kind of complicated and it's not like he's exactly being Mr Chatty. I just don't know what to say to him – but I do know that we both seem to be avoiding each other with the same amount of enthusiasm right now.

'Your hair is amazing, Hannah!' says Cassie, throwing herself into the chair opposite me. 'So why are you looking like someone just died?'

I give her an over-the-top, snarky fake grin. 'God, you're worse than the bloke who walked past me this morning, telling me to *"give us a smile"*. What a twat.'

Cassie holds her hands in the air, exactly like Scarlet did earlier. 'I'm sorry. I didn't mean to offend you.'

I hide a genuine smile behind my glower. I like the way it makes me feel, these domineering women bowing to my whims. Maybe the dominatrix jumpsuit is starting to rub off on me.

'So what *is* wrong with you?' Cassie asks. 'From the look on your face I'm going to guess either Miriam or Nick.'

'Nick,' I tell her. 'Or maybe me. I'm not sure. But I don't want to talk about it.'

She nods sympathetically and pulls a stack of books out of her bag, flipping over the first one and starting to slash through the page with her red pen. We aren't supposed to use red pen anymore – someone on the Senior Leadership Team decided that it's confrontational and aggressive and might upset the pupils. Instead we're supposed to use a variety of neon highlighters to indicate areas of progress and room for improvement and next steps and spelling mistakes and grammatical errors and god knows what else. It takes me longer to mark the work than it takes the class to actually do it, which can't be right if you think about it. Cassie is clearly choosing to ignore this policy in the same way that she ignores every other policy ever issued by the Senior Leadership Team. I have no idea how she gets away with it but she always does. I have come to the conclusion that she must have some serious dirt on Miriam.

We sit quietly for a few minutes but I can't stop the thoughts from whirling around inside my head. If I don't talk to someone soon then I'm going to lose the plot entirely and I can't afford to do that. I check the room for eavesdroppers and then I lower my book and look at Cassie. It's important that I present the information in as factual and unemotional way as possible. She already thinks that I'm a neurotic diva and I really need her to focus and take me seriously on this.

'I think I might be being a bit unfaithful to Nick,' I blurt out.

It certainly gets her attention.

'What are you on about?' She drops her pen and stares at me. 'Either you are or you aren't. There shouldn't be any *thinking* involved.'

I pick up my coffee and then put it back down. I can't believe that I'm actually going to say this but I'm desperately in need of some reassurance right now.

'I think that *Nick* thinks that I've gone off him or even worse, he thinks that I've gone off with someone who *isn't* him,' I say, stumbling over the words. 'And it should be the easiest thing in the world to reassure him and tell him that I would never do something like that. Because I love him more than I could ever love any other man and I only ever want him.'

'So you're not cheating on him then?' Cassie looks mildly disappointed. 'Then just tell him that.'

I shake my head. 'It isn't that simple though. I've been imagining random men as Daxx and my writing has really improved because I've been picturing them *in flagrante*.' Cassie rolls her eyes and I rush to continue. 'And it isn't just that, before you say anything. I've been having these *episodes*.'

'Episodes?' She sounds interested. 'What *episodes*?'

I glance around again and lower my voice, although there's nobody else here.

'I think of them as *sex bubbles*,' I confide in a whisper. 'And they can happen at any time. Like, I'll be in the supermarket or walking down the street and suddenly I'll just see someone and start having really sexual thoughts about them.' I lean back and look at my best friend. 'Are you appalled?'

She doesn't look appalled, to be fair. She looks slightly amused.

'Hannah – we've been here before,' she tells me, smirking. 'You're allowed to think about sex. It's not inappropriate.'

'But I'm not just thinking about sex, am I?' I point out. 'I'm thinking about sex *not* with my husband. And I read an article the other day about micro-cheating and I think that's what I'm doing.' I lean forward. 'I'm committing micro-infidelity.'

Cassie opens her mouth as if she's about to speak but no sound comes out. I've done it. I've shocked her into silence and even with everything that I've just said, I feel a hint of pride that finally, after all this time, I have managed to drop a bombshell that makes her sit up and take notice.

I make the most of the moment and ram the point home.

'I am a micro-adulterer and a sex bubble addict,' I tell her sadly.

Cassie flaps her hands in the air, in a gesture that I can only imagine is supposed to rid herself of my horrific confession. Perhaps I was wrong to confide in her? This is not reassuring me in the slightest. If I've horrified my best friend this much then maybe I've *really* gone over to the dark side. My heart starts to race and I feel my face pale. What if she thinks I'm genuinely at risk of fucking up my marriage? What if Nick leaves me and my traitorous thoughts, and I lose everything? I didn't mean to do anything wrong.

I didn't choose the sex life – the sex life chose me.

'Oh. My. God. Hannah.' Cassie's words come out in small pants and I brace myself for her disgust. 'I can't decide if you're the funniest person I know or the stupidest. Are you actually being serious right now?'

I look at her as she leans back in her chair and roars with laughter. I wait patiently while she snorts and guffaws and then finally, when she's calmed down, I answer her question.

'I am deadly serious. I can't stop thinking about sex and I think it's a problem.'

Cassie wipes the tears from her eyes and shakes her head at me.

'Okay. We're really having this conversation, then?' She sits up straight and takes a deep breath before fixing me with a firm stare. 'I'm going to ask you three questions and I want you to answer them quickly and honestly. Don't think about it – just go with your gut.'

I swallow hard. This sounds hopeful. She has a plan and I like a plan.

'Firstly, are you still in love with Nick?'

'Yes,' I tell her, feeling shocked that she even has to ask.

She nods, her face giving nothing away. 'Second question: Are you ever tempted to act on these *sex bubble* moments? And I'm just going to put it out there, Hannah – *sex bubble* is literally the most ridiculous phrase that I have ever heard.'

I scowl back at her. 'Of course not. Who do you think I

am? I'm not going to just run around fornicating with random strangers, am I?'

She can think what she bloody well likes about the phrase *sex bubble*. I think it works very well.

Cassie rolls her eyes, as if this is all a giant waste of her time. 'Thirdly, are you and Nick still having sex?'

I gulp. I'm as liberated as the next woman but I would normally draw the line at discussing my intimate sex life in the school staffroom. Nothing about this is normal though, including me.

'Yes, thank you so much for asking.' I jut my chin out defiantly and beg my cheeks not to flush with embarrassment. 'We have plenty of sex.'

'And is it exciting, fly-by-the-seat-of-your-pants sex or a quick-fumble-before-you- fall-asleep-sex,' enquires Cassie.

I pause. My answer is entirely changeable, depending on what kind of week it is. I suppose, if I was forced to choose, I would describe it as the safe, comfortable, familiar type of sex. I'm not really sure that flying by the seat of my pants would be either enjoyable or erotic, if I'm truly honest.

On the other hand…

My mind suddenly fills with an image of the fridge door, with two shiny gold stars stuck to my reward chart and it dawns on me, like some kind of sexual eureka, that I am possibly not very honest with myself quite a lot of the time.

I totally chose the sex life.

'We do okay,' I tell Cassie, trying not to smirk as memories start flooding my brain.

'So do you really think that conjuring up sexual scenes

in your head, which I might add, are in response to you writing an erotic novel, is really cause for such angst?'

'No. I suppose not,' I say, grudgingly.

She grins at me and picks up her red pen and we sit quietly for a moment as she resumes her marking.

I feel a tiny bit ridiculous now. I mean, I wasn't even that worried about it until I read that stupid article about micro-cheating. I'd never be unfaithful to Nick and we might be having a bit of a weird time right now but that's because we're stressed about money and the kids and life is relentless. And I'm sure that if he genuinely thought I was cheating on him then he'd say something.

Which means that it's all fine, which is good because I *like* my sex bubbles. They make me feel empowered. I'm glad that I don't have to stop having them.

'I suppose we all have our own guilty pleasures, don't we?' I say, picking up my now-cold coffee. 'There's nothing wrong with it.'

Cassie's head snaps back up to look at me. 'Nothing wrong except for you referring to feeling sexy as a "guilty pleasure",' she says. 'Honestly, Hannah – it's like one step forward and two steps back with you. You're allowed to own your sexuality – the word *guilty* shouldn't come into it.'

I shrug. She can say what she likes – I'm fairly sure that most other woman don't spend their days envisaging raunch-tastic sex scenes with bare-chested hunks glistening with sweat. And if Cassie had any idea of the erotic nature of my thoughts (or the contents of Book Two) then she would most certainly be referring to it as a guilty pleasure.

There's absolutely nothing innocent about it, that's for sure.

'I think you need an intervention,' she says now, putting her pen down again. 'You're speaking at Sex Con soon and you need help if you're not going to make a complete and utter plank of yourself.'

I wrinkle my nose. 'Thanks a lot, Cass. I'm completely dreading the entire thing as it is. I don't really need you making me feel more freaked out about it.'

'Well, luckily for you, I happen to know *exactly* what you need.' Cassie glances at her watch and stands up. 'There's only one solution and that's a night in with the girls.'

'Oh, I don't know,' I tell her, gathering up my pile of books and pushing back my chair. 'That sounds like a lot of effort and I'm on a deadline, you know?'

Cassie puts one arm around my shoulder as we make our way towards the staffroom door. 'No effort at all. Your house, Saturday night at seven o'clock. I'll arrange the nibbles and everyone will bring drinks. I'll sort it all, okay? All you have to do is provide the venue and turn up!'

'But who will we invite?' I ask, feeling my resolve weaken. It *would* be nice to have something to look forward to and a chilled evening at home with a couple of friends does sound quite appealing. Nick will no doubt be spending his evening in his shed anyway and it'd be nice to have some decent adult company for a change.

'I'll sort that too,' Cassie assures me. 'Do we have a deal?'

I nod. 'I suppose so. But I don't want it going on too late, alright? I really have got to do some writing on Sunday.'

Cassie winks at me. 'Trust me, Hannah!'

I absolutely do not.

Benji is waiting for me when I arrive to collect him from after-school chess club. His face is forlorn and I feel a pang of guilt for making him go before reminding myself that a) chess expands the brain and b) I have nobody to look after him on a Monday so attendance at whatever activity is on offer is a requirement, and he should therefore be grateful that it isn't litter-picking club.

'How was your day?' I ask, giving him a big smile. 'What did you get up to?'

'Nothing.' He pulls on his coat and marches out of the door ahead of me. I know that all kids give their parents this answer at the end of the school day and that it shouldn't be credited with too much thought, but when it comes to my youngest child I am always a tiny bit unsure about whether he's giving an indifferent response or if in fact he has actually done nothing all day.

It's a distinct possibility.

'Why yes, my day was fine,' I mutter as I follow him through the hallways. 'Slightly challenging, especially when I had a mini-breakdown in front of my best friend, possibly due to a hormonal imbalance – but generally fine. Thanks so much for asking.'

'Hannah?' I spin round to see that Allegra is right behind me. 'I wasn't sure if it was you for a moment. What on earth possessed you to go grey? And what was that you were saying about hormones?'

I attempt a chuckle. 'Oh, hi Allegra! No, I was talking about—' I pause, rapidly trying out rhyming words in my head. 'More scones! For the next cake sale. I think the children would love that.'

I hate myself. I don't even call them *scones* – it's a hard 'o' all the way, for me.

And my hair is fucking silver, thanks for asking.

Allegra frowns, before remembering that it gives her wrinkles and rapidly smoothing her forehead with her hand.

'Well, that's actually a very good idea, Hannah. I think an Afternoon Tea Party could be an excellent fundraiser for the school. I'll run it past the rest of the committee but you should be fine to organise it for the last week in November. That way we can use the profits to help fund the grotto for Father Christmas.'

'No, I didn't mean that I would—' I start but Allegra sees me coming and shuts me down before I can utter another word.

'And it *would* help to raise your profile after the flapjack fiasco,' she says, her voice sly. 'Which wouldn't hurt Benji, not with all the Christmas parties that are going to be coming up.'

I stare at her. Is she actually implying that my child's social life is going to be impacted by my inability to provide a plate of sugar-free flapjacks for a poxy cake sale? I open my mouth and right on cue, Benji comes hurtling back down the corridor with Auberon, Allegra's oldest child, in tow.

'Mum!' he calls. 'Auberon is having a Winter Wassail, whatever *that* is, and he said that I'm invited! Please can I go this time?'

I nod but he hasn't finished.

'Because when it was his Spring Soiree you said that I couldn't go because a) we aren't pretentious losers and b) you can't have a soiree at two o'clock in the afternoon and you'd have thought that Auberon's mum would know that seeing as she's always banging on about her year in France.'

I close my eyes for a brief second, hoping that when I open them I will have been magically teleported far, far away. But sadly, and also unsurprisingly, I am still standing in the school corridor with two eager-looking boys and one furious-looking woman.

'I didn't say that.' I'm not even convincing myself. And suddenly, I'm sick of pretending. Twinky Malone wouldn't let herself get pushed around like this. The time has come to tell it like it is.

'Okay, I totally said that but in my defence, I was talking to my husband and I was in the privacy of my own kitchen.' I face Allegra, my bravery making me reckless 'And while we're here – I *bought* those mince pies that I donated to the Winter Fayre. But I'm sure you've done exactly the same thing in your time, hey? None of us are perfect, after all!'

Allegra stares me down and I force myself to stand my ground.

'If by "*done exactly the same thing*" you mean have I said hurtful things about other parents behind their backs?'

Allegra's cold-blue eyes shoot frozen lasers at me across the corridor. 'Then no – I have not.'

She's got me there. Allegra has absolutely no problem with saying hurtful things right to your face.

'And I knew that your mince pies were shop-bought.' She hasn't finished with me yet. 'We all did. We could see the dents where you'd hit them with a rolling pin.'

I had it on good authority that the rolling pin trick would make them look more authentic. Thanks a lot, Mum.

'Look, I'm sorry,' I say as the boys run back towards the main entrance. 'I was clearly having a bit of a day when I said that about your Spring Soiree but that's no excuse. I should have made sure that Benji wasn't listening. That was terrible of me.'

Allegra narrows her eyes and I realise my mistake.

'Obviously what I meant is that I shouldn't have said it in the first place,' I correct quickly. 'If you can't say something nice then don't say anything at all, hey?'

If I never want to utter another word again for as long as I live and breathe.

Bracing myself, I await the other woman's wrath. Twinky clearly has a bit of a mean streak and I probably deserve whatever Allegra's going to throw at me. The Afternoon Tea Party is mine now, that goes without saying, but I doubt that I'll get away that lightly.

'I understand about having a bad day.'

Her voice is so quiet and her words so unexpected that it takes me a moment to process what she's just said.

'Lately I've been feeling like all my days are bad days.' She leans against the wall and looks at me with bleak eyes.

'I've been trying to put all my attention into these bloody – excuse my French – school fundraisers but some days I don't even know why I'm bothering. Nobody cares.'

'That's not true,' I say cautiously. I'm feeling very unsure about this new, vulnerable Allegra, and it seems best to keep a safe distance between us in case she suddenly remembers who she really is. 'We're all very grateful for everything that you do.'

'Grateful! Pah.' She folds her arms across her chest and glares at me. 'I don't want *gratitude*. I just want to remember how it feels to be excited about something that isn't organising a worthy playdate for Ophelia or planning some form of enriching entertainment for Auberon. My children have a better social life than me and I just thought it would be different, you know. Being an adult.'

Oh. My. Fucking. Word.

Allegra has actual blood flowing through her veins, not de-icer.

'I'm having a party on Saturday night,' I say before my brain can catch up with what my mouth is saying. 'Well, more of a get-together than a party. Just a few of us round at mine. You're very welcome to come, if you're free.'

She gives me a tight smile and I feel a warm, cosy glow flooding my stomach. This is actually perfect. I get to offer the hand of friendship and make amends for both my ever-so-slightly rash outburst and also my loud-mouthed son – who, incidentally, had better be prepared for the removal of his Xbox when we get home as a consequence for having no fucking sense – and Allegra gets to reject me and my kind offer, which will both remind her of her superiority and restore her state of equilibrium.

It's win-win for both of us.

I pull my features into their best *oh-what-a-shame* position and await her cutting dismissal. Women like Allegra do not hang out with women like me for fun. No way. She probably spends her evenings baking bread and doing enriching activities with her children before cooking a three-course-meal for her loving husband.

'I'd love to come.' By the look on her face, I suspect that it's not just me who is surprised by her reply. 'What time should I arrive?'

'Oh.' I gulp and then rearrange my face into a big smile. 'Well, the others are arriving around seven but you can come whenever. It's not a formal thing – just rock up when you're ready.'

'And is there a dress code for this gathering?' Allegra pushes herself off the wall and starts walking, forcing me either to stay where I am and ignore her or trot along beside her. I'm momentarily tempted by the former but then change my mind on the grounds that I've used up my rudeness quota for today.

'It's more of a get-together than an actual gathering and no, there's no dress code,' I assure her. 'Other than actually being clothed, that is!'

Allegra nods, like this is fair comment.

'So, I'll see you on Saturday then?' I break away from her as soon as we step outside, scanning the car park for Benji. He's over on the far side, trying to entice Auberon down from the roof of the Headteacher's car.

'Bye then,' I say. 'Come on Benji!'

I need to get my kid and get out of here.

'What shall I bring?' Allegra asks, pocketing her phone. 'For the *gathering*?'

God. I'm seriously regretting this already.

'Not a gathering,' I tell her. 'And just bring yourself.'

Benji ambles across to me and I grab his hand, pulling him towards the street where I managed to squeeze the car into one of the few available spaces.

'But I can't arrive empty-handed!' she wails, her voice floating across the car park. 'It's the height of bad manners.'

Lord, give me strength.

'So bring a bottle,' I yell back. 'Something for us all to drink.'

Then I unlock the car and bundle Benji inside, before proceeding to spend the entire drive home giving him a detailed lecture on the importance of loyalty and family allegiance and keeping your bloody mouth shut if you happen to hear your mother say something that she may prefer wasn't shared amongst the school population. And that I am more than capable of sabotaging my own life and his assistance in this matter is absolutely not required.

Chapter Twenty

'Can you please put your skateboard away?' I ask Benji, dashing past him and into the kitchen. 'They'll be here soon and I'd like the house to be reasonably tidy.'

'You need to chill, Hannah,' says Nick, not looking up from his *Land Rover* magazine. 'They won't be here for ages yet. Relax. You've got plenty of time.'

'Yeah, Mum,' echoes Scarlet, glancing up from her phone. 'You need to relax. Also, how would you feel if I started dating someone with a full facial tattoo?'

She's just trying to wind me up. I will not rise to it. I really won't.

I look at the clock and then glare back at my husband. 'They're going to be here in ten minutes,' I tell him. 'That is not *plenty of time*.'

He jerks his head up, his face a picture of alarm.

'Ten minutes? But we haven't had anything to eat yet!'

'Yeah, Mum.' Benji wanders in, his skateboard tucked

under one arm. 'I'm starving. Also, my tooth just fell out and now my other tooth is wobbly.'

I shrug my shoulders and fling open the kitchen drawer, searching for candles. 'Not my problem. I'm having a night in with some friends so you guys are going to have to fend for yourselves. Benji – Dad will help you deal with your tooth, okay?'

Nick stands up. 'I can rustle something up for me and the kids,' he says. 'But aren't we going to get in the way? And what about you? You haven't eaten anything either.'

'It's fine,' I assure him, shaking my head. 'We'll be in the living room so you three can eat in here and Cassie is bringing snacks so I'm not going to starve.'

Scarlet groans. 'God. What an *amazing* Saturday night. Eating one of Dad's *rustled-up* meals in the kitchen while a load of middle-aged women have a party in our house. It's so unfair.'

'It's not a party,' I say.

'What's wrong with my rustled-up meals?' asks Nick at the same time.

'And we're not middle-aged,' I add. 'That was uncalled for. Age is just a state of mind and I think you'll find that I have an extremely youthful outlook on life. I'm really only just beginning my journey.'

Scarlet gives me a condescending look. 'The average life expectancy for a woman is eighty-two-point-five years. So you're right, Mum. You're forty-four, which means that technically you've passed middle-age already.'

Sometimes, just sometimes, I really can't stand my children.

'Don't be so rude.' I glare at her. 'And by the way, if you're considering dating someone with a full facial tattoo then you'd better get a well-paid job because there's no way that they are going to be gainfully employed with a face covered in ink.'

I am so absolutely not middle-aged.

'I was going to get some eggs and bacon and make one of my famous omelettes,' continues Nick. 'I thought you all *liked* my omelettes.'

'I *love* your omelettes,' says Benji, loyally.

'You're such a suck-up,' mutters Scarlet. 'And actually, I'm fairly sure that I'm allergic to eggs because they always make me feel sick whenever I think about the poor little scrambled baby chick embryo. I think I'm going to become a vegan.'

Why are teenagers so determined to be so bloody depressing?

'At least being a suck-up is better than being an emotional vampire,' I tell her. 'Inhaling all the joy in life and feeding on it.'

Her mouth drops open in shock and I feel guilt rush through me.

'You did *not* just call me an emotional vampire!' she gasps. 'Mum! That is totally harsh. Are you having a mid-life crisis or something?'

The guilt disappears.

'Have a wonderful evening,' I tell them all, gathering up my candles. 'And don't worry – you won't even know that we're here.'

I've just managed to straighten up the living room, light

the candles and sort out some glasses when the doorbell rings.

'I'll get it!' I call, dashing out into the hall although there was no need to bother because I can hear Taylor Swift's latest album blaring through the closed kitchen door. I feel a momentary pang of sympathy for Nick before reminding myself that this evening is about me chilling out with some friends and that a few hours dealing with Scarlet and Benji on his own won't kill him. Age him, perhaps – but it won't kill him.

Cassie is standing on the doorstep, her arms laden with carrier bags.

'I got the snacks,' she says, proffering them towards me. 'We just need a few plates and bowls and then we're sorted.'

She goes into the living room and I race back into the kitchen.

'Don't mind me!' I say, opening one of the cupboards. 'Just sorting the snacks.'

'UNO!' yells Benji and when I look across the room, I see that the three of them are engrossed in a game of cards. I stand still for a second, enjoying the scene of domestic bliss and feeling my heart soften. They're good kids, really, and Nick is great with them. I wish that Dylan was here but at the same time, I know he's having fun at uni and that everything is as it should be.

I keep telling myself that anyway, in the hope that one of these days I'm going to start believing my own spin.

'You cheated!' screeches Scarlet, bringing me back to reality. 'That game doesn't count!'

'Have fun,' I tell them, stacking up some plates and walking back towards the door. 'And don't forget to do the washing up once you've finished eating.'

In the living room, Cassie has unloaded the bags and started opening packets. I stare at the food.

'I thought you were bringing nibbles?' I ask, watching as she stacks some fondant fancies onto a plate. 'This looks like a kids' birthday party, not a sophisticated night in with some friends.'

She laughs and opens a packet of the scampi-flavour crisps that I last remember eating in the late 1980s.

'Believe me, Hannah. Everyone is going to love this stuff. All that olives and cured meat canapé crap is totally over. White carbs are where it's at. You wait and see.'

I pop a pickled-onion flavor Monster Munch in my mouth and let it melt on my tongue. She may have a point.

'I invited a couple of mums from Benji's school but who did you invite?' I ask but before she can answer, the bell rings again.

I leave her arranging the chocolate fingers into a tower and go back into the hall to open the door to the first guests.

Who are absolutely *not* who I'm expecting to see.

'Welcome!' I say, hoping that I am successfully managing to hide my surprise from the people who are gathered on my step. 'Thanks for coming. Come in!'

I stand back and they all troop inside.

'Just hang your coats on the hooks and then head into the living room!' I call.

I have to be honest – I wouldn't have necessarily chosen to invite these *specific* people to my get-together. I mean, I've enjoyed the few chats that I've had with Isobel, the young PE teacher at school, and Mrs Knight from Home Economics is absolutely lovely, even if I haven't been able to look at her in the same way ever since we had that cringe-worthy conversation about *Fifty Shades of Grey* in the staffroom last term. But I'm not sure that we've got enough in common to spend an entire evening together. And what the hell was Cassie thinking, inviting Miss Pritchard along? She's an old lady, not to mention the Headteacher's PA. I won't be able to say anything without fear that every single word will be repeated back to Miriam first thing on Monday morning.

'It's the door on the left, Mrs Knight!' I call as I see her starting to head towards the kitchen. She turns and frowns at me.

'For goodness' sake, Hannah, call me Pru! We're not at school now, dear.'

'Hi, Hannah!' calls a voice and I turn to see Logan's mum walking up the path, with Allegra traipsing behind her. 'I love what you've done to your hair!'

'I was lucky to find Lori at the entrance to your street,' Allegra huffs. 'I'd never have found the place otherwise. I don't come to the other side of the tracks very often.'

So *that's* her name. How did I not know that? Our boys have been best friends for the last five years and I've only ever known her as Logan's mum.

'I'm so glad that you could make it,' I say to both women, smiling at Lori. 'And Allegra, I'm glad that you were prepared to brave the wilderness of this side of town!'

I live approximately twelve minutes' walk from both her

house and the primary school so how she can refer to my street as *the other side of the tracks* is beyond me.

I usher them both in and take their coats before leading them into the living room. I've already set up the small table in the corner with wine glasses and Cassie is relieving people of their bottles and lining them up on the side. I always find it interesting to see what different people have brought as offerings and so I wander over to see what delights might soon be filling my glass.

'Who brought this?' I ask, pointing at two bottles of Pinot Grigio, which have been placed next to the two that I'd already put out. 'I've got a few more of those in the fridge.'

'Lori,' answers Cassie. 'A classic, safe choice and it's already chilled. I like her.'

I nod. 'How about this?'

Cassie grins. 'That would be Miss Pritchard. Apparently it's been cluttering up her sideboard since the turn of the century because she's been waiting for an opportunity to share it with others. And luckily for us, tonight's the night!'

I look at the dusty bottle of sherry and have a sudden urge to cry.

'That's so sad,' I whisper, gazing across at where Miss Pritchard is perched on the edge of the sofa, clutching her handbag with both hands as if she thinks she's about to be mugged. 'Do you really think she hasn't been invited out in the last twenty years?'

'I don't know,' shrugs Cassie. 'But I do know that this sherry is definitely not going to have its cork popped tonight. Anyway, never mind that – look what Isobel brought. We should throw her out now.'

Young and trendy Isobel has brought a bottle of something called *Nosecco*, which on further examination proves to be non-alcoholic Prosecco.

'I didn't even know such a thing existed,' I say, reading the label.

'It shouldn't,' Cassie says, flatly. 'It's just another example of hipsters messing with something that's perfectly fine as it is.'

'I don't know,' I say, wanting to defend my younger guest. 'It does seem rather responsible. This generation definitely appears to be less prone to making the mistakes that we made at their age.'

It also seems a bit boring but I keep that opinion to myself.

Cassie mutters something unintelligible under her breath and I pick up another bottle in the hopes of distracting her.

'So who brought the whiskey?' I ask. 'That's a bit of a strange thing to bring for a night in with the girls.'

Cassie points to where Mrs Knight is settling herself down next to Miss Pritchard. 'Who do you think brought it? *Pru* is full of surprises!'

'Where would you like these?' Allegra approaches with her arms wrapped around a cardboard box.

I gawp at her as she starts to offload the contents of the box. Three bottles of gin are followed by three bottles of vermouth and then three bottles of Campari.

'That's a lot of alcohol,' I say, when all the bottles are on the table. 'You didn't need to bring so much, Allegra.'

She puts the box down and looks at me. 'But you said to bring something for everyone to drink. And I didn't know how many people would be attending your gathering so I thought it best to over-cater.' She looks worried. 'Where *is* everyone else?'

'This is everyone,' I tell her, trying to ignore the surprised expression on her face.

Cassie nods. 'Always best to over-cater in these situations, I completely agree.'

Allegra smiles gratefully at her and then turns back to me. 'I just need you to show me where you keep your ice machine and your largest cocktail shaker.'

'I don't have a *small* cocktail shaker,' I confess, 'never mind a range of differing sizes. Nor do I own an ice machine.'

Allegra stares at me as if I've just admitted to not owning a plumbed-in toilet.

'You poor thing,' she murmurs, as Cassie silently cracks up behind her. 'How do you cope?'

'Oh, we get by,' I say, as bravely as I can. 'I just use a bucket to mix my cocktails and if I have an ice-related emergency then we've got one of those little plastic ice trays in the freezer. I can get enough for a couple of glasses of gin and tonic from that.'

'You don't even have a *silicone* ice tray?' she whimpers and I swear, for one brief moment it looks like she's about to make the sign of the cross on herself.

'Anyone for wine?' interrupts Cassie, finally putting me out of my misery. 'Shall we ramp this party up a gear, Ally?'

'It's Allegra. And I was told that it's not a party,' states Allegra, recovering from my tale of woe. 'I thought it was a *gathering*.'

'Not a gathering,' I say, holding my hand out for a glass. 'And please help yourself to a fondant fancy.'

Her eyes roam to the other side of the room where a table is now groaning under a cornucopia of junk food but I am spared her opinion on the lack of low-calorie, paleo options by the doorbell ringing yet again.

'Now, I want you to stay calm,' Cassie says as she follows me out into the hall. 'I know you're a bit daunted about this whole Sex Goddess thing and so I've organised a guest to liven things up a bit and help you get your sexy vibe on.'

I freeze for a second and then spin back to face her.

'You haven't?' I hiss, conscious that my children and husband are currently playing an innocent, family card game only metres away. 'Tell me that you haven't, Cassie.'

'I haven't what?' she says, innocently.

'Organised a stripper!' I snap. 'For god's sake, Cass.'

But if she has, I wonder who I'd most like it to be? Maybe a provocative postman or a bewitching barista? Perhaps an obliging officer of the law? Or maybe, just maybe, a tantalising, teasing, tasty tree surgeon...

She laughs and shakes her head. 'Not a stripper,' she tells me. 'Just open the door, will you?'

The bell rings again and I narrow my eyes at her before

tentatively creeping towards the front door and cracking it open.

'Hello?' I say. 'Can I help you?'

'Hello, love!' trills a voice. 'Are you going to let me in? Only it's bloody freezing out here.'

I crank the door open a little further and peer in confusion at Sandra, the receptionist from the dental surgery.

'Come on in, Sandra,' booms Cassie, yanking the door out of my hand and swinging it wide open. 'Please excuse Hannah – she's had a long week.'

Sandra walks in and plonks a large suitcase down at our feet.

'I've just got to get some boxes from the car,' she says. 'Won't be a minute.'

She hurries back outside and I look at Cassie in confusion.

'What's *she* doing here? And why has she brought a suitcase?'

Cassie grins. 'Well, you know that Sandra is the receptionist at the dentist?'

I nod.

'She's also got another job. A side-hustle, if you like. Something to help bring in a bit of extra money and give her something to do in the evenings.'

I purse my lips and tip my head to one side. 'I still don't know why she's here.'

Sandra comes back into the hall and slams the front door shut behind her. 'I'll just get set up and then we're good to go.' She nods at the wine glass in my hand. 'Oh good, you've already started drinking – that should make the evening go nice and smoothly!'

Cassie picks up the suitcase and shows her into the living room.

'Can I get you anything to drink?' she asks as they walk through the door.

'No thanks, love,' replies Sandra. 'It's best if I keep a cool head.' There's a pause and then the rest of her sentence floats back to me. 'You're going to need at least one responsible adult on the premises!'

I stand very still until my best friend reappears in front of me.

'What the hell is going on?' I hiss. 'What *is* her side-hustle?'

'Okay.' Cassie pulls me away from the living room door. 'So, you know how in the Eighties, people used to have parties at home where they'd get shown a load of stuff and then have the opportunity to buy it?'

'Yes.' I nod. 'Are you telling me that you thought you'd cheer me up by throwing a Tupperware party?'

Cassie shakes her head. 'Not quite but it's the same premise. Just a bit sexier. And Sandra is going to be demonstrating kinky gadgets, not kitchen gadgets.'

I stare at her and then the penny finally drops.

'You've organised a *sex* party?' I gasp. 'In my *home*? What the hell were you thinking? Miss Pritchard is probably going to have a heart attack – she hasn't been out in twenty years and this is the last thing that she's going to be expecting.'

'I was thinking that *you* needed to have a laugh,' Cassie

retorts. 'And also that this was a great way to get you to lighten up a bit. I don't want to offend you, Hannah – but that stuff you were saying the other day about *guilty pleasures* was a bit straitlaced. I'm not sure that you're in the right place emotionally to write erotica, *or* to speak at Sex Con. It's a big deal, you know?'

I stare at her, speechless. She is voicing my every fear.

'So that's why I invited Sandra,' she continues. 'Come on. Live a little.'

'I'm not sure that I have a choice, do I?' I say snarkily. 'Not when she's currently setting up her S&M party on my living room rug.'

'That's the spirit, Hun!' Cassie takes hold of my hand and gives it a squeeze. 'And you never know, you might end up enjoying yourself.'

I strongly suspect that *fun* is the last thing I will be having but Cassie is pulling me towards the living room and I have no choice but to join her. Gritting my teeth, I brace myself for whatever horror show is about to explode in front of me.

However, all appears to be tranquil for the moment. Pru and Miss Pritchard are having what looks like a nice, normal chat while Lori and Isobel listen to Allegra witter on about something that I am thankfully too far away to hear. Sandra is kneeling on the floor, busying herself with some innocuous-looking items of clothing and the room has the gentle buzz of people who are engaged in lovely, perfectly ordinary conversation.

There is not even a whiff of sex in the air.

'See,' says Cassie, topping up my wine glass. 'Nothing to worry about.'

'If everyone would like to gather round, then we can make a start,' calls Sandra. 'I think there's enough room for you all to sit down.'

Allegra marches across to the comfy armchair and settles down as if it's her rightful throne. Cassie goes round topping up everyone's glass before squeezing next to Lori and the two older women on the sofa. I gesture Isobel towards the smaller sofa and sit next to her.

It's party time.

'Now, I'm going to break you all in gently so don't worry!' quips Sandra. 'We're going to start nice and slowly by looking at this season's top range of bedroom attire.'

She holds up a peach-coloured negligee that looks suspiciously flammable and wouldn't be out of place at a 1970s fancy dress party.

'Oh, I used to have one just like that,' sighs Pru. 'Mr Knight used to call it my "come-hither" nightie.'

I take a healthy slug of wine and pretend that I didn't hear her.

'I'm sorry, what *is* this?' says Allegra, as Sandra holds up something hideous in nylon.

'It's a babydoll nightie,' explains Sandra. 'Very sensual, as I think you'll agree. The peach tones would go wonderfully with your complexion.'

'No.' Allegra puts her drink down and stares across the room at me. 'What is *this*?'

She waves her hand expansively, taking in Sandra, the other guests, the entire room.

This shit-show is my life, Allegra, thanks for asking.

I look towards Cassie for support but she's hiding behind her wine glass. Not well enough to hide the smirk on her face though, the cow.

'We've invited Sandra here to show us her...err...her...' I stare at Sandra, willing her to wade in and help me out, and unlike my evil best friend, she actually gets the message.

'I do women-only parties, love,' she tells Allegra. 'The way it works is that I show you the lingerie and the toys and if you want to purchase anything at the end then you can. And then I give a percentage of the sales to the hostess for her to spend on any of the items that I've demonstrated.'

I do not like the sound of a demonstration.

'Did she say that she was going to be showing us some toys?' bellows Miss Pritchard, sitting forward. 'Because I don't know any small children so I might as well leave now.'

'I think they're *sex toys*,' shouts Pru. 'From what I can gather, anyway.'

'Oh, sex toys,' says Miss Pritchard, settling back into her seat and finally relinquishing her hold on her handbag. 'Lovely.'

Allegra glares at me and Cassie splutters some of her wine back into the glass.

'I'm going to kill you,' I silently mouth at her.

Sandra holds up another pastel-coloured item of nightwear in a strange fabric and we all make polite, appreciative noises. The atmosphere in the room is stilted and it is this more than anything else that makes me get up and start creeping round, filling up everyone's glasses again.

'Oh, no thanks,' whispers Isobel when I reach her. 'I'll stick to the Nosecco.'

I smile and nod because of course I respect her right to make her own decisions when it comes to drinking but good god, if ever an occasion called for alcohol then it has absolutely got to be this one.

Sandra carries on for a few more minutes and then puts the last piece of lingerie back in the bag and claps her hands.

'Right then – it's time for an icebreaker game! Drink up ladies and get ready to use your brains!'

'Not much call for an icebreaker in a house without an ice machine,' mutters Allegra, swigging from her glass.

'No, but it might thaw *you* out a bit,' I mutter back, too quietly for her to hear me but loud enough to make Isobel giggle.

Sandra walks around the room, handing us all a piece of paper and a pen. Her organization skills are very impressive and I wonder if she's ever considered a career change. She'd make an excellent teacher.

'Okay. This is a really fun game called Sex Bingo and it goes like this.' She stands in front of us all and beams. 'Each of you need to write down every single sexual position that you have ever heard of on your piece of paper. Then I'll call out names and if you've written that position on your paper you can tick it off. The person with the highest score at the end wins a prize. And not just *any* prize – it's a gift that keeps on giving. You could say it's the prize of a lifetime, in fact!'

I look across at where Miss Pritchard is sitting and something inside me dies a bit. For this innocent old woman, who hasn't been out in over two decades, to be subjected to such depravity in *my* home is almost too much to bear. I doubt she's ever had a sexual relationship, let alone experimented with wacky positions. Cassie has gone too far this time and I'm going to have to do something about it.

'You've got five minutes to write them all down,' calls Sandra. 'Your time starts now!'

I blink my eyes and try to focus. Perhaps I'll just take Miss Pritchard into the kitchen and ask Nick to drive her home. I'm sure he wouldn't mind too much. Yes, that's definitely the solution. She should go now before any more damage is done.

'Miss Pritchard?' I call softly. 'Can I have a word, please?'

'Think of your *own* words,' she barks, hunching over her piece of paper. 'I want that prize.'

It's only now that I see her hand, scribbling like lightning across the paper. Next to her, Pru is writing with equally alarming speed. In fact, when I glance around the room, everyone is deeply engrossed in the task and it seems to be only me who has a blank page.

'Can I just clarify?' asks Pru, pausing for a second. 'Does it have to be positions that we've personally experienced or just ones that we've heard of?'

'Ooh, let's see,' laughs Sandra. 'I think it's more fun if

we say that you can only write down words that you are intimately familiar with, if you catch my drift.'

There is a murmur of approval from my assorted guests and the scratching sound of pens on paper intensifies. Fine. Nobody can say that I didn't try. If Miss Pritchard ends up traumatised by tonight's goings-on then that's on her. This is *my* sex party and I'm damned if I'm going to let someone else walk away with the prize of a lifetime.

Chapter Twenty-One

For a few minutes the room is silent other than the occasional gasp of pleasure when someone remembers another sexual position. I wonder briefly about what memories are being relived amongst my guests and then realise that unless I want to come last, I'm going to have to think of a few X-rated names of my own. Obviously, I've got The Butter Churner, but I'm going to have to do better than that if I want to win. Casting my mind back, I think about the ill-fated evening several months ago when Nick and I were researching for *More Than Sex* and trying out a variety of sexual positions. Despite the fact that there is little to no hotness attached to the awkward memory I can still remember some of the positions, and I scrawl them down.

After a while, Sandra puts her hand up and tells us all to stop writing.

'Now, no cheating,' she warns us, looking sternly around the assembled women. 'If I say a word and you've written it down then you may tick it off your list. But I *will* be checking and if there's any funny business then you will forfeit the prize of a lifetime.'

We all mumble our assent and she starts to reel off a list of sexual positions.

'Missionary,' she begins and most people put a mark on their sheet.

'How did I forget that one?' moans Cassie.

'It's understandable,' Pru reassures her. 'It's not my favourite position either on account of the fact that it's incredibly difficult for a woman to—'

'Cowgirl!' calls Sandra with impeccable timing. 'Spork!'

'What did she say?' asks Miss Pritchard.

'She said *Spork*!' shouts Pru. 'And no – I have no idea what that is either. Now turn your bloody hearing aid on.'

'It's an eating utensil that is both a spoon and a fork,' Allegra informs them, her tone slightly too patronising for my liking. 'Hence the word *spork*.'

'I don't know what that's got to do with sex,' huffs Pru and I see Allegra open her mouth before rapidly clamping it shut again. I don't know why she's still here, to be honest. She is clearly hating every single moment and I can't even begin to think about how this is going to impact on my reputation with the PTA.

'The Wheelbarrow!' announces Sandra and I wince, remembering our disastrous attempt to reenact that position.

'Not with my gammy knee,' states Miss Pritchard, having obviously complied with Pru's instructions.

I catch Cassie's eye across the room and have to look away before I lose it completely. This evening is turning out to be far weirder than anything I could ever write in a book.

Sandra rattles off a whole load more names and then asks us to tot up our scores.

'There are fifteen points up for grabs,' she tells us. 'So who has got more than four?'

Everyone except Isobel raises their hand, which gives me a moment of smug satisfaction. I *knew* that being youthful and gorgeous and trendy wasn't as great as people make it out to be. Although I would have thought she'd have done a bit better considering it was her who leant me the *Fifty Shades* books in the first place. She must have picked up a *few* things, surely?

'Never mind,' I whisper. 'I expect the prize isn't that great.'

'Ooh, you're a saucy lot, aren't you?' teases Sandra. 'Okay – how about anyone that got more than seven.'

I put my hand down along with Pru and Lori. We give each other sympathetic looks and then I take in the remaining contenders. I'd have voted on Cassie being in the top three but never in a million years would I have predicted the other two.

'More than ten?' asks Sandra and Cassie puts her hand down.

The tension in the room is suddenly palpable as Allegra fixes her rival with a look that is pure competitiveness.

'More than twelve?' ventures Sandra and Miss Pritchard sighs and lowers her hand.

'Never mind, dear,' says Pru, patting her hand. 'You did very well to come second.'

'Story of my life, love,' quips Miss Pritchard. 'Story of my life.'

I snort so hard that half of my wine flies back out through my nose.

'I'll just need to verify your score, Ally,' Sandra says, as if this is some kind of Olympic event.

'It's *Allegra*, actually,' the other woman informs her, in a slightly haughty voice.

'Maybe you should ask for a urine sample too?' suggests Cassie but Sandra is too involved in checking the authenticity of Allegra's list to respond. After a few, tense moments she raises her head and smiles.

'We have a winner!' she declares and we all cheer.

'All hail Allegra, Queen of Sex!' whoops Lori and we raise our glasses to an extremely embarrassed-looking Allegra.

'I hardly think that I deserve that title,' she protests.

I agree. This is my sex party and if anyone in this room is being crowned Sex Queen that it should be me.

'As promised, here is your prize of a lifetime,' Sandra says, handing Allegra a discreet box.

Allegra takes it and glances down at the item in her hand.

'Oh, I'm not sure that I—'

'What is it?' yells Cassie, even though I'm fairly sure that she's thoroughly aware of the contents. 'Come on! Tell us what you've won!'

Allegra shuffles the box from one hand to the other as if it's a hot potato. 'Well, I don't think that I—'

'It's a mini vibrator,' declares Sandra proudly. 'It's one of our bestselling products, actually. And don't let the size put you off. This little beauty can go for hours and hours without stopping and it never asks for anything in return except a few fresh batteries from time to time.'

'Don't you want it then?' asks Miss Pritchard, fixing her beady gaze on Allegra's flushed face. 'Because I came second and I'd be happy to take it off your hands.'

'It's fine, thank you,' says Allegra and we all watch as she rapidly stuffs the box into her handbag. 'I'm happy to take it.'

'You know you are!' crows Cassie and the room erupts in an explosion of laughter.

Allegra freezes for one second and then her shoulders slump forward and her head drops. I stop sniggering and the room goes quiet again. I feel awful for the second time this evening. Allegra is a pain but she doesn't deserve to feel humiliated and we shouldn't be amused at her expense. Not everyone is as liberated as I am or thinks like I do – I doubt Allegra has ever had a *sex bubble* incident in her entire life. She's far too uptight for that kind of thing.

Her shoulders start to shake and then her head whips up and a burst of laughter tears itself from her immaculately made-up lips.

'At least it isn't going to demand that I go along to its stupid football matches!' she stammers. 'Or ask me to collect its dry-cleaning or listen to it droning on about interest rates and mortgage deals. And it might actually come in quite handy next time Derek is out and I have a Keanu Reeves movie marathon, if you know what I mean...'

From the cackling that fills my living room, it is quite obvious that we are all fully apprised of exactly what she means. It is also becoming increasingly clear that I may have made a few incorrect assumptions about the women here this evening.

She makes a buzzing sound and starts laughing again and the evening kind of descends from there. Or ascends, depending on your viewpoint.

Sandra clearly knows how to work the room and when she suggests that we mix some cocktails, the response is overwhelmingly positive.

'I'll do it!' yells Allegra. 'I can mix an incredible Negroni.'

'What about the ice situation?' I remind her. 'We've already ascertained that I am sadly lacking in that department.'

'Sod the ice!' she screeches. 'Now grab that bucket!'

I stand and weave my way rather unsteadily out of the room and into the kitchen.

'Where's our bucket?' I ask Nick. 'Hi, kids – are you having a nice evening with Dad?'

'You're being very loud,' Benji tells me. 'It sounds like a good party. Can I join in?'

'No!' chorus Nick and I at the same time.

'It's no place for a man,' Nick tells him. 'In fact, I think we should probably all go upstairs now. It's safer.'

'I didn't know that you were friends with Sandra from the dentist,' says Scarlet, staring at me quizzically.

'I'm not,' I tell her. 'Nick – the bucket?'

'So why is she here then?' persists Scarlet. 'I saw her arriving.'

'Did you see anything else?' I round on her, my eyes flashing. 'Did you? What did you see?'

Scarlet puts her hands up. 'Chill out, Mum. I didn't see anything.'

I stare at her suspiciously but her face looks innocent enough – which would definitely not be the case if she had the slightest inkling of what was going down in our living room.

Nick has moved across to the sink and is pulling something out from the cupboard underneath.

'Did you mean this bucket?' he asks, waving it in the air. 'Is there a problem?'

'No problem,' I say, taking it from him. 'Thanks.'

'Does someone feel sick?' asks Benji. 'That's the bucket you always give me when I'm poorly.'

'Everyone is fine,' I assure him.

'Is the living room radiator leaking again?' asks Nick, frowning. 'Because you're on your own if it is – there's no way I'm going in there to sort it out.'

For fuck's sake. I come in here for two seconds and get my buzz well and truly killed.

'There is nothing wrong,' I tell him. 'We're making industrial amounts of cocktails and as I sadly do not possess a cocktail shaker then I am going to have to take this bucket.'

'The *sick* bucket?' clarifies Scarlet. 'That is disgusting, Mother.'

'At least they'll have something to throw up into when they've drunk the contents,' mutters Nick. 'So that's one benefit.'

'It's not the sick bucket,' I snap, although I do give it a quick rinse under the tap with some cold water, just to be on the safe side. 'Nobody has ever actually been sick into it.'

'I was.' Benji sounds proud. 'Last year when *you* said that I was fine but *I* said that I was ill and then *you* said that I was just trying to get out of school and then *I* was sick in the bucket and *you* had to say sorry.'

'That doesn't count,' I tell him. 'You weren't *that* ill.'

'Gross,' moans Scarlet. 'You're totally going to end up in A&E.'

'Alcohol kills germs,' I say sweetly, shaking the last few drops of water out and turning back to the door. 'But thank you for your concern.'

'Just take it easy, Hannah,' says Nick as I reach for the handle. 'And call me if you need me.'

I turn to look at him, my gorgeous, kind-hearted husband. His face is lined with exhaustion and yet he's right here, making sure that I'm okay. I don't know how I could ever have doubted what we have together and whatever it is that's going wrong between us, we'll sort it out. We always do.

'I will always need you,' I tell him, dashing back to land a quick kiss on his lips. 'But right now I have one piece of advice. Stay away. When you leave the safety of the kitchen you need to walk briskly through the hall and do not look back. And no matter *what* happens, Nick – do NOT go into the living room.'

I open the kitchen door and a wave of raucous laughter barrels through. Nick gulps.

'What are they laughing at?' asks Benji.

Nick puts his hand on our son's arm. 'Better that we never discover the answer to that question. Now get anything you think you might need and let's go upstairs. We can barricade the bedroom doors if necessary.'

Scarlet rolls her eyes but I see her glance nervously towards the open door, her face uneasy. I'm glad to see that she has some survival instincts. She may be female but she is in no way ready for what is happening in that room. I was wrong to have concerns about Pru and Miss Pritchard – if anyone is at risk tonight then it's Isobel, with her fresh-faced enthusiasm and naivety. She's clearly still at the starting point of her sexual journey, although I have a sneaking suspicion that if she sticks around, tonight might be an eye-opening experience.

Giving a cheery wave to my family, I head into the hall and back into the carnage with Dogger at my heels. Allegra whips the bucket out of my hand the instant that I step over the threshold and starts enthusiastically opening bottles while Lori hovers next to her, sharing her own opinions on the perfect way to mix a Negroni.

Cassie walks over to me and thrusts my wine glass into my hand.

'Drink this,' she instructs. 'While we wait for Allegra to create her magic.'

I take a hearty swig and then experience a two-second

debate about whether to swallow the burning liquid or spit it back.

Swallowing wins out, like the professional that I am.

'Uh. What is this?' I brandish my glass at Cassie. 'It's foul.'

'It's Miss Pritchard's twenty-year-old sherry,' she tells me. 'We're toasting her coming second so it seemed appropriate.'

'It's stale,' I say, taking another more tentative sip. 'It tastes like mothballs.'

'Like I said, it seemed appropriate,' repeats Cassie. 'Drink it all – Allegra is ready to cock you up.'

'Seriously?' I splutter, wondering if I can pour the rest of the sherry into a nearby pot-plant before remembering that this is *my* house and I actually don't have any plants because I've killed them all. 'Did you really just say that?'

'What's that you're talking about?' asks Miss Pritchard, walking up to us and thrusting out her glass. 'Have you organised some gentlemen to join us?'

'No, Miss Pritchard,' I tell her, directing her to where Allegra is waiting with the bucket. 'But you can have a delicious cocktail if you'd like one?'

Her face falls. 'Well, if that's the only thing on offer then I suppose it will have to do. But are you sure that there are no men on the premises, dear?'

A movement catches my attention and I turn, just in time to see my terrified husband scurrying past the door. For a brief, evil second I'm tempted to drag him in here to say hello – but then I come to my senses. He wouldn't last two minutes in this room.

'No men,' I tell her.

'No men needed!' calls Sandra from the front of the room. 'That's my motto. Now get your drinks and let's get this party started!'

Everyone starts to settle back down but something has shifted in the atmosphere and the seating arrangements have changed. Allegra sprawls casually in between Pru and Miss Pritchard on the sofa while Cassie and Lori sit on the floor, closer to the action.

'Hannah?' Isobel's voice is quiet and when I look at her anxious face, I know exactly what she's going to say.

'Of course you should go,' I tell her. 'I'm sorry that I didn't warn you what it was going to be like – I had no idea that Cassie was planning this. Thanks so much for coming though.'

Isobel blinks. 'I don't want to leave. I just wondered if I could possibly have some of that cocktail?'

She holds out her glass and a sudden image of my daughter pops into my head.

'You do know that it's quite alcoholic, don't you?' I say, as gently as I can while still being heard over the noise being made by the rest of the room. 'Maybe you should stick to the Nosecco?'

'The Nosecco is shit,' she says. 'I need a proper drink.'

And while a tiny part of me feels that I should be advising her on the importance of responsible drinking and explaining that alcohol is not required for one to have fun, a larger part of me is cocking up her glass with huge enthusiasm.

'Cheers!' she says, taking a swig.

We clash our glasses together and grin and I relish this moment of connection. It's not about the drink. It's about *female solidarity* and *living for now* and *reveling in our womanly bond.*

And it's a bit about the drink, yeah.

'So we're going to start with what I like to call, the risqué attire,' says Sandra, once we're all gathered around.

Allegra was right. This *is* a gathering. Arse it.

She holds up a black, lacy item and we all stare.

'It's faulty,' states Miss Pritchard.

'That's the problem with clothing today,' agrees Pru. 'It's all badly made tat. This *whatever-it-is* was probably made in a sweatshop by small children who get paid tuppence, at the end of the day. It's criminal, it really is.'

'It isn't faulty,' soothes Sandra. 'And I can assure you that it wasn't made by small children. We have a very strict policy when it comes to treating our workers fairly.'

'It's got two holes in it,' points out Lori.

'They're for your nipples,' says Cassie. 'It's the style.'

The room goes quiet as we all contemplate the item before us.

'Is it for breastfeeding mothers?' enquires Pru. 'Because I suppose it could be quite practical.'

Sandra's face goes a funny colour. 'It's not supposed to be *practical*,' she says. 'It's supposed to be *provocative*.'

'How do they know where your nipples are, though?' I muse. 'I mean, there's quite a large surface area of possibility. It's like those face-in-the-hole photo boards that you get at the seaside. If you're not the right height then your face won't match up to the hole.'

'You make a good point,' says Cassie. 'I reckon my nipples are way higher than yours.'

Bitch, I mouth at her, smiling contentedly when she chokes on her drink.

'Well, maybe the peephole camisole isn't for you then,' says Sandra, valiantly ploughing on. 'But what about this little beauty?'

She holds up a pair of cute, black, lace knickers and we all make an *oohing* sound.

'Now they're nice,' says Allegra. 'Very tasteful.'

'They're on offer right now,' says Sandra, sounding pleased. 'Buy one, get the second pair half price.'

'Well, you can definitely put me down for two pairs of those,' I say. I know that it was Cassie who arranged this whole evening but I *am* the hostess and I feel like it's probably my responsibility to ensure that Sandra actually makes some money. If I order something then perhaps the others will follow my lead.

Plus, the knickers really are lovely.

'Me too,' says Allegra and I smile at her gratefully.

'Fantastic!' Sandra beams. 'I think you ladies are going to love the sheer lace paneling and the playful open crotch!'

'The playful open *what* now?' I ask, my mouth dropping as she demonstrates the gigantic void where the crotch should be. Dogger gives a small whine and slinks out of the room, which is probably for the best. I don't want her being subjected to anything inappropriate and it would appear that shit is about to get real.

'Is that in case you need a wee and you're in a hurry?' booms Miss Pritchard.

'But why?' I whisper. 'What earthly reason would I have for letting it all hang out?'

Cassie raises an eyebrow at me. 'Come off it, Hannah. You're not that sweet and innocent.'

I shake my head. 'I just fail to see the appeal. And what if you need to use a sanitary towel? It'd just fall straight through the hole.'

The room falls quiet as we all contemplate this conundrum.

'The younger generation love them,' says Sandra, her voice wheedling. 'They see this kind of underwear as an opportunity to show off their grooming. They're all waxed and stripped and neat nowadays.'

Cassie scowls. 'What a bloody waste of time and energy.'

'It's true though, isn't it?' says Allegra. 'I saw a documentary on it. All the teenagers have access to all the porn and so they think that's what real bodies look like.'

'I hope *you're* not going to buy into this crap, Hannah,' says Cassie, narrowing her eyes at me. 'Porn should be real. It should be hairy and messy and awkward.'

'I totally agree,' I say quickly, hoping that nobody questions her reference. 'Who has time to wax down there? I can barely be bothered with shaving my legs.'

'I hate the idea of my kids seeing anything like that,' adds Allegra 'We should just ban porn altogether.'

The room explodes in a riot of noise but I sit back, unwilling to engage in what feels like very dangerous territory. I know that I have nothing to be ashamed about but the fear of being identified as Twinky Malone silences me.

'You can't just get rid of porn!' yells Cassie. 'And we shouldn't want to. That's like saying we should get rid of sex.'

'I don't think porn itself is the problem,' agrees Lori. 'It's more the message that it chooses to send.'

'What we need is *real* porn,' shouts Isobel suddenly, making me jump. 'Porn that shows it's okay if you don't know what you're doing and that doesn't objectify women as sexual commodities. We should have porn that shows women having orgasms and men listening to advice about what works and what doesn't work.'

'But would anyone actually watch that?' ventures Allegra.

'I would!' screeches Cassie.

'I would absolutely watch it!' confirms Pru.

'And me!' I yell. 'Real porn with all the sex.' I punch my fist in the air. 'So. Much. Sex.'

Twinky Malone is apparently not prepared to stay silent.

'Lovely, furry, bushy, shaggy porn!' calls Lori. 'With genuine people showing realistic scenarios.'

'We should *do* it,' says Cassie and the volume dials down a few notches. 'We should make our own Porn Production Company. By women, for women.' She looks across at me and lifts one eyebrow. 'We've totally got the skills covered between us. Hannah is an excellent writer.'

'Oh, do you dabble in writing too?' asks Allegra, sitting up and staring at me. 'What kind of thing?'

Actually, Allegra, I have written an erotic novel and in fact, the entire purpose of this evening is to connect me with my inner Sex Goddess because I'm struggling to remember that I am more than just a mum and that I do actually exist as a passionate, seductive temptress even if it is a bit tricky to identify with the sensual me when I'm up to my eyeballs dealing with life.

'A bit of this, a bit of that,' I say, waving my hand dismissively and taking another big sip of my drink. 'So Cassie, what skills are you going to be bringing to this venture?'

She grins wickedly at me. 'I'll be the advisor. You know, for the sex scenes. I doubt that there's an awkward sexual encounter that I haven't experienced. I'm perfect for the role.'

'I'm very good at organising things,' contributes Allegra.

'It's true,' I nod. 'She is.'

'I have a wonderful eye for costume,' says Pru. 'You know, if we wanted to include bondage scenes?'

'I could help with that,' offers Lori. 'I'm pretty handy with a sewing machine and it'd be a nice change to make something that wasn't for bloody World Book Day.'

'So that's almost everything sorted,' I say, waving my glass in the air. 'We'll just need someone to make a website and do the filming. You're young, Isobel – I bet you could do that!'

Isobel nods and gets up to refill her glass. 'I've just got a new iPhone and the recording facilities are exceptional. I could totally do that. And making a website would be easy.'

Cassie claps her hands in excitement. 'So that's everything covered,' she says. 'What shall we call our production company?'

'Excuse me,' sniffs Miss Pritchard. 'But I rather think you're forgetting someone.'

'Oh, I'm sor—' starts Cassie but she is cut off by Miss Pritchard's hand being waved imperiously in her face.

'You're going to need to find some hot men to star in these films,' she says. 'And luckily for you, I have a phonebook filled with numbers. All you have to do is give me the specifications, including height and girth, and I'll hook you up.'

'What exactly does she mean by *girth*?' whispers Isobel, returning to sit next to me.

'Just drink your drink,' I advise. 'And try not to think about it.'

'We still need a name,' slurs Cassie, her drink sloshing onto the carpet.

I lift my hand. 'I have it. *Proper Porn*. You know, as in *right and proper* but also *properly pornographic*.'

Sometimes I amaze myself with my own levels of erotic genius, I really do.

Everyone cheers and raises their glass.

'Shall I show you the vibrators now?' asks Sandra, rather timidly. 'Or are we done for the night?'

'The night is only just *beginning*!' roars Miss Pritchard and we all descend on poor Sandra who, rather wisely, opens her suitcase of pleasure and then beats a hasty retreat to the corner of the room while we scream and cackle and generally act like feral children in a sweetshop – except that the average age in the room is fifty-three and our sweets have names like *Rodeo Rider* and *Tickling Tornado* and *Bullet of Love*.

After an hour of drinking and shrieking and more drinking and generally ridiculously hedonistic behavior, Sandra calls time.

'I've got some forms here if anyone would like to order anything,' she says, just as Cassie prods me in the arm with a *Rampaging Rabbit* and I retaliate with my *Satisfied Queen*. For several seconds we are absorbed in our lightsaber/vibrator battle until Sandra clears her throat disapprovingly and I realise that we're probably not being very respectful with the merchandise.

'There's no pressure to buy,' she says, starting to gather up the vibrators from around the room. They seem to have got everywhere, into every nook and cranny.

'I'd like to purchase a few things,' mumbles Allegra. 'Pass me an order form.'

We all take a form and a pen and I sink onto the floor, trying to decide what to buy. A few hours ago, I wouldn't have dreamt of ordering *any* of it in front of these women but everything has changed now. I'm not the only woman in the world who thinks about sex and I am buoyed up with the feeling that I'm somehow part of a collective. It's been a bit lonely, thinking that I was the only one.

I eventually tick the box for a satin negligee (without holes) and something that I can give Nick on his next birthday. I mean, it's a present for me really but he doesn't have to know that. And quite frankly he should feel lucky to get anything after the amount he's spent on Betty. The memory of the last big bill that arrived for Land Rover parts makes me scan my eyes down the order form again and choose something else that, while perhaps not being a *guilty pleasure*, is one hundred percent going to be a hidden pleasure. That's actually the name of it too, which is a happy twist of fate.

'What was the name of that nightie that you showed us at the start?' calls Allegra. 'The one that you said went with my complexion? I want to add it to my order.'

Sandra goes across and shows her the appropriate item and then finally, everyone starts to gather their belongings and gets ready to leave.

'Thank you for a lovely evening, Hannah,' says Miss Pritchard, leaning against Pru. 'It was wonderful to get out of the house for a change.'

'Can I order you a taxi?' I say, as the two women wobble towards the front door. 'It's quite late and it's ever so dark out there.'

'Oh, bless you!' chuckles Miss Pritchard. 'Pru and I have already ordered an Uber to take us into town.'

'The night is young!' adds Pru. 'Even if we are not!'

'You're as young as the man you feel,' Miss Pritchard tells her. 'Come on – I want to go to that club you were telling me about. The lovely one with the rainbows and all the men.'

'She thinks she'll have more fun at a gay club,' Pru tells me. 'I'm not entirely sure she understands the current meaning of the word.'

'Is that fair?' I ask. 'To the men?'

Pru grins. 'They're big boys. I'm sure they can handle little old Miss Pritchard over here.'

They link arms and totter out into the night and I send a

silent prayer into the sky, advising gay men everywhere to stay at home tonight for their own safety.

'It was a fab evening,' says Isobel, coming up behind me with Allegra and Lori. 'Thanks, Hannah.'

'Are you okay getting home?' I ask.

Allegra nods. 'It turns out that Isobel lives in my street so we'll walk Lori home first and then go back together.' She peers out through the open front door and sniffs. 'It's just as well. You really do live in a dodgy part of town, Hannah.'

'It was lovely to see you all,' I smile. *And it's even lovelier to see some of you leave.*

Allegra darts forward and pulls me in for a hug. It isn't comfortable or warm or even particularly friendly – she's all sharp edges and points – but it's still more physical contact than we've ever had and I appreciate the step forward in our relationship.

Then she pulls away and smooths down the front of her coat. 'I meant to tell you, Hannah. You've got a green light to go ahead with the Afternoon Tea Party. Let me know if you need any help although I'm sure you're more than capable of throwing together a few hundred homemade, gluten-free, dairy-free, sugar-free, soy-free scones, scone-free scones.'

I am pretty sure she did not mean to say that last bit.

She gives me a tight smile and then turns to the other women.

'Let's go. I've got to be up at six to take Auberon to his street dance competition and it's a three-hour drive. Lovely gathering, Hannah – thanks ever so!'

She sails out of the house and after a quick goodbye, Lori and Isobel scurry after her.

'It wasn't a *gathering*!' I call after their retreating figures. 'It was a *sex* party, FYI!'

A man walks past with his dog and shoots me a very dirty look so I hastily close the door and go back into the living room where Cassie is helping Sandra to pack up the last of her stuff.

'Fantastic evening!' she says as I walk in. 'I've had a quick peek at the order forms and I've never made so much money in one night before. One of your friends has spent two hundred and fifty quid on vibrators alone! You've got a great discount heading your way, Hannah!'

I widen my eyes and look at Cassie but she shakes her head. 'Not me. I reckon it was your crazy friend, Allegra.'

I laugh and pick up Sandra's suitcase. 'No way. My money is on Miss Pritchard! So who was it, Sandra?'

'I'm afraid that I can't divulge that kind of information,' Sandra tells us as we head out through the front door and walk towards her car. 'Client-Party Organiser confidentiality, and all that. Can I offer you a lift home, Cassie? You're on my way.'

Cassie nods and then wraps her arms around me.

'Tonight was brilliant!'

'*You're* brilliant,' I tell her. 'I haven't laughed so much in ages. And you were right – I did need this.'

'I am always right,' she says, stepping back and opening the passenger door. 'And rest assured, I'll get Sandra to tell me who spent so much money on sex toys.'

'I heard that,' says Sandra, slamming the boot. 'And my lips are sealed.'

I wave them off and then go back into the house, suddenly exhausted. The clearing up can wait until tomorrow. Right now, the only thing I want is my bed and to sink into sleep.

Chapter Twenty-Two

Nick wakes me up on Sunday morning with a cup of tea.

'We need to talk,' he tells me, his voice serious.

I sit bolt upright and then regret the rapid movement. 'What is it?' I ask. 'What's happened? Is it the kids? Is Dylan okay?'

'Hannah.' He puts his hand on my arm. 'Calm down, okay. The kids are fine. But I need to tell you something and I need you to listen.'

I put the tea on my bedside table and twist to look at him. His face is drawn and he looks like he hasn't slept properly. My stomach churns, which could be due to the appalling amount of alcohol that I drank last night but I'm more inclined to assume it's abject terror.

I think he's leaving me. All this time I thought that I was the one trying to reinvent myself and he's been quietly discovering his own life, away from me. This is what happens when you spend all your time trying to 'find' yourself – you lose the things that are most important. My constant attempts to add some spice to our marriage have pushed him away. I am so utterly stupid.

'I've been trying to find an answer but I just don't think that I can.' I can feel his hand shaking and I resist the urge to yell at him to just put me out of misery and spit it out.

Shouting at him is not going to encourage him to rethink divorcing me, though. I'm going to have to be cleverer than that. Unless of course he's already found someone else in which case, he would be wise to prepare himself to meet the wrath and vengeance of Twinky Malone because my god, she will not go quietly into the dark night. Hell no. She will start by cutting up his clothes and finish by cutting up his heart. Metaphorically speaking, obviously. Twinky or not, I am not a psychopath.

'Hannah? Are you listening to me?' His voice pulls me reluctantly back to reality. I don't want to listen. I don't want to hear the love of my life tell me that he's had enough of me and is throwing me away like a used dishcloth.

'I'm listening,' I say, wrenching my arm away from his hand. I can't stand the feeling of him touching me, not when I know that it's for the very last time. 'When are you going then?'

His face screws up in confusion. 'Going? Where am I supposed to be *going*? I said that I didn't get the forestry contract and I know that it's going to put us in a really tight spot, financially. I'm so sorry.'

Oh. Right then. It's not quite the disaster I was anticipating. Thank god for that – I am not feeling in any way equipped to deal with any drama this morning. I'm also never drinking. Ever again.

I mentally put my scissors away and lean across to wrap one arm around his shoulders. 'It's okay,' I tell him. 'Honestly. I thought you were going to say something terrible, from the look on your face.'

He pulls away and stares at me. 'It *is* terrible, Hannah. I was banking on that contract to help us pay off the credit card, for starters. I know that I'm lucky to still have other jobs on the go but they aren't enough for us to cope with all the emergencies that seem to happen on a semi-regular basis, you know that.'

He stares down at the bed and a thought hits me.

'When did you find out about this?' I ask him gently. 'How long have you known?'

His eyes flicker towards me. 'It's been quite a few weeks,' he says. 'I wanted to figure something else out before I told you because you've been so focused on your writing. At one point I was sure that you'd guessed what was going on but then you didn't say anything and I didn't know if that meant that you were pissed off with me and didn't want to talk about it and—'

He stops and gazes at me, clearly out of words.

'When?' I ask. 'When did you think I'd guessed?'

'That night when you met me at the wine bar,' he tells me quietly. 'You were going on about us getting reconnected and then you were so angry with me for messing up your surprise – but not as angry as I was with myself for doing anything that would ever make you feel like I don't find you attractive.'

A few weeks. All that time when I thought he'd gone off me and I couldn't figure out why things felt tense between us and it was because of this. I love my husband very much but quite frankly, he can be a bit of a knob sometimes. Not that I'm any better.

'Look at me.' I pull myself up onto my knees and put my hands on either side of his face. 'Everything is okay. It really is. I'm just glad that you finally told me. It explains a lot. Perhaps we both need to be a bit more truthful with each other from now on, yeah?'

He raises his head and looks me in the eye. 'It's been awful.' His words come out in a big rush. 'I wanted to tell you but I just couldn't. Not until I had a solution. Which as of last night, I actually do.'

I frown. 'What is it? Have you found another decent contract?'

He shakes his head. 'No. But I put an advert in the local paper and last night I got a buyer.' He pauses, as if the words are hard to say. 'I'm selling Betty. She'll clear the credit card and give us a bit left over to help with any future disasters.'

I don't even have to think. I'm off the bed in seconds, standing with hands on my hips and my feet planted firmly apart.

'No way. You can't sell Betty. She's part of the family now and she makes you happy. So what if we've got a bit of debt on the card? We'll save a bit harder and sort it out. Maybe Miriam will give me some more hours at school or maybe I'll sell a few more copies of my book. I don't know. But I do know that we are absolutely not at that stage, so you can phone up your buyer and tell him that you're very sorry but Betty is not for sale.'

Maybe he should have told me the truth as soon as he knew about the contract. But maybe I should have been more honest about how I was feeling too. Both of us have been faking our way through the last couple of months and perhaps if we'd talked about it we would have found the answer together. We usually do. We've had enough practice.

Nick gets up and comes across to where I'm standing.

'Are you sure?' he asks, and I can hear the hope in his voice. 'Because I really will sell her if I have to.'

It might not make it into the plot of a Hollywood film but quite honestly, I am struggling to think of a single gesture that could be deemed as more romantic than this one. You have truly not been loved until someone offers to sell their precious Land Rover for you.

'I'm sure,' I assure him. 'But maybe we should buy a lottery ticket this week.'

He wraps his arms around me and we hold each other tightly and it feels like it always has done. Safe and warm and solid and loving – like my whole world is right here and there is nowhere else that I would ever want to be. And then my body remembers that it is actually still mostly operating on alcohol fumes and could do with a rest after all the excitement. I stagger back onto the bed and Nick walks across the bedroom to the window.

'I was almost too scared to go downstairs this morning,' he tells me, opening the curtains before sitting down next to me. 'Just in case one of those women was lurking somewhere.'

I wince as the daylight hits my eyes and pick up my cup, sipping gratefully at the tea.

'It did all get a bit out of hand,' I confess. 'But it was a total laugh.'

'You were going on about something called *Proper Porn* when you finally came up to bed.' He looks at me quizzically. 'What was that all about?'

'Oh god.' I shake my head. 'Cassie had this idea that we should create our own porn production company and make films that show the reality of sex. You know – to combat the unrealistic, misogynistic stuff that kids see nowadays?'

Nick nods seriously. 'I can see there being a market for that.'

I laugh and punch him half-heartedly on the arm. 'Oh yeah – and what do you know about it?'

He frowns. 'I'm not a Neanderthal, Hannah. I read the news. I know how different it is for kids these days and it worries me a lot that they're getting these awful messages. It's why I made sure that I spoke to Dylan about it, once he started showing an interest in girls.'

'You spoke to our son about porn?' I ask, putting down my cup. 'When?'

Nick shrugs. 'I don't know. In the car or when we were walking Dogger. Whenever. It wasn't a big deal, Hannah. Just conversations about respect and consent and that if you want to know about real women then porn isn't the best source of material.'

'But what if it *could* be?' I ask, twisting to face him. 'What if genuine, honest, proper porn could actually exist and then people could satisfy their curiosity without causing damage to women?'

'Do it,' he says, giving me a grin. 'You're a Sex Goddess so you're qualified for the job! And I definitely won't ever have to sell Betty if you make your fortune in the X-rated movie industry.'

'You're an idiot,' I tell him, getting out of bed. 'But all this is really going to help with *So Much Sex*, you know? Bella Rose is already kick-ass and won't take any shit. Now she just needs to get her own orgasms in hand.'

'Muuuuuum!' Scarlet's howl of anguish sends shivers down my spine and I glance at Nick who is already off the bed and heading for the door. 'Muuuuuuuum! Daaaaaaaaad! Get down here now!'

I'm two steps behind Nick as he hurtles down the stairs, intent on rescuing our daughter from whatever disaster is currently occurring. She is standing outside the living room, holding onto the door handle for dear life and my heart leaps into my mouth.

'Is there an intruder?' I ask, as we approach her. 'What is it?'

Scarlet shakes her head. 'I heard a noise,' she gulps. 'When I went in there to get my iPad. It sounded like hundreds of angry wasps or bees or something.'

Nick groans and starts firing questions at her. 'Did you see anything? Where exactly was the noise coming from? Could it have been outside the window?'

Scarlet scowls and moves away from the closed door. 'I don't know, do I? It sounded like wasps so I ran. I wasn't going to hang around and locate their specific location – I could have been stung!'

'That was very wise,' I say, nodding at her. 'And you were right to call us.'

'What's going on?' yawns Benji, stomping down the stairs. 'Why is everyone shouting? Again.'

'We've got a wasp invasion,' Scarlet tells him. 'In the living room.'

'Well, we don't know that for sure, do we?' I say, smiling reassuringly at my youngest child.

'There's only one way to find out.' Nick puts his hand on the doorknob and twists it.

'Do you want me to come with you?' I ask, hoping that he'll decline my generous offer.

He shakes his head. 'No point in us both putting ourselves at risk. You wait out here with the kids and I'll call if I need you.'

And then he opens the door and quickly slips inside and the hallway fills with silence as we all stand very still and wait.

Thirty seconds pass and then one minute but no sound comes from the other side of the door.

'What if they're killer wasps and he's dead?' murmurs Benji.

'Don't be stupid,' huffs Scarlet. 'There aren't killer wasps in this country. But he might have been stung and had an allergic reaction. *That* could kill him.'

'Nobody is dead,' I snap, although I do press my ear against the door to listen for any sign of life. There's no sound though, so as the good wife that I clearly am, I make a decision.

'I'm going in,' I whisper to the children. 'If I'm not out in five minutes then do something.'

'Do *what?*' Scarlet whispers back. 'What do you want us to *do?*'

'I don't know!' I hiss, my pulse speeding up as I turn the handle. 'Just do something, okay?'

Then I push open the door and slip inside, my eyes searching the room for Nick. And then I notice his socked feet sticking out from behind the sofa and for one moment my heart misses a beat.

'Nick!' I yell. 'Are you okay?'

The door behind me flies open and Scarlet and Benji spill into the room.

'Dad!' howls Scarlet.

The feet move and a second later, Nick's head pops up.

'What are you all yelling about?' he asks. 'And can you stop, because I'm trying to locate the source of the noise. There aren't any wasps in here but I can definitely hear something.'

We all listen and he's right. There is a buzzing sound and I can see why Scarlet assumed that it was an insect invasion. It definitely sounds like some kind of animal, that's for sure.

'Spread out and try to find it,' instructs Nick and I move forward, tilting my head so that I can pinpoint the exact location of the noise. It seems to be coming from the direction of the armchair but as I start to walk towards it the buzzing suddenly drops in frequency, as if it's losing energy. Which is odd because animals don't usually run out of power like that.

Not unless they're rabbits.

Not unless they're battery-powered rabbits.

'Everybody out of the room!' I scream, spinning round to look at my family. 'Get out now!'

Benji is just reaching the armchair and my shout makes him leap in terror, right on top of the cushions. He scans the floor with wide eyes.

'What happened?' screeches Scarlet. 'Why are you shouting?'

'What is it, Hannah?' shouts Nick, rushing to my side. 'Have you found something?'

'No, but I-I just think that...maybe there's a...'

I do not have the words to explain what is happening right now. There is a very real possibility that the words do not even exist in the English language.

'I've found the noise!' proclaims Benji, bringing his hand out from behind a cushion and waving it in the air.

Of course he has.

I close my eyes and pray briefly that I am wrong. But when I open them again, it is all too obvious that I am right.

Of course I am.

'What *is* this?' he asks the silent room, gazing at the item in his hand. 'And why is it making that buzzing sound?'

My brain finally shifts into gear and I launch myself towards him, grabbing the offending item from his innocent, childish hands.

'It's a massage wand,' I say, the words tumbling from

my mouth. 'It helps to relieve tension if you have stiff muscles. Look!'

I turn to face Nick and start frantically poking him with the wand. 'There! I bet that feels lovely and relaxing, doesn't it?'

Nick pulls away from me, his eyes widening.

'Don't go prodding me with that thing,' he says, wrinkling his nose. 'Who knows where it's been?'

'Oh. My. God.' Scarlet narrows her eyes at me. 'You are actually disgusting, Mother – are you aware of that?'

'Who would like waffles for breakfast!' I chirrup wildly. 'Benji – why don't you go and see if there is any maple syrup in the cupboard and then we can have a lovely Sunday morning breakfast together?'

Benji gives me a suspicious look but the allure of waffles makes him leave the room. I wait until he's gone and then I turn to face my husband and daughter.

'That wasn't very helpful,' I hiss at Nick. 'You made that far more embarrassing than it needed to be and for your information, it hasn't *been* anywhere.'

Nick has the good grace to look slightly sheepish.

'Sorry,' he mutters. 'I just thought it was pretty funny that we were all searching for a wasp nest when really it was—' He breaks off and gestures to the item in my hand. '*That.*'

Scarlet shakes her head. 'You are actually deranged,' she tells me. 'What kind of mother leaves a vibrator in the living room for her kids to find? In fact, what kind of mother owns a vibrator in the first place?' She flings herself into onto the sofa and rolls her eyes. 'Honestly, I'm going to be scarred for life.'

I stand in silence for a second, staring at her.

I am a mother.

I am *her* mother.

But that is not all that I am.

'Firstly, I agree that it is less than ideal that this has happened,' I say, my voice quiet. 'However, it was left here after the party last night and that is absolutely not the same thing as me leaving it for you to find.'

Nick clears his throat. 'I might go and help Benji with the waffles,' he says. 'If I'm not needed?'

'That's an excellent idea,' I say, not breaking eye contact with my daughter. I wait until he has left the room and then I step forward and stare down at her.

'Secondly, and most importantly – you asked me what kind of a mother owns a vibrator? Well, I'm going to ask *you* a question. Do you think that this kind of item shouldn't be available for women? Do you think that pleasure and fun are just for the men?'

I gulp slightly as I say it but then I square my shoulders and be the woman that I know I need to be. The woman I *want* to be. I've spent years telling the kids about the importance of making good choices and staying safe and consent but I'm not sure that I've ever let the word *pleasure* slide from my lips. And it bloody well should have done. Because what's the point, otherwise?

Scarlet scowls. 'No. Of course not! I'm a feminist and I think that women should be able to do whatever they want.'

'Women who aren't mothers though, yeah?' I raise one eyebrow at her. 'Women should be able to do whatever they want until they become *mothers*, at which point investing in their own happiness and pleasure is purely a selfish act? Actually – you said it was *disgusting*.'

'That's not what I said,' insists Scarlet. 'You don't even understand.'

'But it's what you meant,' I tell her, remembering how free I felt last night and how wonderful it was to spend the evening having fun and laughing about sex stuff without anyone being judgemental. 'You talk all about the women you admire who are working for equality and feminism and recognition but you don't even realise that you're being a hypocrite and that feminism starts at home.'

She leans back against the cushions and appraises me. 'You think you're so liberal and with-it and woke but you don't have a clue about what it's like nowadays.'

And I snap.

'I *do* have a clue!' I wail, pointing at her with the vibrator. 'And if you want to see a real-life example of feminism in action then open your eyes, young lady – because the real feminists are not just youthful, gorgeous, skinny legends with verified Instagram accounts.'

I turn away and start to pace the room, punctuating each point that I am making with another stab of the vibrator. 'They are also the women in their forties who are working the triple shift of parenting and trying to maintain a home while holding down a job. They are the women who can't have or don't want children but are forced to explain themselves over and over again to a society who cannot understand any other role for them. They are the women born into the wrong bodies who have to fight every day just to be acknowledged. They are the invisible women who don't think that being eligible for a pension should mean that they have to give up their sexual selves. They are called angry and hysterical and neurotic and bossy and they still don't give up! They are every different size, shape, colour and age. They come from every walk of life. And none of them will stop fighting for equality and fairness until we live in a world where it is okay for a *mother* to own a vibrator.'

I pause to take a breath and see Scarlet cowering where she sits. I think that there is a slim possibility that I might have lost the flow there for a moment but it doesn't matter because every word is true.

'And also, I am totally *woke*.'

It's good to end an argument with a strong statement. Unfortunately for me, I don't know when to stop.

'I am woke and I am with-it and I have the scars to prove it.'

Scarlet frowns at me. 'Would these be metaphorical scars that you're talking about?'

'No!' I howl, advancing towards her. 'They are not bloody metaphorical scars. They are real, genuine scars that have been inflicted upon me by my offspring, *actually*.'

I brandish the vibrator in the air and heroically manage to resist yanking up my pajama top and showing her the scars that lick at my stomach like flames and which are the permanent result of my skin being forced to stretch to the size of a large beach ball *three times* to accommodate my quite frankly, completely huge babies.

'I'm sorry, Mum.' Scarlet stares at me with wide eyes. 'I didn't mean to make it sound like I don't appreciate you.'

I deflate slightly and slump onto the sofa beside her, throwing the vibrator down next to me. I know that she's trying to make an effort but I still feel churned up and cross. I don't *want* her to appreciate me. I want her to *see* me. But I know that if I want that then I'm going to have to show her that I exist as a real person who has more to offer than just cooking the supper or doing the laundry.

I have to show her that I understand the current issues of the day and that it doesn't matter how old we all are because being female is a lifelong condition. I'm also completely on a roll now and I don't want to lose momentum. Who knows when I'll have the opportunity to talk to her like this again?

'I think that we should have a chat about genital waxing,' I tell her, ignoring the way her mouth drops open in shock. Or horror. Or possibly a combination of both. 'I hope you know that there is absolutely no requirement for you to wax that part of your body. Ever. Even if a boy says that he prefers it like that. In fact, *especially* if a boy says that he prefers it like that.'

'Mum!' Scarlet's face lives up to her name. 'We totally do not need to have this conversation now, okay?'

'It's important that we can talk about this stuff,' I tell her. 'I know you think the older generation has nothing to offer you but we've quite literally been there, done that. You can learn a lot by listening to the words of older, wiser women.'

Scarlet stands up and looks down at me.

'I know.' She flashes me a forced smile and starts to back out of the room, like I'm some kind of unexploded bomb. 'That's why I've been chatting to Granny.'

And then she's gone, leaving me alone with a dodgy vibrator that has started pulsating again, albeit with slightly less enthusiasm that it had previously. I pick it up and give it a good, long stare. I should probably give it back to Sandra. That would be the moral thing to do in this situation. Then again, I'm not sure what the returns policy is on sex toys.

I shove it back behind a cushion and wander out into the kitchen, wondering vaguely where I might find a stash of batteries.

Chapter Twenty-Three

I am on a roll. It's like I have unleashed a whole new side of myself and I spend every spare moment feverishly writing about Bella Rose and Daxx's new life in Tulsa, Oklahoma. I channel all the conversations that I've had over the last few weeks about the need to portray honest, real, messy sex and I let Bella Rose and Daxx take their relationship to a whole, new level. I still don't think that I can be deliberately funny and I know that's a potential problem but at least I've finally mastered *sexy*, so that's something.

And success clearly breeds success, because yesterday I had a rather interesting email from Binky. She said that she didn't want me to get overly excited because it's all at the very initial stages right now and these things often fizzle out before they can ever amount to anything – but that a production company has enquired about the performance rights to *More Than Sex* and she wanted to keep me in the loop. She said that there probably wouldn't be any more information for months and that I should put it of my mind, which obviously, I totally have.

And even better is that I finally have a title. It was right there when I woke up the morning after the sex party and it's so perfect that I can't believe it took me so long to figure it out. If my first book was called *More Than Sex* because it was supposed to be an exploration of the deep emotional connection that two people can have (well, that wasn't my actual intention at the start but it sounds good now) then my second book is an expose on how those same two people can plunge the depths of their sexuality and learn about themselves in the process.

I'm calling it *So Much Sex*.

Because there is. So freaking much that it makes me want to squeal in excitement. I am a genuine writer of erotica and I am ready to embrace it all. I'm even imagining a life where my books are made into bonkbuster, blockbuster movies and I can spend my days wandering around on set, drinking Triple-Venti-Soy-No-Foam Lattes in an ecofriendly cup. I know that writing books hasn't exactly made me a ton of money but I'm pretty sure that selling the performance rights would be a tasty deal. Especially when what I'm writing now is so damn steamy.

And who in their right mind *wouldn't* want to see a scene like the one I've just written on the big screen?

Bella Rose was lying in bed reading her book when Daxx entered the room. His eyes lit up at the sight of her and she suppressed a small sigh. It wasn't that she didn't find him sexy – she really did. It was just that she'd got to a really good bit in her book and was reluctant to put it down.

'What are you doing?' murmured Daxx, sliding in between the sheets and moving his hand across her body.

'What does it look like?' she retorted, rolling her eyes. 'I'm enjoying my book.'

Daxx flexed his arm muscles, which were becoming surprisingly well developed since he'd taken up competitive lumberjacking. 'How about you enjoy me instead?'

Bella Rose peeled his hand off her thigh and shuffled further to the left.

'Get back on your own side of the bed,' she told him, trying to focus on the page. 'You're distracting me.'

'We don't have sides of the bed,' Daxx said huskily, leaning closer to her. 'We just have one giant playground of luuuuurrrrve.'

Bella Rose tried not to rise to the bait. He knew exactly how she felt on this subject. Only fools or psychopaths didn't have their own side of the bed, everyone knew that. The jury was out on which one applied to Daxx, but Bella Rose rather suspected that he didn't have the intelligence to be a psychopath.

She continued to read for another minute, ignoring Daxx's presence at her side. There was a plot twist imminent, she could sense it, and there was no way that she could stop reading now. Clutching the book firmly in her hands, her eyes widened as she turned the page and eagerly scanned the words.

'Who is King Duncan and why does Lady Macbeth want him dead?' Daxx's voice jolted her back into the room.

She lowered the book and glared at him. 'Because he was an irritating sod who read her book over her shoulder.'

Daxx grinned. 'I bet he'd have made it up to her if he'd had the chance.'

Bella Rose shook her head but she couldn't help the smile that tugged at the corners of her mouth.

'Fine,' she told him. 'But it'd better be worth it.'

Daxx pulled her towards him and she closed her eyes, letting him do his funky thing. It wasn't unrelaxing lying here, she mused to herself. Daxx was a creature of habit and, like a lot of men in Bella Rose's experience, had a signature move. It was a bit like a sexual version of dot-to-dot – his hands went here and then they went there and in a second he would move down to—

'Is that good?' he asked, his voice laden with desire.

'So good,' Bella Rose replied, like she always did.

But then she had a thought. And it was a thought so radical that she almost laughed. She had no idea what Daxx would think and the last thing she wanted to do was make him feel insecure – but he was a big boy and he'd cope. And he had disrupted her reading time – he owed her.

'Actually, Daxx,' she muttered. 'Move to the side, just a bit.'

He stilled and she could feel his panic.

'It's good,' she assured him. 'But it could be better. If you just move a teensy bit to the right.'

'Better?' Daxx seemed to be struggling to understand.

'Better for me,' she explained. 'Sexier. Look – I'll show you what I like and then you can copy me.'

Daxx's head snapped up. 'What?'

Bella Rose shrugged. 'I know what works for me.'

Daxx blinked rapidly and then nodded. 'Show me what to do,' he breathed. 'I want to pleasure you and send you to the

headiest of heights. I want to be the greatest lover that you have
ever had. Show me how to make you—'

　　'Less talking,' suggested Bella Rose, placing one finger on his
lips. 'That would be an excellent start.'

　　And then she put her hand on his head and gently guided
him down the bed where she could only hope that he would be
taking mental notes because as far as she could tell he wasn't
equipped with either pen or paper. Not that it mattered if it took
him some time to get the hang of it. She would be happy to
demonstrate for as long as was needed.

I spend the next week either writing or teaching and by
Friday I am almost two thirds of the way through my first
draft. Which means that I can allow myself to take a bit of
time off and start preparing the house for the weekend. I
drop the kids at school and then I race home and start the
first load of laundry going in the machine before grabbing
the vacuum cleaner and blitzing the entire house.

　　It. Takes. Forever. I know that I've been busier lately and
haven't had as much time to get housework done but I did
have a big chat with Nick, Scarlet and Benji about them all
pulling their weight and they assured me that they would.
From the state of the house, however, I think it is safe to
assume that they have mostly been pulling their weight
from the sofa to the fridge and back again.

　　I've finished with the vacuuming and am making a start
on the bathroom when Scarlet barges in through the door.

　　'Can I have a shower?' she asks, as way of greeting.

'No.' I turn and wave a sponge at her. 'Nobody is using this bathroom before he gets here, is that understood? Also – how come you're home so early *again*?'

'I told you I had a free period, last lesson,' she moans. 'Honestly. Nobody ever listens to me around here. It's like you all go deaf when I start speaking. Also – how would you feel if I started dating someone who had a nasallang piercing?'

I bend back over the sink and resume my polishing of the taps. 'I'm pretty sure that they're called *study* periods, not *free* periods,' I say, ignoring her other comment. 'On account of the fact that you're supposed to stay at school and do some studying during that time.'

'Why are you doing all this?' she asks, dumping her bag on the floor and perching on the edge of the bath. 'I've never seen the house look so tidy, not even at Christmas.'

I rub determinedly at a lump of toothpaste that has clearly been attached to the tap for half a decade, judging by its refusal to be removed. 'It's his first weekend home,' I tell her. 'I just want everything to look nice and welcoming.'

'He's going to think he's walked into the wrong house,' mutters Scarlet. 'You do know that he's been living in a flat with seven other people, don't you? I really don't think he's going to care about how shiny the bathroom taps are.'

'I care,' I snap back. 'Now instead of hanging about here making stupid comments you can go and put the kettle on.'

Scarlet nods dolefully and stands up.

'I should have known that it'd be like this. It was foretold in biblical times. The prodigal son is returning and so I, Cinderella, have to spend my time in the kitchen.'

'You are aware that those are two different stories?' I ask, moving onto the mirror. 'And that Cinderella isn't a character from the Bible?'

Scarlet shrugs. 'Whatever. I'm going to my room, unless you've decided that Dylan should have two bedrooms and I have to sleep in the garden shed? Maybe I'll just move in with Granny and make it easy for you.'

She picks up her bag and flounces out of the bathroom and I reminded again of the need to force my mother to tell me exactly why Scarlet has been asking her for advice.

'Put the kettle on before you go!' I yell after her. 'And don't touch anything else in the kitchen. And don't eat any of the food – it's for the weekend.'

I am waiting in the hallway when Nick arrives home with Benji.

'Shoes off!' I bark, the instant that the front door opens. 'And hang your stuff in the cupboard under the stairs.'

'What's wrong with the hooks?' asks Nick, walking across to where we normally hang all our coats. 'And hello to you, too.'

I reach up and give him a kiss. Things have been so much better between us since we talked last weekend. And while I share his worry about what we're going to do for money, I'm trying not to stress about it too much. Right now, I'm just enjoying the knowledge that my marriage isn't about to go up in flames. Our financial plight is on my list of things to panic about but it's way below my imminent appearance at Sex Con, for which I am woefully unprepared.

'Nothing's wrong with them,' I tell him, yanking his

jacket out of his hand and opening the cupboard door. 'I just want there to be plenty of space for Dylan to hang up his coat when he gets here later.'

'How many coats is he bringing?' asks Nick, looking confused. 'There are five hooks, Hannah. There's always been five hooks – one for each of us.'

'Don't try and reason with her, Dad,' advises Scarlet, descending the stairs. 'And I sincerely hope that neither of you need to use the bathroom in the near future.'

'I do!' shouts Benji, hopping up and down and clutching at the front of his trousers. 'I've been desperate for a wee since one o'clock.'

'So why didn't you go at school?' Nick asks him. 'That was hours ago.'

Benji scowls. 'Miss said that I couldn't go to the toilet because we'd only just had lunchtime and *that* was my time to go. And that if I wanted to go in my *learning time* then she was a bit disappointed about my attitude. She did say that if I was really desperate then I could ask her again in two minutes. But I forgot.'

'So you weren't really that desperate then, were you?' I mutter.

'I was,' insists Benji. 'But we were doing a science experiment with yeast and water and balloons and it was really fun. So I just kind of made the wee go back up so that I didn't miss anything. But now it's all pressurised and if I don't go soon then it could be a medical emergency.'

Scarlet makes a delightful retching sound. 'You're an animal,' she tells her brother. 'I can't believe that I have to put up with this kind of foul conversation.'

'Well, you'd better get up there now,' says Nick, grinning at Benji. 'It sounds like the situation could turn nasty at any moment.'

'No!' I cry, stepping in front of our son. 'I've just cleaned the bathroom for Dylan. I'm not having your explosive wee messing it all up again.'

'Hannah!' Nick grabs my hand and gently but firmly pulls me out of Benji's path. 'He's allowed to use the toilet.'

I nod resignedly and slump my shoulders.

'Just clean up after yourself,' I mutter. 'Properly.'

'What time is Dylan arriving?' asks Nick. 'Have I got time for a cup of tea before I go to collect him?'

I stare at my husband. 'I thought I was collecting him.'

He shakes his head. 'No. I definitely remember saying that I'd go and get him in Betty.'

'I was hoping to have a chat with him though,' I say. 'Before we get back here and everything is chaos, as usual.'

Nick looks at me. 'If it's that important to you then of course you should get him,' he says. 'But I've missed him too.'

I hadn't even thought that Nick might want to spend some time with Dylan on his own. We talk a lot about what Dylan might be doing at uni but after that first day, Nick has seemed to take the whole thing in his stride and hasn't really shown any sign that he might be finding it as difficult as I am.

Maybe I'm just a bit louder about my worries than he is.

It's a possibility.

'You can go,' I say.

'I want to go too,' Scarlet interrupts.

'And me,' shouts Benji, leaping back down the stairs. 'I've been excited all day.'

Nick grins at me and I smile back. I don't know what I was thinking. Of course we'll all go and collect him. Anything else just wouldn't be right.

So it's the four of us waiting on the platform as the train pulls into the station. I scan the carriages as they pass but can't see Dylan anywhere. The doors open and people flood out and still there is no sign of him. I stand on tiptoe and peer along the length of the train, looking desperately for my little boy whose face I have missed so very, very much and whom I haven't seen for four, whole weeks.

And then he's there, striding towards us in a new jacket with a slightly bedraggled bunch of flowers in his hand.

We run. As in, we literally sprint down the platform, dodging travellers and suitcases and commuters and briefcases. I reach him first and pull him into my arms, the bulk of him feeling at once so familiar yet so different.

'My boy,' I whisper, holding him tightly as Nick joins our hug, followed rapidly by Scarlet and Benji. 'We've missed you.'

'I can't breathe,' rasps Dylan and we laugh, loosening our hold. I step back to take a proper look at him, drinking in the grin on his face.

'How was the journey?' asks Nick, taking his bag. 'Are you hungry?'

'Starving,' Dylan tells him, thrusting the flowers in my direction. 'These are for you, Mum. And I love your hair!'

It's highly likely that at least one person has sat on these flowers at some point in his three-hour journey. They are tired and drooping and squished. They are quite possibly the best flowers that anyone has ever given me.

Back at home, Dylan settles into his room while Nick cooks his favourite chicken curry and I open a bottle of wine. The sound of Benji laughing as he races between his room and his brother's room floats down the stairs and I feel a lovely warm feeling spreading through my stomach that is only partly down to the Prosecco.

'This is good, isn't it?' I say to Nick, pouring him a glass. 'It feels like everything is back to normal.'

He nods and tips some coconut milk into the pan.

'It's like he's never been away,' he agrees and we toast our glasses, silently thanking the universe for making the Thompson family complete again.

'So what have you actually been doing?' asks Nick, once we're all sitting down to eat. 'Is all your time taken up with studying?'

Dylan laughs and loads up his fork with some chicken.

'I wouldn't say *all* my time, no.'

'How's Zoe doing?' Scarlet's voice is sly and instantly gets my attention. 'Have you guys been visiting each other?'

Dylan shakes his head and puts the fork in his mouth.

'We broke up,' he mumbles around his food. 'It was the right thing to do.'

'I knew it!' screeches Scarlet. 'I've been looking at her Insta and she's taken down all the photos of you and she's been posting loads of motivational stuff about what to do when the world gives you lemons blah, blah, blah.'

I put down my glass and look at my son.

'When did this happen?' I ask, concerned. 'Why didn't

you tell me?'

He shrugs. 'It was after the second week,' he says. 'And I didn't tell you because it's not a big deal.'

'Well, that's good,' I tell him. 'But I *am* still your mum. I'm here to help you, even though you're at university now. And I have *so* many good suggestions on how to get through heartbreak and trauma and angst. I've been saving them up to share with you at a time when they were needed. I'm actually quite good at talking about this stuff, aren't I, Scarlet?'

Across the table, my daughter shudders and spoons some curry into her mouth.

'I wasn't heartbroken, Mum.' Dylan sounds amused. 'But I'll remember that for next time.'

'You'll have to convince someone else to go out with you before there's any remote possibility of another time,' mocks Scarlet through a mouthful of rice. 'What's the chance of two girls in the universe being that dumb?'

Dylan grins at her and reaches for a poppadum. 'Well, based on evidence, I'd say the chance is one hundred percent likely.'

'Have you got a new girlfriend?' Scarlet's mouth drops open. 'Who is she?'

'Give the boy a break,' says Nick, passing Dylan the jar of mango chutney. 'I'm fairly sure that he doesn't want to share all the details with us.'

'Sharing is caring, Dad,' Scarlet tells him. 'That's what you always say, isn't it, Mum?'

Everyone looks at me.

'Dylan's new girlfriend is not really the kind of thing

that I'm referring to with that phrase,' I say, chuckling lightly. 'I'm sure he'll tell us in his own good time.'

It's exactly the kind of thing that I'm referring to. And there is no way on this planet that I am prepared to let this mealtime finish without finding everything there is to know about this mystery girl.

My eldest son smiles at me. 'I'm glad that you can respect my need for privacy,' he tells me. 'I was a bit worried that you'd still try to baby me when I came home instead of treating me like an adult.'

I wave my hand dismissively in the air.

'Of course I'll treat you like an adult.' I smile back at him and pick up my glass. 'As long as you behave like an adult, obviously.'

He nods. 'Obviously.'

I take a sip of my drink and eyeball him over the rim of the glass. 'And part of adulting is sharing important details of one's life with the people who love you most.'

He opens his mouth to speak but Scarlet's whoop of triumph beats him to it.

'I've found her!' she crows, waving her phone in the air. 'I am literally a genius!'

'I thought we agreed no devices at the table?' complains Nick. 'Put that away, please.'

'But—' she starts.

'I'm serious, Scarlet,' snaps Nick. 'We're having a nice family supper and there are rules about looking at your phone while we're eating. Either you put it away or I'll confiscate it for the night.'

Scarlet juts her lip out and rams her phone into her back

pocket. 'Fine. If you aren't interested in Dylan's new girlfriend then I won't tell you what I've just seen on her Instagram account.'

'Good.' Nick gives her a nod of approval. 'It's not healthy, all this online stalking and snooping and prying into other people's business.'

'It's really not,' agrees Dylan sanctimoniously, dolloping mango chutney onto his plate. 'I worry about the impact on young people these days, living their lives on the Internet instead of interacting in person.'

Scarlet glares at him. 'Well, that's not a problem for your new girlfriend, is it? She does a lot of *interacting in person*, from what I've just seen. She certainly isn't shy, is she?'

I don't know what she's on about but I need to know what she saw.

'That's exactly what I'm talking about,' says Nick, looking at Dylan. 'Young people are losing crucial skills by having the majority of their communication online. I was reading an article the other day that said the workplace is really suffering from an intake of young employees who don't know how to handle real-life situations face to face because they're all too used to hiding behind a screen.'

'Okay, Boomer,' mutters Scarlet. 'Like your generation is doing a stand-up job of running everything.'

I do not want this evening to turn into a debate on which members of our family are more responsible for the destruction of the planet and life as we know it (mostly because Nick and I never end up coming out of these discussions well).

'Have some lime pickle,' I say to Scarlet, offering her the

jar. 'And what did you mean about Dylan's new girlfriend not being shy?'

She shoots a look at Dylan and then shakes her head. 'Dad said that I wasn't allowed to use my phone while we're eating.'

'It's not true, anyway,' Dylan informs us, breaking up his poppadum and scattering crumbs across the table. 'She's actually quite demure and reserved.'

Scarlet snorts loudly. 'Oh yeah, those are totally the words that I would use to describe someone who takes off their clothes for a living.'

I choke on my rice.

'What do you mean?' I splutter, gesturing at Nick to pass me some water. 'Who takes off their clothes for a living?'

'That's a rubbish job,' states Benji, staring at Scarlet. 'Why would someone get paid to do that?'

Dylan starts laughing but I can't see anything remotely funny about this conversation.

'Perhaps you should tell us about this new girlfriend after all?' suggests Nick, taking a big gulp of wine. 'Just to put your mother's mind at rest.'

'I don't need to tell you anything,' Dylan says, smirking. 'Scarlet has clearly got it all figured out.'

'Her name is Harley.' Scarlet whips out her phone and I lean closer to peer at the screen. 'This is a photo of her.'

Oh good god. Of all the things that I worried about when Dylan headed off to university, this was not one of them. I've been so concerned about his mental wellbeing and his nutritional intake and his ability to stick with his degree course that I have forgotten to worry about the most important thing of all. And this is what happens when mothers aren't in control of every aspect of their child's life.

They start dating pole dancers.

'Where did you meet?' Nick asks, raising his eyebrows when Scarlet shows him the screen.

It's an excellent question. All those nights that I was imagining my little boy sitting alone in his room feeling homesick and missing his family, the reality was clearly very different.

'You do know that strip joints reinforce the sexual objectification of women, don't you?' snarls Scarlet, glaring at her brother. 'She might think that she's in control but until there are as many men as women being paid to take off their clothes while other people watch then she's just being used by the patriarchy as a cheap thrill.'

'I have to agree,' I say, leaning forward to stare at my son. 'I can't believe that you've been frequenting establishments like this. And if she's your girlfriend, then what does that make *you* if you've been paying her to perform?'

'It makes him her pimp,' snaps Scarlet. 'And it's disgusting.'

'I didn't meet her in a strip joint,' says Dylan. 'And for your information I have never been inside a place like that.'

I breathe a sigh of relief. Of course my boy wouldn't go to a strip club. He's a nice, decent clean-living young man. He probably met her somewhere completely innocent like the supermarket or the library.

'I met her in the Student Union,' he continues. 'At Sexploration Society.'

'What the fuck?' asks Scarlet and I know that I should admonish her for her bad language but she's only voicing what the rest of us are thinking.

Dylan nods. 'Yeah – that's their motto.'

There is a moment of pause while we all absorb his words.

'Can I go and play on my iPad?' asks Benji.

'Absolutely!' I trill.

'Just go!' urges Nick, at the same time.

I wait until the kitchen door closes behind him and then top up my wine glass with the rest of the bottle, sending a silent apology to my liver while I do so.

'So,' I start, 'this society. What exactly is it about?'

Dylan grins at me. 'I'd have thought the clue was in the name, Mum.'

Nick clears his throat. 'Maybe this isn't something that we should be talking about in front of Scarlet?'

Our daughter scowls at him. 'Oh, that's nice. I'm the one who found out that your child has turned into a sex addict and now you're going to leave me out of the best bit of the conversation?'

I saw an article on Facebook the other day that featured people with all different kinds of addiction and the ones who were sex addicts could barely live a regular life because they kept having to stop what they doing and get it on. At the time I did briefly wonder if my sex bubbles were an indicator that I may be in the early stages of addiction but on reflection, I have decided that I'm more of a hobbyist rather than addict.

'I'm not a sex addict,' Dylan sighs, as if we're all being

very boring and the whole *sex* subject isn't a big deal. 'Sexploration Society is about exploring and challenging sexual norms and engaging in conversation that identifies the stereotypes and myths around sexuality.'

'Oh.' Scarlet doesn't have very much to say to that.

'That all sounds very responsible,' I tell him. 'I'm very proud of you.'

See? I can engage in a non-awkward conversation about this, especially as he's being so grown-up about the whole thing. We're clearly evolving as a family and this is how life is going to be now. Adult conversations about real-life topics, all without any judgement or shame. Just sensible people with mature attitudes.

'I only went once,' Dylan confesses. 'It was the Condoms and Cupcakes Social and I hadn't eaten all day.'

Not that mature, then.

'It still doesn't explain why your new girlfriend is a stripper,' announces Scarlet, bringing our attention back to the actual topic.

Dylan reaches across and grabs her phone, swiping the screen and then turning it so that we can all see.

'If you actually look, you'll see that she is fully clothed. There's no stripping going on here.'

'But she's halfway up a pole,' I point out, keeping my voice calm and mild like the progressive, liberal parent that I am. 'How do you explain that?'

He swipes the screen again and I blink, trying to make sense of what I'm seeing. Which is my oldest child, dangling from a pole in a position that looks both striking and uncomfortable.

'Is this how you're funding your degree?' I whisper. 'I-I-I just—'

I am speechless. This is what it's come to. Our child has had to resort to desperate measures to keep himself in beans on toast. If this is how life is going to be from now on then I did not sign up for this.

'You should have told us that you were struggling,' says Nick, his face pale. 'We'd have helped you out, son.'

'Who'd pay *you* to pole dance?' scoffs Scarlet, gazing at the photo. 'Although, that is quite impressive.'

'I'd forgotten how ridiculous you lot are.' Dylan sits back in his seat and smirks at us. 'But you can all stop freaking out. Harley and I both decided to join Pole Dancing Society. We aren't strippers or anything – it's just a club and it's actually a major workout. Pole dancing is a hell of a lot harder than it looks!'

'So Harley isn't a stripper?' I clarify, just to be sure.

'And you aren't selling yourself for cash?' adds Nick.

Dylan nods. 'Harley is a student on my course and I'm actually not doing too badly for money,' he tells us. 'Although the train ticket home cost an absolute fortune.'

'We'll pay for that,' I say quickly. 'Just let us know if you're running out of cash and we'll figure something out.'

He smiles at me. 'Thanks, Mum.'

'She's actually very pretty,' says Scarlet, taking her phone back and swiping back to the picture of Harley. 'I can see the attraction from your side but what's in it for her?'

Dylan shrugs. 'I'm a catch,' he tells her. 'What can I say?'

I stand and walk across to open the kitchen door. 'Benji! It's time for pudding!'

'Is it safe to come back in?' he calls back, plodding out of the living room. 'I'm not coming if you're all still talking about disgusting stuff.'

'Sex isn't disgusting, darling,' I tell him, removing the iPad as he walks past me. 'It's natural and normal and—'

'Can we just not?' demands Scarlet, gathering up the plates. 'Just for once, can we pretend to be a nice family and talk about something ordinary?'

'Here, here,' agrees Nick. 'Dylan – you can get the ice cream out of the freezer and Scarlet, you can get some bowls and provide us with our next topic of conversation.'

'Okay.' Scarlet beams at him. 'How would you feel if I started dating someone with a criminal record?'

I sink into my seat and close my eyes. I will not dignify her with a response. I am better than that.

'I'd be concerned,' Nick tells her mildly, opening the dishwasher out of habit before frowning and stacking the plates in the sink. 'And it would obviously depend on what the criminal record was for.'

'But would that really matter if he'd done his time and served his sentence?' Scarlet probes.

'Err, yes it would matter,' I inform her, my eyes flashing open. 'It would be highly relevant to anyone who is considering dating someone who has been in prison.'

'But if he's been let out of prison then he's obviously not a concern,' she insists, slamming the bowls onto the kitchen counter. 'And everyone deserves a second chance, you're always saying that.'

'That's naive and shortsighted,' I snap back. 'And you know it.'

'Even criminals deserve love, *Mum!*' she shouts. 'I can't believe that you're being so tabloid-y about this.'

'Does he actually exist, then?' mutters Dylan as he brings the ice cream over to the table. 'Because he sounds made up to me.'

'And if he does exist, would it be a fair assumption to presume that he rides a motorbike and is covered in tattoos and has strange piercings?' I ask. 'Because I don't want to leap to conclusions.'

Scarlet scowls at me. 'Why are you so judgemental about people?' she asks. 'Honestly. Just because you live a boring, middle-class, middle-aged life doesn't mean that everyone else wants to be like you.'

I flinch. 'Do you really think that I'm boring?'

She shrugs. 'I'm not trying to be rude, Mum. But look at you. You're a mum and a teacher and a wife. You go to school and you come home and you don't really do anything else. You're just a lot of *middle*, you know? Average.'

She pauses and then sees the look on my face.

'And all of that is totally fine,' she rushes on. 'If *you're* happy with only being those things, then that's all that matters. I'm just saying that I hope my life is a bit more exciting than yours is when I get to be as old as you.'

I open my mouth.

Boring?

Old?

Average?

Let's see what she thinks about her boring, old, average mother when she finds out that I'm actually a successful writer of erotic (tasteful, non-offensive) fiction and there is the tiniest of possibilities that I'm going to sell the performance rights for my first book and probably become a zillionaire.

I clamp my lips together. Actually, let's not. It's not worth the thirty seconds of satisfaction that this announcement would allow, for the lifetime of trauma that would be sure to follow. It's one thing for me to start feeling more chilled out about this stuff and I *have* been thinking that the day is coming when I might possibly relax my rules around remaining completely anonymous, but it's quite another to contemplate Scarlet discovering my alter-ego. She would never cope and I'll let the entire universe find out who I am before I risk her getting wind of it.

But bloody hell – it's harder than I possibly thought it could ever be to sit here and let her think that I'm a washed-up waste of a woman.

'Watch yourself,' warns Nick and for a second I think he's talking to me until I see him giving Scarlet a firm look. 'God knows that your mother is many things but boring is definitely not one of them.'

I think there's a compliment in there, but it's a little hard to tell for sure.

'This *crime lord* sounds like a bit of a dick, if you ask me.' Dylan sits down and stares at his sister. 'An *imaginary* dick.'

'Can we get back on topic, please?' snaps Scarlet. 'It doesn't matter whether you think he exists or not. It's the principle of the thing. You guys act like you're so liberal but then you can't cope with the idea of me bringing anyone home who doesn't fit into your perfect idea of who I should be dating.'

'It was you that freaked out first when you thought Harley was a stripper,' points out Dylan.

'I don't mind who you bring home,' adds Nick, passing Benji some bowls. 'But if you could preferably choose someone who has the skills to fix the bloody dishwasher then that would be a bonus.'

'I've missed this,' Dylan says, sitting down next to me. 'Uni is great and I've met so many excellent people but there's something about the crazy of home that I don't think you can find anywhere else.'

'And don't you forget it,' I tell him, patting his hand. 'You can travel the world and stay up all night debating the big questions in life but you're never going to find this level of sophisticated conversation anywhere else on the planet.'

'I think I've just swallowed my wobbly tooth!' howls Benji, dumping the bowls onto the table and clasping his hand to his mouth. 'Will the tooth fairy still give me money if I can't leave it out for her?'

'Don't worry,' I say, getting up. 'Let me have a proper look.'

'Did you just assume the gender of the tooth fairy?' snipes Scarlet, pulling the tub of ice cream towards her. 'God – the stereotyping in this family is unbelievable.'

'I don't care what gender it is,' whimpers Benji. 'I just want my money.'

'Open your mouth.' I tilt his head back gently and peer inside. He's definitely lost another tooth. I'm going to have to liquidise all his meals if he keeps going on like this.

'You're going to have to wait for the tooth to pass through your system if you want to get paid,' Dylan tells him, leaning across the table to take a big spoonful of chocolate chip. 'And then you'll have to fish it out of the toilet and give it a good clean before you leave it under your pillow.'

'Would that work?' asks Benji. 'How am I supposed to find it?'

Dylan shrugs. 'Maybe you could make some kind of filter system?' he suggests. 'You need to find something that you can push your poo through and leave the tooth behind.'

Scarlet shoves her bowl away from her.

'Stop talking!' she shrieks. 'Mum! Tell them to stop being so foul!'

'Don't be so uptight!' shouts Dylan back at her.

I pass Benji a tissue to dab his mouth and then sit back down, smiling at Nick as he tops up my glass. Our offspring start screeching at each other but I'm not going to let it spoil my evening. I'm getting better at standing back and letting them get on with it. They don't need me to micro-manage their every discussion and action. They can deal with things themselves and I can remove myself from the conflict and let them develop important independence skills. I can let the cacophony of sound wash over me.

I can rise above.

'Would *this* work?' Benji's voice wafts up to my higher level of being, yanking me back down to reality and I shove my chair back and wade into the chaos, desperate to save the new shiny and unsullied sieve, that I treated myself to from Ikea, from being used as a poo filter.

Chapter Twenty-Four

Year Ten, Class C are waiting for me when I walk into my classroom. Well, perhaps *waiting for me* isn't exactly the right phrase. They are actually engaged in what can only be described as warfare. Elise and the rest of the girls are gathered on one side of the room while Brody, Vincent, Wayne and the boys are huddled on the other. Missiles are flying through the air and the floor is littered with balls of paper.

'What is going on in here?' I yell, slamming my hand down on the desk and making them all jump. 'May I remind you that you are Year Ten now – not aged ten.'

They mutter and mumble under their breath but I stand there until every single one of them is seated. Then I perch on the side of my desk and reach for The Box.

I have not been looking forward to this lesson. Not one bit.

'Are we doing that today, Miss?' calls Elise, her voice

sounding nervous. 'Because I think I might be on library duty if we are.'

I shake my head at her. 'Yes, we're doing it today and no, sadly for you, you are not on library duty.'

She sinks despondently into her chair. I can't say I blame her. I'd rather be somewhere else too – anywhere but here. But Adele, in her infinite wisdom, has convinced Miriam that we are failing to address the students' personal, social and emotional needs and that the solution is to have a weekly session where the kids can submit anonymous questions which I then have the misfortune of attempting to answer.

What could possibly go wrong?

I reach through the opening of The Box. We had a staff meeting on this last week and Adele was adamant that we have to read out every single query. Apparently there is *no such thing as a stupid question* and if we start to censure what the kids are asking then we will be *failing to build an environment of trust.* I politely reminded her that I teach Year Ten and that every word that ever comes out of their mouths is ridiculous and pointless but she wouldn't budge.

I pull out the first piece of paper, holding my breath. But the gods of educators are clearly looking out for me and this first offering isn't too bad.

'So, our first question is about the range of healthy food available in the canteen,' I start before Brody interrupts me.

'You have to read it out properly, Miss,' he announces. 'Exactly how it's written on the paper. Miss Wallace said so in assembly. Otherwise you aren't *giving us a voice.*'

Excellent. The one time that Brody actually chooses to

pay attention in one of Miriam's boring assemblies and it's this one.

'Of course,' I say, smiling at him. 'I was just paraphrasing for speed. The precise wording reads: *"If I eat chips and a jacket potato for lunch, does it count as two of my five a day?"'*

I resist the urge to sigh. According to Adele and Miriam, it is crucial that we do not project any negativity about their questions, for fear of invalidating them.

'And does it?' asks Vincent. 'Does it count?'

I stare at the ceiling for a second and then plaster on my most sincere smile.

'No. It does not. Next question.'

I reach into the box and wince as my fingers touch something that is clearly not paper. Pulling it out, I hold it aloft in front of the class, filled with relief that it is still in its packet.

'I wondered where that'd got to,' yells a boy at the back of the class. 'Thanks Miss – chuck it over, will you?'

'As if *you've* got a use for a Johnny!' screeches Wayne. 'Come on lads – whose is it?'

The room fills with howls of hysterical laughter from the boys. The girls all fold their arms and scowl. I walk across to the bin and drop it inside, making a mental note to give my hands an extra good scrub at break time.

'What makes you think that this belongs to one of the boys?' I ask, making my way back to my desk. 'That's a big presumption to make.'

'Err – cos girls don't have willies, Miss?' offers Vincent, causing yet more hilarity from his side of the room.

'How old are you?' demands Elise. 'My little brother calls it a willy and he's four.'

'I am *so* sorry,' Vincent says. 'I obviously meant to say that girls don't have dongers.'

'Or cocks!' shouts Brody.

'Or todgers!' calls another boy.

'Or wing-wangs!' yells Brandon Hopkins, silencing the room in a heartbeat.

'Did you just say *wing-wangs*?' asks Elise, her face screwed up as if she's in pain.

'Knobs!' roars Wayne, and the room erupts once more.

It is the first time that Wayne and I have ever agreed on anything.

'I am aware of the fact that girls do not have a *penis*,' I inform the class at large, once the noise has died down. 'But contraception is everyone's responsibility. This could easily have been bought by a girl.'

There is a bit of disbelieving murmuring and I glance at the clock before reaching into The Box for a third time. With any luck this will be another random question about food or acne or the meaning of life. If I take my time and pretend that I know what I'm talking about then I can probably spin the next question out until the bell rings.

Lady Luck is clearly not playing ball today though. Not with me, anyway. I pull out a crumpled piece of paper that looks like it was written in a hurry and read the words before closing my eyes and praying for a miracle to whisk me away from this place. I am not paid enough for this crap.

'What does it say?' The clamouring voices inform me

that despite my best attempts, I am still standing here in front of Year Ten, Class C. 'Is it a good one?'

I can't read this out. It's not appropriate. I'm just going to have to shove it back in The Box and choose another one. There's no way that I can have a conversation about this with a class of fifteen-year-olds.

I hover my hand over the opening in The Box and then I pause. Somebody wrote this and yeah, sure – it's ninety-nine percent likely to be a way to disrupt the lesson and embarrass me. But what if it wasn't meant as a joke? What if someone wrote this because they really want to know the answer and they don't have anyone else to ask? There's no way that I could have talked about this with them a few months ago but maybe I can now. Maybe I just need to treat them like the mature young adults that they are becoming. Maybe I don't have to bluff my response. Maybe what the person who wrote this really needs is some honesty. Can I really afford to take the risk and dismiss it? Even if there is only a one percent chance that it's a genuine question?

I turn back to face the class.

'This question is a bit more personal,' I start. 'So I hope you will all be sensible and respectful. Because it takes great courage to seek advice about matters that may be of a more private nature and whoever wrote this, I admire your courage.'

'Just read it out!' shouts Brody.

I clear my throat and read from the paper, ensuring that my voice is as neutral sounding as possible.

'The person asks "*How do I get someone to have sex with*

me?'" I lower the paper and look at the class. 'Now, I think the most important thing here is for us to—'

'Loser!' bellows Vincent and it's the signal they've clearly been waiting for. The room descends into chaos as the boys bang their hands on the desks and the girls rock back and forth, clutching their stomachs and howling with laughter.

I give them a minute and then I raise my voice above theirs.

'Alright, settle down!' I call.

Nobody responds. If anything, the noise increases in intensity. I wait for another minute, hoping that their mirth will die down but it becomes clear that they are utterly unable to control themselves without some kind of intervention.

'Anyone still making a sound in five seconds time can expect to be in detention for the rest of the term,' I holler, and finally they listen. The room quiets down and I fix them all with a hard stare. 'That was a highly inappropriate response. I thought you were better than that, I really did. I'm very disappointed in you all.'

Elise drops her head and I feel a pang of regret. They might behave like chimpanzees at a tea party most of the time but the one thing they do actually seem to care about is having people feel proud of them. It's like teaching a class of overgrown toddlers.

'Sorry, Miss,' mutters a voice and then a few others join in. I stand and glare at them until I'm sure that the insanity has well and truly passed and then I relax my shoulders and drop the paper onto the table, intending on telling them to get their books out for the rest of the lesson.

A hand shoots up in the middle of the room. It is Brandon Hopkins, no doubt about to tell me that he desperately needs the bathroom and that if I don't let him go then he can't be held accountable for the resulting carnage. We have this conversation about three times a day and it never ceases to remind me that it's time I got a new job.

'Yes?' I raise an enquiring eyebrow. 'What is it?'

'I just wanted to know,' he says, staring me right in the eyes. 'How *do* you get someone to have sex with you?'

They say that people see red when they are provoked into full-blown anger. I do not see red. I see a generation of kids with no respect or consideration for anyone but themselves. And I don't know what Twinky would do if she had the misfortune of being faced with a class of insolent fifteen-year-olds but I know what Hannah Thompson is going to do.

She is going to give it them straight.

'You want to know how to get someone to have sex with you?' I ask, my voice sharp. A few kids laugh nervously but on the whole they keep quiet and I am glad to see that they have understood the gravitas of the situation. 'Well, firstly we need to address the use of language in this question.'

I stride into the middle of the classroom and sweep my eyes around the room. 'A person can *get* many things. For example, they can *get* a McDonalds if they feel in the mood for food. Or they can *get* pregnant or *get* chlamydia if they feel in the mood for unprotected sexual intercourse. The term *get* implies an acquisition of some sort. But it is very wrong and immoral to try to acquire a person for the sake of sexual activity. Do we all understand that?'

The room stays silent.

'Do we all understand that you can't just *get* someone to have sex with you?' I bark.

'Yes, Miss,' they mutter in unison. I can tell by their slumped body language and lack of eye contact that they are not entirely in their comfort zones right now. And I'm about to push them a bit further because I am an educator and this is what we do. We create a safe environment where challenging discussions can be enjoyed without fear or humiliation.

Well, perhaps *enjoyed* is too strong a word.

'So, moving onto the next issue with this question.' I head across to the window and lean against the glass. 'You are all still fifteen years old. It is, in fact, a legal offence for any of you to be involved in any sexual activity.'

This gets little reaction other than an unimpressed huffing noise so I move on.

'It's also important to consider the emotional and psychological impact of engaging in sex before you're ready,' I say. 'You have your whole lives ahead of you and believe me when I tell you that you're going to be grown-up for a very, very long time. There's plenty of opportunity for you to explore the world of adulthood but your time as a child is limited.'

I gesture up at the clock on the wall. 'Time is ticking, Year Ten, Class C. Make the most of being a kid while you can because before you know it, you're going to worrying about money and relationships and your own kids and global warming and whether the best years of your life are behind you and *that's* the time when you are free to engage in whatever consensual and legal sexual activity takes your fancy. And even then, you're going to be beset with neurosis about how often you're doing it and whether you're doing it the way everyone else is doing it – it's an endless battle against hormones and self-esteem and fatigue and body-confidence and don't even get me started on what happens when you have a mid-life crisis. You guys are definitely best holding off for as long as you can.'

I pause to take a breath. 'And I can't pretend that I have all the answers. Of course I don't. I'm a teacher, not the Internet.' I wave my hand in the direction of The Box. 'You can put whatever questions you like in there and the chances are that fifty different adults would answer them in fifty different ways. But what I do know is that when you're ready and of legal age, then engaging in sexual activities with a consenting person who cares about both your physical *and* mental health can be both meaningful and enjoyable. And it doesn't have to be about swinging from the chandeliers or setting the world on fire. It's about more than that. It's about knowing that you are safe and cared for and that you're part of something with a person who likes you for exactly who you are.'

'You're really selling it, Miss,' mutters Brody.

'I did *not* know that a conversation about sex could be so boring,' adds Vincent. 'Like, no offence Miss, but that was seriously dull.'

Brandon Hopkins nods. 'I wish I'd never asked now.'

I smile. I was right. All they needed was the honest truth. Something to cut through all the noise of being a teenager.

It's at times like this that I really do feel like *Teacher of the Year*. I am at the top of my game. I can tame the wild beast. I know no fear.

Maybe I'm not as much of a phony as I thought I was?

Chapter Twenty-Five

It is T-minus two days until Sex Con and I am struggling to maintain my composure. A million potential disaster scenarios are whizzing around my head and I am finding it hard to channel my thinking. I don't know what questions I'm going to be asked on the *Real Sex Talk* panel but I do know that I've done everything I possibly can to bring forth my inner Sex Goddess and I'm just going to have to cross my fingers and pray that some of my research has stuck. I still have the issue of what I'm going to wear but that's a problem for my day off tomorrow. I've debated the pros and cons of the dominatrix jumpsuit but there's no way that I'll be able to relax in it and I think that the entire event is going to be challenging enough without me feeling like mutton dressed as lamb. I've got my silver hair and my new, sparkling attitude. That's going to have to be enough.

We all gather in the kitchen at suppertime and I dish up lasagna (shop-bought, naturally). Nick opens a bottle of wine and the four us sit down at the table for a lovely, relaxing Thursday evening family catch up which is exactly what I need.

When will I ever learn?

'So – how was your day?' I ask Benji, passing him his plate. 'Did anything interesting happen?'

Benji shakes his head. 'Not really. Except the tooth fairy *still* hasn't come which means that I'll probably be owed a load of interest when it finally pays up.'

I gently blow on my lasagna to cool it down and look across at Benji. 'I'm fairly sure that interest rates are at rock bottom right now. I wouldn't get your hopes up. Now eat your supper.'

For a blissful moment the room is quiet. And then Scarlet decides that we're obviously a bit too relaxed.

'Can I go out on Saturday night?' she asks. 'With someone that I met at Petra's party, before you ask.'

Oh, it was a party, was it? Only I distinctly seem to recall you referring to it as a casual get-together.

'Sure,' I say. 'As long as you tell me where you're going and what time you'll be home.'

'I'm going to chill at their place for the day and I'll make sure that I leave you the address and I promise that I'll be home by ten o'clock.'

The speed of her answer makes me sit up straight and give her my full attention. This is not like Scarlet, not one bit – and I have a heightened awareness to any changes in my children's behavior.

'Is this a date?' I ask, looking her in the eye. 'Do I need to have more information about this *someone*?'

'Hannah,' says Nick. 'Do we need to find out every single detail?'

I look at our daughter and see her fidgeting uneasily in her chair.

Yes. Yes, we absolutely need to find out every single detail.

'How about I help you out?' I say, reaching for the salad bowl. 'I'll ask you questions and you can answer them. How does that sound?'

'Like a particularly torturous way to spend Thursday evening,' mutters Scarlet.

'I think it sounds great!' says Benji, picking all the beef out of his lasagna like he's excavating for treasure. 'It'll be like a real-life game of Guess Who! I'll start – do they wear glasses?'

'Somebody put me out of my misery,' groans Scarlet.

Nick snorts. 'Just answer her questions and then we can all get on with a nice evening,' he advises her. 'Hannah – you can ask her three things and that's it, okay? We have to start respecting her need for privacy.'

'That's fine with me,' I tell him.

A person can discover most things if they ask the right three questions and I'm no rookie.

'Question one: What are you going to do all day?'

This is a good starting point. It's not too threatening and I can learn a lot by her answer.

Scarlet shrugs. 'Dunno. Hang out. Play video games. Get some food. Stuff.'

Maybe not the rich source of information that I was hoping for but I still have two questions left.

'How old are they?' I look smugly at Scarlet. I've made the mistake before of assuming the gender of someone we're discussing and it'll only take one sniff of political incorrectness on my part for her to go off on a tirade about my lack of woke-ness. And then I'll have lost my opportunity for parenting…and snooping.

She sighs loudly. '*He* is older than me.'

I narrow my eyes.

'How much older?' I snap.

'A bit,' she volleys back.

'That's your three questions done,' Nick informs me.

'You didn't even ask any of the good ones,' complains Benji. 'Like does he have a beard or does he wear a hat?'

'How much older? More than one year?' I ignore them both.

'Why does it matter?' she asks, wrinkling her nose. 'Age is just a concept created by humans.'

I bloody hate it when she quotes me back at myself. Especially when the words sound so ridiculous.

Scarlet picks up her fork and puts some lasagna in her mouth.

'I don't know why you're making such a big deal out of all this,' she mumbles around her food. 'Granny was totally chilled about it when she met him.'

I narrow my eyes. 'Granny knows that you're hanging around with an older boy and she's okay with it?'

Granny knows that you're hanging around with an older boy and she DIDN'T TELL ME? What the actual fuck? She's gone too far this time. My mother and I are going to be having a challenging conversation in the very near future. Challenging for her, anyway.

'What does he do for money?' asks Nick, bringing me back to the moment. I'm impressed a) that he's finally caught up with the gravitas of the situation, and b) with his line of questioning. It's an important detail. And maybe a change of tack will trick her into sharing some information.

Scarlet stops scowling and grins. 'A bit of this, a bit of that.'

'That's not an answer,' I snap. 'Stop being difficult.'

She looks at me and shrugs. 'I'm not being difficult. That's what he told me. If I knew any more then I'd tell you.'

I seriously doubt that.

'What's his name?' I ask. I can't lie – I am not hopeful that the answer will bring me any relief.

She pauses, making sure that she has our full attention. 'It's *Skinz*. With a z.'

Of course it is.

She's on a roll now. 'And you were right, Benji. He *has* got a beard.'

Fuck. My. Life.

'We need to meet him before you can go over to his house,' I tell her.

'Absolutely,' agrees Nick, who seems to have gone rather pale. 'Why don't you invite him over here tomorrow evening instead?'

'I'd rather have a date in hell,' snarls our darling child, her smile dropping from her face.

'Park your attitude!' I bark back. 'We are trying to be

351

accommodating here but we can always just say no to you seeing him altogether.'

I'm lying. My parenting credentials might not be exactly stellar but even I know that banning her from hanging out with him is both pointless *and* dangerous. I know my daughter and it'll take only the slightest provocation to drive her underground. I might not like this latest turn of events but now, more than ever, Nick and I have to behave rationally.

'Fine.' Scarlet loads up her fork with more lasagna. 'Whatever. I'll just see Petra tomorrow then.' She puts the food in her mouth and chews slowly while switching her gaze between the two of us. 'Assuming you've not suddenly decided that I'm not allowed to hang out with my friends, now?'

'Of course not,' Nick assures her. 'And I'm sure we can come to some sort of agreement about this, this – *boy*.'

She smiles at him and the atmosphere in the room starts to thaw.

But that doesn't stop my stomach swirling and my head fizzing with unanswered questions, most of which start with '*what the hell*' and end with '*why yes, I'd love more wine...*'

We finish the rest of the meal in peace and I start to think that the evening can be saved. But our oldest child leaving home has clearly done nothing to diminish his ability to tag-team with his siblings in order to cause us maximum stress and the phone rings just as I'm getting into bed.

'What's wrong?' I ask, leaning back against the pillows. 'Why are you calling me so late?'

'Hi to you too, Mum!' He sounds exuberant and I can hear other voices in the background. 'I'm doing great! And what are you on about? It's not late. We haven't even started the evening yet.'

I glance at the clock and wince. It is late. If I don't go to bed now then I'm never going to get my eight hours' sleep.

'I'm just about to head out with the rest of the flat but I thought I'd give you a quick ring first to tell you my news.' Dylan's voice is trembling with excitement and I sit up straight and swing my legs off the bed, readying myself for action. I have no idea what he's about to say and that bothers me. It bothers me a lot. It's one of the strangest parts of your child leaving home – you go from being absolutely involved in every aspect of their daily life to not knowing what they're doing or thinking or feeling apart from the things that they choose to share with you.

It makes me feel constantly on the back foot and I do *not* like it.

'Is everything alright?' I enquire, as casually as I am able.

He laughs again. 'Mum. I told you that I'm doing great. Do you think I'd say that if I was ringing to tell you that there was some kind of disaster?'

I shrug. 'You might. If you were trying to soften the blow and let me hear traumatic news in a gentle way.'

'Well…' He pauses and I hear him take a deep breath. 'I've been really giving this some thought and I know that it might freak you out a bit but I promise that I'm not doing it on a whim and I think it's going to be something that changes me for the better.'

This situation just got a whole lot buggering worse. Images explode into my head, one after the other like fireworks being detonated by a toddler.

He's asked Harley the pole dancer to marry him.

He's got someone pregnant.

He's dropping out of university to become a monk.

'Spit it out,' I rasp into my mobile. 'What is it?'

'Drum roll, please,' he demands and I resist the strong urge to scream at him. 'I've signed up for a charity trek. I'm going to Everest, Mum – isn't that amazing!'

'Amazing,' I whisper, my voice weak as I flop back onto the pillows. 'Utterly amazing.'

'Don't start stressing out,' he tells me. 'It's all super-organised and everything.'

'Totally not stressing out,' I assure him. Nick comes in with two cups of tea and offers one to me.

'Get rid of the tea and put some wine in there,' I hiss, covering my phone with one hand and waving him away. I'm doing him a kindness – far better that he hears this revelatory news with something alcoholic in his bloodstream.

'So, just to clarify,' I say, once Nick has left the room. 'Are we talking about Everest as in *Everest*, Everest? As in *Mount Everest*?'

'Yes, Mum!' Dylan sounds more excited than I've ever heard him. 'Everest as in *Nepal*. We fly out to Kathmandu and then we fly from to Lukla. You should Google it – apparently it's the world's most dangerous airport and you only get one shot at landing and takeoff because the airstrip is right on the edge of the mountain and if the pilot gets it wrong then it's *Hasta La Vista, baby*.'

'Lovely,' I say, ignoring his terrible Schwarzenegger impression and willing Nick to hurry up with the wine. 'I will most definitely look it up online.'

And then I will no doubt be haunted by whatever horror stories the Internet has to offer me from now until your safe return.

'So you're okay with it, then?' he asks and it's only now that I can hear the nerves in his voice.

No. I am one hundred percent *not* okay with this. Not even a tiny bit. He is my first-born child and I am barely coping with him being a few hours away. The idea of him being in a different county is hard enough, never mind a different continent. I am his mother and it is my job to keep him safe. I could tell him that I hate the idea and I don't want him to do it and the chances are that he'll listen to me. He's always been good like that.

'It sounds like an incredible opportunity,' I tell him, reaching out and accepting the glass of wine that Nick is now proffering towards me, a questioning look on his face. 'Good for you, Dylan. Now you'd better tell your dad all about it.'

I hand my phone to Nick and take a big gulp of wine. I could have stopped him but I didn't. Just because I *could* doesn't mean that I *should*. And it's not just his physical safety that matters, I know that. This is the very first big decision that he's made for himself, all on his own.

It isn't about me. All Nick and I can do is stand back and

watch and pray that we've given him the wits to survive when we aren't there to catch him.

Nick ends the call and turns to face me. We say nothing for a moment, just stare at each other while everything that Dylan has said wraps itself around us and pulls us closer together.

'Well done,' he says after a while, raising his glass towards me. 'I heard what you said to him and I know it wasn't easy. But you did the right thing, Hannah.'

'I'm glad you took him out on all those climbing trips when he was younger,' I say, clinking my glass against his. 'At least he'll have a vague idea about what to expect.'

Nick smiles and puts his arm around me. 'He's trekking to Base Camp, not climbing to the summit,' he tells me. 'And he'll be fine. He's not a duffer. He just wants an adventure, that's all.'

I take another swig of wine. Dylan isn't a duffer, I know that. None of our kids are. It's just hard having to take a step back and watch them get on with their lives when what they want to do doesn't involve me.

But what I'm doing right now doesn't involve them either. Maybe I need to stop constantly focusing on their lives and sort my own out. They aren't the only ones allowed to get out there and have adventures and take risks and I have got to stop waiting for someone to give me permission to live my best life.

Sex Con is happening and I can step up and start behaving like a grown-up or I can faff around worrying about whether or not I really deserve to be there and waste this incredible opportunity.

I wake up on Friday morning and leap out of bed with a spring in my step. If Dylan can go to Everest then I can climb my own mountain. I will take charge of the things that are bothering me and I will stop waiting for someone else to solve my problems. It's time to take control. This morning I will deal with the small issue of finding clothes that will be appropriate attire for a Sex Goddess and this afternoon I will address my other issue and turn myself into an effective, proactive parent and finally deal with what's going on with my daughter.

Town is absolutely heaving but I am a woman on a mission. We're going to be eating baked beans on toast for the next six weeks to make up for my purchases but I am determined to have no regrets. This is absolutely the last spending I'll be doing for a while and I intend to make it count. I know that this is utterly reckless when we're so low on cash and I recently spent out on the jumpsuit but it was payday yesterday and I just can't see any other options. Besides, I'm intending on buying an outfit that will make me feel good, not like a sex fetishist. I'm bound to be able to get tons of use out of whatever I buy today.

Two hours later I am heading home laden down with bags. Once I'm back in the house I go straight upstairs, drag out my author shoes from under the bed and put everything on. Then I stand in front of the mirror in order to admire the full effect.

I've bought a new pair of black, skinny jeans that are, quite frankly, a revelation in denim. Jeans manufacturing has obviously come on somewhat since my last purchase and it is highly possible that I will be living in this particular pair for the rest of my days. They were marketed as being 'uplifting and slimming' and they certainly live up to the hype. My arse hasn't looked so firm in two decades.

And things aren't looking too shoddy up top, either. I've invested in a sleeveless black top with tiny little black beads and sequins stitched onto the fabric. I look sparkly and shimmery while also managing to exude (I think) a slightly moody, gothic look which is definitely enhanced by the incredibly trendy black leather jacket that I bought at the last moment because I've always wanted one but always thought that they're for other people.

Because fuck that. I can totally be *other people* if I want to be.

———————————

My mother arrives at one o'clock. I take a moment to compose myself and remind myself of the strong, feisty woman that I now am and then I fling the door open and usher her inside.

'Let's go into the kitchen,' I suggest, following her down the hall. 'The kettle's on.'

She starts to walk towards the battered old sofa where Dogger is stretched out, but I pull out a chair and wave her towards it. This is not a social call. I've invited her here for one reason and one reason only and I am determined to have my say.

'How's the writing going, darling?' she asks.

I ignore the question and sit down opposite her at the table.

'Why does Scarlet keep coming to talk to you?' I have debated many opening sentences and this was not one of them – but it seems that my Twinky mouth would just prefer to dive straight in.

Mum smiles at me.

'I can't tell you that, Hannah. It's like I said last time you asked, I can't break the Circle of—'

'Yes, yes – I know all about the bloody Circle of Trust,' I snap, not letting her finish. 'And I couldn't care less about it. She's been hiding stuff from me and then I found out last night that she's been seeing an older man and that you knew all about it – yet you said nothing to me and where's MY arsing Circle of Trust, hey? Tell me that! Because I'm her mother and she should be talking to me and you should be helping with that, not coming between us.'

Mum's face drops but I plough on. I should have said all of this weeks ago. Hell, I should probably have stood up to my mother *years* ago.

'She is seventeen years old and she thinks that I have nothing to offer her because every time she disagrees with me you're right there, with your right-on vibes and your liberal views and your bloody lust-for-life and quite honestly, I can't compete with it all because I haven't got the time or the energy to be a hip, funky mother as well as all the other people who I'm supposed to be right now.'

I stop and glare at her. 'So, are you going to tell me why she's been spending so much time with you and why you didn't tell me that she was seeing an older man?'

My mother nods. 'I'm not really sure what you're so upset about, Hannah – but I think in this instance I can probably bend the Therapist-Client rules a little.'

I nod stiffly, gesturing to her to continue.

'First of all, I don't know what Scarlet has been telling you but I had no idea that she was seeing someone older. I may be a Sex Therapist but I'm also her grandmother and I wouldn't ignore something like that.'

'You're not a real Sex Therapist,' I mutter unkindly. 'And she said that you'd met him.'

Mum looks puzzled for a moment and then smiles. 'Oh! Do you mean that lovely young man she was with when I bumped into her in town the other week? The boy with the funny name? Barbara's grandson?'

'I don't know about any of that.' My teeth are so gritted that the word struggles to push itself out of my mouth. 'But his name is Skinz.'

Mum nods. 'That's the one! Well, I really don't know what all the fuss is about, darling. He's the same age as she is.'

I shake my head firmly. 'Nope. That's definitely not right. She said that he was…'

I stop and think back to our exact conversation. She said that he was a *bit* older.

'She said that he earns his money doing *this and that*,' I tell my mother.

She nods. 'That's true. He's been mowing Barbara's lawn for a few quid every Sunday. And last week he cleaned her downstairs windows.'

I narrow my eyes. 'She said that he has a beard.'

Mum chuckles. 'That bit of bum-fluff sticking out of his chin?'

'So I assume that the motorbike riding and facial tattoos and criminal career are all completely bogus as well?' I hardly need to ask.

My mother looks at me pityingly. 'I doubt that boy has ever been in trouble with the law in his life,' she tells me. 'He was riding one of those silly push-along scooters though, if that sheds any light on the matter?'

The devious, sneaky madam.

'I think she's been having you on, Hannah!' she tells me helpfully. 'I wouldn't pay any attention to what she says. You were the same at her age. It's like teenagers think telling their parents the truth is the equivalent of handing over their soul.'

'So what has she been coming over to talk to you about?' I ask, trying to get back on track. 'Because this is all very well and good but she's always at your house lately. If she isn't asking you for advice about boys then what *is* she doing?'

Mum finally has the grace to look a bit abashed and I brace myself for whatever is coming next.

'I really don't think that I should tell—' she starts.

'Just say it!' I narrow my eyes and glower at her. 'Show me that Circle of Trust, okay, Mum?'

She sighs and puts both hands on the table. 'Fine. If you absolutely insist. But don't breathe a word of it to her and don't blame me when you wish that I hadn't told you.'

That is not going to happen. I am a strong tigress of a mother. I can handle whatever she is about to reveal and I will do whatever it takes to make sure that my relationship with my daughter is secure and robust.

'Knitting.'

The word takes me by surprise and I tilt my head to one side, trying to understand what she is telling me.

'Scarlet wanted to learn and she didn't want you to know about it. She's been coming over to my house several times a week and we've been working on something together.'

'Knitting?' I snort. 'Okay, Mum – very funny. I might be a rubbish parent whose daughter never talks to her anymore but I know her well enough to know that she wouldn't do something as lame as knitting for anyone.'

'She'd do it for you,' Mum stares back at me, her face impassive. 'She's knitting something for you because, contrary to what you may think, she doesn't think you're a rubbish parent. She thinks that you're feeling a bit sad since Dylan left and she wanted to do something nice to surprise you.'

'Oh.' I whisper it so quietly that the word is barely audible. 'That's...that's...'

That's the most insane and yet wonderful thing that I have ever heard. I feel warm and also ashamed. I feel moved by her thoughtfulness and also furious that she made me think all of those things about that boy. I feel relieved and loved and stupid and frustrated.

Basically, all the emotions that I have felt on a daily basis since giving birth to Scarlet, seventeen years ago. You'd think I'd be better at this by now, you really would.

'What is she knitting for me?' I ask and then I shake my

head. 'Actually, don't tell me. Whatever it is and however hideous it may be, I will wear it with pride. Unless it actually isn't that hideous and I won't actually have to wear it?'

I stare at my mother with hope in my eyes and she smirks.

'Oh, Hannah. It is more awful that you can possibly imagine. And you absolutely are going to have to wear it. In public and on a daily basis.'

I guess I can't win them all.

'I'll make that cup of tea now, shall I?' I get up and walk across to the now-cold kettle. 'Sorry for having a go at you, Mum. I was just really worrying about what Scarlet was up to.'

Mum shrugs my apology off like it's no big deal, just like she's always done. I was wrong to get so angry with her – she's only ever tried to look out for me and I should have known that she'd never do anything to jeopardise my relationship with Scarlet. I *would* have known that if I hadn't been so tied up with all of this book stuff. I guess I'm just going to have to do a better job of compartmentalising my roles in future.

'So how's Book Two going?' she asks, repeating her question from earlier as if the last ten minutes didn't happen. 'Have you nearly finished it yet?'

I put two teabags into some mugs and turn to look at her, thinking about what I can tell her. I don't want to rebuff her again after how I've just behaved but this is exactly the kind of conversation that I can't stand having with her. She'll dig and dig until I've divulged some personal information about myself or my emotions and then act like she knows everything there is to know about how I'm feeling. Sometimes it's easier just to lie to her and feed her some misinformation, just to keep her off my case.

Oh. For fuck's sake.

I have turned into my mother and Scarlet is turning into me.

'Well,' I say, pushing myself off the counter and resolving not to conform to type. What's the worst that can happen if I trust her with my innermost thoughts? She's my mother. She wants the best for me. 'I took your advice about pushing myself out of my comfort zone and, while the results have been a bit mixed, I'd say that I've had more successes than failures. I think I've learnt a few things about myself – and my sexual self.' I smile at her bashfully. 'Including when I should be listening to my mother!'

Her snort of laughter makes me jump. 'Oh Hannah! I don't have the first clue what I'm talking about! The last thing that you should be doing is taking advice from someone like me, especially when it comes to your sex life. Look at me – I'm not exactly a good role model for long-term relationships! The only good thing that I ever got from a man is you.'

I frown at her, not understanding. She gets up and walks across to where I'm standing, reaching past me to pour hot water onto the teabags.

'But you're training to be a Sex Therapist,' I say weakly, moving out of her way. 'I thought it was a Sex Therapist's job to give advice about – you know – sex?'

'Absolutely not,' she declares, shaking her head from

side to side. 'I've just completed *Module Four: It's Not About You* and it turns out that I've been slightly premature in my instruction and top-tip giving. Apparently, being a Sex Therapist isn't about telling people what to do after all. It's about listening to their problems and writing them down and then letting the clients find solutions for themselves.'

They didn't think it might be a good idea to introduce the *Let's Talk About Sex, Baby! Foundation One, Access to Counselling* course with a section on not proffering your inexpert, bogus opinion to all and sundry? I've spent all this time trying to follow her advice and *now* she's telling me that she didn't know what she was talking about?

Not that I can complain too much. I'd have never thought about making a star chart if she hadn't told me about rewarding myself for being brave and the seven shiny gold stickers that are now brightening up my fridge are also indicators of my much more sparkling sex life. I can't really grumble.

She adds the milks and then turns to hand me a mug.

'I've decided that it's not for me, Hannah. As I've told you before, I'm a do-er, not a writer or a listener.' She shudders. 'And if I'm completely honest I found it very difficult to understand what they were going on about, most of the time. I just kept hoping that some of it would sink in and I'd start to feel less of a phony, but there comes a point when you just have to admit that you don't know what you're talking about, doesn't there?'

Yes. I think there probably does. And I think I am possibly about to hit that point with an almighty bang.

Mum takes a sip of her tea and then glances up at me.

'I hope you won't mind, darling – but I've transferred the rest of the online credits that you gave me and I've started a new course.'

'Doing what?' I ask, grasping hold of my mug tightly.

'It's called *Hot Flush: Own your Menopause* and I think it's going to be really informative,' she tells me, walking back over to the table.

'I thought you went through that years ago, Mum?' I follow her and sink down into a chair. 'I'm not sure it's going to tell you anything you don't already know.'

She laughs brightly and reaches across to grasp my hand. 'It's not for me, silly! It's so that I can help you! Nobody talked about it in my day but it's time we broke this ridiculous taboo. Everyone gets old and everyone's body goes through changes, whether they're male or female. You should be able to shout about your shriveling ovaries and your sweaty chest from the rooftops, Hannah! And I'm going to be right there alongside you. We'll start a revolution, darling!'

Fuck. My. Life.

Chapter Twenty-Six

I feel like a woman who hasn't slept a wink, which is understandable. I was awake for most of last night, stressing out about what today is going to bring and it took me more than an hour this morning to put on enough concealer to hide the enormous bags under my eyes. I'm just praying that the bright, letterbox-red lipstick I'm wearing will distract from the exhaustion that I'm sure is plastered across my face. Hopefully the four coffees that I mainlined on the two-hour train journey here will kick in soon and I'll find some energy because right now, I'm running on fifty percent adrenalin and fifty percent fear and it's not making me feel particularly calm about the scene in front of me.

At least this event is taking place a long way from home and there's no risk of bumping into anyone who might recognise me. I'm fairly sure that nobody I know will be at an event like this, even though Cassie offered her wonderful support by suggesting that she bring Miss Pritchard and

Pru and the others on a *girls' day out*. I'm going to be doing her detention duty for the next two months as payment for declining her generous offer but it's worth it. This would be so much more terrifying if any of them were here.

'If you can just put this lanyard on then I'll take you through to the Green Room,' says the young girl who has been signing me in. 'Sorry about the rush but it's one of our busiest days of the convention today and everything is manic!'

She's not wrong. The foyer is packed with bodies and it's complete chaos. I've been elbowed in the back at least eleven times since I arrived and I've only been here for five minutes.

'Which hall is the Beginner's Guide to Swinging?' yells a girl in front of me.

'Hurry up!' screeches someone else to their companion. 'We're going to be late for Psychic Sex if you don't get a move on.'

My friendly guide gestures for me to follow her and we start to move through the room. This place certainly isn't what I was expecting, that's for sure. The visitors range from appearing as if they've just stepped off the set of an X-rated movie to looking like they've wandered in here by mistake, like the middle-aged couple in front of me who are standing right in the centre of the foyer, heads bent together while they consult their programme.

'I think it's saying that Porn for Parents is in Room 69,' says the woman. 'But I haven't got my reading glasses on – can you see it, Donald?'

I weave around them, wondering whether I should be

checking out that particular talk. I probably should be keeping abreast of the latest developments, just so that I can make sure that I'm aware of the things that the kids might be seeing. Unless I've got it wrong and Porn for Parents means something else entirely.

My guide pushes open a door and leads me inside. The noise level instantly drops and I relax slightly.

'If you wait in here then someone will be with you as soon as we're ready,' she tells me. 'You're all here nice and early so I'm afraid you're going to have a bit of a wait.'

That suits me. Just getting this far has cost me everything that I have. I am in no way prepared to get out on the stage yet.

'Thank you,' I say and then I step forward, taking in the room. I've never been in a Green Room before and I have to admit that despite the nerves, I'm excited. Part of me wishes that I'd had the forethought to really make the most of this experience and demand a rider. I could have asked for twenty white kittens and one hundred white doves, like Mariah. Although actually, the idea of a having a load of birds flapping around my head and shitting on my new leather jacket doesn't sound that great so perhaps it's just as well that I didn't bother.

'Are you in the right place, love?' asks a voice and I stop fantasising about Versace towels (Kanye) and brand new toilet seats (Madonna) and turn my focus to the other people in the room. There are three of them, all women – and while one of them is giving me a friendly smile, the other two are staring at me like I'm not supposed to be here.

I *knew* this would happen. There's only so long that a

person can fake it before they're found out and it would appear that my time is up. This event was for Sex Goddesses and even though I've tried really, really hard, I'm clearly an imposter. Not even my new leather jacket can hide the fact that I don't belong on this panel.

'Err – probably not,' I stutter, waving my hand in their direction. 'Yet here I am!'

'You're Twinky Malone, aren't you?' The smiling woman stands up and walks towards me. 'I've read your book. This *is* the right room – we're all here for the *Real Sex Talk* event.'

She puts her hand on my arm and gives it a quick squeeze. 'They won't bite,' she tells me quietly, leading me across to a small table that holds a few cups and a hot water urn. 'Don't look so scared!'

I swallow hard and smile back at her. 'Is it that obvious?'

'Maybe a bit,' she says. 'Now drink this coffee and come and say hello to everyone.'

I take the cup that she is offering, even though more caffeine is probably the last thing that I need right now and head across to the sofa area. There's an empty spot next to a petite-looking woman with a bright purple mohawk and I sit down, self-consciously patting my own hair into place.

'So, what do you do?' asks one of the women on the opposite sofa. Her voice is a tiny bit aggressive and quite honestly, she reminds me of Miriam.

'I'm a teacher,' I say automatically, sipping my coffee.

Mohawk turns to look at me, looking interested. 'Me too! What do you teach? I specialise in Tantra and discovering more about your sexuality through connecting your spirit and body. I run residential workshops in a healing environment with a focus on pleasure and opening our hearts and bodies to love.'

'Oh,' I say, attempting a chuckle. 'I teach English in a secondary school. With a focus on getting through the day and not causing too much damage.'

All three women stare at me and then the nice, smiley one leans forward and helps me out.

'That's not why you're here though, is it?' she says. 'I read your bio. You're an author. You write erotic fiction.'

I nod gratefully.

Of course that's why you're here. Get a fucking grip, Hannah.

'Why are you here?' I ask Miriam-lookalike.

She smirks at me. 'I'm an erotic masseuse,' she tells me, with a tone that suggests I should be impressed. 'I won an award last year for my services to the sex industry.'

'That's nice,' I say weakly. She scowls at me and I rush to sound more enthusiastic. 'And do you enjoy the work?'

Thankfully, I am saved from having to hear her reply by the door opening and a young man ambling into the room.

He plods over to where we're standing and does a quick head count.

'Good. You're all here. I'm supposed to take you to Hall Five.'

I totter after him and the others in my author shoes, desperately hoping that a) my lipstick hasn't smeared itself across my face as it is often prone to do and b) my bladder can hold out for the duration of the event. There doesn't appear to be time for a visit to the bathroom and I've had three natural childbirths. It's not a given.

We wind our way down long corridors and up several

flights of stairs and then the bored young man leads us through a doorway and onto a stage, where four stools are lined up in a horseshoe shape in front of a closed set of curtains, like we're in some kind of cheesy girl band. There's no time to think about anything before I'm hoisting myself onto a stool at the end and he is shoving a microphone into my hand. And then the lights go dim and a loud voice booms over the speaker system.

'And now – the event you've all been waiting for! Please give a very warm Sex Con welcome to our panel for this afternoon's *Real Sex Talk* event!'

There is a smattering of applause, the curtains swish open and the spotlights flash on. I blink rapidly, trying to get my eyes to adjust to the brightness. This is the moment that I've been feeling most anxious about. Sitting up here and being looked at by a hall filled with people. The air heavy with the expectation of the crowd. The knowledge that any words that come out of my mouth will be heard by a critical gathering of Sex Con delegates who have all paid to hear what I have to say.

Last night, when I couldn't sleep, Nick tried to help me out with some strategies for dealing with this situation. And by *help me out* I mean that he told me to stop worrying and just to imagine the entire audience naked, before rolling over and going back to sleep. I didn't think much of his suggestion at the time but right now, with a heart that is beating at twice the normal speed and a line of sweat breaking out on my forehead, I figure that I've got nothing to lose. So I take a deep breath in, exhale as slowly as I am able and look out at the assembled throng.

I do not know what the official number of people has to be for them to be counted as a *throng*. I do know, however, that it is probably more than eight. Maybe they would look a bit more *throng-like* if they were all sitting together instead of spread out across twenty rows of chairs? Then again, maybe not.

My brain starts whirring. Binky assured me that my presence at this event was going to boost the sales of my book but I can't see how it can possibly do that. Not unless every member of the audience is planning on buying several hundred copies each, which seems unlikely.

A woman bounces out onto the stage with a microphone in her hand and gives the audience a cheery wave.

'Good afternoon, Sex Con!' she shouts perkily, as if she's at the O2 Stadium. 'I'm Marigold and I'm your host for today's panel, which is part of our *Real Sex Talk* theme and is titled: *Sex Goddesses Tell All*. Are you having a good convention so far?'

There's a bit of muttering from the third row but other than that, the hall stays silent.

'Tough crowd,' mutters Mohawk, who is sitting next to me. 'Let's hope they warm up a bit.'

I let my eyes roam across the hall while Marigold proceeds to explain the health and safety procedures and that, as there isn't a fire drill scheduled for this afternoon, we should all respond immediately to the sound of an alarm. The attendees at this talk seem to have come from all walks and stages of life and seven of them are women. The one man present is sitting right in the very middle of the front row and it is instantly apparent that he wants to be here even less than I do. The woman sitting next to him has her hand clamped to his thigh and I suspect that if she were to release her grip then he'd be off faster than a ferret up a drainpipe.

'So – now the boring bit is over, let's get down to business!' trills Marigold, once she's finished pointing out the emergency exits. She turns to look at the four of us on stage. 'Let me introduce our Sex Goddesses! First we have Ma-lady, a world-renowned dominatrix and an expert in her field.'

My jaw drops open as I stare at smiley, friendly Ma-lady. I did *not* have her down for that job.

'And next we have Celia Fox, who is a highly sought-after sexual masseuse.'

I'm slightly disappointed that she isn't called Miriam, after all.

'And next we have Elaine Muttridge, a Tantra Practitioner Level 2, with ten years of experience.'

I glance at the woman sitting next to me. I don't wish to be judgemental but I have never met a person whose name is such a terrible fit. I have met *Elaines* before and she is definitely not one of them. There's no way it works for her. I shall continue to privately refer to her as Mohawk.

'And last but not least, we have Twinky Malone. Twinky writes books that are a mash up of humour and erotica.'

I feel myself flush with embarrassment but it could have been worse. She could have said *porn*.

'Goddesses!' calls Marigold, striding to the front of the stage. 'Are you ready to share your secrets and tell all?'

'Hell, yeah!' calls Celia, punching her fist in the air.

'Bring it!' yells Mohawk.

'I was born ready!' shouts Ma-Lady.

They all turn to look at me.

'I think so,' I say, holding the microphone too close to my mouth. The loudspeakers emit a high-pitched shriek and everyone winces.

'Then let's get going with the first debate point,' says Marigold hurriedly, glaring at me. 'And we're diving straight into it with question one. Sex Goddesses – which position is guaranteed to make you end the evening with a smile on your face?'

Celia raises her microphone and looks around at the rest of us. 'I'll start with this one, if that's okay with all of you?'

We all nod our agreement. It is possible that I nod a little too enthusiastically because she shoots me a strange look before turning back to face the audience.

'As a sexual masseuse, I am highly experienced in manipulating the body into a variety of positions,' she begins. 'I will never forget this one time, when my client was—'

Movement further down the hall distracts my attention and I strain to see what the woman in row five is doing. She's leaning over and I can only see the top of her head as she rummages about with something that is, thankfully, out of my view. I really hope that this isn't supposed to be one of those interactive talks where the audience gets involved, like 4D cinema where you get pelted with liquid and the seats vibrate.

Then she sits up straight again and I can see what she was doing. Or rather, what she was getting out of her bag. I expected to see some unusual things at Sex Con but an elderly lady getting on with her knitting while a sexual masseuse regales us with lurid tales of kinkery was not actually one of them. I'm pretty sure she's my imaginary reader, Valerie, actually. I always knew that she'd be hardcore.

'—and so that's why I always recommend that particular position to any of my clients who are failing to reach orgasm,' finishes Celia.

Damn it. I missed what she said and now I'll either have to face the embarrassment of asking her later or forever miss out on sexual fulfillment.

'That was a wonderful start!' coos Marigold. 'Our next question is all about getting in the mood. So – what are your top tips for getting your sexy on?'

She turns to look at us and for one chilling moment I think that she's directing the question at me. But then Malady raises her microphone and starts to speak and I sink back onto my stool, the relief making me almost giddy. These women clearly know their way around the business end of an orgasm and I'm feeling very unqualified to be here. I just need to stay quiet and look goddess-like and hope that I can get away without being exposed as an imposter.

'Well, I can only speak for myself,' she says, her gentle voice floating around the hall. 'But when I need to get myself in the mood for love, I turn on the music and I dance.'

'Me too,' agrees Mohawk. 'I put on something slow and sensual and then I get sultry as hell.'

'And if my partner is there too, then all the better,' says Ma-Lady. 'She loves to watch me dance for her.'

Marigold turns to face the audience. 'I think we'd all like to see a demonstration of this X-rated dancing, wouldn't we?'

The lack of response suggests that nobody gives a shit about seeing anyone's sex dance but this doesn't deter Marigold, who reacts like they've just given a standing ovation.

'Yes! Let's do it!' she cries, signaling to a man at the back of the hall who flicks a switch. The room fills with the recognizable strains of *Lady Marmalade* and Celia, Mohawk and Ma-lady all leap off their stools and start gyrating on the edge of the stage. Marigold whoops and hollers into her microphone and in the fifth row, Valerie rolls her eyes and starts a new line of her knitting.

I sit on my stool, trying to look composed and completely in my depth while inside my head I am doing the equivalent of hiding under the duvet. It's just like the staff meal that we have every Christmas when someone puts on some music and everyone gets up to dance. It's just not my thing and I hate that the only options are to join in and feel ridiculous, or sit it out and look like a killjoy. So I do what I always do in these kind of situations which is to smile too brightly and tap my foot in time to the beat and attempt to look like I'm having a wonderful time watching everyone else while hoping that the fire alarm goes off and puts me out of my misery.

And just when I think that the whole scenario can't get any more awkward, Marigold ramps it up a notch.

'Twinky!' she calls. 'Come and join us!'

I smile so hard that my face hurts and then I shake my head but I'm wasting my time. She sashays across the stage towards me and takes hold of my hand.

'Show us your sexy!' she shouts as the singer asks if I *want to give it a go*, which I absolutely do not.

'I'm fine here!' I tell her. 'I've got a bad back.'

'All the more reason to show us your sexy moves,' she says, yanking me onto the floor. It's a good job that my bad back is as fictitious as my book because otherwise I'd be in agony right now.

She grabs her microphone and speaks over the music. 'And for those of you who think that a disability or physical impairment might be a barrier to using dance as a sexual enhancer, then think again. Twinky is going to show you how, even with terrible back pain, she manages to get both herself and her partner in the mood.'

She steps away and gestures at me and the other three women stop dancing and retreat to their stools.

'Take it away, Twinky! Shake that sexy booty.'

I *should* take it away. If I had an ounce of sense then I would shake my sexy booty right out of here and I would keep on shaking until I was far, far away from this insanity.

I start to dance. Well, dance is possibly a bit of a strong word to use for what I am doing but I am moving and that's a start. The music increases in volume and I try to ignore the eight people in the audience and the other women on the stage and just let my body do whatever comes naturally. And actually, it isn't that bad. I close my eyes and I stop thinking and as the chorus floods the room, I let it all out. I shimmy and slink and then finally, in a burst of last-minute brilliance, I run my hands across my body and down my thighs. I am flowing and graceful and loose. I only hope that there aren't any complaints about the explicitness of my presentation.

The music ends and I return to my stool, slightly out of breath.

'Well, what a performance that was!' says Marigold to the audience. 'We can certainly tell that you like to keep things light-hearted and humourous! And I think it's fair to say that we could all see just how stiff and stumbling you were, so thank you, Twinky – Sex Con is all about promoting sexuality for everyone and that includes those with mobility issues.'

Humourous? Stiff and stumbling? Screw you, Marigold.

That's the last time that I am going to dance.

Ever.

For the rest of my life.

'So, moving on to the next question,' she says. 'What's the best place to have sex?'

'Outside, where Mother Nature can bestow you with her bounty!' says Ma-Lady.

'Somewhere public!' adds Celia. 'Where there's the constant thrill of being caught.'

'In a sauna,' contributes Mohawk. 'Especially if you like things hot and steamy.'

'In a bed?' I ask, before I can stop and think. 'Where it's comfy and warm. Both of those things are pretty important, don't you think?'

'You heard it here first, folks!' Marigold tells the

audience, chuckling into her microphone. 'Apparently comfy and warm is the new sexy!'

The other women laugh and I shuffle on my stool.

'And what about the best thing to wear in bed?' asks Marigold. 'Do you wonderful Sex Goddesses have any helpful suggestions for our audience about how to liven things up on those rare occasions when the only available location *is* the bedroom?'

'I think it's important to sleep in the nude,' says Mohawk. 'There is no item of clothing that can ever rival the beauty of the naked, human form.'

'I disagree,' says Celia. 'I think a soft, sensual piece of lingerie can enhance the body and our own feelings of sexuality. I've always found that wearing something luxurious, especially in silk or satin, can make me feel like a Goddess even if I'm just wearing it to perform household chores. The right underwear can get me in the mood, every time.'

I sit forward and peer at Celia.

'Come off it,' I say, because there is only so long that I can sit here and listen to this utter crap. 'Are you telling me that you can turn doing the laundry or making the packed lunch into something sexy just because you're doing it in a pair of scanty pants? Because if you are then I'm not buying it.'

'True sexiness comes from within,' she tells me, frowning slightly. 'You need to invest in yourself and if you do that then anything can be a journey in sensuality.'

'I think you're right with the first part,' I agree. 'Sexiness *should* come from within. But are you honestly saying that you feel sexy just because you've put on some fancy underwear? Because I've tried that and honestly, it wasn't as sexy as a nice pair of flannel pajamas.'

A muttering of agreement spreads around the hall.

Cassie told me a while ago that women need to have all the answers; that knowing everything about everything is our one true power. But I think she's got it a bit wrong. I think it's okay *not* to know what you're doing sometimes. Maybe if we admitted that we aren't necessarily in control every goddamned minute of the day then we might feel a bit less governed by the need to be perfect.

Nobody can be a goddess all the time.

'I thought we were here to talk about real sex,' I say tentatively. 'It just isn't honest to pretend that everyone is constantly in touch with their sexual selves or getting it on, Hollywood-style, at every available opportunity. Some of us are too knackered at the end of a long day to do anything other than put on our pajamas and watch Netflix and drink wine before falling into bed. And what happens after that isn't usually planned out or orchestrated. It just happens.' I pause and think about what I've just said. 'Or not.'

'Here, here!' shouts Valerie from the fifth row and when I glance across I see that she's finally put her knitting down.

The room goes quiet and then Marigold clears her throat.

'So – in your *expert* opinion, what should we be talking about?'

I ignore her snarky tone and try to explain.

'The truth. The messy, uncomfortable truth because sex

is messy and it *can* be uncomfortable and that's just the way it is.'

'You're doing it wrong if it's uncomfortable,' Mohawk tells me.

'Am I?' I ask her. 'Or do we all just think that everything has to be perfect, one hundred percent of the time?'

Celia nods firmly. 'When it comes to sex, we have to demand that it is absolutely as perfect as it can be. We deserve that. That's what being a Sex Goddess is all about.'

'Hell, yeah!' Mohawk punches her fist in the air in solidarity with Celia's proclamation.

'Is it, though?' I pause, trying to find the words for the thoughts that are whizzing through my head. Maybe I should just shut up but for the first time in forever I feel like I'm finally starting to get it. 'Or is being a Sex Goddess about trying to have sex as silently as possible so that you don't traumatise your children?'

Someone in the audience laughs.

'Or being able to laugh when you try to introduce something new and neither of you can figure out where your legs are supposed to go so you end up kneeing your partner in the face?'

'That doesn't sound remotely sexy,' says Mohawk.

I nod. 'No, it doesn't. But it should because there's nothing sexier than being confident enough to laugh when it all goes wrong. I thought we were here to share our secrets but I think that this might be the biggest secret of all. We're all faking it and we're all quietly scared that everyone else has got it all figured out. Maybe if we stopped bullshitting about this stuff then we'd all be a bit more relaxed about the whole thing.'

'And this is what we love about Sex Con!' declares Marigold, facing the hall and not looking as if she is loving this conversation in the slightest. 'A bit of healthy debate. And now, moving on to our final question for the panel. If we're looking to our diets for improved sexiness, which aphrodisiac foods should we be eating?'

'Oysters, for sure,' states Celia.

'I swear by Maca powder,' says Ma-lady. 'It really boosts your libido and it's perfect in a smoothie.'

'It's got to be Tofu,' insists Mohawk and it takes everything I have not to tell her that this is the most ridiculous thing I've heard (in the last minute, anyway). It's like they didn't hear a single word that I said.

'And what about you?' asks Marigold, looking at me.

'Pie and chips,' I tell her. 'It's warming, it fills you up and the only thing you have to do is bung it in the oven. That's the definition of sexy food for me.'

The hall erupts in laughter.

I grin and give Valerie a wink.

I'll get my coat. My work here is done.

Chapter Twenty-Seven

T he weak winter sun is streaming through the window when I wake up on Sunday morning. I stretch out my legs and look up at the ceiling, reveling in the fact that yesterday is finally over and I don't have to worry about it anymore. In fact, I think the chances of me being asked to anything like that ever again are less than the chance of me winning the lottery, which is only a good thing.

Marigold couldn't get me out of there fast enough after yesterday's talk was over. I had intended to have a little look around the rest of the convention and pick up a few top tips for *So Much Sex* but on reflection, that wasn't really necessary. I might not be a Sex Goddess but I know what I want to write and I don't need any experts to tell me what it should look like.

'How's the head this morning?' Nick walks into the bedroom and puts a cup of tea down on my bedside table.

I sit up and smile gratefully at him. 'No worse than I deserve,' I tell him. 'It turns out that drinking all of the coffee and then all of the wine and forgetting about the food isn't such a great idea after all. Although I do recall that the evening ended on quite a positive note.'

He grins at me. 'We don't do too badly, do we? For an old, married couple?'

I cringe. 'You're sounding a bit self-satisfied there, Mr Thompson. Please can we not turn into the stereotypical smug, old marrieds?'

'I reckon I'm entitled to a bit of smugness this morning.' He gives me an over-the-top wink. 'And *you* were pretty satisfied last night, if I remember rightly?'

I shrug. 'Meh. It was okay, I suppose.'

I'm lying. It wasn't okay. It was no-frills, happy-go-lucky, stripped-back marital sex. No props, no tricks, no circus.

And it was absolutely bloody brilliant.

'You're clearly still under the influence of yesterday's drinking and experiencing memory loss,' Nick tells me, still smirking. 'You should get a bit more sleep. I can take Benji to his swimming lesson and Scarlet is still in bed. I suggest you leave her there – I know you're going to want to grill her about last night but maybe leave it for a while, yeah?'

I frown. 'We need to talk to her properly though. It was really late when she got back last night and I'm not convinced that she was with Petra. She was far too perky and smiley for my liking. We need to find out what the deal is with this *boy* – and I need to get her to tell me the truth for once.'

He looks unconvinced. 'Of course we do. But can we at

least try to have a nice, quiet Sunday lunch together before the Spanish Inquisition begins?'

I scowl at him and reach for my tea. 'It's not an inquisition. Merely a gentle questioning about her life choices.'

Nick raises an eyebrow. 'If you say so. Are you still planning on doing some writing this morning?'

I nod. 'I'm ready to get it done,' I tell him. 'Bella Rose and Daxx are going to explore the true meaning of their relationship, warts and all.'

Nick pulls a face. 'Is that genital warts? Because I don't think anyone could make them sound erotic, Hannah, not even you.'

He ducks as I throw my alarm clock at him and I can still hear him laughing as he heads out of the room and down the stairs.

After a long shower that goes some way to refreshing my tired body, I find my laptop and settle down at the kitchen table. I've been struggling so much to finish this book after Binky told me that I need to combine my *trademark humour* with increased sexual content, because I just couldn't figure out the way forward. But I get it now. I don't have to try to be funny. Sex *is* funny all on its own, as long as you stick to reality. And even though I thought I'd got it nailed, I've not really been writing the real truth.

And that's all that I have to do.

I open up my laptop and think about everything that has happened over the last couple of months and all the things that I've done in my pursuit of sexiness. Some of them have been quite fun and some of them have been mortifyingly embarrassing and what none of them has done is turn me into a Sex Goddess. But that's okay and it isn't necessarily my fault because I'm starting to suspect that she doesn't actually exist. Not just inside me – but in anyone. I think that there is a distinct possibility that Sex Goddesses are as mythical as Aphrodite herself and that attempting to become one is as realistic as attempting to become the tooth fairy.

Which reminds me – Benji's grotty tooth is still loitering under his pillow. If I don't remember to replace it with the obligatory one-pound coin soon then it's going to become a serious health hazard. I never did find out how he rescued it after the accidental swallowing but I'm starting to come to the conclusion that there are some things that a mother doesn't need to know. Although I probably should ditch that sieve, just to be on the safe side.

I flex my fingers and let my mind transport me to Oklahoma. A state of prairies, forests, plains. A state that invented the shopping trolley. A state where the number one export is (allegedly) sperm. A state where Bella Rose and Daxx are currently trying (and failing) to understand both the emotional and physical boundaries of their relationship.

And then I write. I write about all of the fabulously awkward things that can and will happen whenever two people attempt to get their groove on.

Once Bella Rose had stopped panting, she looked suggestively down at Daxx and raised an eyebrow.

'Come with me?' she asked him.

Daxx smirked. 'I just did,' he told her but his words were wasted. Bella Rose had already flung on a robe and was outside on the magnificent balcony and after a moment he rolled off the bed, threw on some clothes and joined her.

'Look that that sunset,' he purred. 'It's almost as beautiful as you.'

Bella Rose gazed at the sky. Daxx was right – the Tulsan sunset was spectacular and only slightly marred by the knowledge that the brilliant red hue was mostly caused by pollution as the light interacted with nitrogen and oxygen in the air in a phenomenon knows as Rayleigh scattering.

'It's so hot out here this evening,' he said, turning to face her. 'Why don't you cool down a little?'

Bella Rose nodded. 'I was just about to have a shower,' she told him.

Daxx pouted. 'I was more suggesting that you lose the robe,' he said, running his hand down her bare arm. 'Let's get it on, baby.'

Bella Rose stepped back and looked at him in disbelief.

'Again?' she asked. 'Out here? On the balcony?'

Daxx smiled his most seductive smile. 'Let's live dangerously for once, sweet thing.'

Bella Rose took a hefty slug of wine and then lowered her glass to give Daxx her sternest look.

'You're already living dangerously if you honestly think that I'm going to get down and dirty out here with you.'

She shook her head and stuck out her thumb.

'Number one: It is a well-known fact that having sex in a high up place comes with the obvious risk of falling off that high up place. I do not want sex with you enough to risk dying.

Number two:' She stuck out her index finger. 'Under the Oklahoma Code Indecent Exposure Laws, Section 21-1021, it is a felony to lewdly expose your genitals in public. It can be punished with incarceration between thirty days and ten years, fines up to twenty thousand dollars or possibly community service. I do not want sex with you enough to risk either a decade in prison, making myself poor or picking up litter. You should have relocated us to a more relaxed state if you were planning on getting frisky al-fresco.'

Daxx opened his mouth to speak but Bella Rose hadn't quite finished.

'And number three: I can tell you right here and now that I will get absolute zero pleasure from a hurried, frantic shag up against that railing. You might get a kick out of feeling as if you're doing something a bit risqué but I am a grown ass woman and I know what I like.'

She turned and stepped back inside the penthouse. Daxx stayed outside on the balcony, clearly unsure about where he stood after her strong reaction. Bella Rose deposited her wine glass by the sink and then checked the time again. He was an irritating twat a lot of the time but she probably had got a spare fifteen minutes.

'I'm on for another session,' she called through the open window. Daxx jerked his chin up, a hopeful smile flooding across his face. 'But we have a perfectly comfortable bed in here.'

She headed into the bedroom. Daxx was hot on her heels and they were both naked in seconds. Well, Bella Rose was. Daxx, as always, struggled to take off his socks and Bella Rose made a mental note to suggest that next time, he removed them before taking off his boxer shorts. She may well have seen the most intimate parts of him but there was nothing sexy about being confronted with his arse in her face.

Once he was finally undressed, he advanced upon the bed where Bella Rose was quickly checking her phone, just to make sure that she hadn't missed anything exciting on Facebook.

'Do you want to try—' he started.

'No.' Bella Rose cut him off mid-sentence. She didn't know what he was about to propose but if it was something new or quirky then she was absolutely not in the mood. She was delighted that he'd been so receptive to learning some new moves but as always, he was trying to run before he could walk and she was keen for him to master the positions that gave her some pleasure before he got all sex-god on her. 'Let's just do the stuff that I showed you, yeah?'

She put down her phone and rolled towards Daxx. He clasped her body to his own and then, in an act as old as time itself, they joined together in a blissful liaison.

'No! Not there!' shrieked Bella Rose, pulling away and glaring at Daxx. 'Are you trying to be funny or something?'

'Sorry!' he gasped. 'Sorry, sorry, sorry. That was totally unintentional.'

'It'd better have been,' Bella Rose muttered darkly. 'There are probably laws about that in Oklahoma too and if you try that again then I'll report you myself.'

Daxx sighed deeply and rolled onto his back.

'Now what's wrong with you?' demanded Bella Rose, before glancing down and seeing the problem.

The sun had sunk lower in the sky and it would appear that it had taken Daxx's enthusiasm and vigour with it.

Bella Rose patted his shoulder kindly.

Don't worry, honey,' she told him, her voice kind and reassuring. 'It's really very common.'

Daxx looked up at her, his eyes hooded and dark.

'But what kind of a man am I if I've lost that?' he whispered. 'It's my entire identity.'

Bella Rose snorted and swung her legs off the bed. 'You can be a bit of a dick sometimes,' she agreed. 'But I think there's a bit more to you than a five-and-a-half-inch copulatory organ.'

Daxx flinched.

'Fine,' Bella Rose said patiently. 'Six inches.'

And then she blew him a kiss and gave him a smile before dragging him off the bed and towards the shower. Daxx drove her crazy most of the time but he brought her a cup of tea in bed every morning and rubbed her shoulders after a long day and bought her chocolate when she was on her period. And when the whole world felt a bit crappy, he was always there for her.

Just like she was for him. And she knew that he might need a few minutes to recover but there was no reason for that time to be wasted. She had needs too. You can't keep a good woman down for long.

I stop typing and lean back in my seat. I don't know if this is what Binky wants and I'm still not convinced that it's really that humorous but it's *got* to be hitting all the right notes on the sexy front and that's just going to have to be good enough. The clock on the wall tells me that I've got half an hour before Nick returns with Benji and, as I'm feeling on a roll, it's probably time to do something about the other issue in my life.

I push back my chair and walk to the bottom of the stairs.

'Scarlet!' I yell, loudly. 'Time to get up!'

There is no response so I shout again, even louder. And then a third time, this time really letting my vocal chords have a workout.

There's a grunting sound from the vicinity of her room and then the ceiling above me shakes as something stomps across the upstairs floor. Scarlet's bedroom door flies open and a bleary-looking teenager appears at the top of the stairs.

'Why are you screaming?' she demands. 'Is the house on fire?'

'Good morning, sweetheart!' I trill. 'I'm just about to put the kettle on. Would you like a cup of tea?'

'It's the middle of the night,' Scarlet snarls.

'It's eleven o'clock in the morning,' I point out, reasonably. 'Put some clothes on and come downstairs. I want to talk to you.'

Scarlet mutters something that I can't quite hear and goes back into her room, slamming the door behind her. I walk back into the kitchen and start making tea, taking my time because I know she won't appear for at least another fifteen minutes.

I'm sitting at the table waiting by the time she finally makes her entrance.

'There's a cup of tea for you,' I say, pointing to the chair opposite me. 'Sit down and let's have a proper chat.'

'What is there to chat about?' she asks, looking at me suspiciously as she sinks into the seat. 'Has something happened? Are you having an affair? Are we going to be products of a broken home?'

'What?' I shake my head and frown. 'No! Why would you say that?'

'Maybe because you've been acting even crazier than usual recently,' she mutters. 'There's definitely something going on around here. You keep dashing off to London on random trips and you're always bashing away at your laptop.'

Both of these things are true but that is absolutely not the conversation that I am intending on having with her.

'So – how are things with you?' I say, bringing the focus back onto her. 'Anything exciting happening in the world of Scarlet Thompson?'

She rolls her eyes at me. 'No, *Mum*. Nothing exciting.'

'Oh, come on!' I lean forward and give her my friendliest, least threatening look. 'You're seventeen years old! The world is your oyster! You must have lots going on.'

Scarlet wrinkles her nose. 'I don't know what life was like when you were seventeen but I can assure you, I do not have *lots going on*. Unless you mean lots of homework or lots of stress or lots of constant harassment by my mother about what I'm doing and who I'm doing it with – in which case, yeah. I've got a butt ton of stuff going on.'

Excellent. I knew that if I played this right I could get her onto the subject I want to discuss.

'And how *was* your evening?' I ask, leaping right in with the hope that I can catch her off guard. 'Did everything go okay with *Petra*? Was anyone else at her house?' I lean forward. 'Any boys?'

She leans back in her chair and sighs. 'Okay, whatever. I went to Petra's house like I already told you and yes there were a few other people there too. Including boys. Are you happy now?'

I am feeling quite content, actually. I think last night's exploits with Nick have released some kind of endorphin rush because I feel calmer and more relaxed than I have done in ages. So yes, I am happy – and I am also surprised that she's revealed this so easily. It's clearly too early in the day for her to relish torturing me with a lack of information and I make a mental note to always interrogate her before noon in the future.

'And was *he* there?' I enquire.

She frowns. 'His name is Skinz. You can say it, you know?'

I can. But that doesn't mean that I want to.

'Fine.' I stare back at her. 'How was your evening with *Skinz*?'

Scarlet raises one eyebrow. 'Okay.'

Clearly no more dirt is going to be dished. I'm going to have to try harder.

'He sounds very interesting,' I tell her. 'Why didn't you tell me that he was in your year group at school?'

She shrugs. 'I didn't *not* tell you that. You just made an assumption.'

I think about the fact that she is secretly knitting me a gift to cheer me up and swallow my harsh retort. I get it. She needs to control something in her life and if not telling me everything makes her feel good then I'll just have to deal with it, like the respectful, understanding mother that I am. It's okay for us to have parts of our lives that we don't share with the entire world. I know that, better than anyone.

On the other hand, I could also keep on seeking out information with my subtle questioning and mild-mannered interest and if that fails, tracking her phone and roping in my mother to keep me appraised of any new developments.

'So.' I smile at her encouragingly. 'Are you dating him now?'

Scarlet holds one hand against her forehead, as if I am being incredibly frustrating.

'God, Mum. Why do you have to put a label on everything?'

'So you're *not* going out with him then?' I am undeterred. Yesterday I talked about sex in front of a whole room of strangers. I am having this conversation with my daughter.

'Why do you want to know so badly?' she asks, scowling at me. 'How can this stuff be so important to you? It's like you think you have to know everything.'

And there it is. The million-dollar question. Why *do* I want to know? Why *am* I prepared to go to such extreme lengths to find out what's going on in her life? Does it really matter if she's talking to me or to her grandmother, as long as she's talking to someone?

I pause and think about the best way to explain to my teenage girl how it feels to be a mother. How to tell her that I only ever want the best for her but that I'm constantly aware of the fact that I am *not* the best. Not even close. But that the one thing I can promise her is that I will never stop trying to be better.

'I've never been a parent of a seventeen-year-old daughter before,' I tell her, reaching out for her hand. 'I'm making it up as I go along, Scarlet – and I definitely do *not* know everything. But I love you and I want to know about the things that are important to you. But you're right. I'll back off.'

Scarlet's hand tightens in mine. 'Don't do that.' Her voice is so quiet that I have to lean closer to hear her. 'Don't back off. I like it that you care enough to ask about what's going on with me. Petra's mum couldn't care less what she gets up and Petra makes out like she thinks that's a good thing but it isn't. Not really. It's lonely if you don't think anyone's bothered about you. And living in this house is a whole hot mood but it's never lonely.'

I am lost for words. But that's okay.

'So, you asked if we were dating,' she continues, pulling her hand away from mine and pushing her hair out of her face. 'It's not quite that simple. There are things that you can be doing other than dating or not dating. There's stages, you know – and he could be eliminated at any point.'

It's my turn to raise an eyebrow. 'Stages? What are they?'

She sits up straight and holds up her hand, counting them off on her fingers.

'There's the *Getting to Know You* stage,' she tells me. 'Then it's the *Talking* stage. After that comes the *Exclusive* stage and *then* you get to the *Dating* stage. It's really quite simple. And before you bother asking, I'll bring him home if and when he manages to reach the *Dating* stage.'

I frown, trying to make sense of what she's saying while simultaneously silently singing the 'Hallelujah' chorus at the declaration that she's amenable to bringing him home. 'So there's three stages before you actually kiss each other?'

It seems like quite a long time to wait but I have to say, it warms the cockles of my heart to hear her say this. I did read something the other week commenting on the fact that this generation of kids do appear to be very restrained and sensible in their approach to relationships and it's reassuring to know that Scarlet has such a mature attitude. Although it does make me feel like we were all a bit wanton back in the day, by comparison.

Scarlet shakes her head. 'Of course not. How else are you supposed to decide if they're someone who's worth starting on the *Getting to Know You* stage?'

My cockles drop a few degrees in temperature.

'So which stage are you and Skinz at then?' I enquire, hoping that I'm going to be able to handle the answer.

Her face flushes slightly. 'We've moved on to the *Talking* stage,' she admits. 'I need to make sure that he's more than just a good snog.'

Never a wiser word was spoken. Maybe I'm not such a rubbish parent after all.

Chapter Twenty-Eight

I t's quite a relief to go back to school on Monday. I make my way through the next few days doing the usual things. Sighing in despair at Year Ten, Class C's ability to use *all the words* in their loud and frequent discussions but then *none of the words* when it comes to committing their thoughts to paper. Laughing with Cassie in the staffroom as Peter comes up with new and ingenious ways to leave teaching and escape to his desert island. Trying to avoid being in a room alone with Miss Pritchard in case she tries to engage me in yet another conversation about our Proper Porn production company. Just a regular three days at school which, after all the excitement of last weekend, I am more than happy to float my way through.

Nick brings pie and chips home for supper on Wednesday night and we're just putting it onto plates when Scarlet comes flying through the door with her laptop held tightly in both hands.

'I'm with them now!' she yells, crashing the laptop onto the kitchen island and twisting the screen to face me.

'Hi, Mum,' says a voice and I smile at the welcome sight of my oldest child.

'Dylan! We weren't expecting to FaceTime with you tonight. Is everything okay?'

'You tell me,' he answers. 'Scarlet just called me and said she's got something big to show us, only she won't tell me what's going on.'

I glance at Scarlet who spins the laptop so that it's facing away from us and then starts typing rapidly onto the keyboard. 'What do you want to show us, sweetheart?'

'Is this going to take long?' asks Nick. 'Shall I put the oven on to keep the food warm?'

'Hi, Dad!' calls Dylan. 'Is Benji there too?'

'This isn't appropriate for Benji,' says Scarlet. 'I've bribed him with my phone and told him to stay upstairs until we call him down. I don't want to be responsible for ruining his childhood.'

Now that I look at her properly, I can see that her eyes are shining and sparkling like particularly twinkly stars in the night sky. She looks almost manic with excitement and my heart rate starts to speed up.

'Scarlet? What is it? What's the big thing?'

She ignores me and instead clicks something on her laptop. It makes the whooshing email sound and I start to walk around to the other side of the island so that I can see what she's doing.

'What's going on?' I demand. 'What have you done, Scarlet?'

She smirks at me. 'It's not *me* that you need to be worried about right now, Mum. And to think that I thought you were boring!'

'Scarlet!' Nick glares at her. 'I've warned you before. Your mother is the least boring person that I have ever met.'

'Well, I know that *now*, don't I?' she drawls. 'I shouldn't have been wasting my time knitting her a stupid scarf to replace the one I lost. She'd probably prefer something a bit more risqué.'

Scarlet is knitting me a scarf. Despite the increasing tension in the room I feel a warm glow of maternal love flooding through me, combined with the tiniest bit of justified wrath and fury. I bloody knew that she'd lost my expensive birthday scarf.

Scarlet leans closer to the screen and I refocus on the situation at hand. 'Dylan – you should have the email with the link by now.'

'I'm just clicking on it.' His voice sounds strangely disembodied and I suddenly have a very, very bad feeling.

'Got it. What am I looking at?'

'Just click *play*. We're going to watch it here.'

She swivels the laptop back round to face us and presses the mouse. The screen is split into two – one half filled with Dylan's face and the other with my very worst nightmare.

'Mum? Is that you?' I can't tell if the shake in my oldest child's voice is trauma or hysteria or a combination of both.

I shake my head and stumble onto a stool. 'No. It's not me.'

Nick comes up behind me and puts his hand on my

shoulder and together we watch in silence as the camera zooms in on my face and I start to speak.

'I thought we were here to talk about real sex.'

It's worse than I thought. Just kill me now.

'It just isn't honest to pretend that everyone is constantly in touch with their sexual selves or getting it on, Hollywood-style at every available opportunity. Some of us are too knackered at the end of a long day to do anything other than put on our pajamas and watch Netflix and drink wine before falling into bed. And what happens after that isn't planned out or orchestrated. It just happens. Or not.'

'I think we've seen enough,' says Nick, leaning over towards the laptop. 'Turn it off at your end please, Dylan.'

'No way!' His face is scrunched up with laughter. 'This is brilliant!'

It is not brilliant. It is a total disaster.

Scarlet pulls the laptop out of Nick's reach and raises her eyebrows at me. 'I'll pause it if you tell us why you were there,' she says. 'I'd like to hear in your own words what were you doing at Sex Con and why has this clip already got twenty thousand likes on YouTube? And why are they calling you the *Queen of Sex*?'

And for one beautiful moment I think that I can see a way out. My brain goes into a frenzy as I try to construct a plausible reason for why *me*, their boring, middle-of-the-road, average mum would possibly be speaking at Sex Con. Maybe I could convince them that it was somehow related to their grandmother and her sex therapy course? Or I could say that Miriam wants me to teach Sex Ed and I was there to learn about what I'm supposed to be telling the younger generation?

'Mum?' Dylan has stopped laughing and is gazing at me from the screen, looking confused.

'Mum?' repeats Scarlet, and I can see the stars in her eyes burning like fires. My feisty, fearless girl who needs to know that forty-four-year-old women can be just as feisty (if perhaps not quite as fearless).

I look up at Nick. He squeezes my shoulder and gives me a grin.

'That was an interesting speech,' he says, nodding at the screen. 'I'm looking forward to hearing the rest of it later.'

So I take a deep breath and then I say the words that I never, in a thousand years, imagined that I would be saying to my teenagers.

'Once upon a time, in a land not so far away, there lived a woman. She had a wonderful husband and three marvelous (if slightly irritating) children and everything was just as it should be.'

A snort comes from the screen. 'This is clearly a fairytale because in real life, she has two bloody annoying kids and one talented, brilliant son who is away at university.'

'Shut up, Dylan!' snaps Scarlet. 'Just so you know, I got my predicted grades the other day and they're way better than yours were.'

'Do you want me to continue with my story?' I enquire. 'Or would you both rather go to bed early without any supper?'

Scarlet nods at me regally. 'Continue.'

I nod back and resume from where I left off. 'But, even

though the woman had so many good things in her life, she was missing something important. And that was her own identity.'

I wave the hand in the air, getting into my stride. 'Yes – while she was grateful to have been given the opportunity to be a wife and a mother and a teacher, she felt adrift in the world – like she was floating alone on a raft out at sea and every time she tried to paddle towards land, she would... erm, she would...'

I pause. This analogy would have worked better if I'd had some time to prepare.

'She'd get tired?' suggests Dylan.

I shake my head. 'No – not tired.'

'She'd break the paddle?' offers Nick, putting a glass of wine in front of me.

'No!' I scowl at him. 'That's totally not what I'm trying to say.'

'She'd just keep going round in circles?' says Scarlet tentatively and I beam at her.

'Yes! That! Thank you, sweetheart!'

'No problem.' Scarlet sits down next to me and pats my arm. 'Keep going.'

'Now, the woman was feeling that something was missing.' I gaze into the middle distance and put everything I have into explaining this unusual situation through the non-threatening and relatable medium of storytelling. 'And she also knew that her three charming (and slightly tiresome) children were going to be bleeding her and her husband financially dry over the coming years. So she decided that, as life is for living and should be seen as a magnificent adventure, then she needed to jump off that raft and start swimming – and see where her journeying took her.'

I smile gently, pick up the glass of wine and take a big sip. 'And there you have it.'

There is silence and then both Dylan and Scarlet erupt, their words flowing over each other.

'What? You haven't told us anything!'

'How does this explain what you were doing at Sex Con?'

I shrug my shoulders. 'Well, if neither of you were bothering to listen then I'm afraid that I'm not prepared to say it again. I've explained very clearly why I'm on that video and I don't think we need to say any more about it.'

Scarlet pushes back her stool and reaches for the laptop.

'Dylan, start Googling,' she calls towards the screen. 'Her pseudonym is Twinky Malone. It shouldn't take you too long to catch up.'

I stand too and look at Nick. He raises his glass of wine and gives me a mid-air cheer and I am reminded of the evening, not so long ago, when we discovered that Twinky Malone, and her manuscript, had been accepted by an agent. So many things are different since then but even more things have stayed the same.

Some things will never change and for that I am truly, truly grateful.

'Okay, fine.' I give him a rueful smile and then I twist the laptop so that I can see both my teenagers at the same time. I hadn't planned to tell them this way; I hadn't planned to tell them at all but, as Scarlet is so fond of saying, *'it is what it is'* and I just have to make the best of it.

'I've written a book. It's an adult book for grown-ups and you are one hundred percent not allowed to read it because it has a few rude words in it and the characters may, on the very odd occasion, engage in consensual, loving relations.'

'What do you mean?' Dylan stares out of the screen, his eyes wide. Next to me, Scarlet stifles a snort.

'I mean that I have written an erotic book that contains some scenes of a more sexual nature,' I tell her. 'We don't need to make a big fuss about it.'

There is silence. It starts quietly and then it gets louder and louder until I am desperate for someone to speak and drown it out, even though I have no idea what their reaction might be and I'm already trying to figure out how we can afford to pay for university fees and driving lessons *and* counseling sessions for the entire family.

'Dylan?' I ask quietly. 'Are you okay?'

His hands are clasped over his face and I can hear a snuffling, mumbling sound. If he's crying then I will never be able to forgive myself.

'Oh my god.' His voice is breaking into tiny pieces and my heart is breaking with it.

I did this to him.

I have broken my own children.

This is what comes from my selfish attempts to *have it all.*

'Scarlet – are you hearing this?' His voice is muffled.

Scarlet moves around so that she can see the screen. 'I am absolutely hearing this.'

'You know what this means, don't you?'

She nods and I see her mouth trembling. I'd reach out to comfort her but I don't know if she'd welcome my touch right now.

'I know what it means, Dylan.'

Scarlet blinks hard and looks down at the floor, as if she's trying to compose herself. Dylan makes a gasping sound, like he's struggling to breathe – and then the room erupts with a screech of hilarity as he pulls his hands away from his face and starts howling with laughter.

'Our mum has written a porno!' Tears of mirth are rolling down Scarlet's face and on the screen I can see Dylan clutching his stomach as he cracks up.

Not broken then. That's a bit of a relief.

It's not what I was expecting but on reflection, it could have been a lot worse. And this probably isn't the right occasion to explain the difference between erotica and porn. That can wait for another time and another day, when I've had a lot more wine to drink.

For now, I'll have to settle for trying to explain to my still-hysterical children that, despite being an erotic author who somewhat bewilderingly appears to be something of a YouTube sensation, I am still very much their mum. And if they think this diminishes my power and authority over them, *in any way*, then they are very much mistaken.

I am Hannah Thompson. Wife, Mother, Daughter, Teacher.

I am also Twinky Malone. Writer of *always* factual, and *occasionally* funny, Erotic Fiction.

I have no idea what my newfound Internet fame is going to mean for *More Than Sex* and *So Much Sex* but I suppose it might make selling the performance rights more of a possibility, which is both nerve-wracking and wonderful in equal measure. And my book being turned into a film could be the opportunity that I've been waiting for. My chance to stop being a 'bit' part in my own life and take the starring role for a change.

Not literally, obviously. That's a horrifying thought.

And I might not be a Sex Goddess but based on what Scarlet just said about the comments on YouTube, I think there's a vague chance that I could be a queen of sex and that sounds way more appealing. Trying to be a Sex Goddess was super-exhausting and incredibly time-consuming and there's just too much other stuff to be getting on with. Like informing Dylan and Scarlet that if they don't stop laughing in precisely two seconds flat, then I'm going to have them sent to the bloody tower.

The Goddess is dead – long live the Queen.

Acknowledgments

I have faked many things in my life and writing a sequel was never going to be the easiest thing that I've pretended I can do. But here we are and I really, really hope that you enjoy faking it as much as I do.

I need to thank a few people for supporting me on my FAKING IT journey.

First, my fabulous mum, **Kerry** and my incredible little sister, **Elizabeth**, both very funny and hysteria-inducing women. Next, my brilliant friend **Polly** who is always ready to read an early manuscript and tell it to me like it is. If I want the truth then I go to her – and if I want a hilarious sex story then she's pretty good at those too, as is **Kym**, who never fails to make me splutter my Prosecco onto the table.

I also want to thank the **One More Chapter** team but especially **Hannah**, my wonderful and talented editor. She made this book the *most* fun to write and I did not know that working on my edits could be so uproarious and awkward and generally entertaining.

I'm going to thank my kids (**Z, G & R**) who I know will not be reading this, if their reaction when they heard me explaining the vibrator scene is anything to go by. They are generous and kind and incredibly supportive and this book is absolutely not about them.

Lastly, I need to thank my husband, **Adam**. We met when we were 21 years old and our entire life together has been about making it up as we go along. He constantly encourages me to move out of my comfort zone and to stop waiting to be given permission. He makes me brave and the one thing I will never fake is how in love with him I am (and no – he is NOT Nick!).